About the Author

Gill was born in Reading but moved to Fareham where she now lives.

Having always been a 'reader', she particularly enjoyed stories with dark themes. After joining a creative writing group in 2001 she began writing short stories, most of which reflected the 'dark theme leaning'. She was encouraged when she was lucky enough to win some writing competitions and have stories appear in Writers magazines.

She based one of her short stories on a childhood memory. Whilst lying awake at night in her parents' house, she used to wonder and worry about the weird sounds she often heard through her bedroom window. She believed they were the plaintive voices of children that were lost and crying for their parents. Later she realised it was just the wailing of the foxes that lived at the bottom of the garden.

This memory proved a base for a tale, but the story took on a life of its own and propagated. The characters needed to tell their story and a novel called 'Diamonds are for Never', the first of a trilogy, was born. It outlines Reading police's efforts to eradicate paedophiles from civilised society.

Diamonds
ARE FOR
Never

Gill Wallbanks

ISBN 978-1546475255

Book design by The Art of Communication www.book-design.co.uk
First published in the UK 2017

Dedication

Brian, where ever you are.

Acknowledgements

My thanks to June Hampson who encouraged my interest in writing, and taught me the skills of putting pen to paper. Thanks also to the members of the Café Writers Society and The Porchester Writers Circle for their help and support during the writing of this book.

To the three 'geeks' who helped me on technical issues: Emma Heath, Jack Wassell and Guy Merry. Also a big thanks to Christine Hammacott of The Art of Communication for helping me publish and being so helpful.

Last but not least, my husband Bob for often having to finish cooking dinner because I needed to write a few more lines.

PART 1
GENESIS

I was seven when mum drowned on our holiday in 1993.

Our family drove to Cornwall for two weeks. Dad drove us in his clapped out red Cortina, a hand-me-down from Granddad. Every time he changed gear, especially towards the end of the journey, there was a high-pitched crunching sound. Typical kids, my five-year-old sister Jane and I giggled and rammed our fingers into our ears to stop the grating noise that rattled our teeth. Four-year-old Emma, gazing out of the window, rocked gently in her unreachable autistic world.

Mum sat in the front with Dad, and despite Jane and I arguing because we were bored, I remember watching mum's long, wavy ginger hair. It reminded me, even at that tender age, of a Martian river. My mate Tommy and I were big into space, but did not know then there was no free flowing water on the red planet. Typical boys, and many years before NASA's Phoenix Space Probe found ice beneath the surface, we envisaged furious torrents of raging blood red rivers swirling over Mars' landscape.

Three days into the holiday and our lives changed forever. We went to the beach, and despite the windy weather, mum went in for a swim. Dad told her to be careful, but was not worried as she was a strong swimmer. He would not let us three kids even paddle, said it was too dangerous for little 'uns. Mum laughed as she ran to the sea, her long hair swirling out behind her in the wind.

We could hear the rollers breaking on the shore, and excitedly waved when she turned towards us, her head bobbing up and down between the waves.

Dad was giving us marmite sandwiches for our lunch. We kids jumped when suddenly he shrieked, "Christ, she's in trouble."

He ran into the sea, with Jane and I trailing behind, whimpering in terror. We stood at the seas edge while he waded in, and was up to his waist when a lifeguard suddenly appeared and strode in after him; dragging him back to the beach. I now realise it was so they could do their job properly without worrying about him. He stood on the edge of the sea, a crowd forming round us, and I remember his screams to this day, whilst Jane and I sobbed in horror. Emma slumped to the ground, and rocking gently, she closed her eyes, put her hands over her ears, and retreated to her safe place.

The lifeguards jumped into an inflatable boat and sped towards her, but she disappeared beneath the grey waves.

I still recall my feelings. The world slowed down; there was a shrill ringing in my ears. I bit my tongue and could taste salt. Dad's shrieks hurt my heart. Pushing the terror away, I dug my toes into the sand. Dad had taped a TV documentary about the cosmos that maintained there were more stars in the Universe than grains of sand on every beach on earth. I started counting the grains, anything to take away the horror of the moment.

A long time later, or that is how it seemed, the inflatable came to shore with mum's body in it. My heart beat so fiercely I thought it would burst from my chest and explode onto the sand. The disbelief and terror as I saw my mum's beautiful hair, wet and dishevelled, fanned out over her face and spilling onto the beach, was indescribable. Her mouth was half-open; eyes dulled of life, staring blankly. The lifeguards pumped her chest, but no light sparked from her eyes. Young as I was, I knew they would never see me again.

Jane and I stood clutching each other's hands, quiet

4

sobs and trembling body now the only signs of her distress. Emma's behaviour changed. Still slumped on the beach, she started frantically humming to shut out the unacceptable. I wanted to hug her but mum had warned us not to touch her as that caused her distress. Until that day, I'd considered all girls, especially little sisters, were only on this world to antagonise and provoke. I learnt early to appreciate my family.

Just occasionally through my childhood I would have a nightmare, and hear dad's heart-wrenching pleas as he watched the lifesaver vainly trying to rekindle her pulse.

I do not know how they got mum's body home. I just remember the funeral. My sisters did not go; they stayed with a neighbour. Perhaps at seven, I was considered old enough to be there or because dad wanted a hand to grasp. We sobbed together; a childish blubber coming from me, whilst dad's heartbroken moans were low and subdued. My hand was sore for days afterwards, but I had not minded, and I remembered feeling quite grown-up because he had relied on me.

Three years later, he married the neighbour who had cared for the girls on the day of the funeral. She was a good mum, but throughout my childhood, I felt guilty. Naturally, I loved my real mum the most, but after a while, unless I looked at her photograph, I could not recall her face. Dad put away all her photos that had covered the walls and sideboard once he married Sandra, although he gave me the one of mum sitting on a donkey in Majorca, and I kept it by my bedside. I took it with me to University and when I studied her face, I remembered her loving touch, and it provokes a dilemma.

The day when mum drowned was the worst day of my life... I think. I say that because the next year paedophiles abducted me. I was attempting to fly my kite in the park. Grandma had gone shopping and her friend Elsie was minding me. She was close by on a park bench, reading the paper. A

5

lady with long, dark hair and a big smile came to help me get the kite up in the air. That was all I recall until I awoke, tied up in the back of a van that stunk of petrol.

Experience now tells me they drugged me. The next thing I knew I was naked in a room, surrounded by bright lights and a camera. Two big kids burst in, and there was a lot of shouting and chaos. They snatched me and we ran. I remember shivering as we dashed into the night.

Taking me to the corner of the road where I lived, wrapped in the boy's jacket I think, they told me to 'run like fucking hell' to the police car parked outside my house. They said they could not take me because the police would think they had kidnapped me. I obeyed. Kids do not argue with 'adults'.

Here is my dilemma. The days after my kidnap in the park were comparable to the fear I had felt standing on that golden beach, shivering and terrified, knowing my mum would never hug me again. The wound still lingers in my heart, opening occasionally, and the unhealed gash throbs, but if I'm truthful, time has eased that loss, despite my tender age.

Although I've done my best to shrug off the horrors of the abduction experience, I know those days in captivity were the ones that actually shaped the path of my life.

However, both incidents, which ever was the worst, mean I will not go to Cornwall, and *I hate fucking nonces with a vengeance!*

2001

The eleven year old girl climbed into the sturdy cupboard in the bedroom and drew across the heavy bolt. She was safe now. Sitting down amongst clothes suspended neatly from the hangers over her head, she tip-toed her fingers towards the hiding place. Deft from previous training, her fingers located the mobile and the small torch.

Switching on the purposely slim torch, the sudden brightness made her blink. As instructed, she placed the end in her mouth, shone the torch at the mobile phone, and touched the On switch.

The thump on the door made her jump. Her hands trembled but practice had made her resolute even though her heart felt as though it were a startled bird, wings thrashing, trying to escape the cage of her ribs.

"Open this door, you fucking bitch," her mother yelled.

The child carried on with her task, and when the phone came to life, she dialled 999. The answer was prompt.

"Emergency service. Which service do you require."

"The police, please," she answered.

"What the fuck do you think you're doing," her mother shrieked.

"My name is Polly Ayres," she stated clearly to the voice that answered. " I live at 16 Beverley Gardens, Tansworth, Norwich, NW18 4JS. I need your help. My mother's just killed... " The girl, paused here. She shook her head to clear her thoughts. They hadn't practiced this bit word for word. The police woman on the other end of the phone started to speak, but Dad had said time was of the essence. She loved that phrase and smiled when she thought of him saying it. The thumping and shrieking from outside the cupboard made her focus. "Umm, sorry, she's killed Dad, Timothy and Paul. They're seven and four. Please come quickly. Mum's outside. Dad built the cupboard real... umm... stout he said... ummm... and the bolts sturdy... but nuffink lasts forever." She repeated her name and address, and switched off the phone.

"I heard that, you cow. You haven't got a bloody mobile, so..."

As instructed, Polly did not answer. Despite the bird's wings still fluttering madly in her chest, and her stomach churning like the lava in a volcano she'd seen on a TV documentary recently, she sat, still cross legged, staring at the blackness of the door.

Retreating into her safe world, she ignored the crashing and hammering sounds from outside her sanctuary. Eventually, silence fell, and she closed her eyes and waited. She must have dozed. She heard a loud voice she didn't know call out, "Christ, I don't believe it..."

There was more talking. She stopped where she was. Dad had been adamant. "Don't move. Don't open the door. She's crafty. Wait till it's safe."

There was more noise. Someone tried the door handle. Eventually the golden glow seeping round the door faded. She was desperate to go for a wee-wee but dad had said, "Just wait. She'll pretend she's the cops."

So she waited. She dozed. Light flaring like a camera flash round the door startled her awake. She heard voices. A lady and a man's. They sounded soft, gentle voices, like her teachers. She was really desperate for a wee now.

Standing up, pushing the clothes aside, she gently eased back the bolt. Peering round the door, she was surprised to see two strangers dressed in funny white overalls. The man was taking photographs. The woman was kneeling and picking up stuff.

They didn't looked like police but perhaps they knew them. She pushed open the door. The two people looked at her with round, staring eyes.

"I'm Polly Ayres. Are the police here yet?"

The Present

Lucy could not believe her bad luck. All she wanted was a quiet life, keep a low profile, enjoy her exercising, and occasionally get pissed with Freddy. That was not asking a lot, was it? Then, on an enjoyable jog on a day off from school, admittedly suffering from a hangover, under a tree, Higgins, her beloved dog, had found a hand. From its size, she guessed it was a man's hand, crawling with white, squishy, disgusting maggots. What a bummer.

The daft mutt had looked so pleased, and no doubt then wondered why she'd puked all over his paws. Her first instinct was to run, which she did. Unfortunately, the day, so pleasant to start with, was turning into a bastard, because as she got to the edge of the grove of trees where they'd been ambling home after their daily run, she'd bumped into a couple strolling through the park. From their concerned expressions, she knew the fact that a woman, face as pale as bloody Snow White, and a dog, no doubt a big grin plastered all over his chops, if that was possible whilst holding a human hand, was not normal. Hell and damnation, life had been pretty OK until this point.

She could not just skiddaddle. The moment the rest of the body remains were found, which was highly likely as Higgins had left quite a few bits and pieces strewn over the path, they would remember her behaviour, and the cops would be very interested as to why, if innocent, Snow White had fled the scene. Double Bummer!

Part 2
Turn a different
corner

Chapter 1

From the park entrance, the jogger sped along the path that led to the top of the hill. The elms and oaks' foliage on either side was still green, although small golden leaves were sneaking in to warn the waning season that although colourful autumn was still weeks away, their battle for inevitable supremacy was beginning. The complacent greenery was unaware its time was limited, and that a reign of gold and red would soon govern the park.

Lucy Hamilton, intent on her own regimes, was also oblivious to nature's battle. Jogging up a slight gradient, she paused on reaching the crest to admire the emerald vista before her whilst vigorously running on the spot, legs pumping like pistons. Slowly reducing her speed, and allowing her breathing to return to normal, she checked her watch and noted with pleasure that this was her best time for the first three miles of the day.

In the early misty morning, the sun struggled to shine, resembling a blurred golden orb just visible through a thin, grey duvet of diaphanous clouds, its energy waves vainly battling to warm her shoulders through the damp haze.

The young woman stretched her arms above her head; then bending double, touched her toes before placing her fingertips onto the ground between her feet. She felt the stiff muscles in her back extending, and the resultant sensation of being supple and fit was a satisfying one.

Her running partner, a skinny greyhound, flopped down beside her and panting heavily looked at her with large, pained eyes, giving the clear message that his days as a runner were over, so what was he doing here, competing with her when he could be curled up in his very comfortable basket, thank you!

From her bowed position, she patted his firm, silky-smooth head.

"Told you not to come, Higgins. I was quite prepared to run alone, but you insisted, which is a miracle in itself, so don't blame me if you're knackered."

Higgins looked away, shaking his head as he did when she so blatantly fibbed. The tall, slim woman straightened up, noticing another runner dressed in red shorts and vest who nodded a greeting to her. Waving back, she smiled contentedly; deliberating that you tend to see the same people exercising in this part of the park most mornings. They acknowledged one another, usually with a nod, but that was the extent of their association. They had no personal knowledge of fellow athletes, but like Lucy, were happy to be exercising in the fresh air in pleasant surroundings.

Completing more stretching exercises, thus giving her doggy companion time to catch his breath, she bent over again and fondled his silky ears, informing him that he was *so* unfit for an ex-runner. From his relaxed position on the ground, front legs crossed and head flopped over them, his large brown eyes held a bored look that conveyed he really didn't give a toss.

This planet's star that gives life suddenly won its battle with the clouds, and its rays streamed to earth like molten spears, ironing out Lucy's tight shoulder muscles. She stopped exercising, put her hands on her hips, closed her eyes, and tilting back her head and shoulders, letting the warmth caress her face, knowing once the clouds returned, so would the chill. The short-lived sun's embrace totally de-stressed her whole being, and she decided to stop the work out for the morning.

An elderly couple sauntered past with a small dog and remarked on the lovely morning. Lucy smiled back and agreed; the conviviality of the sun, her relaxed muscles and general well-being making her content with life.

"Come on, mutt, enough's enough. You're just not as fit as me."

The dog stood up, shook himself vigorously, and Lucy could see from his expression he thanked his doggy god the punishment was finished. Habitually, Higgins walked a few steps ahead of his mistress, and he knowingly turned into a narrow path in a small grove of trees, their short cut home.

As Lucy arrived at the path turn-off, she glanced back, often experiencing in the park an impression that someone was watching. She could see no-one.

For God's sake, stop being paranoid.

Shrugging off the feeling, she followed Higgins into the thicket. The pair ambled back towards their apartment, taking in nature's delights by way of this wooded area lining the southern part of the park. Here the trees were smaller, their scrubby appearance no contest to their beautiful brothers outside. Only weeds, dried mud, and the tattered remains of last year's dropped leaves covered the floor and as Lucy walked, her running shoes kicked up an aroma of woody decay.

She picked a blackberry from a stubby bush, but the shadows cast by trees outside the copse had discouraged the fruit to grow and sweeten. The berry was hard and sharp tasting and Lucy winced, quickly spitting the offender into the undergrowth.

Humming as she meandered, Lucy felt pleased with herself. The junior school where she taught had closed due to local elections so she was determined to make the most of the extra day's leave. Also a late summer 'flu virus had devastated both staff numbers and pupils, but so far she had avoided the outbreak, so felt this day and life in general was definitely for enjoying.

She had arisen early, and not fallen back to sleep, her first inclination, when the alarm had woken her at six thirty. Anticipating her leave with pleasure, she had forgotten to reset her alarm clock the previous evening after drinking too much wine with Freddy, her friend who lived in the flat above.

Before climbing into her bed about midnight, she'd covered Freddy with a blanket, who, before flopping onto her sofa, had described himself as 'smashed as a rat', and then promptly fallen asleep. Glancing into the living room when she had left for her morning run, Freddy had already gone.

Suddenly aware of a pressing silence, and realising she could not see Higgins anywhere, Lucy called his name, fully expecting him to bounce up with a twig in his mouth and a silly grin all over his chops. That was the normal routine. She would throw a stick, he would retrieve it, indicating how clever he was, and what tremendous fun they were both having!

Twice she swivelled through three hundred and sixty degrees, scanning the area, with a sensation that a lump of concrete was building in her chest. After five minutes of searching and appealing to him, the concrete was now building into an indigestible brick wall. The oppressive hush did not help, and her over-active imagination fired itself up into a mind-blowing anxiety.

Get a grip of yourself; you're in the middle of a busy park, stop getting so work up!

The mental scolding did not help one bit because Higgins, if nothing else, was pathologically transparent and predictable due to the ill-treatment he had suffered from his previous owner when his days were over as a champion runner. Normally when out running, he rarely let his saviour out of sight.

Widening her search, and with a further five minutes

of calling, her voice sliding from impatient to begging, the relief on hearing his answering *woof*, albeit some distance away, was huge.

Following the sound of his enthusiastic barking, Lucy eventually tracked him down to a part of the woods away from the normal path for home. Flies were swarming despite the coolness of the season. Batting them away as she approached, she was surprised to see only his rear end as he frantically dug beneath a hedgerow struggling for survival behind a gnarly oak tree. He was hurling the earth into the air behind him. She wrinkled her nose and shuddered as she detected an unpleasant odour of mould, mingled with another obnoxious, musty smell that caused her to gag. Despite her relief on locating him, her voice held an edge sharp enough to cut through hardened steel as she snapped.

"Higgins, you stupid mutt, you had me damn worried. What the hell are you doing? Come away." She attempted to drag the dog away from his frenzied work, but Higgins, usually obedient, with snout snuffling inquisitively beneath the hedgerow, was intent on his quarrying.

The tunnelling completed, the dog looked positively delighted when he withdrew an object and showed his treasure to his running companion. Expecting a pat on the head and the usual praise, when his beloved mistress fell on her knees and puked smelly food onto his paws, Higgins' doggy intellect didn't appreciate that a severed human hand crawling with maggots, invariably produces this outcome.

Lucy was still trembling despite the police officer who had introduced himself as Detective Inspector Roy Cole placing his overcoat over her shoulders. Standing about thirty metres from the place where Higgins had made his discovery, through the trees she could see police cordoning off a large area.

"Feeling better?" asked Cole. He nodded at her 'yes

thanks' reply, but she had the distinct feeling he wasn't endowed with the policeman's equivalent of a doctor's bedside manner, and his voice was testy as he said, "Can you tell me how you came across this find?"

Before Lucy could reply, a redheaded giant hurried up and interrupted.

"Got here as soon as I could, Guv. D'you want me to take over here? SOCO's just drawn up behind me."

"Good. Yes. This is Miss...," he referred to his notes, "Hamilton. Her dog found the severed hand. I'll pass you over to Detective Sergeant Blake." Without further explanation, the DI walked abruptly away.

"Sorry about this Miss... "

"Hamilton," Lucy snapped, now feeling more in control, and fed up with being passed from the proverbial pillar to post. " As in... Lewis... or... Lady Hamilton!"

This was the fourth police officer she had spoken to in the last hour since she had hysterically fled from the find. Unfortunately, a passing couple had seen her distress, so she could not just sneak away. Knowing that eventually the other body bits would be discovered and become news-worthy, the couple would certainly recall her anxiety; then the search for her might start because she had obviously witnessed something.

Act cool, normal, or the nightmare will begin again. You'll get through this. Remember, you're an unfortunate witness. You did the right thing. Told the couple to ring 999 and stayed.

Lucy snapped her mind back to the present. Her eyes travelled up the police officer. At five foot ten inches, Lucy was tall for a woman, but she craned her neck to make eye contact with this police officer.

Feeling lightheaded, she forced herself to act as natural as possible in this situation, realising she needed to get home and drink a large mug of comforting tea.

Higgins was pulling on his lead, the prospective breakfast

within smelling distance for him, and his rumbling stomach still anticipating the meaty delights disappointingly snatched away by his mistress.

"Sit down, Higgins. Behave," Lucy ordered, attempting to bring him to heel.

Retrieving his notebook and pen from his pocket, the officer half smiled and his white even teeth, plus she noticed he was good looking in a rugged, unshaven sort of way, made her thankful she had not reacted like a snarly old bag.

"Hang on Higgins, this won't take long," the police officer murmured. He turned to Lucy, pen poised over his notebook, and continued. "As my colleague informed you, I'm Detective Sergeant Blake. Can you tell me exactly what occurred?"

As Lucy related her story again, the police officer's unrelenting stare was distracting. Fighting the feeling of unease that arose when under the spotlight, and not in control of a situation, she took a deep breath to master the feeling that spikey-winged insects were cutting her stomach lining to shreds.

Don't let your imagination go berserk. Stare back, the innocent have nothing to hide he'd told her.

With wobbling innards, not actually in tune with the defiant glare she shot back, she could not decide if *his* stare was because he did not believe one word of her story, and was convinced she had deposited the body part under the hedgerow herself, or if this was his normal look. Either way it was unnerving. Drawing on her courage, she dismissed the slashing insects, encouraged her coping streak to rise up like a soaring eagle, and resolving not to be intimidated, matched his intensity with her own fiery gaze.

By the end of their conversation, she realised his eyes were greener than any cat's and his eyelashes and facial hair were blond compared to the mop of thick dark red hair which looked well overdue for a cut. The only word she could think of to describe his hair was wayward. It stuck up at various angles, and a cool youth might well have spent an hour before a mirror and a whole pot of gel to achieve a similar effect. Lucy had the distinct feeling the resultant hairstyle was more chance than intention.

As she watched the officer finish scribbling his notes, she thought of her close friend Freddy, who would gleefully point out his amazement that in the middle of this nasty experience she was doing a 'typical woman thing' and noticing a man's looks.

She shivered as she metaphorically pinched herself to focus, and realised, despite the benefits of the good-looking copper and the thick coat round her shoulders, that the cold and shock from her find had finally sneaked in, and she could not control the quivering and tremors that shuddered through her body.

A concerned look passed over the police officer's face.

"Thank you for your help. You're cold, shocked. I'll arrange for one of the team to give you a lift home," he offered, tucking his pen and notebook away in his jacket pocket.

"Don't worry; I live just ten minutes away. Higgins and I'll jog home. A good run will soon sort me out."

"You're sure?" He paused for a second before adding, "Have I seen you at the Fairways gym?"

"Gym?" The sudden change of subject and his knowledge took her by surprise. The insects returned and morphed into giant, man-eating, shark- fanged vampires, slashing her innards. Desperation to be back in control made her dizzy.

"Fairways Gym. I'm a new member." His voice jolted her back. "Think I've seen you there?"

"Oh, um... yes... not noticed you." *Strange... usually good at spotting trouble. Jeez, why's this happening?*

"Yeah, well, I'm usually too busy to get there often enough." He shrugged, unaware of her turmoil. "Just trying to get fit."

"Oh... I'll make a point of noticing you next time. Come

on, Higgins, breakfast time." Taking the coat from her shoulders, she handed it to him, explaining it belonged to DI Coles. She hurried away, the dog at her heels, now obedient at the mention of food.

"We'll need to speak to you again," he called after her.

"You've got my address," she said, waving her hand dismissively, not turning round; praying her voice was steady. She forced herself not to run.

Don't hurry, be natural, you're an unfortunate, innocent spectator. This will pass.

But the bastard killer moths whipped out their razors, and now the pain in her innards was making her feel distinctly sick. A second sense informed her that his face had hardened with suspicion as she walked away, and panic spiralled like a whirlwind through her body. It was all she could do to walk steadily on her trembling legs.

What a bloody, sodding, bastard bummer!

Dan, eyes screwed up with suspicion, watched the woman and her dog until they were out of sight. Forcing his mind back to police mode, he hurried back to the frenzied activity around the immediate area.

"What've we got, Guv?" Dan Blake asked his senior officer who was standing outside the newly erected yellow crime scene tape watching the activities of the white suited Scene of Crime Officers.

"Got a cigarette?" said DI Cole, ignoring the question, and beckoning Dan to follow him. Trailing behind him to the edge of the zone, Blake gave back the overcoat and his boss slipped it on, pushing his hands deep into the pockets. He hunched over against the cold, his foxy face creased in concentration.

"We're near a crime scene... thought you'd packed it in," Dan faltered. The bosses' look nearly sent him reeling. His subordinates reckoned he'd never need a gun, his look could kill from a hundred yards.

Dan handed his boss one of his last two cigarettes. He did not dare mention again the SOCO's would consider the fag as contamination even outside the yellow tape area, but no-one argued with the Guv. He had planned to quit smoking himself this very evening, intending to have a pint of beer and savour the last two fags, on the understanding, of course, that events allowed him to get to the pub.

"When there are no more murders, violent robberies, or muggings in this bloody town, I'll succeed in giving up. You not having one?" Cole snarled.

Blake shook his head, not bothering to explain. He repeated, "What's turned up?"

Roy Cole took a deep drag of the cigarette and exhaled. Dan caught a whiff of the smoke and had to fight not to suck it into his starving lungs.

"You listening or not?" Coles' bark made Dan jump. "They've just found two feet, another hand, finger tips also chopped off like the one the dog found, two matching ears, and a penis. No head or torso. Dog appears to have unearthed most of it. Oh yes, and some bollocks."

"Also a matching pair?"

"What?" The heat-seeking missile glare that accompanied the question would have sliced off the top of Dan's head had it landed. He almost ducked it was so menacing. He had worked with Roy Cole for three years and still found it hard to believe his boss did not have a sense of humour, something sorely needed to remain sane in their job.

"I assume they belong to the same person?"

"Probably. Pathologist will pack up the bits once the SOCOs and photographers have done. We're closing off the whole park as I speak and the team will do the usual sweep. Thanks for coming at short notice." He took a deep drag of the cigarette, and slowly blew out the smoke before continuing, "How's Kennedy's undercover operation going?"

"Seems good. He joined the gym five weeks ago. I've

joined recently so it's not apparent we know each other. Don't acknowledge each other obviously. On the application form I'm a civil servant, although I understand from the Fitness Assessor they don't tend to inspect those." Dan wrapped his arms round his body, the cold now beginning to penetrate his thick coat. Taking another discreet gulp of the lingering smoke from his boss's cigarette, he continued, "He's talking to Tomas already. Noticed yesterday morning when Adam was on the rowing machine, Tomas arrived and before he even went to his office, walked over and chatted."

"Good. Keep me posted. How're you contacting each other, usual?"

"Yeah, mobile mostly. Simple coded text message we've worked out. I'm his 'mum'. I see him at the gym as much as I can. I'll up the visits now he's making progress. These are nasty bastards."

Dan watched as Cole pinched out the cigarette butt, and was relieved to note he obviously now remembered the need to keep even the outer area of the crime scene contamination free as he conscientiously wrapped it into his handkerchief before slipping it into his pocket.

Dan continued, "Anything else I can do here, Guv?"

"No. I'm back to the station, nothing more I can do until we get the pathologist's report. Only came because I knew you were in court. D'you need a lift?"

"No, thanks. My cars at the edge of the park. I want to view the crime scene before returning to the station to complete the witness's report. Weird coincidence, Guv, I've seen Lucy Hamilton at the gym. Under the circumstances, I'm gonna dig deep, find out if she's got form; check her history."

"I don't believe in coincidences in our line of work and you're meant to be there keeping an eye on Kennedy and the developing situation, not drooling over a young, lithe body. Just do your job. "

"You noticed the lithe body then." Dan instinctively

ducked but his boss only gave him one of his famous enigmatic looks and walked away.

"See you at the station, Guv."

He stood for a few minutes undecided whether to have the last remaining cigarette now or save it for later. Checking his watch, he chose not to smoke, as he was eager to check the crime scene, but momentarily his thinking wandered back to Cole's question about the undercover investigation.

In a Police investigation named Operation Centaur, Dan was working alongside a fellow officer, Detective Sergeant Adam Kennedy, who was operating undercover and attempting to infiltrate a paedophile ring suspected of operating in the area. Contacts had suggested it was a large, well-organised ring called 'The Brotherhood', spread out over the country but divided into small, manageable cells.

Two years earlier there had been a similar police operation code named Operation Rawhide, but the Police Officers involved then had been less knowledgeable and experienced, and arrests had been premature, resulting in shambles. The majority of the ring members had escaped and the few arrested then released because an idiot judge, in the Police's opinion, had ruled at the beginning of the trial that the 'entrapment' process used at the time was inadmissible. Other 'cells' had by then been alerted and their members gone to earth or got themselves cast iron alibis. The operation had been a costly failure so it was imperative that this time they proceed cautiously.

Adam was slowly getting to know Gerry Tomas, manager of the local gym and suspected as being the leader of the local paedophile cell. Dan was the undercover officer's handler.

He snapped his mind back to the present, and hurried towards the crime scene, taking in the activities of the SOCOs as he did so. He admired their meticulous procedures, their methodology leaving nothing to chance, and despite the diligent and bustling activity, their movements were totally organised, no-one getting in another's way.

Checking his watch again, he realised that if he was to get his own scrutiny, he had better do it now, as he ought to get back to the station to complete his report.

Pulling the white protection suit over his clothes, his thoughts returned to Lucy Hamilton. She acted innocently enough, but Dan knew criminals could get an Olympic Gold for acting. When he returned to the station, he could not wait to start digging on the inscrutable Lucy Hamilton.

Still, first things first.

Ducking beneath the surrounding yellow tape, he felt excited. He inevitably found his own take, what to take on board, what to dismiss, what to pursue on a crime scene more valuable than any written reports from the white suited experts.

Chapter 2

The Watcher

Carefully positioning his car so he would not be noticed, the watcher ensured he had a good view of the school's playground. It was ten thirty and the kids were due out to play at any moment. He glanced anxiously at the sky, crossing his fingers that the heavily pregnant grey clouds would not give birth to a downpour because that would mean the children would take their break indoors.

A bell peeled in the distance, the clouds held onto their load, and his eyes widened with anticipation as his little delights, dressed in identical bright yellow jumpers, swarmed out of the school doors into the playground like bees from a hive. The noise escalated from a gentle buzz to ear splitting decibels in ten seconds. The hubbub composed of screams of laughter, joyous calls to friends and ecstatic shrieks greeting long lost friends not seen for at least an hour. The babble and clamour overwhelmed the playground and the monitors winced with pain.

Spotting the faction he'd dubbed 'the outsiders', centre left of the playground, he noticed they were grouped together for support as usual. Their uniforms showed the most wear, and their knees bearing the normal wounds of childish play were uncared for, presumably by either overworked or neglectful mothers. These children and their shabby state were the result of poverty, and their pauperism made them more vulnerable, and that was what he wanted.

Their richer cousins wearing well turned-out jumpers that contrasted to the dullness of the day, were banding together confidently at the playground centre. He appreciated they may not necessarily be more loved than the poorer kids, but experience had shown him they were not such easy prey.

During previous surveys he had meticulously noted mums who were late picking up their children from school, or the kids who regularly hung around the playground or just outside the school gates because mum had missed the bus, maybe worked late, or perhaps just did not care about being prompt.

'Careless Mothers' was what a Kenyan guide had once told him that he dubbed Giraffe mothers. They left their young unprotected in the open, whereas the wily lioness hid her youngsters away from prey. Her genes, evolved over the millennia, ensured she trained her offspring to stay concealed from predators and not stray. Her large teeth and watchful golden eyes also guaranteed she regularly fed her hidden young, ensuring their survival. The giraffe children, exposed, gormless, unwatched, were unprotected. The watcher liked the 'Giraffe Mums' better; they made his job easy.

He had memorised the teachers who were in charge of four to eight year old children, and not released until the parent or nominated person arrived to claim them from school. The watcher then noted the teachers stringent in applying this technique. Two 'frumps', one with a big nose and a grey hair-bun, and also a young, black teacher who always wore unfashionable skirts, never released the children in their charge without rigorous checking. They promptly escorted children back into the classroom to await their parent's arrival if they were late.

Happily, for the watcher, there were also the 'lax lot'. One nerd in particular was particularly careless; the short, skinny teacher with John Lennon look-alike glasses often became involved in conversations with other parents anxious to ask questions. That allowed other charges keen to flee the confines of school to slip away without teacher noticing whether or not their guardians had arrived. The watcher liked this type as well.

It was the watcher's duty to study and assess. 'The Brotherhood' told him the best schools to survey and he had duly studied two from a poor part of town, and another one from a better class estate.

The 'better class estate' school had been a fruitless exercise. The mums mostly turned up in cars and whisked away their offspring in a timely fashion. The 'poor' school he was watching today was definitely the best choice. His research confirmed that many kids were regularly left on their own for a few minutes too long. That's all he needed to know.

He was the only one performing the job in this area, and if any watcher was late reporting in, circulated messages in code ensured cast-iron alibis were available or disappearing acts performed until it was safe to re-surface. That way, the Brotherhood was not at risk.

There were more watchers in other villages, towns, and cities doing the same job, but he liked to think he was the best. The Leader of his cell had told him that the Elders of the Brotherhood admired his perfection. That made him proud.

Forcing his thoughts back to the present, he spotted the little boy who was his likely target. He had reported his findings about him to the Brotherhood, and they agreed he sounded perfect for their needs.

Timmy, the prey, was streetwise but that would not necessarily save him. Whilst the Nerd was talking with another parent, as he invariably did, Timmy regularly slipped behind his back and ran into the playground, and freedom! Feedback at local cell meetings suggested there were many 'Timmys' around the country if you watched and waited patiently.

Taking it slowly over many weeks, he began chatting with Timmy, casually explaining he was meeting his grandson, a fictitious child of course. Later, when Timmy recognised and obviously trusted him, the watcher had given him a few sweets. On another occasion, the boy had run over to him and realising that could be troublesome, the watcher now parked where Timmy could not see him unless he wanted him to.

Sensing he'd parked long enough, he rewarded his hard work by allowing a few moments of enjoyment; ogling at chubby legs or girls' thighs when their skirts swirled up as they played with their skipping ropes.

Noticing the Nerd who was on playtime duty looking in his direction, he got out of the car, walked to the boot, opened it and lifted out a box, and placed it into the car. This was a pre-planned move to avert doubt should someone eye him with suspicion. Made it look like he had stopped for a purpose, and he was careful to walk round the nearside of the car so he could not be identified clearly. He drove away, noticing in his side mirror the Nerd had looked away, already disinterested.

Never mind, I'll be back. This job isn't a burden, I love looking through those railings and watching those delicious sweeties. A paradise of Turkish delight. A whole shop of kiddy candy.

Chapter 3

Adam Kennedy walked into the gym wearing a navy blue tracksuit. He had joined the gym five weeks ago; received a fitness assessment that had shaken him to the core and immediately panicked him into giving up his twenty-five cigarettes a day. Then determination had kicked in, and he now painstakingly worked through his Fitness Assessor's suggested routine every other evening. 'Emphasis on the pain bit', he had informed his amused work colleagues. Amused, because as long as they had worked alongside Adam, and for some that was almost three years, fitness had not been his top priority.

The ribbing had been good humoured. His colleagues were aware his life over the last few years had been harrowing. His wife had died from breast cancer two years ago, leaving him with twin girls who were only a year old when they lost their mother. The new practice of keeping fit seemed to have given him something fresh on which to focus outside of work than just the caring for his children.

When Adam had first heard his remit of becoming acquainted with the gym's manager, he had groaned aloud. The thought of rowing machines and lifting weights was definitely not his idea of having fun. However, a few weeks into the operation, and he was beginning to enjoy the discipline and its benefits. The weight was slipping away, he had more energy, and the normal morning cough due to the cigarettes had virtually disappeared.

He put his leather holdall and tracksuit top into the locker, inserting the required pound coin to lock it. Another member, his locker still open, was sitting nearby on the bench, tying his shoelaces. He had merely nodded to Adam and an outsider would have maintained the two men were strangers and the brief acknowledgement was that of occasional recognition but not friends. Shoelaces tied, the second man, tall with dark red hair, glanced around the locker room. As his study indicated they were the only people present, he rose, walked to his locker alongside Adam's and deposited his wallet. Without glancing at Adam, he quietly asked him about progress.

"Yeah, fecking good. Making headway," murmured Adam, his words still laced with an Irish accent despite living in the U.K. for ten years. "The bastard told me he's coming in later. Maybe that'll be the time to hint at my having done time."

"OK. Give me a bell afterwards. Don't push it though." He secured his locker and walked to the gym entrance, not giving his companion another glance.

Anyone inspecting the images on the recently installed, poor quality security cameras, thieving had been rife in the locker room over the last few months, would think the two men had not recognised or communicated with each other.

DS Blake, groaning inwardly, walked into the gym and glanced round; trying to decide which of the array of torture machines in front of him would give him the least pain.

He spied Lucy Hamilton and once again wondered at her obvious obsession for keeping fit. Knowing he was nowhere near as fit as he should be, he winced as he surreptitiously watched her as she stood near the water dispenser, left leg bent at the knee, foot touching her backside as though it was the most natural position in the world. Conscious that if he attempted this move he'd be very likely to acquire a severe thigh strain, Dan flinched at the thought. Finishing her drink, he watched as she tossed the plastic cup into a rubbish bin, and walked to the cross-trainer.

It was just over a week since Higgins had dug up the body parts; Dan had been to the gym twice and on each occasion, Lucy had been there. They had nodded at each other but so far had not talked. Dan did not want to encourage conversation because on his joining form he had described his job as a civil servant in case Tomas should inspect them. He did not want the manager to be suspicious that a cop was now a member. Dan knew after the previous failure two years ago, Tomas would be extremely vigilant and suspicious.

Not keen to do any exercise, Dan walked away from the rowing machine to the water dispenser, deciding a drink of water would kill a few more minutes. Sipping the water, his eyes flicked between Adam trying to kill himself on the running machine, and the large windowpane on the upper level that Adam had told him was an observation window that ran along the front of Tomas' office. He was startled when Lucy suddenly appeared in front of him, hands on hips, and not looking best pleased.

Having experienced a number of sleepless nights, instead of letting things ride, as she knew she should, when she saw Dan at the gym again, she was convinced he was watching her, especially as he had previously said he did not often have time to get to the gym. For her peace of mind, and a night of desperately needed sleep, she needed to settle her disquiet. She glared and asked, "Am I a suspect?" Her eyes, dark as black treacle, flashed as she spoke.

"What?"

"When you interviewed me just over a week ago, I got the impression that I could be a suspect. Is that why you're here, keeping an eye on me?"

Aware she had caught him off guard, he stared at her for a second too long before saying quietly, "Obviously I can't comment on an on-going investigation but let's just say..."

he paused before continuing, "Well, no-one's ruled out at this stage. We're just continuing with enquiries."

"Um." *He appears to be telling the truth. OK, change the subject away from yourself.* "I thought you said you weren't fit because you couldn't find the time to get here often. I'd have thought an ongoing murder enquiry would have meant you were up to your eyes in work."

Another wary look flashed across his eyes. He recovered immediately, but she was glad he had re-acted like that. She felt in control now and his discomfort definitely took the attention away from her.

"I've worked non-stop for twelve hours. This hour in the gym is instead of my kip time."

"Well maybe you're more dedicated to fitness than you make out. Anyway, back to it, just another hour and I can go home."

Dan lurched between horror and amazement as she walked away to an empty rowing machine.

Another hour! Bloody hell, she's totally, fucking obsessed.

Looking round for Adam, he noticed he was now madly heaving away as though out to beat the world record on the other rowing machine. Still sipping the water, and knowing this was just an excuse to kill time, he took a deep breath to get motivated, and actually exercise. He must not draw attention to the fact he was not really here to get fit. If Lucy Hamilton had spotted him idling, then a wary Tomas might also notice.

Wandering to an empty 'torture' machine that conveniently gave him a view of both Dan and Lucy without being too obvious he was observing them, he re-set the clock displaying time and pressures, taking into account his capabilities. His eyes, as though attached to a piece of string, swivelled to Lucy, and he noticed the shimmer of perspiration that silvered her legs. He dragged his eyes away, but could not help admitting she was very attractive, obsessed or not!

Two minutes later Gerry Tomas walked through the gym

on his way to his office. The police officer persona over-powered the man, and Dan focused on the job he was there to perform. He forced his loathing for the man not to show on his expression.

She'd been relaxed, now she was uneasy. *Is he coming here to check on me? He says he isn't... um, he acts like getting fit isn't for him, yet he's always hanging around this gym. If I'm not a suspect... shite... why doesn't he bugger off. I'm going to glug down a very, very large wine as soon as my derriere hits the sofa tonight.*

Her thoughts spiralled and an uneasy feeling of panic slithered snakelike up and down her spine. She rowed like a demon possessed. Memories zigzagged through her mind, like interference on an old black and white television.

She'd been a plump child. Her end height had not been obvious then. *You can change your appearance in endless ways,* he'd said. He looked her up and down, not with any bad intent, just being practical. *'I think you've got the fat genes of the family. It'll be hard, but eat sensibly, no crisps or cakes, play games at school. Netball, hockey, tennis. Then when you're old enough, join a gym. Work hard and you'll be slim, quite unrecognisable.'* So she had. The fact that she suddenly shot up six inches in her mid-teens from a mere five foot four to five ten was a bonus.

Now her hard work seemed to be slipping away. *I hate not being in control. What the hell's happening? First Higgins finding the bones, now this cop's suspicious. Must find out what he's thinking. Bloody bummer!*

Thoughts lurched like tumblers in a lottery drum, her panic made her unaware of the perspiration slithering down her back, and shimmering on her legs.

1994

The girl stood on her usual patch, desperately trying to look sexy and inviting. Business hadn't been good for the past three hours; the punters weren't buying tonight. The unseasonably cold weather that had just arrived was probably keeping them indoors. Pulling her lightweight coat tightly around her slim body didn't prevent the spiteful wind penetrating the thin material and whistle viciously round her legs. She massaged the right one, trying to rub the goose bumps away. Her skirt was too short for the cold and damp evening.

"Men like to see a lot of leg. Skirt right at the top of the legs. Easy to fantasise about the heaven just above it," Winston, her pimp had told her right at the beginning. "Makes them think of schoolgirls. Punters like a bit of young."

He'd picked her up three weeks after she had arrived in London. She'd not eaten for three days and her pride had flown away like an escaping bird. Absolute necessity, if she was not to starve, forced her to go on the game, but two years down the line and she still hated it. The other girls told her she'd get used to it, maybe even like it in the end, but she never had. They were all more experienced so she listened and remembered their advice.

"Suck their dicks but don't kiss 'em full on the lips. That's for real love."

Most of the girls did it to feed their habit, but she never did drugs. Winston did all he could to force her, but that one bit of pride in herself saved her sanity. He wanted her hooked because then she'd be completely in his power. She suffered because of her strong will, and his resentment meant she got more kicks and thumps than the rest.

Strange thing was, he never' 'touched' her. He fucked

all the others, but her aloofness made him uncomfortable. She'd been the only girl he'd ever controlled that wasn't using. According to Winston's outlook, girls were only good for domineering, shagging, and slapping around if they got lippy. Still, she'd rather have an extra slap or kick than his sweaty hands all over her tits and his breath, reeking of tobacco, pumping into her face as he shagged away. Acting enticingly for slimy punters was bad enough, but Winston would have made her sick to her guts.

The air smelt damp and the rotting leaves clogging up the gutters wafted along the street competing with the pong of the drains. Looking again at 'the bastard's' watch as she referred to it, she hoped for the umpteenth time her stepfather was dead and had died a slow, painful death. She'd nicked the watch from the hall table the night she ran away from home. His wife's wedding ring, he'd married her after her real mum had died, had been lying beside the watch so she'd nicked that too, and tossed it into a neighbour's dustbin as she'd sprinted down the road. She wasn't streetwise then. Now she knew she should have kept the ring and hocked it.

Glancing up and down the empty street, she mumbled to herself,

"Sod it, another ten minutes and if I haven't scored by then, damn Winston, I'm going home." She vigorously rubbed the other leg to get the circulation going.

"How's business?" a voice asked. Turning round and seeing it was only the local rent boy, she shrugged and turned away. She'd often seen him hanging about her patch near the government buildings. The bum boys also got a lot of trade there.

"Not very talkative, are you? I heard you wus stuck up. Think you're better than the rest of us."

"Sod off. I just don't wanna talk to any rent boy. 'Specially not you,"

Despite her words, she thought he was dishy. Tall and thin with spiky black hair, always grinning as though everything *in his life was perfect. The girl knew that his life could not be that good: his trade was only for desperate characters. Still, his cheerfulness was contagious, and when he'd whistle at her and then wink, she'd put her nose up in the air and turn away, but inside she was grinning.*

"Treat 'em mean, keep 'em keen," Dana, her best mate, had told her. She was right because he kept coming!

"Ooh, they're right. Really stuck up. So what's wrong with me?"

"For one thing I can't stand the sight of you," she lied. "Secondly, if Winston sees me, I'll get another kicking 'cos you're not a punter. I don't need that, so bugger off."

"Winston? Big Maltese guy with the black Merc?"

"Yep! You deaf? I don't want to talk to you."

"Yeah. I'm deaf. So let's go and get a bite to eat. Nice greasy bacon sarnie at an all-nighter, 'bout ten minutes away. Whad you say?"

She turned round, hands on hips, ready to give him a mouthful when she caught sight of his expression: eyes frightened, and pleading. Not the usual cocky grin ruling his face. She hesitated and remembered; her face had probably looked like that once, begging them silently not to hurt her any more.

From the drains nearby the dank smell assailed her nostrils again. This time it reminded her of dead flowers. She saw wilting flowers on a grave, her mother's grave. An image of a young woman with hair like straw flashed through her mind. Touching her hair, 'fair and wiry' Dana had described it, she felt elated. She had the same type of hair as her real mother. Why had she suddenly remembered now? She'd read somewhere all sorts of things could revive memories; smell, music, colours. His words broke her reverie.

"I said, what'd you say?"

She didn't realise that her answer would change her life forever. "You buyin' then?"

His cocky grin returned for a second and then faded. He

said "Yeah, I'm buying. Gotta talk to someone. I've done something terrible."

"What's worse than a bloke shagging blokes?"

"Yeah, I do that 'cos I've got to. This, well... "

"Come on, tell me over the sarnie. Oh yeah, I want lots of tea as well."

As they walked along in a comfortable silence a wailing noise from one of the nearby gardens made them hesitate.

"Christ, what was that? Sounded like a kid wailin'. But sort a weirdish like."

"It's a fox," she said.

"How do you know? Fox! In bloody London."

"They live everywhere. London's probably a paradise if you're a hungry fox. Suburban foxes they're called." She remembered the dirty, torn curtains at her bedroom window, so thin they'd looked like tattered cobwebs and hearing the lost children crying. Only now she was older she knew it wasn't lost children, it was the weird cry of the foxes in the garden. She stopped. A child's face slipped across her memory. They were both sobbing and waving goodbye to each other as the child was dragged away. They called out but their frantic words were lost in the wind, then she was bundled into a car and gone.

"I've got a sister too."

"So, I had loads of the buggers. What of it?"

"I've just remembered. I'm going to find her someday."

"Don't bother. You'll only be disappointed."

He took her hand as they walked but she snatched it away. "Sarnie and tea, you said, that's all."

CHAPTER 4

The men drove through the council estate for the third time and checked again the group of children playing in the dusk on the small patch of scrubby land situated to the north of the closely-knit streets. At the edge of the piece of land were twenty tightly packed council houses.

An hour earlier, when the weak autumn sun had not quite lost its one-sided fight with the looming evening, there had been eight children on the play area. Half an hour later, the orb's battle virtually lost and over, the number had reduced to four. Now, at four thirty pm on a Wednesday in late September, only one little girl was left playing.

Michelle Foster was six years old, not very bright, but with the face of a cherub, and her blond, bouncing curls completing the angelic picture, she looked adorable. Patsy Foster, her unmarried mum, known locally to be 'extremely friendly' after three vodka and cokes, was twenty-one, and had three children by three different fathers. Brad was four years old with skin one shade less than ebony. Shaun, the redheaded three-year-old and the rascal of the family, was the literal product of a one-night stand. Patsy had been leaning open legged against a pub wall enjoying the thrusting of a man with a red beard from the Highlands of Scotland. Michelle's actual conception was an alcoholic blur although Patsy recalled it had been a great evening.

Patsy was a good mum considering her circumstances, and was having a quiet cigarette whilst her sons were engrossed in watching SpongeBob's antics on the television. The last time she checked on her daughter, she had been playing with the two girls from next door who were vainly trying to teach Michelle to skip.

As she walked to the front door to eventually call Michelle to come in, the phone had rung, and her friend Mandy, who was a right scream, took her mind off the darkness now galloping over the horizon, ecstatic at its success. When Patsy casually glanced at her watch in the middle of Mandy describing in great detail about the shag in the back of her car with a dishy black fellow she'd been chasing for the last month, her heart did a painful jump as she realised it was five past five.

Looking immediately through the doorway to the play area, dismay overwhelmed her when she realised that even despite the two street lamps situated either end of the green patch of land, she could not see her daughter.

Without explanation, she put down the receiver in the middle of Mandy's 'coming' for the second time in ten minutes, and rushed to the green. Michelle was nowhere to be seen.

Running haphazardly around the edge of the play area, hysterically screaming her daughter's name, Patsy's heart thumped with an ominous fear. Despite the recently installed double-glazing in the council houses' windows, her shrieks were heard and she was soon joined by six more equally panic stricken women. The noise and searching proved fruitless; Michelle had vanished. Patsy fell to her knees, her daughter's disappearance causing the pain in her heart to escalate to such a violent level; she found it hard to breathe.

Unaware of the furore her disappearance had caused, Michelle was sitting in the back of a black car with darkened glass windows eating fruit gums. The driver glanced at his companion in the back seat who was stroking the child's hair and licking his lips. It had been so easy.

Chapter 5

The elderly couple were using the microfiche sited in a room at the back of the library that housed the two microfiche machines and eight computers. The information they wanted wasn't available on the computers the librarian had informed them.

Despite the warmth of the building, they both wore outdoor coats buttoned up to the neck. The man had deigned to remove his flat cap but his companion kept her woolly hat rammed firmly on her head. They were scanning old newspapers for the relevant information they needed. The students from the local Technical College were downloading data for their studies from the near-by computers. It was as though the very air in the room was aware of the need for concentration, and the hush rivalled the silence of outer space.

As Miss Brown, the Chief Librarian, entered the room, arms topped up with books and magazines that needed replacing in this area, she found the silence almost tangible.

"You OK?" she whispered to the couple, not wanting to disturb the nearby students' absorption, although their wrapt expressions suggested only an atom bomb would achieve that. "Anything else I can help you with?"

"No, we're fine," replied the man quietly, quickly

switching pages as though not wishing her to see his perusals. "Thanks very much for your help. We've found what we wanted."

Miss Brown smiled, nodded, and mouthed a silent 'Good', deciding she was being overly fanciful that the man had switched to the next page so promptly. She remembered them from previous frequent visits and wondered what it was that caused them to research so diligently.

At ten minutes to six, two junior librarians waved cheerio to Miss Brown and left the premises. On checking the upstairs floor that contained the non-fiction books in the library, the newspaper room, and the toilets, Miss Brown hurried downstairs to complete her scrutiny and turn out all the lights as she did every working day after closing time. She was therefore surprised to see the lights still glowing in the back room. Distinctly remembering to ask Deborah to switch off those lights unless anyone was still using the room, and to inform them the library was closing in fifteen minutes, annoyance at the girl's failure coursed through her stocky body.

Someone had obviously been using the room, and the scatter-brained girl might well have issued the warning, but then forgotten to switch off the lights after they had left.

That twit will never make a good librarian, totally disorganised with the memory of a goldfish.

Miss Brown was fifty-two, and a spinster through and through. She had nothing in her life but her work, three cats and her knitting. Forgetting to switch off lights or inform her of such was a mortal sin in her eyes. She was 'tsking' loudly as she walked into the room and discovered the 'microfiche couple' still there. They were in the process of switching off the viewer and gathering together their numerous pieces of notepaper, but she still fought a hard battle to be polite.

"So sorry," whispered the man, although the need for hushed conversation was now unnecessary. "We were so near completing our findings, we decided to press on and not have to return another day."

Good manners, top of the list in Miss Brown's narrow life, came to the fore and she smiled forgivingly and whispered,

"That's absolutely fine. I just hope you've found everything you needed?"

As she followed them out of the door and nodding again at their enthusiastic thanks, she locked the door, then shook it three times to ensure it was totally secure, and felt satisfied she'd obviously been a great help to the lovely couple.

Fifteen minutes later, sitting with knees tightly pressed together on the six twenty bus to Caversham, she wondered what had been so interesting to the couple that they had spent almost three hours searching back microfiche-copies of various national newspapers. If she realised her assistance was helping with the planning of another murder, she would have suffered an apoplexy.

Chapter 6

Bloody hell, another evening exercising, this is killing me.

Dan needed to time it just right. He had finished exercising, or rather, the exercise had finished him. He organised his routine, although not always in the same order, so he could check on Adam's activities. Firstly a quick scull on the rowing machine, then onto the cross trainer which was unbelievably knackering, aiming for ten minutes non-stop action, although he usually only managed five. Then onto the running machine, with the whole process normally taking twenty minute, at the end of which time his aching muscles were giving him gyp.

Lucy had arrived just after Dan, and now familiar with her schedule he knew it would be another hour at least before she would conclude her exercising. Adam was running on the other machine, totally focused and not appearing to notice his female companion.

Glancing up, he noticed the glamorous two had ceased their running and were chatting to each other. An unexpected spike of jealousy skewered his body. He looked away, trying to shake off the feeling.

Walking to the water dispenser where he was very aware he spent more time than ever actually exercising, he poured himself a long, cool drink and fantasized as it slid down his dry throat that it was a double whisky, a Jameson's or something equally smooth, and after downing it, fantasying a deep draw from a cigarette.

"You did very well on the rowing machine, DS Blake."

The words startled him; the cold water spurting out of his mouth and cascaded down the front of his tee shirt.

"Damn. Sorry, you made me jump." He pulled up his tee shirt to wipe his mouth. When he saw her looking at his exposed chest, he hauled it down quickly, wishing the sight would have revealed rippling muscle. Glancing up at his face, her expression was inscrutable.

He noticed her eyes move to the tattoo on the top of his arm. It was a Chinese symbol and Dan wondered if she would ask its meaning, but she did not comment.

Glancing back from the tattoo to his face, she said, "Are you going to be long?"

"Long?"

"I need to talk to you about something. I'm not going to be here long tonight, but... if you're busy it doesn't matter. It'll keep."

Dan had planned to go to the local jazz club, knowing if he did not get there by 7.30, he would never get a seat. He had promised to save a seat for Luke whose shift did not finish until eight, and by then all the seats would be taken.

"Is it police business?"

"I wouldn't be asking if it wasn't." She gritted her teeth, and snapped as she continued. "Forget it. It's not important."

She turned her back, and went to walk away but something about her worried expression pricked his conscience. He always prided himself at being good at reading people, but he felt confused by this lady. There was something about her that he could not figure. DC Meena Mesbah, a member of his team, had carried out a deep background check, but nothing showed up; she seemed as clean as a religious zealot. That in itself was not unusual, most people just led ordinary lives, but a completely clean sheet, not so much as a speeding fine was scarce, and curious in Dan's opinion. Dan's conscience moved from a slight pricking to a sharp jab. Maybe she was in some sort of trouble.

He called after her. "Miss Hamilton... Lucy, look I'm going passed your place on the way to the Majestic rooms. Did you drive here?"

"No, I jogged."

"OK, how about I give you a lift, and we can discuss it on the way."

She turned slowly, obviously considering his offer. Staring momentarily, as though she was unsure of his intentions, she said. "You sure? Have you finished exercising? You haven't been here long, and I don't want to..."

"No, its fine. I do need a shower though. Meet you by the front entrance, in say, twenty minutes."

"Thanks. I need a shower too, so twenty minutes is fine."

He watch as she walked to the door

"Get your eyes off her arse," a voice with the softest velvet southern Irish drawl whispered. "Randy bastard. Only here five minutes and you're chatting up the local talent." Adam's head, bent over as he filled a plastic cup with water making it not obvious he was speaking.

Dan answered just as quietly, cup over his mouth. "Just police business, mate. Though she's not a bad piece of woman, I must admit. Anyway, enough of your sexual fantasies. Things progressing OK?"

"Yeah, fine. He's starting to talk to me. Give you a bell later. I'm off home in ten minutes." He walked away.

Hurrying into the men's locker room, Dan stripped off his clothes and was in and out of the shower in five minutes. Glad he had made the effort to change from his working suit into jeans and what he hoped was a trendy looking sweater, he panicked when he could not locate a comb. Inspecting his hair in the mirror, he groaned when he saw the spiky mess.

Shit, it'll have to do. Christ, it's not like it's a date. You're only giving the girl, a suspect at that, a lift home.

He ran his fingers through his hair, hoping for a miracle,

but they were all out because it sprang relentless back into its original prickly points. Grabbing his bag, he got to the door before he realised he had not cleaned his teeth. Having read some-where that the biggest put-off for women was dodgy breath, he had carried a spare toothbrush, toothpaste and mouth wash in his leather holdall ever since. Not that he had to use it recently; he had not managed a date offer for some time. In fact, he reluctantly admitted he had only managed two dates in two years since his divorce.

I repeat, it's not a bloody date!

He hurried to the basins, scrubbed his teeth, and gargled until he had coughed. When he eventually got to the front entrance, showered and peppermint breathed, he realised he was quite looking forward to giving Lucy a lift. *Maybe find out something about her background. Blake, who're you kidding, randy sod.*

She was standing with her back to him, gazing out of the glass doors, and he noticed her trim figure in her jeans.

They walked to his car in silence. He sprang the boot and chucked in his hold-all. Taking her offered backpack, he placed that in too.

Opening the door, Lucy asked, "Majestic rooms. Isn't that where they hold the jazz evenings?"

He waited until they had got in the car and belted up before answering. As he drove away, he said,

"Yes, I'm meeting DC Luke Steiner and my mate Alex there. You have to get there promptly or you don't get a seat. Not that I manage to get there often. As often as we make arrangements, something invariable turns up, and we miss it."

"A friend of mine works there some evenings behind the bar. He's also involved with the Tribute evenings. He's in the Queen band; and does the George Michael sessions."

Glancing across at her, Dan said. "I know him... um, Freddy..."

"Heath. He lives in the flat above. Occasionally I go

running with him. Not often though, he's a lazy git mainly. He's just got a job at the gym as the physio."

This piece of information made Dan prick up his ears. He did not pursue this point but thought it might be worth investigating. "Right, you wanted to ask me something."

"It something that's been bothering me for a week or so, but when I say it out loud, you might think I'm an idiot."

"Well, I won't know if you don't tell me."

"As you know, I go running quite often. Most days in fact. Just recently I've had this feeling... I know you're think I'm crazy, but it's spooky. When I'm in the park particularly, I feel like I'm being watched." She glanced at him and he looked back, a slight frown crossing his forehead. When he did not comment, she continued, "See, sounds stupid like I said."

"Is there any reason you think that someone should be watching you?"

Until he said those words, Lucy did not realise just how worried she was that someone had recognised her. Deciding she did not need any investigation into her life, she knew she was stupid to bring any attention to it. Shrugging in a nonchalant manner, and speaking casually that was not in line with her feeling, she said, "Forget it, I'm just being silly. I always did have an over-active imagination."

Silently cursing the fact she had used the reason to check whether he was suspicious of her in any way, she changed the subject.

"Tell you what, don't drop me off at home, I'll come to the Majestic rooms. I keep promising Freddy I'll drop by and see him. Don't worry, I won't interfere with your evening. Is that OK?"

"Course it's OK. I'll even treat you to a glass of wine or coffee, which ever you'd prefer."

"No-way. I'm bumming a lift, I'll treat you." She was silent for a moment, then continued. "You said your friend Alex. Freddy has a friend Alex who he goes there with sometimes. Alex King. Same Alex?"

Dan glanced round at her, eyebrows raised in surprise. "Yeah, that's him. How do you know him?"

"I met him first through Freddy when I went to see him perform at his Queen Tribute Night. Turns out he's married to my friend, Sara."

This time, besides his raised eyebrows, Dan's eyes widened, showing the whites. "Sara, you know Sara. Christ, that *is* a coincidence."

"Why? Anyway, I always understood the police didn't believe in coincidences."

This time, Dan laughed. "No, you're right. That's my bosses favourite quote. Course, we all know, sometimes they do happen, and I reckon this is a case in question. How do you know Sara?"

"Met her about... oh, four or five years ago at yoga lessons. We got talking, then we both got a bit bored with it and used to go drinking after the lessons, which rather defeated the object." She glanced at him. "How long have you known Alex and Sara?"

"Oh, we go back years."

He did not offer any more, and Lucy did not push. Sympathetic to anyone who did not wanted to enlarge on a subject, understanding too well how uncomfortable it was when someone kept probing.

A light rain started, and as Dan switched on his windscreen wipers, they smeared the screen and produced purple and green halos around the lamplights lining the road. The traffic was light, and consequently, within ten minutes they were driving into the car park by the side of their destination.

Dashing from the rain, they entered a large, noisy room that in the nineteen sixties had been a dance hall. Having fallen into disrepair, it was redeveloped five years ago, and tonight was teeming with people listening to a small group playing modern jazz. The music percolated and corkscrewed into the corners of the room. Squeezing through the tightly packed tables bursting with the jazz fanatics, heads nodding enthusiastically in time with the music, the couple eventually found an empty table in the corner.

Dan insisted Lucy join him, as she could not see her friend anywhere. He ambled to the counter with their order, his spirits high and buzzing with the sound of the music, and he reluctantly admitted to himself, although suspicious of supposedly 'clean-as-crystal-white-virgin-snow' Lucy Hamilton, she was a very attractive young woman, and he reminded himself again he had not socially enjoyed female company, excluding the two disastrous dates, since his divorce. Weaving his way back to the table, two cappuccinos precariously balanced in his hands, the ring of his mobile dampened his mood.

Shit. Work! No-one else phones me. Christ, it's my night off.

Putting down the coffees too heavily on the table, causing some of the contents to splash into the saucers, he took the phone from his jeans pocket and gruffly snapped 'Blake.'

"Boss, it's Meena. Luke asked me to call; he won't be coming. Get yourself back here, all hell's broken loose. A young girl's gone missing."

The police officer felt guilty about his unprofessional thoughts. Silently cursing whilst slurping down his coffee, he was aware that the chance of discreetly investigating Lucy Hamilton was slipping away at Mach II speed. In a relaxed atmosphere, she might make a careless remark, but this opportunity seemed to be lost forever.

She sipped her coffee, gazing intently into his eyes, and before he could say anything, she said "I can see by your expression, your jazz evening's just come to an end. Get going. Don't worry about me. Freddy will be here soon, and can give me a lift home."

Draining the last dregs of the drink, he stood up, shaking his head with frustration at missing another jazz evening.

Dan apologised and left, cursing himself that he always

prided himself on being a good gauge of character, yet this sexy lady was totally unreadable. He was convinced that her excuse about feeling watched was some sort of excuse, yet unless she lusted after his body, which he very much doubted, why did she want to talk to him? If he was honest with himself, he *was* suspicious of her, yet he did not know why. Plus, annoyingly, she was dishy. He strode from the room, realising he had to focus on his job and not on her appeal.

She watched him go, a frown covering her face. She had decided, during another sleepless night, that if he were a threat to her present existence, then she needed to get to know him better, and discover his true intentions towards her. She knew he was not interested in getting fit, yet he kept coming to the gym. Did he suspect anything? She sipped her coffee. *And I haven't learnt a damn thing tonight other than he drinks cappuccino.*

Chapter 7

Donald Taylor felt distraught. He had not seen his friend Nigel Matthews in weeks. Normally they were as thick as thieves. They travelled to cell meetings together; appreciative that they were not meant to know each other's identities, and therefore careful not to reveal their friendship, Nigel would drop off Don a couple of streets away, depending on the meeting's venue. The locations were never the same, ensuring difficulty for anyone not involved in the operation to pinpoint meeting places and attendees. Don would then walk into the meeting, a different entity to Nigel, no connection, no acknowledgement.

At the meetings all the attendees had code-names, secret, unique titles. Don was Atlas and Nigel was Argonaut. No other attendee should know another's true name, ensuring that should the police question them, they could not reveal anyone's true identity. It was all about security, but Nigel and Don's friendship meant that they had no secrets from each other.

They had met at one of the cell meetings three years ago. When a police operation two years ago had resulted in the arrest of four of the members, Nigel and Don had been two of those four. Luckily, some doddering old judge had not agreed on how the police had conducted the investigation, and had released them. They could not believe their luck.

After their release, Brother Samson, the leader of the cell, warned all four to be especially vigilant. He also cautioned everyone within the cell that they had been lucky, but now plans for Operation Hobbledehoy were almost complete, everyone should be alert. Providence may have smiled on them before, but the police have long memories. Brother Samson suspected the police would constantly scrutinise everyone known to them whilst they had sufficient resources.

The two friends were well aware of this, and had been careful. Even though Nigel had now moved in with his friend, they only treated themselves to an occasional peek at certain websites for a little titillation when their feelings got the better of them. They had avoided schools, letting the selected watchers do that job. They did not photograph kids in parks or ogle them in the street. They had obeyed orders, and not attracted any undue attention, but now Nigel had disappeared and Don was sick with worry.

Two weeks ago, Nigel had gone to see his sick mother who was in a nursing home. She had recently become very forgetful and diagnosed as having the first stages of dementia. She had gone downhill unusually quickly, and Nigel had placed her into suitable nursing accommodation.

He had never returned after the last visit. Don had phoned the home to see if Nigel was still there but they said he had not visited recently. Don felt as though his heart had been ripped from his chest.

After a few more days, he considered whether he should report Nigel's disappearance to Brother Samson, but as he should not have a relationship with any cell member, it made it difficult. How could he report his disappearance under those circumstances? Agonising about it for a week, eventually he gave in and phoned his leader.

To alleviate suspicion, Don explained he and Argonaut lived near each other, and despite wearing masks at the meetings, Don had recognised him when he saw him in a local Supermarket. He assured Brother he was very security conscious, but was worried about his disappearance, suspecting the police may have picked him up. He therefore decided he ought to warn Brother Samson in case of repercussions. When Brother Samson started to sound suspicious about their relationship, Don assured him he did not know him well, and they never acknowledged each other.

Brother Samson was silent for a few moments, then snapped,

"Just act as though nothing has happened. Don't attend any meetings until you hear from me, and don't ever phone me again. Now you've contacted me I'll have to get rid of this phone. You've been told never to communicate with me unless it's an emergency."

"But this is an emergency," Don had protested and then realised he had said too much. He was furious, and though always nervous of the all-powerful Brother Samson, his friendship overrode his fear and made him brave.

"It's not a bloody emergency. If the law have picked him up and if he's done nothing, then they'll let him go. Don't panic. Be patient, wait! He'll turn up eventually. As I said, don't phone or speak to me again. I'll contact you if and when necessary."

Nigel didn't appear, and Don had not heard from him for so long that he felt bereft. He knew the reception he would receive if he reported him missing to the cops. The duty copper, once he knew who he was and that he had form, would smirk, take the particulars and then whisper quietly in his ear,

"Good, one less nonce to worry about makes the world a better place."

Bastards! I hope all nosy coppers fry in hell.

As he turned into the quiet road at the edge of the council estate where they now lived, Don felt deeply despondent. He and Nigel had lived so happily here after residents hounded them from their comfortable flats on the Coley Bank Council Estate following their unexpected release due to the 'entrapment' technicality. Neither Don nor Nigel exactly understood the meaning of that term, but they had not cared, they were free!

Head down and deep in thought, he did not immediately notice the car drawing alongside until the driver, an elderly gentleman, called to him through the lowered car window.

"I've got a message for you." The man smiled gently and an old woman on the back seat sitting behind the man waved in a friendly fashion. "Nigel asked me to speak to you."

Don's heart leapt with joy. He leaned over and peered into the car.

"Nigel. Nigel Matthews. You've seen him. You know where he is?"

The old woman patted his hand.

"Course we do, dearie. He's been proper poorly. We've been looking after him for the past couple of weeks. He's a bit better now. Asked us if we'd fetch you? He's *dying* to see you again."

"That's great news. I've been out of my mind with worry. Where is he?"

"Get in the car, mate, here in the front. We'll be there in ten minutes."

Don opened the passenger door. Nigel was safe. Relief hurtled through his body with the speed of an Intercity train

The elderly lady in the back offered him a lemon sherbet sweet, his absolute favourite; his feelings soared with happiness. As he was selecting the sweet from the paper bag, the elderly man started the car engine and then turned and smirked at him. When a strong, clinical smelling pad was pressed onto Don's face from behind, he was so surprised that he waited a second too long to push it away. Someone held his arms as the inside of the car floated to the stars sparking before his eyes, and then on to the end of the universe.

Chapter 8

Dan caught up with DC Meena Mesba as she climbed the stairs to the meeting room.

"Thanks for the call. What's going down?" he said.

"Like I said on the phone, young girl's gone missing from the Coley Bank Estate at tea-time. DI Black's getting us all together."

"You better now? Over the flu' bug?"

"Nearly there. I had to come in, Paul Fletcher and about eight others at least are still off sick. At least I'm on the mend; they're just going down with it. If they feel anything like I felt, we won't see them for a couple of weeks."

"Who's leading the case if Paul's off?"

"DI Cole's the Delegated Officer answering to DCI Jacobs. With Adam Kennedy working on Operation Centaur, we're still thin on the ground."

Walking into the meeting room, Dan appreciated Meena's comments about the lack of staff. Normally at such an important meeting, the whole team would be present for a briefing but half the chairs were empty.

DI Roy Cole was standing at the front of the room. He nodded briefly as Dan and Meena entered and took seats in the front row.

"Just started. I'll recap. Michelle Foster is six years old." He pointed to a large photograph pinned at the top of a white board behind him. An angelic face surrounded by a mop of fair curls smiled down at the audience. "Uniform have just obtained the photo and it's recent. She lives on the Coley Bank Estate and was playing on a piece of ground about fifty feet from her house. Her mother, Patsy Foster, a single parent, said she was checking on her every few minutes and was about to call her daughter in at around five o'clock when the phone went and she became distracted for about ten minutes or so. When she glanced out, the child was nowhere to be seen. She and some neighbours quickly formed a search party and combed the area, but couldn't find her. She then phoned us. Uniform responded immediately as the hysterical phone call suggested a highly vulnerable missing person situation."

"Who's there now, Guv?" interrupted Dan.

"DC Luke Steiner, DC Mel Stubbs who will act as the FLO should it be deemed necessary." DI Cole scratched his head and his eyes swept the room. "OK, you all know what this means. A lot of hard graft with long hours but this child has to be found."

He turned and looked at his second in command. "Dan, I've got a list of Actions you need to classify. I want you to organise the manpower for road blocks, stopping and questioning local traffic in a designated area, friends to whom Michelle may have gone, addresses of all known nonces, house-to-house, tracker dogs, and whatever else you know is needed. Distribute the copies of Michelle's photos to all the teams. I know we're short on resources at the moment. Just do the best you can.

"When you've finished, join me at the house. I want you leading the team on this one. Paul's on sick leave. Meena has the address and more details." He turned back to the rest of the team. "OK, we're short on manpower, as I've said, but we give it our best. If she's not located by tomorrow, or heaven forbid, a body turns up, the chief's alerting other stations for immediate back-up." He picked up his coat from the back of a chair and walked towards the door, calling over his shoulder, "Dan, keep me and the DCI updated."

"Yes, Guv."

As the team dispersed, Dan and Meena hurried back to their desks, discussing the details of organising the task that would take them well into the night.

By ten thirty, pleased that he and Meena had efficiently delegated the tasks, he had to blink away the bucket of grit he felt scratching at the surface of his eyes. Fighting to stay focused, he was not sure the new regime of knackering exercising was helping his stamina.

His last task was to alert Guy Peterson, the local police dog handler, as searcher dogs would be needed by first light. He had phoned but there was no reply from his mobile or land line. Deciding to email him, Dan was confident, knowing Guy well from their Police College days, that he would check his messages first thing in the morning.

Rubbing his eyes again, Dan was grateful when Meena appeared with two cups of coffee and chocolate bars.

"For energy. I heard you grinding your teeth. I can tell you're dying for a ciggy. Maybe this'll stop the craving."

"Cheers, Meena, you're a mind reader and an angel. Anything back yet from the pathologist about the body pieces from the woods?"

"The reports on your desk." She took the top report lying in his in-tray and waved it at him.

"Anything? DNA match? Summarise save me reading it."

"No, nothing back from the data base yet. That could take a few days at least."

Someone tapped him on the shoulder and on looking up, saw it was the young policeman, PC Simon Leadbetter, from the front desk.

"Been trying to ring you. Somebody's at the front desk asking for you, DS Blake."

"I'm busy. Who is it?"

"A Lucy Hamilton. Apparently left her hold-all in the boot of your car." The young man could barely hold back his smirk.

"Shall I get it for you, Boss, and give it to her? I know you're busy," said Meena, eyebrows raised, eyes open in innocence.

Dan stood up, feeling in his pockets for his car keys.

"No thank you, comrades. It's nothing like what your dirty minds are thinking."

"I'm not thinking anything, sir," said the young police constable, who in Dan's eyes looked like he should be at home doing his homework.

"Nor I, Boss," added Meena, her joking voice concealing her feeling of disappointment.

"Yeah, yeah."

As Dan walked into reception, Lucy was walking up and down impatiently.

"I'm sorry. I'd have dropped it round as soon as I realised," he apologised."

"My front door keys were in the bag."

"Christ, how did you get here? No, don't tell me, you jogged."

Lucy lifted her foot, pulled her trousers up above her ankle slightly, exposing stiletto-heeled boots.

"Hardly think so. Hobbled the last bit. Left my running shoes in the holdall."

"Why didn't you phone, I could have returned it?"

"I had the feeling my needs weren't an emergency."

"Thought you said your friend would give you a lift home."

"Yes, I know. He didn't turn up. I phoned him but he didn't answer. Anyway, I was pleased to have the exercise... well, until the feet starting hurting."

"Wait here. Take a seat. I'll grab you a coffee. I'll be ten minutes and I'll run you home."

"There's no need really, I... "

"No, I insist. Ten minutes. I'm going to Coley Bank. Your place is on my way. Simon," Dan turned to the young police constable who by this time had returned to the reception and was listening avidly to their conversation. "Get Miss Hamilton a coffee."

He headed for the door and called over his shoulder to Lucy, "Ten minutes, tops."

Fifteen minutes passed by the time he returned to reception. Lucy was deep in conversation with PC Simon Leadbetter and didn't appear to mind the wait.

"OK," said Dan. "Through here, my car's parked below."

As he drove out of the underground car park, the rain, just to be spiteful, fell in cold torrents.

"Glad I'm not walking home in this. By the way, on my way here, I cut through the high street. My television's on the blink; I'm on the look-out for a bargain. I looked at the news on a tele in the Co-op window and saw a news flash passing across the bottom of the screen. Apparently a young girl's gone missing locally. Coley Bank Estate."

Dan did not reply. Lucy looked sideways at him, wondering at his silence.

"Oh my God, you said you were going to Coley Bank! Is it about the missing girl?"

"Sorry, I can't comment. The facts aren't clear at the moment."

"Of course, I understand. You shouldn't have offered me a lift. I've probably delayed you."

Dan said nothing more until he turned into her road and pulled up outside the block of flats where she lived.

"You didn't delay me. It was on the way."

After exiting the car, Lucy turned and smiled at him, saying. "Thanks, I'm very grateful. Hey, I didn't tell you my address. How did you know where I lived?"

"You gave me your address when I interviewed you in the park, remember?" *And I noted it. Always remember things when I'm wondering... speculating...*

61

"Of course, you've got a good memory. Thanks again for the lift. Hopefully see you in the gym... if you ever find a minute." As she walked to the front door, she hoped he was telling her the truth and once again her thoughts tumbled in panic. *He'd never remember my address from that interview. He must write down loads of addresses. Does he suspect? Damn, I'm getting paranoid again. Bummer, bummer!*

As Dan drove away, the mystery whirled in his mind. He shrugged it away. Probably she was just a normal, innocent member of society. Yet there was something he could not put his finger on.

Jesus, I'm as obsessed with her as she is with her exercising. He tried not to think that it was, in fact, her rather appealing slim body.

Nearing Patsy and Michelle Foster's house, he pushed all romantic thoughts from his mind. This poor kid was missing, and her mum was probably in hell. He needed to focus.

Chapter 9

"Miss, can I tell you some'ink well dodgy?"

Lucy looked up from marking the writing books that belonged to her class.

"Course you can, Jade, what's wrong?"

"S'not me, Miss, it's 'im." Jade Thompson thumbed at her companion, a very scruffy boy called Genghis Simpson. On first hearing his name, Lucy thought it was a joke or a nickname. It apparently wasn't and Lucy decided whoever inflicted the poor child with that moniker ought to be severely punished; the boy would have his leg pulled for the rest of his life. Ironically, his classmates accepted his name without a flinch and called him 'Gengy', which also caused her to wince, but the boy tolerated his nickname without comment.

"What's happened, then, Genghis?"

The boy shrugged. "Nuffink really, Miss. She's just a goody goody. Making a fuss 'bout nuffink."

"Well, one of you tell me what this 'nuffink' is about?"

"I will, Miss. He's been on the Internet. Gone into a chat room or some 'ink."

Lucy was immediately alarmed.

"Does your mother know that you're doing this, Genghis? You have to be careful of these places, you know."

"His mum ain't there, Miss. She buggered off with Tommy Atkin's dad. My mum says she's a cruel tart, leaving kids without a mum."

"OK, Jade, let's hear what Genghis has to say." Lucy turned to the boy. "Firstly, when you go into this chat room, are you monitored?"

"Am I wot, Miss?"

"Who looks after you when you get home from school and then assists... helps you when you with the computer usage?"

Jade, who was hovering from foot to foot and couldn't wait to add her bit again, said, "He don't need no 'elp, Miss. When we doos 'is computer studies, Mr Frankham says he's a whiz at it. He gets ten out of ten every time, don't you Gengy?"

"Thank you, Jade, but I need to hear from Genghis. When you get home from school, is that when you go on the Internet?" The boy nodded, and if Lucy hadn't just been told he was a 'whiz', she might have concluded he was prone to being on the slow side. Certainly in class he didn't contribute a great deal.

Mustn't judge by appearances. Look at Einstein... wild, bushy hair... "And who looks after you and your younger sister...?"

"Boudicca?"

God, Maybe it's a good job your mother's gone if that's the sort of names she's metering out.

Lucy tried very hard but just couldn't resist asking,

"Have you got any other brothers or sisters?"

"Only Bonnie-bluebird, she's thirteen but she lives with mum sometimes."

Bonnie-bluebird ! I rest my case.

"Right. Who looks after you and..." Lucy couldn't bring herself to say it.

"Boudicca."

"Yes. Bo... yes."

"No-one. I'm ten so I waits for Boudy. She's in year three."

Lucy shuddered, *Boudy, almost as bad as Gengy!*

The young boy added, "She's nearly eight. I waits for 'er. I got a key. Me Nan sometimes tries to get round but she's got arth... arth something."

"And your dad?"

"When he gets home with the fish and chips, we're OK."

"Where does your dad work; very far from home?"

"He don't work much, he has to look after us kids. He's usually up at the betting shop trying to get some dosh."

"Right. When he gets home, does he monit... check what you're doing on the computer?"

"Nah, he can't use a computer," Jade interrupted. She'd been silent too long.

"Is the computer yours? Was it bought specifically for you, Genghis?"

Looking ill at ease, he glanced at Jade for support, who, most unusually, didn't add anything and looked equally uncomfortable. Lucy decided not to pursue that line of questioning in case it was an 'off-the-back-of-a-lorry', and that didn't seem pertinent at the moment.

"Let's get back to the original point. Why, Jade, did you come and start telling me about Genghis talking on this chat-line. What's happened that you think you ought to tell me?"

"'Cos this perv wants to meet Genghis. Says he can get him into films and he can earn loads of money. I told me mum and she said it were a load of bollocks."

"Thank you, Jade. Please don't use that language in school." She turned back to the boy. "Have you told anyone else about this? Told your dad or your Nan?"

"Nah, Miss. Please don't tell him, he'll clip me round the ear. "He turned to his friend. "I told you not to tell her. I said I'd get into trouble."

"It's dangerous talking to pervs," Jade retorted firmly, hands on her hips. "Tell him Miss, they comes and meets you and takes you away in cars and rapies you and murderers you and fings, me mum said so. Never take sweets from 'em or nuffink. Just kick 'em and run me mums says. They're well dangerous."

"Yes, Jade, thank you. It can be dangerous although I don't want to unnecessarily alarm you." Lucy turned back to Genghis and looked deeply into his eyes, hoping he would take on board the seriousness of the situation. "Genghis, you need to listen and do what I tell you. Firstly, please do not go into that chat line again. Secondly, you must report this to someone in your family. If I come to your home and explain to your dad or your Nan, would that help?"

"He said Gengy ought to bring Bouddy with 'im. They could make a film and they'd be famous and make tons of money," Jade said, her big blue eyes getting bigger and bigger and her voice getting louder and louder. "It ent no good telling Mr. Simpson, he'll only wallop him and won't do nuffink. Nanny Simpson's deaf as a post and don't know computers. I think we should report it to the cops, Miss."

Lucy smiled at the streetwise girl's wisdom. Looking at Genghis, she realised how vulnerable he was, motherless and more or less coping for himself. She'd noticed previously that his clothes looked old, and on occasions none too clean, but he was a likeable lad and she tried not to judge. The school was in a poor part of the town and most of the parents were caring and responsible, despite their obvious lack of cash.

"I tell you what we do. Don't go into that chat room again. Promise me." After Genghis' solemn nod, she continued, "I'll speak to Mr Donahue, this needs to be dealt with immediately. Don't look so worried; you won't get into trouble, I promise. By the way, what was this man's name, did he tell you?"

"Sherriff or Lawman or some 'ink.," said Jade, who might not have her friend's computer skills but certainly was blessed with a working tongue and obviously the leader of the two children. "I said that's not a proper name. That's a perv's name. We've 'ad pervs on our estate. They got booted out after they got out of jail. Me mum says we don't want those buggers living near us."

"Why is Sheriff, Lawman, a... why isn't that his correct name?"

"Obvious, ennit. When those pervs was caught last year, they all had funny names."

"How did you know this, Jade? Don't tell me, you mum says..."

"That's right, Miss," said Jade, missing the irony. "She heard it on the news and 'er friend works in them courts and 'ears fings and when those pervs comes back to our estate, my mum got up a 'tition to get rid of them."

"Thank you, Jade. Now I think you'd better run and get your lunch, at this rate, you won't have time to finish it. I'll speak to Mr Donahue and I'll talk to you again tomorrow. Hurry and eat your lunch."

"Thanks, Miss," said Jade. Genghis merely nodded, his eyes thoughtful and Lucy knew now a lot more went on behind those eyes than she'd previously realised.

Jade called back as they left the room. "We'll finish our lunch easy. Gengy sometimes forgets to make 'is sarnies so I share's mine wiv 'im."

At the door, Genghis turned and said quietly, "His name's Lawman, Miss, not Sheriff."

Lucy thanked the boy, a pain of dismay filling her chest, realising she must investigate the possibility of getting the boy on the free-school-meals list as soon as possible. The dad probably never realised that facility was available. She slipped the books into her desk drawer and hurried away to the Head Master's room to report her conversation with Jade and Genghis. Some things were more important than catching up with your marking.

Chapter 10

Dan put the phone down and Meena noticed he looked pleased with himself. They had returned from Michelle's house, distributed the job action forms, and until any results came in, they were carrying on their investigations into the body parts left in the park.

"OK boss?" asked Meena, as she put the third cup of coffee in two hours on his desk. It was past midnight, and the caffeine and the stale cheese sandwiches bought previously from the station's canteen, were the only things available to keep them going.

"The DNA results are back from those body parts."

Meena, checking her watch, stared back him, amazement beaming from her huge Persian eyes.

"It's turned midnight. How in the world did you get DNA results so promptly, and at this time of night? I was told they'd be days."

Dan, eyes focused on his PC, mumbled "It's who you know that counts, my dear."

"And they've got a hit?"

"Yes, apparently he emailed me before he left work," muttered Dan, pushing aside the pile of folders in front of him. "Mate realised I might not be picking up emails as we're up to our eyes in searches and what not, and knew I wanted the info as soon as, so he phoned, good lad."

Meena walked round and stood behind her boss, sipping her coffee. She noticed how his hair, overdue for a cut, curled up over his collar. She would have liked to have tucked in the hair but turned away to avoid the inclination.

"Drink your coffee, boss," she said quietly as they waited for the computer to boot up, conscious her boss only saw her as a colleague.

Dan automatically obeyed, subconsciously aware that the policewoman was unable to drink her coffee if it got cold. If she made a drink for anyone and they allowed it to go cold, she was reluctant to make that person another one. Her colleagues pulled her leg about the obsession but always drank their coffee while it was hot to ensure a supply of future drinks.

As the information appeared on the screen, Dan highlighted the subject and they both leaned forward to read the contents.

"The DNA is a match for Nigel Matthews." As Dan read the rest of the file, he muttered, "Nigel Matthews. Where do I know that name... ?"

Meena straightened up. "I know, boss. He was one of the nonces who got off because of entrapment a couple of years ago. The nonces operation."

"Alleged entrapment. Christ, you've got a good memory. That was before your time here."

"And yours."

"No, I'd been here a few years then."

"You're right."

"What?"

"I have got a good memory."

"OK, clever dick, what are the names of the other three that got off?"

"Umm, umm. Hang on; I'll get them in a minute." Meena's face took on a glazed look, her eyes focused on something in the distance, moving slightly from side to side as though reading from a book. "Joseph Bates, Marie

Grainger, and Donald... can't recall his last name."

Dan leaned back in his chair, staring at Meena, his mind elsewhere.

"Motive... maybe... retribution... payback? Could be," he murmured. "If I recall though, no kids were taken at the time."

"Not quite true. A boy went missing around that time and his body was never found."

"That's right, well remembered. OK, see what you can dig up for me. I know, don't look like that, you're up to your eyes in it but you're a technical whiz, you'll get something about the case in five minutes."

"I was just off home. I'm due back to organise more house to house enquiries at seven thirty," Meena protested to his back as he grabbed his coat to go home.

"Delegate then," he called back through the door just before it closed.

"Yeah, like you just bloody did," she muttered to the swinging door.

Chapter 11

Donald Taylor slowly returned to consciousness. He could hear nothing but was aware his eyes, sticky and heavy, would not properly focus on the two blurred faces peering at him from either side. He was flat on his back and shivering with the cold. Whatever he was lying on was freezing, and rock hard, and certainly wasn't his comfortable, warm bed. His fingers tips caressed a smooth surface, reminding him of the steel table he'd seen on a TV drama used by a pathologist when examining and cutting up a body.

"Hello, luvvie," a woman's voice said, interrupting his pondering. Donald squinted, forcing his eyes to concentrate on her face. Despite the gooey mist still lingering before his eyes, he could see she was the elderly woman from the car. Lines came from her eyes cascaded down her cheeks as though gouged out with a sharp stick.

She's either a heavy smoker, well into the seventies or not wearing well.

Donald wanted to giggle at his stupid thoughts, so unimportant in his present predicament that he sensed was far from normal or desirable.

"Are you comfortable, son?" asked a male voice.

Attempting to turn his head to look at the speaker, he discovered he couldn't, something tight around his throat prevented much movement. His eyes weren't so confined, and they confirmed this voice belonged to a man as senior as his female companion. Dennis remembered the elderly couple telling him they knew where Nigel was; then seeing the lemon sherbet before the pad pressing into his face.

"Where am I? What's happening? Have I been in an accident? You said you knew where Nigel was."

"Yes, we do. Would you like to see him?"

"Yes, please. He's OK then? I've been so worried."

"I expect you have," said the man, his voice held a sympathetic tone. "Just lie there, we'll go and get him."

The two heads disappeared from view before Don could explain that he couldn't move anyway. Attempting to wriggle his hands and then his legs and feet, he could feel hard leather or something similar, chaffing his wrists and ankles.

I'm so cold; it's numbing my brain. Can't work out what's happening. What's going on?

Donald forced himself to relax. He needed his thinking to be clear.

The couple offered to take me to Nigel. Said they knew where he was. Why'm I tied down like this? Maybe Nigel will explain.

"Here we are then," said the woman, her face appearing in his limited field of vision.

"You're looking forward to seeing him so much, we know," said the man, his face appearing as before on the opposite side. "We've done a lot of research over the last couple of months. We've found out you and ol' Nigel were good mates. Mind you, once they run you off the Coley Bank Council Estate, we had a bit of a job tracing you. Anyway, we persevered and found you again."

"And here we are all together, isn't it fun," added the woman. "Come on Donald, say hello to your friend Nigel."

"Looking forward to this moment, are you?" said the man. "Bet you were worried about him. Don't suppose you could sleep wondering where the little rascal was? Isn't that right?"

Donald was puzzled. Why were they stretching this out so long? Why didn't Nigel just say hello and put his mind at rest. His friend wouldn't normally taunt him; he'd know how frantic his disappearance would make him. Donald decided he'd better play along with this game, even though it was beginning to annoy him. Lying here, strapped down, and with the distinct feeling he was bollock naked, his fingertips couldn't detect any clothes, and he was in no position to argue. He forced a grimace.

"Yes, I'm really looking forward to seeing him." *So stop sodding about and get on with it.*

He was really going to tell off Nigel when they got home, mucking about like this when he'd been out of his mind with worry.

"Here we all are then. Say hello to each other, Don meet Nigel, Nigel meet Don." The woman cackled as she spoke.

The elderly man held what looked like a badly made wax-work model of a head, resembling a poor replica of Don's face. The smell was awful, like rancid, sickly pork.

Jesus, what the hell... bloody reject from Madam Tussards. Why the hell are they showing me a waxwork model, stupid idiots? They don't know where he is at all.

Don inspected the model, trying to control his stomach, which was churning and burping like lava heaving slowly up from a volcano crater. The model's hair was dark, greasy, sticking up as though shocked. The skin was greenish and the mouth gaping open in an 'o' shape. The teeth, resembling the white and even ones in which Nigel took such pride, contrasted totally with the rest of the horror before him. There were no eyes, just bloody holes where they once were. The bottom of the neck was ragged, as though crudely hacked or sawn from the body.

It sort of resembles Nigel, but they haven't really done a good job if that's a model.

Don wanted to tell them to stop buggering about and just let him see Nigel, but the contents of his stomach weren't reacting too well to the stench and he knew if he tried to speak, he'd puke for an Olympic gold medal if puking was an Olympic sport.

"Come on, ducky," said the woman. "You're not saying much. How does your friend look? Bit on the dicky side, I'm afraid."

"Yes, sorry about the raggedy neck. Think I've lost my touch there," said the man, beaming proudly by the side of the model. Don dragged his eyes from the model to gaze uncomprehendingly at the speaker. "Didn't have the right tools. Was a time when I could slice through a side of beef so it fell apart with both sides as smooth as silk."

"I did the eyes," boasted the women. "Stan told me how to do it, how you prise them out without bursting them, but I was useless. Might be better with yours. More experienced now. Look, this is what I used. This special one-pronged fork. Had hell of a job getting it. Couldn't even get one over the internet. Stan had to go the wholesalers in the end. Still, determination pays off."

"Come on, Don, say hello to your mate. Don't waste time because you could be saying goodbye as soon as we get started if you don't co-operate. Mind you, that won't be for a couple of days. We'd like you to lie here and contemplate your future."

"Take another look. Don't worry though, you will see him again." The woman waved the long, thin hook before his face. "Just before I poke your eyes out with this, I'll let you have one more look at him."

Don moaned and lost the battle with his stomach contents. They spewed out of his mouth but due to his prone position, gravity pulled them back over his face.

"Why are you doing this? What have we ever done to you?" Don whimpered through slimy lips that were covered artistically in carrot coloured vomit.

"Don't you know?" said the man. He bent and whispered lengthily into his ear.

"Don't know what you're talking about. I swear I don't know where he is, truthfully. I'd tell you if I did."

"Just what dear ol' Nigel said. Someone knows. Eventually we'll find out."

The man walked away and placed Nigel's head on a shelf that was just within Don's vision. As he heard the door shut behind the couple, he whimpered and then felt the hot urine puddle at the top of his legs before trickling down to pool beneath him.

Chapter 12

"OK, let's consider what we have. Try and make some sense of this."

The buzz of muted muttering from the dedicated task team gathered in the briefing room stopped immediately. Dan Blake walked to the left side of a white board divided neatly in half by a thick black felt pen line. On one half of the board was a photograph of a man, and on the other, Michelle's smiling face beamed down at the assembled men and women committed to finding her.

Pointing to the image of the man, he said, "Collating and disseminating the information and facts from these two events supplied by you to date, there is a suggestion there's a tenuous link between them. The DNA retrieved from the body parts discovered in the woods on the side of Elmpark identifies this man, Nigel Matthews. Anyone remember him?"

Dan looked round the room still sparsely populated due to the flu outbreak. There were four detective constables present including Jim Davison, and Tom Carter, both men in their early forties who Dan considered experienced and reliable. Meena Mesbah, who had joined the team a year ago and the newest recruit, Luke Steiner, a likeable young man well known for his good humour and an eye for the ladies. The others present were uniformed police brought in to cover the staff shortage, and had been involved in the necessary searches carried out over the council estate and the surrounding areas.

Jim half raised his hand and replied to Dan's question.

"Boss, d'you mean one of the nonces that got off with so-called entrapment after Operation Rawhide failed."

"That's right. You probably remember it too, Tom. Meena and Luke weren't around then but even so, Meena, diamond brain, recalled his name instantly and has been doing some digging around." He turned towards the woman detective constable and asked, "Dug up anything else yet?"

Meena shook her head. Dan turned back to the white board and continued, "The picture below is a photo of the remains. No torso, fingers chopped off, so no finger prints, and no head." Dan moved to the right hand side of the board and pointed to a photograph of a young, smiling girl. "Michelle Foster, six years old. As you all know, taken from near her home five days ago. Despite extensive house-to-house enquiries, dragging the quarry lake at the back of the estate, questioning all known nonces, immediate traffic blocks... zilch.

"She hasn't been seen since and we have no witnesses who saw anything. Some of the neighbours, trying to be sensitive, hinted that Michelle was a sweet kid but a bit slow. Her mum, apparently, had told her time and time again about the dangers of going off with anyone, but admits Michelle probably wouldn't remember. DCs Steiner and Mel Stubbs, now the official FLO, have been liaising with the mother and built up a good relationship considering the circumstances. Mel is with the mother at the moment.

"Realistically, after this amount of time, we know statistics suggest the chances of Michelle being found unharmed are unlikely. However, that mustn't stop our efforts."

"Boss, these two cases, side by side, what's the link then?" said Tom Carter.

Dan pushed his fingers through his hair, causing it to

stick up even more than usual.

"There is no hard evidence and I know we have to keep an open mind, but I think it's a bizarre coincidence. A nonce's remains turn up and the next day a child goes missing."

"So the link is 'nonce'. Is that what you're saying?" said Jim. "'Cos I think we must all be assuming the same thing, the chances are some perv's got her."

Dan shrugged. Adam's undercover work certainly suggested the paedophile ring was active, but currently this information due to Adam's involvement was on a need-to-know basis only at the moment, so he just commented, "Yes, the link has got to be 'nonce'. Our enquiries need to focus on whether the body parts and those responsible for Michelle's disappearance are members of the same group or it's a nasty coincidence. The Guv's least favourite word.

"Pressure is being exerted on all locally know nonces but nothings come up as yet." He turned and pointed to three names listed below the Nigel Matthews column. "Joseph Bates, Maria Grainger, Donald Taylor. These were the three others also released due to the alleged entrapment inadmissibility. Uniform are checking their last known addresses. We need to speak to all of them."

"I know that trial hardly got to court before it was thrown out, but there were other nonces we know about that got away, or suddenly had rock-solid alibis," said Tom Carter.

"Yes, I know. I repeat, all known paedophiles are being checked, but what we need to find out is whether there is a link. One step at a time" He turned and pointed again to the names of Bates, Grainger and Taylor. "We need to speak particularly to these three in regard to the Matthew's case as well as Michelle's. We've been promised more resources if we need them, but at the current time we're coping and information's coming in steadily, so we press on." He pointed to two piles of job lists.

"OK, right pile here, Actions for the Day; left pile is a list of actions I want you to be considering in the longer term. Take one of each. I know it's hard working long hours, but Michelle is our top priority. If we can tie in a link with Matthews, so much the better. OK, get to it."

The room cleared quickly. Dan gathered up his papers and with one last look at the whiteboard hurried from the room, grabbing a coffee from the drinks vending machine on the way.

He dropped the papers untidily onto the pile already spilling over much of his desk, and spied a note written in large red writing sitting in his filing tray. Reading the message, he experienced alarm and unease at the content.

DI Blake

Telephone message taken at 0830 from a Miss Lucy Hamilton.

She wanted to speak to you about something that alarmed her at the school yesterday where she teaches. A young boy, Genghis Simpson (I'm not kidding) aged 10, apparently has been going into a chat-room and speaking to someone who calls himself 'Lawman !!!'

This man is trying to persuade the boy to meet him, offering him money, saying he can get the lad into films.

Lucy (hold-all on the boot of the car lady?) Hamilton hopes she has persuaded the lad not to contact this fellow any more but thinks she ought to report it anyway. She's reluctant to report this to his father (apparently a one parent family situation) because the boy's scared he'll get a thump from his dad. She's now spoken to the Headmaster who is at a meeting in London and he has agreed she will act as the liaison point.

Wants to know if you think this should be investigated further?

Signed PC S Leadbetter

It was the name 'Lawman' that worried him. The hairs pricked at the back of Dan's neck and a knot of deep concern tied in his stomach. The evidence was growing by the minute that the link to current events was 'paedophile'. He bit his lip as he re-read the note. One child missing was bad enough, two would be catastrophic!

Chapter 13

Lucy opened the door to DC Meena Mesbah, startled by the police officer's stunning looks. Her hair was tied back in a severe bun, but it didn't detract from her attractive appearance in any way. Obviously of Middle Eastern extraction, her skin was honey brown and her eyes, fringed with lashes so long they looked false, were the colour of golden syrup. When she smiled and introduced herself, flashing her warrant card at the same time, her teeth were tiny, like a child's first set, and so startlingly white, Lucy decided she could make a fortune on adverts for toothpaste.

"Come in," said Lucy. She walked ahead of the policewoman, indicating the door to the living room and inviting her to sit down while she made them coffee.

"Thank you for agreeing to see me when I phoned at such short notice," said Meena as Lucy placed the coffee cup and a plate of ginger biscuits on the low table in front of the sofa. Patting Higgins' head, Lucy urged the policewoman not not to be fooled by the big eyes suggesting he was starving as they pleaded silently for a biscuit, he'd just been fed.

"Poor Higgins, never mind." She sipped her coffee before saying, "Thank you for phoning us with this information and agreeing to see me. As I explained to you or earlier on the phone, DI Blake is very concerned about this man that is talking to..." Meena consulted her notes, "Genghis Simpson, who I understand is one of your pupils." She continued at Lucy's nod of agreement. "Perhaps you would go over exactly what you understand went on in this communication between the boy and this person on the internet?"

Lucy explained the conversation she'd had with Jade and Genghis, emphasising that she didn't want to get the boy into trouble with his father, but felt that she would never forgive herself if he came to any harm just for the sake of a possible clip round the ear for doing something he should not.

"You've made a sensible decision in contacting us. I ought to tell you some background facts. Regarding the man contacting Genghis..." Meena looked hard at Lucy. "Excuse me, I don't want to appear rude, but is that really his name, a foreign name perhaps, or is it some sort of nickname?"

Lucy grimaced, sipped her coffee, and then chucked.

"It's his real name. You don't want to know what his two sisters are called."

Meena laughed in return. "No, don't tell me. People often look surprised at my name." She picked up her notebook, the moment of frivolity over. Knowing what she was about to say may alarm the teacher, she consulted her notes, giving Lucy time to finish her drink before continuing. "The contact is worrying in itself, but another aspect for concern is the name used during their communication, 'Lawman'".

As the failure of both the paedophiles' operation and the police fiasco in apprehending many of the suspects had been well publicized at the time, Meena wondered if Lucy was aware of the case and remembered the news associated with it, but may not make the connection now.

The telephone rang and Lucy excused herself and while she left the room to answer it, Meena felt compelled to surreptitiously slip a biscuit to Higgins whilst putting a finger to her lips, indicating he had to eat it quietly. She needn't have worried, the biscuit was bolted down in one gulp and both the dog and Meena looked innocent when Lucy returned.

"Sorry, a talkative friend. Do continue," said Lucy.

"What I'm about to tell you is in the public domain already. Two years ago there was a police operation during which four people were arrested, but eventually released due to a technicality. The press speculated widely on these events but didn't get all the facts right. However, be that as it may, the four were released." Giving Lucy a second to digest these facts, Meena sipped her coffee, refusing the offer of a biscuit. Higgins whined but Lucy ignored him, nodding to Meena to continue. "What I am about to tell you now is not public knowledge but I have been given permission to explain in order that you may help us with our enquiries. Please do not repeat to anyone what I am about to say. One of the four people arrested, hoping for leniency and not realising he would be released on the technicality, gave us some facts. Part of that information was that at certain meetings, unique codes names were used for security purposes. The name 'Lawman' was one of the unique titles."

"Oh, hell, so when a young boy is contacted by what sounds like a predator to me, and uses that name, it's worrying to say the least." Lucy's eyes opened with horror. Her heart was beating so hard she could hardly breathe.

"I can assure this affair is being taken seriously, and an investigation is underway. DS Blake has asked me to deal with this side of it. I'll need to interview Genghis Simpson."

"Mm, don't know how police procedures would sit with this, but I phoned Mr Simpson earlier and have arranged to go and talk to him this evening about what has happened," Lucy said. "The Headmaster has asked me to deal with this matter as I'm the lad's teacher. Mr Donahue's unfortunately not around for a few days, a matter he can't avoid, but feels we should sort this worrying situation as soon as possible. If it were convenient, we could go together."

Meena momentarily considered Lucy's suggestion.

"Mm, that may be an excellent idea. I think you should phone them to prepare them for my arrival with you.

Naturally I don't want to unnecessarily alarm the family and for some people a police officer turning up on their doorstep makes them...anxious. As they are already expecting you, my arrival with you may make them less uneasy, and help with their co-operation. What time was your appointment?"

"Just after seven. The father's explained he wouldn't be home until then. His mother's looking after the kids but he obviously wants to be present."

"Meena glanced at her watch. "Almost six thirty. That's worked out well. Although this is police business, as you made the report and being Genghis' teacher, your presence may encourage the lad to talk." The policewoman stood up. "We'll use my car. I'll drop you back here afterwards."

Lucy stood up and picked up the two cups. "Good. I'll phone Genghis' father and check that he is happy for you to accompany me." She stood up and picked up their cups, heading for the kitchen. "Won't be a minute."

Meena stroked Higgins silky soft head, listening to Lucy's voice as she talked on the phone. On her return, Lucy explained he was quite happy for Meena to come along too. As Meena stood up, Lucy continued, "A friend of mine and his friend, a chef, are coming to cook dinner but we're not eating till eight thirty so time-wise it's just right. I've already left a phone message explaining I'll be out for an hour. Freddy, my friend, has a key so they'll let themselves in. Should take us fifteen minutes to drive there, so we could get going now if you're ready."

"Thanks very much for your co-operation. Accompanying you is a real bonus."

At that moment the doorbell rang three times.

"That's Freddy and Peter now. Freddy always rings three times like that." Lucy glanced at her watch. "They're early. I'll let them in and we can get going."

The two men standing in the doorway armed with groceries didn't fit the 'boyfriend' role, although Meena silently and instantaneously scolded herself for stereotyping.

Introducing the men and explaining they were in a great hurry, Lucy, rubbing her hands at the thought of the meal, told the men to carry on with the preparation and she'd be back to eat at the arranged time!

Peter accepted the explanation without question. Freddy, the perpetual gossip, closed the door and stood with his back to it. He shook his head, begging for details, determined the two women weren't leaving without some juicy explanation.

"Freddy, nosy bastard, open the bloody door. DC Mesbah and I are in a hurry."

"Ooh, important business then, ducky. DC Mesbah, a glam police woman. Come on, Lucy, just give your best friend a whiff of the scandal. You know I can't resist it."

Meena was amazed how easily Lucy moved her friend aside even taking into account his armful of ingredients. He was easily six feet tall, and even though Lucy was taller than the average woman, Meena doubted she could have moved him so readily to the side of the hallway, enabling her to open the door again.

"Love the eyes, DC Mesbah," Freddy flirted. "Eyes to absolutely die for. You should be on tele, in 'Mistresses', not a cop."

Meena couldn't refrain from grinning, he oozed irresistible charm. His smile was cheeky and his moustache and closely cropped dark hair reminded her of her dad's favourite singer, the late lamented Freddy Mercury.

"Come on, DC Mesbah, just ignore him." As she closed the door, Lucy called over her shoulder. "And don't feed Higgins. He's already had a biscuit."

"Sorry about the sneaky biscuit," said the policewoman as they waited for the lift. "You were right, I couldn't resist those eyes. I didn't think you'd noticed."

"It's OK. He gets to everybody. I've had him two years. Got him from a dog pound. After his racing days were over he was dumped. I just couldn't resist him. We looked at each other and we both knew we were made for one another."

"I'm surprised you were allowed to have a dog, living in a flat."

"I know the people very well who own the dog pound. I'd had a greyhound from them previously but Brains got ill not long after I had him and died. Although I lived in a house then, even when I moved into the flat, the people running the pound knew I'd take him out regularly. He gets out at least three times a day."

"He certainly looks fit."

As she climbed into the police car Lucy shivered, a finger cold enough to be straight from the Arctic traced a path down her spine. Recently, when getting into her own car, she'd experienced similar weird feelings of being freezing cold, together with great unease. The temperature in the car had plummeted and she couldn't control herself from shivering violently, despite switching up the car heater to maximum. Dismissing the event once she'd arrived home, these repeat sensations were now disquieting, and apprehension crept down her back, following the icy digit's path.

She glanced at Meena who was concentrating on driving, unaware of Lucy's unease. Silently ordering herself not to be a fool and control of her feelings, Lucy concentrated on the task ahead.

Chapter 14

Dan Blake looked at his watch, raising his eyebrows in a questioning manner, as Meena slumped into the chair at her desk.

"I'm knackered," she said. Raising her eyebrows, she wheedled, "I'd love a coffee."

" Kettle's still broken. I'll get you one from the coffee machine if you want but I know you can't stand it."

"It's better than nothing. Thanks, boss."

As Dan put the plastic cup on her desk, he asked,

"Where've you been? Thought you were going to see Lucy Hamilton and interview her about the pupil approached in a chat room."

"I went. I left a voice message on your mobile updating you. It didn't take long to go over the details so we decided to deal with the problem directly, and go and see Genghis and his father straight away. Lucy, fortunately for me, had made an appointment with the lad's father. The headmaster at the school had asked her to sort it. She wanted to do it sooner rather than later, worrying that Genghis may not take any notice of her warnings, and if left unsupervised, may go back into the chat room and arrange to meet this Lawman."

"I can understand that. Still, fortunate for you. Easy way in. Sometimes when we turn up... "

"Yes, I explained that to her. It worked out really well. A

boyfriend was coming round and cooking her a meal at eight thirty so she was happy to go and leave him to it."

Boyfriend. Dan was surprised by a jolt of disappointment that he experienced. *Hell, she's attractive, course she's going to have a boyfriend.*

Meena, unaware of Dan's feelings for Lucy, didn't appreciate how her words had affected him and blithely carried on. "On the way to the house, Lucy updated me regarding the child's family situation. The mother has left the family home. The father's unemployed, and Lucy initially understood that he spent a lot of time in the betting shop, although he looks after Genghis and his younger sister. So often, when they arrive home from school they are unsupervised."

"And they live on the Coley Bank Council Estate." Dan sipped his drink, frowning as he thought about Meena's words, he murmured, "Umm, not the richest part of town, wonder how they can afford a computer?"

"Lucy had previously asked if the computer was for Genghis' use, but she said the kids, even the talkative Jade who had brought the matter to her attention, looked very sheepish. I decided not to go down that path. An old computer that's possibly 'fallen off the back of a lorry' is the least of our worries at the moment. If we start pursuing that side of things, chances are, they'll clam up, and we'll get no-where."

"Wise move. This could be a real break-though and we don't need non-co-operation."

"Exactly." Meena finished her drink before continuing. "Turns out what Lucy was told by Genghis' friend Jade Thompson about the family situation wasn't quite correct. Mr Simpson actually works in the betting shop. We phoned on the way to check he was already home. He seemed relaxed about our coming, but obviously concerned about what was happening.

"When we arrived, Lucy explained that the headmaster

had asked her to run with this, and explained again why I was
with her. He couldn't have been more helpful. I explained we
needed to check out this situation and it would be helpful if
Genghis, under police supervision, contacted this man on his
computer. We can then take over and agree to the meeting
as he suggested, enabling us to check out exactly what this
man's intentions are."

"And if he is, in fact, the 'Lawman' from the previous
Operation Rawhide."

"Or Operation Blunder as it's now known."

"Yeah, well, let's hope we make a better job of it this
time." Dan drained the last of his coffee from the cup and
tossed it into the bin near Meena's desk. It hit the top and
tumbled to the floor. He stood up and retrieved it before
continuing, "Still, the lads did the best they could with the
resources and knowledge they had."

"I know, boss, I'm not knocking it, just passing on
gossip. Anyway, Mr Simpson, James Simpson, proved to be
very obliging and willing for us to be there when his son
attempts to contact Lawman. I explained Genghis will be in
no danger and he obviously wouldn't be expected to meet
this man, we just needed him to set up the time and place."

"Excellent. When's this going to happen? Contacting
Lawman I mean."

"The dad works late on the days there are horse race
meetings. They're not so frequent this time of the year
but the dog racing is in full swing so Mr Simpson is out
a few week-nights at the moment. His mum, the children's
grandmother, comes and babysits when he's working. I've
arranged to meet there at his convenience, actual day to be
confirmed, when Mr Simpson isn't working, but obviously
as soon as possible. According to Genghis, this 'Lawman'
tends to come on line on certain evenings. I have a list of
those here. When you decide who the police presence will
be, I'll contact Mr Simpson to confirm the date. Then it's
keep your fingers crossed this 'Lawman' comes on-line

when Genghis goes into the chat room."

"Good." Dan leaned back in his chair, sipping his now cold coffee, rubbing his fingers over his blond stubble. "I wonder if we ought to involve Adam with this."

"Will it help his investigations?" Meena sipped her coffee, shuddering at the bitter taste

"Might. If a meeting should be set up, I'm sure he'd want to be on watch and get a gander at this fellow. If he gets in deep enough, it might be very useful to be able to recognise a face in case a new one has come into the equation. "

"Boss, I want to run something by you." Meena continued at Dan's nod. "Lucy Hamilton. She found Matthew's body and now she's involved with the Genghis and Lawman case. She's appears to be a pleasant enough person, but it just seems a strange coincidence, don't you think?"

Dan stared at his assistant, not seeing her Arabian beauty, but considering her words and the worried expression on her face. He shrugged. "I understand where you're coming from. Maybe she was in the wrong place for Matthews and the right place for young Genghis. She can't help being his teacher, that's no coincidence. However, that said, we don't dismiss her. Something feels not right. She's been checked out and has no form. In fact, she's so 'clean' it's almost like she doesn't exist. Not even a speeding ticket, nothing, yet no evidence against her. No, something's not right. We sit tight and keep her in our sights."

"OK," Meena agreed. Deciding it might be prudent not to pursue her point further, she continued, "If a meeting's set up, who will meet with this Lawman? We can't send a young child, too dangerous. We need someone with a really young face."

At that moment, PC Simon Leadbetter walked into the room, ready for his night duty. He nodded and once again Dan marvelled that the young man wasn't at home doing his homework. The two detectives looked at his young face and then at each other.

"What? What?" Simon asked, seeing their looks. He became aware they were scrutinising him.

His fair hair flopped boyishly over his face.

Dan stood up, beckoning at the young man. "I want you to come upstairs with me and see DI Cole."

Meena grinned as she heard the now worried young man asking what he had done wrong as he followed Dan out of the room. Few people willingly went to see Roy Cole. He was rumoured to be able to make an angel feel very much fallen.

Walking to a pot plant wilting on a window-sill, she considered pouring the remainder of the foul coffee into the pot. Deciding that was a cruel act she walked to the cloakroom to dump the poison. Glancing at the clock she noticed it was well passed her knocking off time. Grabbing her overcoat and shoulder bag from her locker, she hurried down the stairs and out of the station before her boss returned and found her another job. He might be a workaholic but she wasn't, even if she did fancy him. She hurrumped loudly as she hurried to her car. A twelve hour day was enough.

Chapter 15

Donald could hear pathetic whimpering sounds. Whoever was making them was getting on his nerves and he couldn't concentrate. The noise distracted him and he urgently needed to focus. He couldn't lift his head too high due to the straps round his neck, but by straining carefully and easing the neck enough for a view but not strangulation, he could just see what the old man was doing and he didn't like it one bit.

The other crazy old coon, his wife, was sitting on a breakfast barstool, humming a tuneless song and popping jelly babies into her mouth. After a while, she became aware Don was watching her. She smiled sweetly, got down from the stool, and wandered over to the steel table where he was securely lashed down.

"Sorry, darling, eating in front of you. How rude of me not to offer you one. What colour would you like? Well, any colour but red, there are my absolute, total favourites so any colour but that." As she talked, Don, from his prone position, could see mashed up jelly babies in her mouth. Small bits of the sweets clung to the gaps of her teeth. Red, green, yellow, it was almost as though she was chewing confetti. He could smell the sweet cloying odour of the jelly and he knew he would never be able to ever eat them again, despite the fact until now he had been fond of them, buying them occasionally when he went to the newsagents for his daily newspaper.

"Green one OK?"

He didn't reply. She popped the sweet into his mouth, which was so dry from fear he could not even chew it. It just lay on his tongue, huge and tasteless like a blob of durable fat.

Holding up the infamous fork she'd shown him previously. "I did show you this, didn't I? For popping out the eyes. You'll be pleased to know I won't be using it quite yet. No, we want you to *see* what's going on, besides *feeling* of course. Hold up the drill, darling, and show the young man your pride and joy."

Don did not want to look, but when he heard the old man say 'Here's my baby', it seemed some sort of adhesive was attached to his eyeballs and tugging them in the direction of his voice. What he saw caused him to wet himself again. A drill with a round head, surrounded by teeth, sharp, curved and gleaming. It resembled the grinning profile of a shark with steel teeth and made a red-hot fear burn through him, making his heart pound so hard he thought it would burst from his chest like the alien in the film of the same name.

"Fucking hell," he mewed, the terror ruling his tongue.

"Naughty boy," exclaimed the woman. "What foul language. I'm going to go and get Nigel. He'll soon tell you that such words won't stop the inevitable unless you comply." She disappeared from view again and returned with the now stinking head, which had deteriorated even more in the hours since he'd last seen it. Holding it by its hair; he could see the face had collapsed into itself, the mouth hanging open resulting in a lopsided grimace. The stench smacked of an open sewer.

She waggled the head and put on a high-pitched voice.

"Oh, Don, you mustn't swear like that. It's very naughty and as for wetting yourself, well, you're a bit old for that. Now when we metre out our just punishment I want you to promise not to swear or piddle yourself like a baby. Now repeat after me, I swear not to be a baby and piddle myself, or use bad language and I promise not to scream too loudly. Come on, say it."

"Fuck off. If you're going to make me suffer, I'm buggered if I'm going to play your stupid game." The words were brave but Don could hear the quaver in his voice and knew it did not sound heroic.

The excruciating pain emanating from his ankle a second after he heard the high-pitched whirl of the drill would have made him jump from the table had he not been bound so securely. He screamed.

"Maybe that'll make you change your mind," said the old man, his head coming into view, the blast from his bad breath equal to the stench coming from poor Nigel' rotting head. "Now when my lovely wife repeats her words, and she'll do so slowly because there's a lot to learn, I want you to repeat them. Savvy?"

Don nodded and as the woman repeated the oath, he whispered the identical words.

"Now, we're not entirely heartless. By the way, call me Muriel. Stan, our manners!" The woman turned her head to the man, her face pained with remorse. "Aren't we rude, you've been here almost two days and we didn't properly introduce ourselves. Here's me nagging you for swearing and I'm almost as bad. We brought Nigel to see you and then clean forgot our manners in the excitement. You don't have to call us Mr or Mrs or Auntie and Uncle, its real friendly in this household. Just plain ol' Muriel and Stan. We'll call you Don if that's OK?"

"Good for you, Muriel, reminding us of how we should act. Now, young Don, we'll even give you a choice of where we cut first? We've given you plenty of time to search your memory and to realise we mean business. Unfortunately, you're not being co-operative, so it's down to business. Where would you like us to begin?"

The whimpering started up again and Don realised the sound was coming from him.

"Stan, you didn't explain that very well. I don't think the poor chap understood one word of what you meant. I'm better at those sorts of things, women usually are," Muriel explained, once more leaning over Don with the multicolour teeth on displayed again. "What we plan, unless of course you can tell us what we want to know, is to cut off bits and pieces of you. Nigel's willy, balls, arms, his feet and some ears were cut off. Stan does it very slowly, very methodically. He's an artist at his work, you know, a proper perfectionist." The old woman turned to her husband, her brow wrinkled.

"At least, I think that's all the bits and pieces you cut off. Am I right, Stan?"

"Yes, you got it right, dear. If you remember, we had a discussion about leaving a hand but as Nigel had been a naughty boy in the past, we didn't want anybody to be able to check out his fingerprints, should the body bits be found, so we chopped off his finger-tips."

"Silly me, you're quite right. I'd forgotten that." Muriel turned back to Don. "As I said, we give you the chance to choose what bits come off first. No, nothing to say? You've gone almost as green as poor Nigel. I'd suggest to you that cutting through the bone is the most painful. Stan used to work in an abattoir and is an expert at cutting up carcasses but even with his expertise, it's not going to be painless." She smiled at the terrified man as though they were holding a neighbourly conversation over a garden fence. Any words of protest wedged in Don's throat as though they were comprised of wet clay, clogging and choking his airways.

Putting her head on one side, she continued, "Oh, deary, deary, still nothing to say? OK, what I'd suggest is that we start with your willy. Once that is out of the way, Stan can get to the balls more easily."

"Young Nigel passed clean out when we did that," said the man, his face coming into view once more, his reeking bad breathe still turning Don's stomach despite the situation. "Don't worry, if that happens; we wait for you to come round to enjoy the rest. Dear Muriel washes you face with nice cold water and you feel a lot better. We put tape over your mouth I'm afraid, because the noise gives Muriel a headache. She's very prone to migraines plus the fact we don't want to disturb the young couple next door. They're a lovely pair but lucky for us Alison's stone deaf and Keith works nights. Very convenient, so we mainly work when we know he's not home. Anyway, these old houses have thick walls, not like the modern tat. Those walls as thin as wallpaper. Alison, lovely girl, not long had a baby and is feeling tired and a bit frail so we like to be considerate. Anyway, here we go then, hang on tight."

Don felt his 'willy' being held up and the saw screeched into life. The pain was so intense that for a few seconds his brain could not comprehend what it had never experienced before, and Don felt nothing. It soon learned, and the agony was the sum total of all the discomfort that Don had felt throughout his whole life. It shot down his legs like barbed wire flaying his nerves. It sprinted back up his body like a knife tracing out his nerve endings until it exploded in his brain like a nail bomb, the missiles severing his cells to shreds.

Don did pass out. When he came to, kind Muriel was bathing his face and making soothing noises. Then Stan started on his balls and it began all over again.

Chapter 16

Lucy, after feeding Higgins and assuring him he was her favourite man, switched on the kettle to make some green tea and then dabbed cold water on her aching forehead, hoping together with the two headache pills she had just swallowed they would stamp on the pounding horses hooves that were thumping over and inside her head.

She was still suffering badly because of the wonderful dinner Peter had cooked the night before. The food had been wonderful, but now she was suffering from a hangover.

Walking into the living room with her tea and a pot ready to top up her cup, all thoughts of food forgotten, she flopped onto the sofa, curling her legs under her. Higgins jumped up next to her, taking advantage of his mistress's sad demeanour because normally this was forbidden territory. He eased his head onto her lap. Absent-mindedly stroking his silky brow, she slowly sipped her drink.

Lucy woke with a start; she must have dozed. Higgins was making noises at the front door. She could hear him scratching at the mat and although not barking, making doggy grunting and snuffling noises. Looking at her watch, she was shocked to see it was nine thirty. This was usually one her nights at the gym but the hangover had put paid to that.

"Shut up, Higgins. What the hell's wrong with you?

Making that damn row."

She eased herself up from the sofa, her back creaking from the slouched position whilst dozing. Her mouth was dry and she wandered into the kitchen and poured herself a glass of water.

"Right, my lad," she called as she walked into the hall, "unless you shut up now, there'll be trouble. Or maybe you're dying for a pee, is that it?"

Damn, I'm going to have to take him for a quick walk before I go to bed.

The doorbell rang three times and Lucy confirmed it was Freddy through the spy-hole before opening the door. He had a large black bin liner in his hand.

"Just calling in for a late night drink. Coffee I mean, not booze. Found this on your doorstep. Christ, Higgins, leave it alone, you daft mutt."

Higgins was by this time leaping with curiosity all over the bag Freddy was clasping in his hand. Lucy waved Freddy in and it took all her strength to pull the dog away from the bag. She dragged the dog into the kitchen and closed the door on him, although he insisted on throwing himself against the door and barking.

Freddy dumped the bag onto the floor. "What the matter with him and what the hell's in this bag. Jeez, it's bloody smelly too."

Lucy's stomach did double flip. A cold sweat broke out on her face.

"Luce, you OK? You've gone as white as a ghost."

She knew she must look ill; Freddy normally did not show that much concern. Glancing at the bag, an unseen hand cruelly dug the end of a sharp icicle through her body.

"Dunno. It's just... Higgins acted like that before when..." She tumbled over the words; her eyes drawn to the bag. "Don't look in the bag. Just don't look!"

"What the hell's wrong? It's just a bag, a smelly bag admittedly. You're over reacting, probably the wrong..."

Freddy stopped, even he wasn't brave enough to refer to Lucy's menstrual cycle, having once before made that mistake and his ears almost shorn off in the resulting dynamite blast. "Probably just a hangover thing. Go and sit down in the living room, I'll look and tell you what it is. Feels like someone's rubbish. Bloody cheek, leaving it outside your door, lazy bastards."

Staring in amazement at the usually brave Lucy as she backed into her room, shaking her head, he mumbled to himself about silly, hysterical women, He peered into the black bag. Inside was another bag, a white plastic one securely with thick black tape. Even the double thickness didn't prevent a foul, sickly smell from oozing out and turning his stomach.

All attempts to rip open the tape failed and Freddy didn't fancy getting a knife or scissors from the kitchen as Higgins was by now throwing himself against the kitchen door and the growling had turned to a desperate howling.

"Shite, a hysterical woman and a temperamental dog. Wish I'd gone straight to my flat instead of calling in and telling her about my first few days at work." The man stood up, chewing his lip, annoyed now that he couldn't get into the bag.

Clicking his fingers, he remembering the Swiss Army knife in the side pocket of his holdall dropped onto the floor when he walked in. The knife sliced through the thick plastic easily. As the hole widened so did Freddy's eyes, his stomach turning a complete painful somersault and he wished he'd listen to Lucy's advice. The contents of the bag looked decidedly bloody, gory and disgustingly nasty and for someone who had fainted when he saw his first birth on a video in Biology in year eleven at school, Freddy was proud that he kept his cool on this occasion.

"Fucking hell," he whispered. "Is this someone's idea of a sick joke?" Twisting round the top of the bag to conceal the contents, he noticed an envelope taped just inside he hadn't noticed previously in his haste. Pulling out the envelope, despite it being addressed to 'Lucy, the lovely dark-haired runner', he ripped it open to read the contents. Normally he wasn't brave but his gut instinct told him he had to do this for his best friend.

"What's that?" said Lucy quietly as she appeared next to him. Her colour hadn't improved.

Freddy put his hands on her shoulders and guided her back to the sofa.

"Sit there and wait, ducky, I'm sorting it."

"But what's going on. Higgins is still going mad."

"He'll have to be patient. I'll be back in a minute."

"What's in the bag?" she called after him as he left the room.

"Nothing. Be patient. I said, I'm sorting it. It's just rubbish," he said, closing the door behind him. He read the note.

Dear Lucy

Excuse us for being so forward, but we see you often and feel we know you so well.

As you and your doggy found the first bag of remains, we thought we'd save you the bother of having to search for the second so we bagged them up and have left them for you. Don't open the white bag inside the black one sealed with sturdy duct tape because we don't want to give you another shock.

When the cops come just tell them that both bastards, excuse our bad language, deserved every moment of the pain they suffered. Take care and keep up the keep fit.

Stan and Muriel

Freddy dialled 999.

Chapter 17

"OK, what have you got?" said DI Blake to Meena and DC Luke Steiner. He leaned forward on his desk and rubbed his eyes. It was eleven pm and they all wanted to go home, but he needed to update his facts ready for his meeting with the boss due the following morning at eight o'clock. "Luke, give me something to cheer me up. I've got to report upstairs first thing tomorrow to DI Cole and the DCI and I want to give them something to stop breathing down my neck."

"Wish I could. Michelle Foster; door to door enquiries have still turned up nothing and it's not that anyone is keeping quiet." Luke leaned back in his chair, rubbing his own eyes that looked as sore round the edges through lack of sleep as his boss's. His normal cheerful demeanour was missing. Understanding Dan's concern about the lack of progress, he sighed and continued, "There is great concern and anger on the estate with her disappearance. It's not that people aren't willing to talk. They're talking non-stop, given the chance; expressing their outrage, but the truth is, no-one saw anything. Mums were preparing dinners, dads not home from work and kids watching TV.

"We know she disappeared in a ten to fifteen minute period at the most. Uniform has thoroughly searched the extensive area of scrubland near the house, but nothing found. Again, the neighbours were wonderful in their response and helped with the searching. Beyond the scrubland there's a quarry lake. Divers have searched it. Nothing to report except bicycle wheels, mattresses and the usual shopping trolleys." Luke leaned back and took in a deep breath. He was desperate to give Dan details of progress but despite hours of hard police work, there was none. He finished lamely, "I guess you know all this, I'm not telling you anything new."

"You're dead right. Shite. So, there's nothing new I can report there." Dan turned to Meena who was directly involved in the house-to-house search. "Anything positive from your side of things?"

"Currently, no. Luke's summed it up. In terms of Michelle getting herself to the lake within the time frame when Patsy last checked on her daughter and then noticed she was missing, it's highly unlikely the child could have got there before the mums were out searching. Apparently three mums trekked across the path from the back of the houses to the lake as soon as Michelle went missing, but saw nothing. So we didn't really expect anything from the quarry."

"Despite the unlikelihood, no stone's been left unturned?"

"No, the lads are still out there talking and looking. So far the house-to-house enquiries haven't turned up anything. Do you want us to extend the search area?"

"Not yet. I don't think it would be a sensible use of resources." Dan looked at a map of the area that was lying on his desk. He traced his finger around a red area outlined on the map. "This indicates the houses covered in the enquiry so far. From the report it would appear all the householders have been helpful and forthcoming and going outside that area would be pointless at the moment. Cole agrees with me." He leaned back in his chair, staring at the map. Taking a deep breath, he sighed before he muttered, seemingly to himself. "Nothing from the road blocks set up, Nothing from all the checks of known nonces. Hell and damnation. Zilch!"

"What's the next step then, boss?" Luke leaned forward, putting his elbows on Dan's desk. "Mel Stubbs is still there with the mother and being a great comfort and support but Patsy, understandably, is distraught. She keeps asking about what's happening? What's the progress? Why her daughter hasn't been found?"

"Poor soul. Look, Mel's trained to deal with sort of situation so until we can give Patsy some good news, God willing, she'll cope I'm sure." Dan knew he had to be positive to keep up their spirits. "OK, our next step. Keep looking and keep asking. Meena, got anything to report on the three remaining nonces released on the technicality?"

Meena opened her note book. "Nigel Matthews and Don Taylor lived close to each other on the Whitely Estate. They also lived near each other on the Coley Bank Estate. After their arrest and subsequent release, the neighbours started to threaten them, so for their own safety both were moved.

"Their current neighbours, who from their answers seem unaware of their form, have been interviewed and state they have not seen them for at least a week. Although they have separate addresses, it seems they spent a lot of time at Don's place. Mrs Pearson, his right hand side neighbour says she thinks she might have seen Nigel Matthews about ten days ago but not since. She remembers because her dog went missing round the back of the houses and he went looking for it with her. She saw Don about three or four days ago and he was concerned he hadn't seen Nigel after he'd visited his mother in a nursing home. He told her later he'd contacted the home and Nigel never showed."

"Did this Don ever report this to us?"

"No, I checked our records," said Meena, who, Dan knew, never left a stone unturned. "Maybe he thought as a known nonce he might not get a lot of sympathy."

Dan shrugged, keeping his thoughts about such people to himself.

"And the other two, Joseph Bates and Marie..."

"Grainger," Meena finished. "Joseph Bates moved a year ago from his last known address. He was working so I'm trying to trace him through his National Insurance Number. We have an address for Marie Grainger but her neighbours say she's staying with her sister in Spain. They think she'd due back any time and have offered to contact us should they see her."

"So until we run them to earth, our enquiries have hit a brick wall. If they are in similar danger, let's hope we contact them soon," said Dan.

"Two nonces. Who cares?" said Luke. Dan flashed him a look but it was merely a senior officer's penetrating look and not a loaded missile. Again, Dan kept his thoughts to himself; it wasn't wise to be too vocal in front of his team. The old adage familiarity breeds contempt was true but not many police officers, if they were honest, had any time for paedophiles and he was definitely no different. In fact... he dismissed the thought.

Leaning back in his chair, chewing the end of his biro, Dan said,

"Meena, during Operation Rawhide d'you recall around that time a child went missing, the body never found. If it's revenge, what about *his* relatives? Have you turned up anything there?"

"Jordan Turner, age seven. He was from a single parent family, like Michelle. Perhaps that makes them more vulnerable or just unlucky. Can't trace her mother yet." She flipped over a page of her notebook and her eyes scanned down the page. "OK, she came originally from a small village between Theale and Newbury before she moved to Reading." She frowned as she checked her notes again, annoyed she didn't remember the fact.

"Bucklebury. The local boys are checking for me, seeing if any relatives are still there or anyone is keeping in touch with her."

"So basically I have f-all to report to Cole. Nothing on Michelle and nothing on the body parts." Dan closed his eyes, biting his lip as he contemplated. "Mm, let me think how I approach the Guv with next to nothing... Meena, now the kettles mended, any chance of one of your wonderful brews?"

"The kettle's not mended," snapped Meena, standing up and collecting her files. "It was passed its best. I bought a new one. The invoice is on your desk. I bought the one before and never got the money for that one. This is the last one I buy!"

She flounced from the room. Dan winced. "Oops, give her a hand, Luke. It's equal opps now."

"Boss... " protested Luke.

"Don't argue. Remember, two sugars in mine."

"You never used to take sugar. I should know. I got a bollocking when I put some in your coffee the first time I made it."

"Yeah, but it helps with the nicotine deprivation." Dan reached inside his desk and pulled out a boiled sweet."

"That'll make you fat," said Luke grumpily. As he reached the door, he shot over his shoulder, "Or fatter."

The sweet dangled in front of Dan's mouth. He looked down at his stomach. He dropped the sweet back into the drawer. The phone rang and the horror started all over again.

As Luke and Meena walked back in with the coffees, Dan was putting his overcoat on.

"Boss?"

"As they're in plastic cups, we'll drink as we go. We might have just found a companion for the first set of body parts. You have three guesses, and your first answer'll be right."

Chapter 18

"This note says that this Stan and Muriel see you so often they feel they know you. Do you know anyone with those names?" asked Dan. Lucy was sitting on the sofa, her face so white it looked as though it was dusted with flour. She was looking at her hands lying in her lap, clasping and unclasping them in her agitation.

A tall, good-looking Freddy Mercury look-alike was sitting next to her with one arm around her shoulders and the other resting on her knee. Dan recognised him as the man who worked part time at the jazz club and a buddy of Alex, and was now the new physio at the gym. Despite the seriousness of the situation, his familiarity with Lucy irritated him although he knew he should be more professional. Pushing the thought to the back of his mind that it had been a long time since a woman had provoked such a jealous feeling, he forced himself to ignore the man's attentions and concentrate on his questions, after all, she was still a suspect in his opinion.

"I don't know anyone with those names." Her normally confident voice was a whisper.

"Right. They also tell you to keep up the keep fit. Stan and Muriel are names that most of us would associate with an older couple. I think that probably rules out the gym although of course that will be checked. You do a lot of running. I know you've had a shock but..."

"Yes, she has had a damn shock," said Freddy, who was now stroking Lucy's arm and Dan was shocked with his reaction, that he needed all his self-control not to bop him one.

"Yes, sir, I know, but the sooner I have answers to my questions, the more likely we are to catch these people. So if you don't mind, I must continue my questioning. Perhaps you'd like to go and make Lucy a cup of tea, help sooth her nerves." *And stop crawling all over her like an octopus.*

"I'll make the tea, boss, if that's OK with Lucy," said the ever helpful Meena.

"No," snapped Dan. "I want you here. Would you mind sir? Perhaps a cup for all of us? It's late and I'm sure we could all do with some refreshment."

Freddy's eyes narrowed with suspicion and the darts from his eyes were sharp and aimed straight as laser beams into Dan's orbs for maximum damage. He looked back at Lucy.

"You OK, ducky? Would you like a cup of tea? I just don't want to leave you." He didn't say it but his words insinuated he didn't want to leave her in the clutches of these intruders.

"I'm fine, darling. Tea would be good."

The 'darling' caused an spike to pierce Dan's heart, and he was furious with himself for his lack of focus.

"You OK for me to continue, Lucy?" asked Dan once Freddy had left the room, "or do you want some tea first?"

"No, continue. Don't mind Freddy, he's being a bit over protective. He knows what a shock the first find was, now with this latest..."

"Of course, it must be awful for you, but as I've just explained, the sooner we run this couple to ground, the sooner we may stop any more of this happening."

Lucy nodded at Dan and whispered for the police officer to continue. He picked up a photocopy of the original note, and read. "They wrote, 'They see you so often 'and then 'keep up the keep fit.' After your discovery of the body parts in Elmpark on October 5th, we subsequently interviewed three male and one female jogging in the park on that day. Between them and your information we concluded we'd interviewed everybody exercising in the area at that time. You personally recognised three of them and agreed you often saw the same faces and although not able to supply names, tend to nod and acknowledge each other. Is that true?"

Lucy nodded again, nibbling her thumbnail as she listened.

"However," he continued. "Two of these people interviewed mentioned an older couple walking through the park, one of these people thought the couple had a dog but the other one couldn't be sure. The descriptions were vague so it's not clear if it's two different couples or the same. I've checked your original interview and you never mentioned older people or anyone having a dog with them. The fact didn't necessarily seem relevant at the time, but now I would ask you to think back, particularly to October 5th and to other previous occasions when you were running. Can you recall seeing an elderly couple, with or without a dog or others that you did not recall in your first statement?"

Two parallel lines appeared between Lucy eyebrows as she concentrated. She was staring hard at Dan but he knew she wasn't seeing him. His deliberations were broken as Freddy banged a mug of tea onto the coffee table between him and Lucy.

"Your tea," snarled Freddy and pointed at a bowl of sugar on a tray. He handed a mug to Lucy, and with a softer voice, said, "Come on, drink up, ducky. I put a spot of sugar in it. Read somewhere it's good for shock."

He sat himself besides Lucy, putting his arm round her shoulders again. Dan bristled, not sure if it was the contact or that this bloke was interrupting his work

Glancing at Lucy who had taken the mug but appeared in a trance, Freddy asked sympathetically, "You OK, Luce? Not being bullied are you?"

Dan hackle's rose again and his annoyance obviously showed on his face because Meena glared at him, daring him to be unprofessional.

Lucy, ignoring Freddy's comments, turned to Dan.

"Yes, I did see a couple. I remember, it was a sunny day and I was stretching my muscles in the warmth. They spoke to me and commented that it was a lovely warm day for the time of the year."

"Can you describe them? Think about their age bracket. What were they wearing? Were they white, black, tall, short... anything outstanding that you can now recall about them."

Lucy placed the mug on the table and leaned forward out of Freddy's arms, putting her elbows on her knees, her face in her hands whilst she thought. After a minute, she straightened up and her dark eyes bored into Dan's.

"OK. I'd say they were... maybe sixty-five to seventyish. The woman was wearing a really old-fashioned hat, like you'd associate with something a... grandmother would wear. He wore a trilby, and a three quarter Mac'. Again, sort of out-of-date, again... like a granddad's. They didn't have a dog with them that time... I think, or maybe... "

"Have you seen them before?"

"Yes, I probably have. Just an ordinary looking couple. No, I'm wrong. They did have a dog. I recall them clearly now." Her expression became animated. "They had a little terrier with them. White mainly, brown ears and a saddle shape on its back. It always pulls on its lead."

"Can you remember exactly when you saw them before? Take your time. Something probably happened that could fix the day for you."

"The day I found the body parts was a day I had off work. I remember because it's very difficult when you work in a school to get a day off during term time but it was the local elections and the school was closed for the day. Freddy and I had a session the night before and we'd drunk a bit too much. Thought I'd better still run to run it off. That was right wasn't it, Freddy?"

"If you say so, ducky, you know what an awful memory I have."

"So I went for a jog." Lucy spoke quietly, concentrating on her memory and her words. "Yes, I remember, because it looked as though it would rain and Freddy said not to go, I'd get soaked."

"But she went anyway," said Freddy.

Lucy continued as though he hadn't spoken. "It didn't rain. It was sunny, after all. I definitely saw them that day and... yes, they did have the dog with them, I remember now."

"That's helpful. I need you to come to the station and look at some mug shots... photographs... or help compose a photo fit of the couple if necessary?"

"I'm not very arty."

"Don't worry. Someone will guide you through it. It's computerised in this day and age. All you have to do is check each stage and build up a composite picture of this Muriel and Stan. Thank you for your help, Lucy. I feel we've made progress."

Dan turned to Freddy and started interviewing him about what he had seen, making him search his memory about whether he had passed the couple leaving the building after leaving the bag of body parts. After a short time it was obvious that Freddy hadn't seen them and didn't know anything other than he'd picked up the bag when he'd rung Lucy's doorbell.

Glancing at his watch, he realised it was well past midnight, and decided they probably wouldn't make any more progress. The SOCOs had been and gone with the bag containing the body parts. Now a yellow crime scene tape surrounded the passage way outside Lucy's apartment and a young police officer guarded the area. Lucy looked shattered. Dan nodded at Meena, and the two police officers stood up to leave.

"Thank you for your help. Lucy, will you be alright tonight after the shock you've had? Is there anybody that can come and stop with you?" asked Meena.

"Don't worry. I'll kip here tonight," said Freddy. He then compounded Dan's dislike of him by adding. "I often do. My flat's upstairs but I'll stop with Luce until she's over the shock. If nothing else, I can keep the press away. They'll hear about this latest incident pretty soon, you can bet your last dollar on it. You must have leaks the size of whales pouring out of your police station. How else would they find out about these things?"

Dan opened his mouth to reply, but Meena dug him in the back and he turned quickly to the door before the look on his face could be seen and classed as unprofessional, which he knew it was!

On the way back to the station, Dan couldn't stop grinding his teeth, a habit he had when really irritated.

"For heaven's sake, boss," said Meena, her eyes gleaming angrily in the darkness of the car. "That's such an awful noise. I know you're annoyed. What's made you so cross?"

"I'll stop and look after you, ducky," mimicked Dan. "Christ, that fellow's such a creep. What the hell does she see in him, big poser?"

Meena collapsed into giggles and laughed so long the mirth became contagious and forced a reluctant grin onto Dan's face.

"What so funny, DC Mesbah?"

"Boss, for such an intelligent man who is a brilliant police officer, you're unbelievably useless around women. They fry your brains."

"What exactly does that mean?" Dan asked as he pulled

into a car park space behind the police station.

"You're jealous."

"I'm not. For a start she's a suspect. Not high on our list, but she's still on it. So therefore my feelings are guided by my professionalism."

"If you say so, boss. I'll believe you, many wouldn't. You saw me glaring at you. What would you do if I didn't look after you?"

Meena got out of the door and walked into the station, shaking her head.

Dan slowly got out of the car, feeling a fool. Maybe he ought to be more in control, but the fellow was such a dick. Following Meena into the police station, he forced himself not to think of Lucy Hamilton as an attractive woman, but person on his list of suspects.

Later, as they both fired up their computers, Dan said, "Meena, what about a nice..."

"Cup of coffee," interrupted Meena. She flounced off and called back, "One of these days, a miracle'll happen and you'll make me one."

"Fat chance. You wouldn't drink it, my coffee tastes like shite."

Meena put the coffee down heavily on Dan's desk. "I'll drink shite if you've made it." She sat down and stared at her boss over the monitor.

After a few moments, sipping the coffee but not looking up, Dan asked.

"What is it, DC Mesbah? Why are you looking at me so disapprovingly?"

"Boss, you remember I talked to you about Lucy and the unlikely coincidence of her involvement. Firstly finding the body and then of being Genghis' teacher, the boy approached by a possible predator?"

Dan stared back at her but said nothing, just lifting his

eyebrows.

"Well," she continued, nervous at his silence, but determined to speak her mind. "Now this third thing has happened to her. Just seems too unlikely for her not to be involved, don't you think?"

Dan leaned back in his chair, screwing up his eyes in concentration and steepling his fingers as he considered her words. "I know where you're coming from. Just can't put my finger on it. You've check her out thoroughly. She hasn't form, not even a bloody parking ticket! That's what I can't figure yet... " He paused before sitting forward. "Still you're right, see if you can dig anything else up. I don't think she's our murderer but she's definitely involved." Dan's voice was unusually sharp and Meena shrunk back in her seat as he added. "And when you interview her again, make sure that dick-head Heath isn't around."

Chapter 19

"Is that him?" asked Donna Jackson, Cole's computer whizz kid' as the team knew her. She had come to the Simpson household with DC Mesbah to oversee Genghis' internet contact with the person who had called himself Lawman. Adam, who because of his special interest in suspected paedophiles, had also accompanied them. Meena had introduced him by his undercover name of Tom Reilly.

It had taken the child seconds to go into the chat room and very quickly had contacted their suspect.

Genghis seemed over awed by the four adults and so far hadn't uttered a word. He did manage a nod and a grunt in answer to Donna's question.

"Fucking perv," growled his dad. "If I ever get my hands on him..."

"Don't worry, Mr Simpson, we're as anxious to catch him as you and with your son's invaluable help, we will. However, we have to be careful how we approach the situation," said Adam.

He turned to the lad and assumed what he hoped was a friendly voice that would put the lad at his ease.

"Genghis, you told your teacher that this man had approached you about meeting him. How would you proceed from here if you wanted to start that conversation again?" The child looked blank. "Make out we're not here.

He's on-line now and waiting for you to say something. If you pretended you did want to meet him to talk about those film parts and to make all that money, what would you say to him?"

"Dunno. Suppose we'd start to chat."

"Why don't you do that? If he doesn't mention money again, or meeting you, why don't you remind him."

With that, Genghis proceeded to engage 'Lawman' in conversation. All the adults watched in amazement as the young boy, on the surface not the sharpest knife in the drawer, set about making dynamic, amusing conversation with the man. With astonishing speed, his hands flew over the keyboard as though he was part of the machine. The messages, innocent at first, passed back and forth. Then Genghis cleverly brought the conversation round to the previous conversation and asked if the money offer was still on the table. The trap was set and 'Lawman' drawn into it as gullible as a fly into a beautiful cobweb, glistening with innocent rainbow dew but deadly to the unsuspecting insect.

The group's astonishment grew as the boy then almost flirted with his prey and they knew from the replies that 'Lawman' had succumbed to Genghis' charm. Donna wanted to take over as she was extremely uneasy about his role in this, but when she went to move him aside, Adam held her arm and stopped her. She pulled her arm away in annoyance but knew he was right; she could never have set the trap so cunningly.

"Agree a time to meet him in Palmdean Park near the pond just past the small café." Adam was looking over Genghis' head, eyes wide, and a grin flickering about his lips at the boy's wit. The boy looked up at Adam when the response was positive. "Offer to bring your young brother with you for an extra fifty pound. I know you haven't got one, this is just pretend."

Adam turned to Meena and Donna and explained his thinking.

"He'll think the lad is greedy and therefore vulnerable." Adam suggested a suitable date and time for the meeting, and when Lawman replied and agreed to this, Adam insisted the lad log off as soon as possible. He emphasised to Genghis and his father about the seriousness of the situation.

"I can't begin to thank you enough for what you've done today. However, this Lawman may be a dangerous person as far as children are concerned. We will take over from here. I can assure you this is as far as it goes with your child, Mr Simpson. We need to take this computer to try and trace this person. It will be returned as soon as possible."

"He's not really going to meet him though, is he?" asked Mr Simpson, concern covering his face with worry lines.

"Absolutely not. That was never an option. This is Police business now. However, I must emphasise that it's absolutely vital that neither you nor your son discuss this with anyone. I don't want to alarm you unnecessarily, but for your safety and perhaps the safety of many others, we need to catch this individual. If word leaks out, we may lose him. So tell no-one." He turned to the boy "OK, lad? Not your best mate, your worst enemy, no-one."

The boy, now not attached to the computer on which he was so skilled, returned to being a ten year old, and with eyes open wide, nodded his agreement.

As the three police officers drove back to the station to report their progress, they discussed whether the man in the chat room was who they suspected he might be; the 'Lawman' whose code name was supplied by one of those arrested after the failed police operation 'Rawhide'.

"I think it's highly likely that he is our man," said Adam. "Mind you, he must be pretty thick or arrogant to use his code name that we know is a unique title. He could so easily have called himself something else."

"As you say," agreed Meena, "he must be thick.

Remember though, he doesn't know we were informed about the code names. Still, lucky for us, because it means we have him in our sights. Even if we don't arrest him, just put under surveillance, we can check if he's the nonce. If he's not got form, at least we can keep tabs on him."

"Yeah, although I'm getting in real thick with that feckin' little gobshite Gerry Tomas, I can't pick his brains because I'm not meant to know anything about this."

"You coming in to set up the surveillance on this meeting?" said Meena, thinking ahead as usual.

"No, I don't need to get involved in the organisation but I want to be on the surveillance team."

"Will this Lawman be picked up? He could make out the filming thing is a serious offer. Plus it might compromise your undercover operation." asked Donna. She worked mainly on the technical side of the police work but DI Cole had wanted her present today in case there should be any specialised difficulties. They hadn't counted on Genghis' expertise and she hadn't been needed.

"We'll have to look at the options," said Adam. "If we pick him up when he meets the boy that could alert the cell, alerting them they're back in our sights again."

"But if we don't, that could be dangerous for some other child if he doesn't get successful with meeting Genghis," said Meena, concern painting her beautiful face. "He could go on line again and snare someone else."

"Don't worry; he won't be allowed to walk around unescorted. This Lawman, whether the original one or not, will have a tail on him day and night. Plus I'm sure the technical team will find a way of keeping an eye on his internet dealings, eh, Donna?" At her nod, he finished, "On the positive side, we'll find out where the feckin' wanker lives."

Adam looked out at the purple autumn sky as he talked. The weather was dry and chilly; autumn was leaping into the year having firmly killed the summer stone dead. The sky, clear of clouds, allowed the stars to shine like minute beacons in the blackness and his thoughts turned to his children, tucked up safely in their beds. His mam, who cared for the twins while he worked, believed the stars were the souls of children taken from life before their life span was completed. He didn't have the same beliefs himself, but just in case, he vowed to work all his life towards putting away the bastards that might be responsible for some of those sparkling astronomical objects taken from this world before their allotted time.

Chapter 20

1989

"OK, so tell me. What's so terrible you need to buy someone a greasy bacon sarnie to have someone to talk to?" she asked the rent boy.

"Yeah, where to start? Well, I'd picked up a punter round Westminster. We got in his car and drove to a quiet place I know about half a mile away. By the way, what's your name?"

"Sharon."

"Mm, you don't look like a Sharon somehow. More a... Madonna."

"Idiot. Look, when and if I get to know you better, and I trust you, I might tell you my real name. Anyway, what's yours?"

"Stuart. That my real name. I trust you already or I wouldn't be telling you this."

"Just get on with the story, Stuart."

"Well, after we'd done the business he starts prevaricating and won't pay."

"Pre what? That's a long word. You educated or something."

"Yes, I was once but that was another world." The rent

boy paused and sipped his tea. He glanced through the café windows, biting his lip. He shook away the dark thoughts swirling in his mind and brought himself back to the present, mimicking her voice as he continued. "I quote, 'when and if I ever get to know and trust you', unquote, I'll tell you about that part of my life."

"Touché." Sharon saw sadness behind his eyes and didn't press for more. Her experiences on the streets had taught her that most of the kids on the streets had lived quite different lives at one time. Few talked about their pasts but the ones that did always had a sad tale to tell. She didn't suppose Stuart's life was any different.

"Touche, ooh, now who's getting posh?"

Sharon took a bite of her sandwich, "Stuart, just get on with this story. I haven't got long. I've got Punters to fuck."

"Right. So I said, are you going to fucking pay me or not? 'You're too old for me,' he said. You should have thought of that before I sucked your dick I told him. I was getting annoyed by now. So I shouted at him 'Too old, Christ what do you want, a baby'?"

"Sounds like a perv to me. How old are you anyway?"

"Seventeen. How old are you?"

"Sixteen." Sharon shuffled her feet, bit into her sandwich and muttered, "Well, nearly."

"If he'd fancied girls, you'd have been way over the top in years. I could tell he was weird, fucking really weird. I started stringing him along. 'Come on,' I said to him, 'what age, maybe I can help you out?"

"You bastard."

"Hang on. I can't stomach peados. They make me sick to my stomach. I just wanted him to confirm what I was guessing by this time. ' Well, about five to seven years.' he said. I had trouble controlling myself. Then he made me almost puke. He said, 'Not to do anything to 'em, I just want to save their souls'. What, you some sort of preacher or something I asked. I pulled down the collar of his jumper and he had on a bloody dog collar."

Sharon's voice was full of horror. "A preacher. Now you're definitely kidding me?"

"Save them, my arse,' I said to him. 'Tell me the truth.' He just kept insisting he was going to save their souls. Anyway, I said to him, if he paid me the dosh he owed and fifty quid besides I could take him to where I knew some very young runaways lived, about that age." Stuart saw the horror and disbelief in his companion's face. "Sharon, don't look like that. Course I wasn't going to take him anywhere. Finish your sarnie, woman."

Stuart sat back in his chair and finished his tea. He nodded at the pot and Sharon tutted but filled his cup up anyway. She topped up her own cup, shoved the last piece of the sandwich into her mouth, brushed the crumbs from her hands, put her elbows on the table, cupping her face in her hands, waiting for the rest of the story.

"He gave me my dosh and said if I took him there, he'd pay the other fifty. We drove about a mile out of town to a little green I know that's got a copse of trees in the middle. We stopped in a dark lay-by and I pointed out the place. Mind you, they might be a bit too young, I lied. They're only about five. He was getting so excited I could see the sweat on his brow. He put his hand in his lap and I knew he had a hard on just thinking about it. The wanker."

At this point Stuart leaned his elbows on the table and put his head in his hand. Their faces were almost touching. "Then... I can't believe this. I took him in the trees. I knew there wouldn't be any one much about 'cos the dealers go there after the clubs kick out, so after dark everyone else avoids the place. Then I beat him up and kicked the living shit out of him. I kicked and kicked till he was pulp."

"Is he... was he dead?"

"Dunno. Maybe. I felt good but at the same time I felt sick to my stomach. He might have been a perv but maybe I was a murderer. What's worse?"

"Did you leave him there?"

He nodded. "I pulled off his Dog Collar and stuffed it in his mouth. I searched his pockets and found his driver's licence. 'Father David Quigley. I don't know if he could hear me,' I whispered in his ear,' but I know you now. If you ever touch a kid again I'll castrate you, hypocritical tosser. Then I ran. He had hundreds more pounds in his wallet but I just took the fifty he owed me. I didn't want any more of his filthy money."

By this time, even under the dim lights, Sharon could see tears making his eyes shine. He covered them with his hands. She took his hands away and held them in hers.

"Come on, let's get out of here. Let's just leave."

"Leave? What, back to our fucking jobs?"

"No, leave London."

"Yeah, sounds good, but where'd we go? You said you had to get back to work."

"I know somewhere we could go. My mate Dana. She's off the game. Lives with a really nice black guy. They'll help us I know."

"Why would you do that for me?"

"Dunno. Sometimes you just know you've gotta do something. This is it. We'll both quit. Get jobs, but first we've must check if you did kill the wanker." They walked out of the seedy café together.

"Don't look back," was all she said.

Chapter 21

"Don't you look so pretty in that dress? Give us a whirl," said Lawman to the pretty little girl, her blond curly hair tied into two small bunches by pink ribbons that matched her dress.

"Hold your dress so it swirls out like a princess's dress."

Michelle Foster had been thrilled with the new dress her two new friends, Uncle John and Uncle Roger, had given her as a present. It was off-the –shoulder, fitted into the waist, with tiny white bows decorating the hem.

When they'd given her the dress, she'd told them, "I always wanted a pretty dress like this. When I asks Mummy for one she always said she don't 'ave no dosh 'cos me bastard father don't bloody pay no bloody mainten...some fink or nother."

Michelle didn't know what a 'bastard father' or 'bloody mainten... ance' meant, but as mum usually popped a sweet into her mouth at that point and changed the subject, Michelle soon forgot her longing. Now she had this dream dress and these kind men said it was hers to keep. They took photos of her and then showed her how beautiful she looked.

Swirling round and round, the short dress whirled out like a ballerina's and she knew she looked wonderful. She would have liked to have worn knickers but they said they didn't have any but not to worry because the sparkly strappy sandals that looked almost like real Cinderella slippers made up for that.

"No-one will notice," they had assured her. "There's only us here and we're your friends so it won't matter at all. If you're good and pose for the photos like we tell you, you can have ice-cream, jelly, sweets or chocolate."

Sometimes they got her to dance and sing. Lawman told her the words, and when she sang they laughed and clapped and asked her to keep singing.

'Diamonds are for Never,' she sang.

They kept saying 'ever' not 'never', but she didn't know what they meant and it didn't seem to matter 'cos they laughed some more and hugged her and told her she was a little diamond herself.

She was very pleased with herself, and when they tucked her into bed, her mind was always buzzing with things they had all done together during the day.

Some of the other fings they asks me to dooz is easy peasy. It ent 'ard or nuffink. Just gotta smile, lift me dress up at the front, then turn round an then pick up them apples or some ink. They tells me I'm wonderful. Better than Brad, 'e tells me I'm stupid. I ent 'cos I dooz all these things wot uncles tell me.

Sometimes she had to make out she was a famous television star and sit on their sofa with her legs up on a stool thing and then they made her laugh 'cos Uncle John told her jokes and silly Uncle Roger laid on the floor and took the photos.

They're so daft. They makes me laugh.

Afterwards they all had a party and she had her favourite food for being so good. She must have been tired 'cos she always felt sleepy soon after and when she woke up she sometimes felt very sore in her wee hole. She told them about it and Uncle Roger said he was a doctor and put some nice white ointment on her sore bits so that was all right then.

I misses mum and Shaun an' Brad. Uncle John says a

few more days and I'll get a friend and we'll all have some fun an' then we'll have another party if I'm good. Heard Uncle John say it'll be over soon 'cos I'd outlived me use.

She didn't really understand what they meant but if she could go home soon, that was alright.

Chapter 22

Five men and a woman sat round the table, all wearing masks. After the meeting they would go their separate ways, and because of the disguise, not easily recognisable. Only the cell leader, Brother Samson, knew everyone's identity. Security also determined real names weren't used and all cell members had unique code names. Present on this occasion, besides Samson, were Hawk, Excalibur, French Larry, Wolfbane and Delilah.

Brother stood up and addressed the meeting. "You all know why you have been called."

Looking at each person in turn, he waited for them to acknowledge his question with either a nod or a muted 'yes'.

"Lawman has been stupid. He has jumped the gun. After all our well-laid plans he's put us all in jeopardy with his actions. He knows, historically, when someone has not followed the agreed path they pay the ultimate price." He paused, looked again at each one in turn, waiting for them to digest and consider his words. Eyes flickered nervously from side to side, but no-one spoke.

"He snatched this girl for his own personal pleasure, ignoring the larger strategy. My informants tell me he has also contacted a young boy over the internet and is arranging a meeting. Taking two at this stage is so dangerous; he must have lost his mind."

The tension in the room was almost tangible; their fear of him and his threats making their mouths taste unpleasant, like the dry taste of sleep. Malevolent insects with ice spikes for feet dragged up their bodies and scratched at their nerve endings. The fear and disquiet showed in their expressions, and this was how Brother needed them to be. Total terror of him was necessary because this should ensure absolute obedience with no-one stepping out of line. He was the commanding officer, his soldiers had been brainwashed to obey.

Glancing round the table and confirming all eyes were fixed on him before he continued, "You've all been coached and trained on how to avoid capture. Lawman has this knowledge, yet has chosen to ignore this advice by these stupid actions. He must be eliminated before he is caught and brings us all down with him. And believe me, he will be caught. The full force of the law is already in motion seeking this girl. We must assume his stupidity has blinded him from working as diligently on avoiding capture as we have, ready for when Operation Hobbledehoy swings into action. After all our hard work, I cannot believe he would deceive us in this manner. He must receive the ultimate punishment very soon."

"What about the child?" asked Excalibur. As he spoke, he nibbled at his nails. A small, timid looking man, whose appearance belayed his true nature. "If we manage to rescue her, should we let her go to stop unnecessary investigations?"

"I'm undecided. If we dispose of her, if he hasn't already done so, she can't be a witness. Alternatively, if we let her go, the situation may settle down quickly. That's what we need desperately. Otherwise, we disband again and move on. All our planning wasted. The big day is almost upon us and his foolish actions have severely jeopardised it."

Harsh sounds of frustration and anger rippled round the table like slapping waves on a shore before the breaking of a storm.

"I say we let her go."

All eyes turned to Wolfbane, a young man with long hair tied back in a ponytail. He was handsome unless he smiled. His teeth were long and unattractively discoloured. His main hobby, discounting his predilection for young children, was weight training and he was proud of the muscles bulging and constantly flexing from his tee shirt sleeves. He was a football coach for the local boys at a well-known football club, and this meant his font of young stocks was limitless. Due to the looming operation, and the need for restraint, he'd been extra cautious.

"If we're careful, she'll only be able to identify him. It'll be all over the newspapers for two or three days and then forgotten if she's returned safely. It'll start being a lower priority for the police and they'll move their resources elsewhere".

Wolfbane spread out his huge hands as he spoke, eyes glued on his leader. "If she's murdered and her body found, all hell will break loose. If she's never found, they'll keep digging and looking. As you said, all our planning could be undone again."

Brother frowned and screwed up his eyes as he contemplated the words. Once again the silence was almost palatable

"Thank you, Wolfbane, perhaps you're right. Are you all in agreement?" Brother once again looked at each person in turn, seemingly for their consent although his words alone would, in reality, decide the final action.

"You said he has contacted another a youth. How do you know this?" said Delilah. Her voice held a sulky tone; she was used to Tomas keeping her updated.

Brother stared at her. Once she had been a beauty with long, dark hair and an infectious laugh that had been a honeyed trap. Time had taken its toll. Her hair was now the flat black from constant dying. Her once perfect white teeth were yellowed from smoking. The habit had shrunk back her gums and her teeth were now uneven with unflattering gaps.

He had loved her youth once; even forgiven her an indiscretion whilst her partners had died for their stupid irresponsibility. Her beauty and her special gifts had allowed her to live. Her ugliness now revolted him. He controlled his negative thoughts; she was after all, a long serving member of this cell within the Brotherhood and her total lack of conscience made her an irreplaceable ally.

"It doesn't matter how I know." He turned away from her, his individual knowledge added to his power and he wasn't prepared to share it. "I have decided. We release the girl if she's still alive. However, it's critical we dispose of Lawman before he meets up with the youth. That in itself is a dangerous situation. The kid could identify him and that might lead to us. Maybe the police already know about this second contact. I intend to check that situation. I despair his stupidity."

"Where are Atlas and Argonaut?" said Delilah. "They haven't been to the last two meetings. Do you know if they're involved?"

"They're not involved. Don't trouble yourself about them," snapped Brother, now tired of her interruptions. "Keep focused on our present problem."

"I think that Lawman would not, could not, do this on his own." All eyes turned to Hawk. Despite his public school accent and expensive suits signifying a man that oozed confidence and connections, he still treated Brother Samson with respect, being apprehensive of his power and the knowledge of his predilections. Being a past MP meant watching every step you ever took in your public and private life, but an urge for young flesh endlessly overwhelmed him.

He drew in a thoughtful breath, but seeing Brother nod, he continued. "Think about it. He's taken one, not easy in itself. He's planning to take another you say. How would he control that situation? Someone else must be involved."

A silence plunged onto the room which made their ears

ring. This point made sense, and it was devastating. Brother, normally coldly controlled, sat down heavily. His eyes, pale and maleficent, shone through the eye slits in his mask. Hissing through his teeth as he spoke, he snarled,

"You're right. I ought to have deduced that. We don't leave here tonight until we find that person. We're all present except Lawman, Atlas and Argonaut and those two are not involved. The situation is so dangerous; tonight you will remove your masks. I need to see your faces."

The gasps of astonishment circled the group. They couldn't believe what they were hearing.

"This has been done before in an emergency. Many years ago there was a similar situation. Thanks to our police mole, we dealt effectively with the situation and eradicated the fools swiftly. It allowed that particular Brotherhood cell to move on, away from danger. Everyone escaped capture but the transgressors died for their foolish stupidity. They were in prison by then, but it was no deterrent to us finding and punishing them. Right, remove your masks."

Slowly, hands went to their masks and pulled them over their heads. Eyes lowered, feeling naked and resembling chastened, embarrassed children, they looked into their laps.

"Why just us? How will it help this situation? Aren't you going to reveal yourself?" said Delilah, pouting and her voice defiant.

The others nervously flicked their eyes towards Brother Samson and this woman. No-one normally challenged him but just lately she had become outspoken and overconfident.

"No, I am not. Without masks it will be easier for me to assess what I need," said the Brother, the snap in his voice not permitting argument. His eyes swivelled slowly clockwise from person to person before returning in the opposite direction. His gaze stopped at French Larry. A twenty five year old man of Jamaican descent, he rarely spoke at the meetings. Minute beads of sweat forming on the man's forehead revealed the slow ebbing away of his control.

"However," said Brother, his voice suddenly mellow, his gaze sweeping away from the perspiring man. "I understand this might have been a moment of weakness. Probably brought about by Lawman's persuasive powers. If that person confesses here tonight, telling us about Lawman's future plans, we can forgive and move on. That may save us. Then, as I said, we forgive and forget."

Five pairs of eyes looked at him in horror at the suggestion. French Larry, a hopeful smile playing on his lips, slowly looked up, eyes pleading, grateful for the forgiveness. Brother leaned forward, a gentle smile playing round his mouth, hands held loosely together on the table in front of him.

"Come on, French Larry. I know it's you, my dear." His words caressed like the softest velvet, persuasive yet pleading, making the listener realise he could save them all and be rewarded by his bravery. Brother reached across the table and took his hands in his own. "You can help us now. Tell us the plans and you can still be one of us. All will be absolved."

His voice was hypnotic, every word a lyrical note. Brother Samson was his Father Confessor. French Larry saw and heard his salvation and laid bare the plan. No-one spoke until the end. Brother smiled kindly.

"Thank you," he said softly.

Brother walked round the table and stood behind French Larry. "We must thank this young person for his help. I believe he was drawn into this dangerous situation by an older, more experienced member of our Brotherhood, who should have known better. Stand up; let your Brothers and Sisters embrace you, showing their forgiveness. Move aside Hawk and Delilah."

The members watched as the person stood up, relieved and grateful. He smiled a lop-sided grin as he pushed back his chair, ready to turn and meet Brother Samson, his blessed redeemer.

Momentarily he was confused, not realising the severe pain along his throat was payment. He winced. Still looking puzzled, he dropped like a graceful gymnast to his knees. Blood seeped from the neat slit around his neck and trickled slowly from the side of his mouth. Then he gargled and a huge spout erupted from the wound, splashing the floor. Brother Samson pulled the chair from the table, and as French Larry collapsed sideways to the floor, he didn't feel the pain as his nose broke hitting the side of the table.

Chapter 23

Maria Grainger slung the three shopping bags into her boot of her car and banged the lid shut.

"Frigging shopping. I 'ate it." Standing by the side of the car she lit a cigarette and looked defiantly round the gloomy car park. Before going on holiday she'd lit up in this same car park and someone had called out to her that smoking shouldn't be allowed to contaminate the fresh air. She'd shouted "Stupid turd" in their direction at the top of her voice. That had shut them up. They'd scuttled off.

Having just returned yesterday from a peaceful three weeks in Spain staying with her sister Teresa, the sunshine, and the relaxed attitude to smoking had been a welcome relief. She had returned tanned, stress free and in a great mood ready to face work and the world again. This morning, swirling clouds heavily loaded with moisture had darkened her mood to match the sky. Taking a deep drag of the cigarette, she leaned against the car, trying not to shiver. Although only early October, the chill of autumn was making the air damp, preparing for yet another wet winter.

Shitty climate. Think I'll sell up and move to Spain. Live with Teresa.

"Excuse me, young missy, could I trouble you for the time?" The voice seemed to come from no-where and Maria jumped, the inhalation of extra smoke making her cough.

"Jesus Christ," she exclaimed, "you nearly scared me to death."

"Really sorry, dear. It's just that my watch has stopped. Can you tell me the time?" An elderly man, dressed in an tatty mac' and wearing old fashioned flat hat identical to her Granddad Wilf's, and looking so pathetic, that Maria, known for being a real hard case by most of her associates, felt sorry for the old man.

"It's twenty to seven."

"Oh dear, that means the doctors' surgery not open yet. My missus has taken a turn for the worse. She's in the car."

Maria took a last drag and threw the cigarette away, blowing smoke through the side of her mouth. She didn't feel like being a Good Samaritan, but it was a gloomy morning and as nobody else appeared to be in the car park, she thought she'd better seem concerned.

"What's wrong with her?"

The man shrugged. "I don't know. I'm no good at that sort of thing. Says she feels a bit faint and sick. I suppose you wouldn't have a quick look at her. Just a couple of seconds. She's sat in the back."

"I'm no doctor or nothing."

"Just literally twenty seconds. Just ask her how she feels? She won't ever tell me the truth. Says I worry too much. Maybe she'll tell you and then, if necessary, I'll take her to the hospital. Casualty. Sorry, dear, I don't like to bother you. Just a few seconds."

"OK. I can't be long. I've got to get home and cook for the kids," Maria lied. *Twenty seconds, that's definitely all!*

Maria peered into the car but in the darkness could only make out an outline of someone bent over, possibly in pain. Opening the door, she could hear a quiet moaning interspersed with the odd sob.

"You not well, mate?" Maria asked. "You in pain or something."

The woman, who looked as elderly and feeble as her

134

companion, mumbled something and bent over even more.

"Sorry, I can't hear you," said Maria, bending closer to the crouching figure.

"I don't think she can talk 'cos of the pain," explained the man. "If you could sit by her, comfort her, I'll call an ambulance. Just sit by her for a second and then you can go as soon as I know they're on their way,"

Shit, this is all I need. Bloody Florence Nightingale. I hope she don't stink of pee or nothing.

Maria climbed into the back of the car and tentatively put her arm round the woman's shoulders.

"So sorry to be a nuisance," the woman gasped and then slowly straightened up and looked Maria in the eyes, patting her hand as though Maria was the patient.

"So sweet of you to help me," she murmured.

The man leaned in the car. "I've called an ambulance. They'll be here in about ten minutes."

Maria turned to climb from the car when something was pushed into her face, covering her mouth. Before her panic she saw the outline of a man. At the same time, the patting hands from the woman turned into grasping claws, and she couldn't thrust away the something which smelt like a rubber hot water bottle. Maria leaned backwards, bucking like a frantic bronco, but like a cowboy, the person hung on and wouldn't be dislodged. The ringing in her ears and the stars against blackness was the last thing she saw.

When she woke, uncomfortable on a cold hard surface, Maria, convinced at first that she was dreaming, could see two weird masks propped up on a shelf, leering lopsidedly at her. They looked familiar, but her mind was still confused from the effects of whatever was on the pad shoved in her face. Also, the smell of rancid bacon was over whelming, making her want to puke and puzzling her even more as to what was going on.

That bloody couple. I'll bloody kill 'em when I get my hands on 'em.

Within minutes the dream turned to a nightmare.

Chapter 24

The weather was deteriorating fast. The supposed 'Indian summer' that the weather pundits had forecast and delighted everyone in late September had finally given up the battle after just a few days and the over-all war finally won by the approaching autumn and winter. Now October was trembling furiously with the cold, and the star that warms this planet and gives life had faded from a golden fury to a forlorn sphere hiding behind mist and clouds and feeling very sorry for itself as it slid down below the horizon.

Despite the cold and gloom, Lucy had persuaded a reluctant Freddy to come running with her and Higgins.

"You've not working this evening and I daren't run in the park on my own if it's dark after all that's happened. Come on, you admit you need the exercise. Higgins loves it when you occasionally come out with us," she'd said, sidling up to him, putting her arm through his and giving him a kiss on the cheek.

"Higgins likes it when I run with you!" he said, disbelief at such an obviously stupid remark painted his face. "You do talk bollocks."

"Watch your language in front of Hig. He's very sensitive. Oh please, please, please."

"Course you know I would but Pete's coming round when he's finished his shift. He'll wonder where I am."

"Text him. It's seven now, we'll just run for an hour. What time's his shift finish?"

"I'm not running for a bloody hour and *that's* final."

"Half an hour."

"Twenty minutes and that's final."

"Ok, I'll tell you what, run with me to the gym. That should only take twenty minutes if we hurry. I'll do half an hour on the running machine while you rest and have a coffee. I'll pay for a taxi so we get back in time for Pete. What time did you say he was due?"

"I didn't. He finishes the dinners at nine thirty so he'll probably get here ten thirty latest."

"How about it? Run to the gym and come back by taxi."

"We can't take the mutt if we do that. He can't come in the gym and I'm not sure how taxi drivers feel about letting dogs in their cabs."

"You're right. Blow it; I'll go on my own. I just won't go to the park. Running on the streets should be safe."

They eventually compromised and jogged for half an hour in the park, Freddy flopping on a bench after exactly thirty minutes and watching as Lucy ran further on along the park path and then back again a few more times. Despite the bright moon grinning down on them like a benevolent father, and the light from the street lamps filtering through the naked branches of the trees that lined the park, as Lucy got to the end of the path she disappeared for a few minutes into the gloom before she turned round and came into view again.

Despite his air of indifference, Freddy was uneasy when this happened. Although Lucy appeared to have recovered from the two episodes of the body parts, Freddy knew underneath her calm exterior, an unease lingered in her that hadn't been there before.

Dunno why I feel so protective towards her? Not like she's of my persuasion.

Not that Lucy was small or delicate. At five foot ten,

she was tall for a woman but Freddy sometimes detected a vulnerability about her, especially when she wasn't aware he was watching. She never spoke about her family or past, and on the odd occasion he asked anything she seemed adept at altering the path of the conversation. Freddy couldn't pin down what brought out his protective side, and he admitted he was too possessive on occasions.

Suddenly aware these contemplations had gone on too long and he wasn't checking on Lucy, he stared into the gloom in the direction she'd last run and felt the panic bring up the hairs in his neck when he couldn't see or hear her. At that precise moment the moon proved vindictive and hid behind a dark, impenetrable cumulus cloud causing Freddy's heart to lurch when the gloom and silence became painful, hurting his peering eyes and straining ears.

Freddy jumped up. "Luce," he shrieked. Nothing. "Luce, where the fuck are you?" Higgins had flopped down besides Freddy when his mistress had carried on running, giving her his usual 'my running days are over, thank you' look. "You lazy mutt, dogs are meant to have good hearing, can't you hear her running, for Christ's sake?"

The panic in Freddy's voice pierced the dog's lethargy and as the man ran off towards Lucy's last known direction, Higgins yelped and ran after him, out stripping him before they had gone ten steps. It didn't help Freddy's alarm when the dog disappeared into the dark and he had this awful premonition he wasn't going to see either of them again.

Rounding the first corner, he almost collided with Lucy who was standing with her hands on her hips and deep in an animated conversation with a young man. He couldn't stop himself yelling, not embarrassed one bit by the hysteria in his tone.

"Christ, Lucy, where the fuck have you been? Didn't you hear me calling?"

In the gloom, Freddy couldn't see the shock on Lucy's face, but heard it in her voice.

"Whatever's wrong, Fred. I did call back to you when you yelled. You probably couldn't hear me because you were yelling so much."

Freddy was exhausted, both by the sprint and the anxiety. He flopped forward, hands on his thighs, breathing heavily.

"I was worried. You disappeared out of sight. I yelled and... " He couldn't finish, he hadn't enough breath.

"Oh, Freddy, my darling, you do love me after all." Lucy pulled him upright and put her arms round his waist.

"Stupid cow," Freddy mumbled. "Hope you get strangled by Jack the fucking Ripper next time."

"Don't mind Freddy, he's rather temperamental," explained Lucy to the young man. The moon decided to peer round the cloud at all the excitement and Freddy felt a fool when he saw the astonishment at his outburst on Lucy's companion's face.

"Anyway, Freddy, I've just found out something interesting. Jake meet Freddy Heath, Freddy meet Jake Carter." The two men nodded to each other. "Jake often jogs in this park. We sometimes see each other and nod or wave. I nearly bumped into him in the dark and we got chatting. Seems Jake's read in the papers all about my unfortunate adventure with the body bits. I was telling him about how you found the other bag outside my flat from the mysterious Muriel and Stan. Jake said he's noticed something a bit weird. Apparently for months now he's seen an elderly couple around the park, in all sorts of different places but he reckons that loads of times they're watching me. He didn't know whether to say anything or not."

Freddy, still annoyed about the panic and with the defensive mode kicking in again, gave Jake a look clearly suggesting he was stupid. Ignoring the young man, Freddy spoke to Lucy. "How can you tell if someone's watching anyone else when you're out running? I find that hard to believe." His tone suggested Jake was the village idiot.

This time it was Lucy's turn to throw a look, sharp as an

ice pick and had it landed, would have severely damaged his frontal brain lobe.

"How would you know what Jake's seen and his interpretation of it?"

Twisting the glacial glare a little more for maximum effect and pain, Lucy turned back to Jake. "Thanks for that useful information, Jake. I'm very grateful. As you suggested earlier before we were interrupted, maybe I ought to be careful, not knowing the couples intentions."

Not wanting the evening to turn into a full-scale war, Freddy was obviously in a foul mood, she said goodbye to Jake, emphasising she looked forward very much to seeing him when she ran in the park again.

As they walked away, the cold mood hung between them like an ice sheet. Higgins followed, head lowered, and tail dangling between his back legs, despondent because he hated it when they rowed!

Jake could hear, fading into the distance like floating ghosts, a stage whispered argument that Lucy was definitely winning.

Fancy that beautiful woman being friends with a miserable git like him. Still, things will change pretty soon...

Chapter 25

Lawman was waiting for French Larry who was an hour late. He'd promised to arrive by midnight so they could complete their task before morning. Lawman had set Sky to record certain programmes to watch later if necessary to confirm he'd been watching TV if he needed an alibi.

He wasn't panicking yet, but he felt anxious. The longer he held on to the property, the more dangerous it became.

She's drugged, so won't be a nuisance. Lying on her bed totally out of it, still wearing her precious dress, the silly little cow. She loves it so much she won't take it off.

After about five days of continuous wearing, the dress had looked so tatty and dirty it had shown up on the film and spoilt the effect. They wanted the scene to look as though the child star was rich and famous, not a ragamuffin. Larry was forced to go and buy an identical dress but Michelle was so thick she never twigged. They had allowed her to have a bath so they could swop the dress, which was just as well because she hadn't washed since she'd arrived and was beginning to get smelly. Larry then got inspired and filmed the bathing scene; Michelle getting in and out of the bath had given them some good shots, even if it meant Lawman lying on the floor to get the best angles. She'd splashed him purposely, thinking it was hilarious.

He looked at his watch and went over the schedule again

in his mind. They planned to film each other with the girl and then watch. That should take them up to two o' clock. They hadn't shagged her yet and had tossed a coin to see who should have the virgin. Naturally he'd won; he'd paid twenty pounds for a coin with two heads and Larry was so daft, he never twigged why he never won a toss!

Now having all the films they needed of her revealing herself in her short dress which had been a real turn on in itself, it was nearing finale time. Once they had the lad and all the enjoyment that had to offer, they'd jettison both of them.

Having carefully thought through their plan about disposing of the bodies, he'd have to be meticulous in the actual execution of the task. They'd kept themselves safe from the bizzies and the cell members, but Brother had eyes and ears in unbelievable places, and they didn't want to ruin it now through carelessness.

Walking into the room next door where she was asleep on the bed, he gazed at the sleeping child. Lying on her side, hair splayed out over the pillow, her hands tucked under her chin and her legs pulled up to her body, she looked so angelic. Stroking her legs with one hand, he sighed and loved the sensation only innocence could give him.

He was sorely tempted but pulled himself back from the edge and hurried back into the next room, away from the attraction, groaning with impatience. Pouring a large whiskey, he swirled the glass and the aroma with its hint of silky, mellow smoothness steadied his nerves a little. He took a large gulp of the nectar to finish the job.

Another half an hour passed and French Larry was now very late. This had never happened before. They had stepped outside the rules on other occasions but it had always gone so smoothly.

Perhaps we've grown complacent, careless. Never, we laid the plans thoroughly. We've been trained by the best. I'll have another whiskey and then phone him.

Pouring himself a good measure, he picked up the receiver and started to dial. *No, you fool, don't weaken.* He replaced the phone onto its wall bracket.

Phone calls were easily traceable in this day and age, he mused. Not like the old days, before computer checks on mobiles and bloody great, spying eyes in the sky. Whoever invented satellites should be stretched on a torture machine; it made their lives so difficult. The Brotherhood laid down strict policies which prevented any likelihood of capture and one of those particularly included use of the phone for 'business' unless it was an absolute emergency. If anyone had to contact another and use a phone, certain code words were used, meaningful only to local cell members. Operation Hobbledehoy was approaching and the leaders of the Brotherhood were warning everyone to be extremely vigilant, but he and Lawman had grown impatient.

Just a little fun beforehand.

They'd managed similar 'digressions' before and never been exposed. Anyway, the voice in his head had told him it was right and that persuasive voice was never, ever wrong. The back door bell rang and the relief spread over him like a cool shower.

Thank God. Strange, he's got a key. Stupid sod must have mislaid it.

Hurrying down the stairs, two steps at a time, he almost stumbled in his haste and the gloom. At times like these he left most of the house in darkness so if anyone called they would assume he wasn't home. The blinds upstairs let no light in or out. The 'operation' room, as he called it, had no windows. All the lighting necessary for the cameras came from powerful spotlights. He'd bought the best, and the cost had been worth it because the quality of the pictures produced was outstanding.

Never chancing Internet images, Brother warned them such things were easily traceable. People who should be minding their own bloody business could perhaps check who was accessing certain web sites so another of the Brotherhood's main rules absolutely forbade that sort of thing. However, sometimes Lawman felt a deep urge that wouldn't go away. On occasions he had the odd peek, but not often enough to draw attention. The strict regulations forced him and Larry to do their own thing. After all, being careful was sensible but the Brotherhood took security too far. They had their needs to think about.

The back door bell rang again.

"Wait. Hang on," he hissed. *Christ, he's going to wake the whole neighbourhood with that bloody bell.*

He muttered and swore as he hurried to the door. Seeing the bolts were still secure, he realised why Larry couldn't let himself in. Drawing back the bolts, he muttered, "You're bloody late. We've got another date with darling Genghis in twelve or so hours and you choose tonight to be bloody late."

French Larry stood in the doorway, the vacant expression on his dark face annoying Lawman intensely, and irritation stamped, heavy-booted, through his body. The stupid sod just stood there and Lawman's irritation turned to unease. He resembled a puppet suspended on strings, legs slightly buckled and arms dangling gormlessly. His head was lolling sideways, eyes staring and nose decidedly crooked with streams of what looked like black treacle trickling from his nostrils.

"Hell. What have you done to yourself? Been in an accident or something?" French Larry never answered but toppled forward, almost gracefully, into Lawman's arms. Despite his floppy look he felt strangely stiff and unwieldy, difficult to hold and Larry slipped slowly to the floor.

"You could say it was an accident of sorts. He was a naughty boy and he fell... sort of... onto his sword. Well, someone else was kind enough to hold it for him so there was good contact."

Lawman was still looking at French Harry sprawled on the floor when he heard the posh voice. It filled him with so much fear he thought his heart would burst. The terror started in his toes and inched up his body. Looking up, his jaw dropped as he saw Hawk. Standing behind him, rippling his bulging muscles, and leering over Hawk's shoulder, Wolfbane grinned, showing his yellow, simian teeth.

Yet Lawman knew Hawk was the one to fear. Middle class, public school accent, convinced he was the centre of the universe but what made him so dangerous was a flint-hard heart and vicious psychopathic characteristics.

The Brotherhood had prepared the cell members for such events should they be questioned by the police. The coaching had been excellent. Instantly closing his gaping mouth, Lawman straightened up, ignored his fears, and assumed the look of the amazed and innocent and said,

"What's he doing here? I was just watching the TV. I wasn't expecting visitors."

"If that's all you were doing then you won't mind if we just drop in." Hawk pushed past Lawman, kicking aside French Larry's body as he went.

"Drag him in," he ordered. Wolfbane, glad to demonstrate his strength, smoothly rotated the body into the kitchen as though it were a rolled up carpet.

Lawman, still attempting to act surprised, turned to close the door. A hand pushed against the door prevented him closing it. Standing in the doorway was, even by all the standards of his way of life, evil personified. Delilah, her long hair as raven black as her heart, was looking up at him, smiling like the devil and the man knew all hope was gone. Hot pee from his petrified bladder run down his leg but he didn't notice or care about such incidentals.

She smirked, her crooked teeth not enhancing her looks in any way; Lawman shook to the very core of his being. Licking her lips until they were wet and shiny, then pursing her mouth at him, he mewed like a scared kitten. Hawk grabbed his shoulders and pulled him into the kitchen, pushing him into chair.

Delilah leaned over and whispered into his ear. "Who's been a naughty boy then? Who led silly, daft Larry astray?" She licked his ear. "This is going to be so enjoyable." He whimpered.

"Hurry up, let's get this done. Where's the girl?" snarled Hawk. He turned to the quietly sobbing man. "You'd better pray the kid's not dead. If she is, your agony will go on for eternity. Delilah's a pro, you know that. If she's still alive... "

The woman interrupted, "You'll only suffer for a week." Leering, she rubbed her hands together in anticipation of the enjoyment to come.

Chapter 26

Dan looked at his watch, "What time did you say?"

"I've told you three times. They arranged to meet at two." Adam shook his head in frustration.

"Well, he's late."

"I can feckin' see that," snapped Adam. He felt shattered. Fraternising with Gerry Tomas was beginning to take its toll. Picking up his receiver, he spoke to Luke Steiner positioned on a bench near the entrance of the park.

"Anything your end, Luke?"

"Negative. Simon's still sitting on the bench near the duck pond just passed the point where Genghis arranged to meet him. He's querying in the pre-arranged manner how long should he stay?"

"We're giving it another half an hour. That's an hour late. If he's keen he wouldn't be that late. Anybody else eye-ball anyone that could be Lawman yet?"

"Nope. They're reporting in regularly; wondering what's going on."

"OK. We've enough people in place not to have missed him. Give it another, say, forty minutes, then we call it a day."

Adam rubbed his eyes again. "Got any coffee left in that flask?" Dan poured the remaining dribble into the flask cup and handed it to his companion. "Christ, this tastes like shite." Dan shrugged, giving him a look implying it was better than nothing.

"What happens if he doesn't show?" asked a policewoman from the back seat, shifting the large camera to a more comfortable position on her shoulder. Due to the flu bug still devastating the staff numbers, Dan had temporarily elected DC Mel Stubbs to be the photographer. She was available because Patsy's two sisters were visiting for the day, so Mel was relieved from her FLO job for a few short hours. Mel, although not an official police photographer, was an extremely competent amateur, so the responsibility of taking clear pictures of Lawman from this angle had naturally fallen to her.

"Can't do much about it. We don't have his ID if he's a different person to our Lawman. He told the kid he'd be wearing a navy blue baseball hat. All we do know for sure is that his name was mentioned as one of the code names of a cell member," replied Adam.

"D'you reckon he's the nonce released after Operation Rawhide?"

"Who knows but it's too coincidental not to investigate. We've a long list of suspects but as you know, by the time we got to them they had alibis. Still, we've got some mug shots," Adam held a photo high enough for Mel to see them over his shoulder "That's him."

"Yes, Dan showed all of the team before we left." Mel said. She slumped back in her seat, gazing round the park, the artistic side of her nature wanting to take photos of the autumnal scenes. Despite the low temperature, the sun was alive and well today and its reflection sparkling across the pond. The ducks were disturbing the golden reflection and breaking it into a thousand diamonds. A few leaves scattered between various trees had turned gold and some still clung on precariously to the knobbly branches despite the recent windy weather. She'd have preferred taking these scenes than waiting to snap a pervert.

Noticing a maple tree standing out from the mainly green scene, a sprinkling of red leaves dusting the foliage, she said to Dan, "That reminds me, boss, you still chasing the new recruit with the red hair?"

"Christ, gossip gets around. I've never been chasing the red headed skirt, as you put it so delicately. I'd like to have the bloody opportunity."

"He fancies one with long dark hair at the moment. It's Luke who fancies the red head," offered Adam, his soft Irish drawl emphasising the humour in his voice. He grinned with amusement at the dark look Dan threw at him.

"Not surprised I'm getting the gossip wrong," said Mel, sounding as grumpy as her well-known reputation suggested. "Not that I mind spending the time with Patsy Foster, poor woman certainly needs the support but I'm missing being at the station with you guys."

"Bloody hell, Mel," said Dan, looking over his shoulder to her," I never thought the day would come when I'd hear you say that."

"Why?" the policewoman snapped back. "What are you inferring, boss?"

"That you're not by nature the happiest person I've come across in my experience of being a police officer. Some days you are positively grumpy."

"You saying I'm not an effective officer?"

"Nope. You're an extremely effective officer and your support of Patsy has proved that. What I'm saying is you're not, in my experience, a person who comes into work smiling and laughing."

"OK, let's drop this discussion," intervened Adam who realised the remark was being taken more seriously than Dan had intended. Silently he agreed with Dan, Mel's reputation as a dour personality unfortunately preceded her. "We're here to observe and maybe make an arrest. Not snipe at each other."

"You're right," agreed Dan. "Sorry Mel, forget my

remarks. I was out of order."

"Yes but..."

"Mel, put a lid on it. Dan's apologised. Let's focus."

The silence and mood emanating from the back of the car could have been sliced with a knife, proving the point about Mel's personality.

Adam picked his binoculars from his lap and trained them onto Simon. The young police officer was dressed in jeans and a white tee shirt. His fair hair flopped over his forehead. His lips, full and pouting, were the object of much leg pulling by his older colleagues who called him 'Rosebud'. "Who-ever picked him as an object of attraction for this nonce did a good job. Who's the lad with him, supposedly his brother?" he said.

"Jim Davidson's son, Tommy. He's nine," said Dan. "We thought a real young 'un might add spice to the event. Jim says he's a right tearaway; won't be intimidated by the occasion. Simon might look young for his age but there's no way he's the tender age of ten years this Lawman is hoping for. So if the nonce gets suspicious, saying that Genghis' age range was what he actually needed for his filming, ha, ha, Simon's going to say he's his elder brother, fourteen, and he wants a part in the film as well. There's no way a nine year old, policeman's son or not, would be allowed to sit there as an attraction for that wanker."

"Simon might look young but he still looks older that fourteen," said Adam thoughtfully.

"True, but beggars can't be choosers. All we need is to eyeball the man, get photos for future identification purposes. It'll help your knowledge if he's tied into the local nonce cell, should you get invited to one of Tomas' cell meetings. How's that going?"

"Good. We're as thick as thieves. I've told him about my form as planned. Then acted as though I was concerned it might affect my membership of the gym. Good improvisation I thought."

"Will he be able to check that, your supposed form I mean?"

"Almost certainly. He seems to have moles everywhere but his enquiries will stand any scrutiny."

"Good."

"What about your case of the two lots of body parts? Heard you've identified them. Found out what that's about?"

"Not yet but we suspect it may be payback time." Dan shrugged as he explained. "Taylor and Matthews were two of the four that got off by a technicality from the failed operation two years ago. A young boy went missing but neither the lad nor his body's ever been found. We're looking for his mother but she's left the area so we're not making headway with that line of enquiry. If it is payback, we need to find the other two nonces arrested and then released; a male and female but we can't run them to earth either."

As he talked, Dan scanned the area with his binoculars. Sighing deeply, he lowered the glasses and sat back in his seat. He continued, "It's like a black hole has appeared in the middle of Berkshire and sucking all these people into it and they're never seen again. Regarding the young missing lad, Meena's got Jim Davison helping her with that plus they don't seem to be able to trace the missing two nonces. The woman of the four released, Maria Grainger, was due back from Spain a couple of days go. Apparently she did turn up according to the neighbour who was going to report in when she saw her. The woman came home, dumped her luggage, and went straight out before the neighbour had time to phone us. She hasn't been seen since. So we've no idea."

"And the male?"

Dan clicked his fingers. "Joseph Bates, that's his name. We can't trace him either although Meena's got the local boys in his area keeping their eyes peeled. His national insurance number indicted he was working for a security firm in Didcot but they haven't seen him in weeks. According to them he's totally unreliable and about to get the sack."

"So basically you're just ending up your own arse 'oles?"

"Is that an Irish technical term?"

Adam laughed. "Yes, boyo, I believe it is. But you seem up to your eyes with lines of enquiries and getting nowhere."

Dan murmured his agreement. Rubbing his eyes, then blowing out his cheeks, he said, "Tell me about it. Cole's breathing down my neck; we're short staffed 'cos of the flu bug despite support from other locations and we've heard nothing about Michelle. I know there's a connection but I can't see what it is."

"Something will break, you'll see. Someone will re-member something or somebody will make a mistake and the puzzle will slot together."

"I hope so; you've got more faith than me at the moment. I feel we take one-step forward then two back. The press are giving us hell because we're getting no-where tracing Michelle. We've done house-to-house enquiries, had her mum on the TV begging for news of her whereabouts, or if anyone knows anything, scoured the local scrubland and disused quarry lake. Nada. Absolute zilch."

"She's disappeared into that black hole as well."

"We know by now that statistically we're looking for a body, and not seriously considering a rescue. How do you tell the poor mother that?"

"I can't imagine, but someone's probably going to before long. Assuming we find her body of course. I try to think how I'd feel if either of my girls was taken and I can't even begin to guess the horror and despair she feels. Me mam's over from Ireland looking after the girls as you know. She says she prays every night and morning for Michelle's safe return."

"D'you believe in prayers?"

"I prayed enough prayers to last a life time for Kathryn's recovery. There was no-one listening. No, I guess I don't believe in prayers but if I thought it would bring Michelle back, I'd get down on my knees this very minute."

"Yeah, same as. Just got to hope miracles or good police work aren't all out this year."

Mel leaned forward and tapped Dan on the shoulder.

"Boss, who's that?"

At that instant Dan's receiver beeped. "Yes, we eyeball him," he assured the sender.

A tall, lean man was approaching, sidling up the park pathway and something about his furtive looks made the three police officers sit up and take notice. Mel shifted the camera into position and started to bring him into focus.

"Only thing is, that's not navy."

"Looks navy to me," said Adam.

"It's dark grey, almost black. Whoa, don't think he's our man. Ah ha, here comes the reason for his shifty behaviour."

From the other direction a women smartly dressed in a business suit that was in distinct opposition to his casual appearance, walked towards him. As soon as he spotted her, he glanced round over his shoulder. When they met, the coast being clear, they melted into a romantic clinch as they came together.

"Both married. They're having an affair and they meet here some lunch times. Probably going off for a snog," said Mel. They walked off towards the copse of trees that lined the other side of the duck pond, arms round each other's waists, kissing each other with small, passionate pecks on the lips.

"How the hell can you tell that?" asked Dan. He shook his head in amazement at her reasoning with no hard evidence.

She leaned forward, obviously now having forgiven Dan for his transgression, tapped the side of her nose.

"Women's logic, boss. Can't beat it."

Adam and Dan exchanged glances but didn't comment. They didn't have to; they both knew they had identical thoughts on 'a woman's supposed logic'.

The static from the receiver broke into their thoughts

again.

"Boss, Luke. Nothing happening here except the lovers. Has he sneaked up your end somehow?"

"Nope. The cold's seems to be keeping most people out of the park. There's no-one we can see either side of our viewing area." Dan glanced at his watch. "Ten minutes to go and he'll be... umm... late. He's not going to show now. OK, ten minutes then we stop for the day. Tell everyone to stand down after that time."

"OK, boss."

"You happy with that Adam? He's not going to show now."

"You're right. Ten minutes is enough. What a feckin' waste of time and resources."

"Yep. With all the lines of enquiry we've got going, we waste our time waiting for this wanker not to show."

"Isn't it weird though, boss? From what you told me, he's been chasing this kid for weeks. Do you reckon he got wind of this operation?" said Mel, opening the camera case ready to pack the camera away.

"I'd be surprised if he had. The info was kept on a strictly need to know basis. Maybe he got nervous and thought it foolish to be so blatant, meeting a kid in a park in day light. He must know that's the height of stupidity and asking for trouble. Most kids are street wise now."

"Maybe we'll never know. On the other hand, he could just be someone who's turned on by the thought of a date. All I can say is that if I get to meet the bastard, I'll knee him in the groin for wasting police time," said Adam, thumping his hand on the car steering wheel with frustration.

Silence reigned in the car for the next ten minutes as they waited vainly for Lawman to show. All three officers could almost taste and touch the tension in the vehicle. Lines of frustration distorted Mel's forehead, Dan ground his teeth and wisps of quiet Irish obscenities flowed from Adam's mouth. The screeching of the angry tyres as they eventually drove away equated noisily to the anger and frustration felt by the police officers.

Chapter 27

Dan, totally frustrated after the time wasted waiting for Lawman in the park, had returned to the station. On leaving work later, he decided to check on Adam who had gone straight to the gym.

On arriving at the gym, he was surprised there was no Lucy, and was annoyed that he was disappointed. Adam was also nowhere to be seen, so his efforts on the rowing machine and the chest press were even more half-hearted than usual. After half an hour, despite numerous breaks for water, he couldn't face any more exercise.

Checking his watch for the fourth time in the last fifteen minutes, he groaned when it showed one minute to eight. He could have sworn it was at least ten o'clock and his protesting muscles certainly suggested it was.

That's it, a bloody wasted evening. No Adam... no Lucy... could have sworn Adam said he was going straight to the gym.

What made it worse was that he'd turned down an invite to the pub. It was Luke Steiner's birthday and most of the team were going to the local for a few pints. He wiped his sweaty face in the towel draped round his shoulders, annoyed at the time wasting. Lucy and her constant companion, pain-in-the arse Freddy Heath appeared. Heath nodded coldly in his direction and headed through the gym to the back where

Dan knew the staff quarters were. Lucy nodded an warmer acknowledgement and gave a small smile as she passed to the Ladies Changing Rooms. Dan sipped his drink slowly, wondering whether to call it a day or give it another half an hour. If Adam hadn't showed by then, he'd try calling him on his mobile again.

Can always spend the time admiring the Lucy Hamilton antics.

At that moment, Lucy emerged from the changing area and hurried to the just vacated rowing machine.

Her obsession with exercise and keeping fit was intriguing, curious, and totally amazing. Why would anybody be that dedicated? Shrugging his shoulders, and deciding what she did for a hobby, as long as it didn't spill over into his territory, was her business so why should he be concerned. Yet, what had happened to her recently meant it did spill over and once again he was irritated that he couldn't see the connection. Maybe it was just that she was such an attractive female and if a young man had found the body parts, would he be so curious and uneasy? *Maybe not.*

As there was no Adam to check on, he couldn't seem to stop himself watching her antics. He watched and marvelled at the effort she put into the exercise. She seemed unaware of everyone around her. Allowing the man side of him rather than the working cop to ogle without her being aware, Dan feasted his eyes on her lean and powerful limbs, shining under the light film of perspiration from her efforts, and found her fitness a real turn on.

"For feck's sake give your eyes a rest, you horny eejit."

Dan, so deep into his contemplation hadn't noticed Adam appear and pour himself a drink from the water dispenser. The Irish man's accent, for some reason, besides being constantly lyrical to Dan's ear, never ceased to amuse him as it contained a sardonic lilt, yet tinged with humour. Dan's facial muscles didn't react to the muttered words and the men parted as though no comment was passed, but inside

Dan was laughing although on the outside he was in a frozen pose as though unaware of his companion.

Just seconds later Gerry Tomas appeared, and hurrying though the gym on the way to his office, Dan peering over his plastic cup noticed he had instantly locked eyes with Adam. Putting the cup to his lips again, he realised the drink was long gone. Focusing on his remit, he surreptitiously watched Tomas smile at Adam who gave a nod of friendly recognition.

That fucking pervert's dangerous, I feel it in my guts. I hope I get the chance to smash his face in, cut off his balls and ram them down his throat. Hope Adam bloody fully realises the jeopardy he's in. I know it's his job but...

His stomach jolted uncomfortably as he watched Adam stop his exercising after a few minutes and follow Tomas through the door.

"DS Blake... " Lucy's voice broke his thoughts, brought him back to the present. She was standing in her usual crazy position on her left foot, the right foot being held by her right hand so her heel touched her backside. Dan could not believe the position, knowing he'd dislocate god knows what if he tried that.

She paused for a few seconds. Dan raised his eyebrow and nodded for her to continue. "Can ask you something with your police officers hat on."

"Fire away." Dan was glad Tomas had disappeared to his office. He glanced up to his office window, but he was nowhere to be seen. Dan relaxed. He wasn't around or watching.

Lucy related the incident when running in the park; meeting the jogger who, during their conversation about the 'body parts affair', had told her about his suspicions concerning the elderly couple who seemed to be watching her. She suddenly lowered the right foot, and proceeded to stretch her left leg in the same position. Dan shook his head, finding it difficult to concentrate.

Unaware of the exercises having the reaction it did on the police officer, Lucy drew in a deep breath, raised her eyes brows and shrugged. "Do you think this man's over-reacting? Am I being hysterical, paranoid?"

Initially thinking about this incident, she thought it was related to her past, but realising this was unlikely, she deduced the events happening presently could not be pure coincidence. Attempting to control her paranoia, she was also beginning to believe that maybe DS Blake was keen to get fit, and not suspicious of her.

"It could be quite innocent." His voice interrupted her musings. "I don't think you're being either hysterical or paranoid after what you've been through. Normally I'd think this jogger might be over-reacting, after all, they appear to have only been watching. They might be just enjoying your youth, but after all that's happened to you, it's obvious you're going to be worried."

"What do you suggest I do?"

"Without belittling the event in any way; understand our resources are stretched to breaking point and must be allocated effectively. As these people haven't actually done anything other than look, we can't do anything official. We don't know what this Muriel and Stan look like, so we don't know if it's them."

"Seems a weird fluke though."

"I agree, so I suggest you take care and don't run on your own. I take it you mostly run with Higgins?"

"Yes, nearly always... unless it's raining."

"If he was with you, rain or not, and someone was unpleasant to you, shouted at you or in the extreme, actually attacked you, would he defend you?"

"Mm, can't see it. He's so docile. I mean, he'd get very upset but as for attacking them, or perhaps defend me, I take it that's what you mean, I don't think so."

"Right. What I recommend is to only run in the daytime, preferably with someone else, Higgins being a last resource.

Don't look like that. I understand in the autumn and winter it's probably difficult to have any daylight running with the short days, but you can't take the chance until we know this couple's motives. Keep your eyes peeled and watch out for them. If you do spot them, or any couple or persons who seem as though they are actively watching you or being suspicious, note how they look, their actions and give me a call. I'll alert the team in case I'm not there when you call, and they'll understand the situation."

"Thanks for this. It's probably nothing."

"Let's hope that's the case. What about your mate Freddy, will he come running with you?"

"Who's using my name in vain?" Neither of them had noticed Freddy walk up. Dan turned to go. "Lucy will explain."

As he walked away, he overheard Freddy ask Lucy if she were ready to go for a drink but could not hear her reply. Realising he should not hang around the drink dispenser any longer, and the thought of more exercise was less than appealing, he decided to go home and phone and check on Adam later.

As he strolled to the changing room for a shower, he focused his thoughts.

Not happy leaving Adam with that pervert, but he's a capable officer and doesn't need babysitting I guess. One day, I'll enjoy strangling that bastard manager.

Chapter 28

DC Mel Stubbs placed the cup of tea in front of Patsy. The distraught mum had endured a particularly bad day.

Despite both the Fixed Point Officer located permanently outside the house and Mel ordering journalists out of the garden, one in particular was making a real nuisance of himself. She'd warned him three times if he did it again there would be dire consequences, but he seemed not to care. He wanted an interview with Patsy and was determined to wear everyone down until he got it. He was offering a substantial amount of money for a story and although Patsy had shrieked at him from the window to 'Fuck off', he ignored her pleas and continued to pester.

Mel had suggested they close the curtains but Patsy wouldn't entertain the idea. The moment Michelle appeared, Patsy wanted to see her. Mel's heart went out to the woman because she knew that event was now unlikely.

It was ten o' clock at night. Mel walked over to the window and peered into the darkness. She knew the news people were not far away but for the moment they weren't camped right outside the garden gate. Most of them, about this time she had previously noticed, slipped over to the local for a last pint before sliding off home, leaving the die-hards dozing in their cars in case there was fresh news.

Patsy finished the tea, wiped her mouth on her sleeve

and placed the cup back onto the coffee table. Her whole body language spoke volumes, a listless, unhappy, and traumatised woman.

"Like another cup?" said Mel. When Patsy shook her head, Mel continued, "You taken your tranquiliser today?"

Patsy putting her head into her hands and sighing loudly, shook her head again.

"Why don't you take a sleeping pill and go to bed?" said Mel. "The boys are fast asleep and you really could do with an early night and a good eight hours sleep. I'll be here, and if there is any news I promise to come and wake you immediately."

The young woman nodded and stood up. Except for the two words to the journalist, she hadn't spoken for days. If her two sons asked her a question, she stared at them blankly. Mel had watched the girl, at twenty-one she was barely a woman, slowly slide downhill. The first few days of hysteria had drifted into days of shrieking anger. This last week she had subsided into a black depression and Mel was very concerned about her mental state.

"Yeah, maybe you're right. Them tablets the doc gave me knocks me out proper. The sleeps 'orrible, just black and nuffink, but at least I get a bit of rest from thinking what the bastards are doing to my angle. Fuckers, I hope whoever's got my little darling rots in 'ell."

Mel stood up, pleased that Patsy had at last said something, and put her arms round her shoulders to comfort her. As a police officer she was present to give her total support but it was inevitable you became personally involved. No-one, she decided, if they had a spark of humanity in their souls, could manage to stay detached in this sad situation. Knowing that Patsy was unlikely to see Michelle alive, the sadness and hurt bit deeply into her own heart.

A tapping at the door surprised them both. Before Mel could react, Patsy's eyes, narrowing to slits, with anger shooting from them like missiles, sprinted to the front door muttering that she would kill the bastard if it was that nosey journalist. The young mother wrenched the door open. Mel, a second behind, and desperate to stop a possible homicide, almost collided with Patsy who had stopped dead on the front mat.

"Hello, mummy," a little voice said.

Both women stared at the raggedy little girl in a pink frilly dress who stood on the doorstep holding a skipping rope in her hands as though she had skipped up the garden.

Patsy mewed like a hurt kitten. Niagara Falls changed countries and cascaded down Mel's cheeks. The girl held up her rope.

"I been practisin'. I can skip now."

Mel caught Patsy as she fell back into her arms. She laid her gently onto the floor and took the child's hand. She didn't want the press witnessing this scene.

"She just appeared from no-where," whispered the FPO.

Indicating to the amazed officer, whose eyes and mouth were still open in surprise and delight, that he should immediately contact the police station, Mel closed the door.

"Come in, darling. It's so cold, let's close the door."

"What's wrong with mum, she asleep or some'ink?"

Mel knew Patsy should be the first to cuddle the child but she couldn't resist wrapping her arms round her and hugging her close.

Chapter 29

It was weird, he was in the gym, his least favourite place. He was on the rowing machine and doing so well that Lucy Hamilton was timing him with a stopwatch in her hand and telling him he still had ten minutes to go before breaking the world record. The watch kept ringing and ringing, which he thought was strange.

He woke suddenly and realised it was his mobile that was on the coffee table next to a large whisky he had poured himself. Leaning forward, elbows on his knees, he rubbed his face, and forced himself to fully awake. The drink was untouched so obviously he had dropped off to sleep almost as soon as he'd sat down.

Glancing at his watch, Dan realised it was after ten. Who the hell would be ringing him at this time of night. *Shite, it's work.*

"Blake, he said brusquely."

"It's Cole. Where are you?"

"Home, Guv. Kipping."

"Just got back from London. Go straight to Michelle Foster's house. She's just turned up, alive...You there, you've gone silent?"

"Shock. So much for statistics. Thank God. She OK?"

"Far as I know, on the surface, as right as rain. Fifteen minutes."

"I'll be there in ten."

He leapt up from the seat, his smile so big it was almost slipping off the side of his face.

Despite the gusting wind and the rain hammering down that, according to the weather people, had swept in from the continent, Dan made good headway to Patsy Foster's road. Hoping to get there before the news of Michelle's unexpected return had spread, he knew immediately as he turned into the road that he was wrong. The foul weather hadn't stopped the gathering of neighbours and God knows who else.

A car carrying DI Cole, DCs Mesbah and Luke Steiner drew in behind him as a uniformed constable beckoned both cars into a cordoned off area in front of the house. Outside this barrier, a street party was in full swing; celebration time had arrived.

Despite four police cars parked at both ends of the road attempting to keep the area clear, half the people from the estate had wormed their way passed the roadblock and were standing around drinking champagne. Party time had hit Westfield Road. Bottles and cans of lager were being passed around. A man in an old-fashioned plaid dressing gown with tears running down his face, which looked odd against the contrasting grin, leaned over the cordon tape and offered Dan a drink. Someone else attempted to shove a glass of something bubbly into Luke's hand. They both smiled and graciously refused. A flashlight momentarily blinded Dan. He checked the area and became aware of TV cameras.

"Christ, the press have got here before us," he said to his colleagues as they walked down the garden path.

"No, they haven't left the road since she went missing." Cole pushed Dan from behind and as they entered the house they walked into more celebrations.

The whole family were in the living room, Michelle firmly ensconced on her mother's lap. She was hugging her as though she was never going to let her go. The two young brothers in faded dressing gowns were standing in front of their mum, arms also wrapped around their sister.

DC Tom Carter who had responded to Mel's call, look frustrated. "I'm trying to bring some order. It's awkward. You can see the relief and joy but I know we need to get the kid away to the Special Unit," he explained to DI Cole. "Mel and I thought we'd give them a few minutes till you got here and then you can bring a little realism into the situation. It's not that we've let it get out of control."

"Don't worry, Tom. Anyone phoned the Child Protection Office?" At Mel's nod, he continued. "Get the mum making tea or maybe putting the two youngsters to bed, they look shattered despite the excitement. As soon as the CPO gets here we can get her away and start questioning Michelle. Has she spoken to anyone yet? Has there been a 'First Disclosure?'"

"No, as you can see, we can't prise her out of Patsy's arms and Michelle is overwhelmed with the attention but hasn't uttered a word. They're just pleased to get her back. I've made sure no-ones spoken to her."

Despite the desperate need to get information, all the police officers crowded in the small living room, watched a joyful scene they never thought they'd see, a little girl returned safely to her family. Michelle, thumb in her mouth, still clutching her skipping rope, was smiling coyly, surprised yet pleased about the unexpected attention.

Mel slowly unwrapped Patsy's arms from around her eldest child.

"Hey, Patsy, let's make the guys some tea. Maybe get Michelle and the boys a drink as well, I think we'll all toast the occasion with tea and lemonade, what do you say?"

Chapter 30

Maria Grainger's eyes were firmly closed, and she had no intention of opening them. If she even so much as peeked, the nightmare might return and she was determined that wasn't going to happen. She shivered; the hard bed or whatever she was lying on was metal cold. The noise of a door opening and someone padding across the room almost broke her resolve to concentrate on getting back to reality; her nice comfortable life in her two bed roomed semi. When she returned to it she vowed never to moan about it again. It was paradise in comparison to her present predicament.

"Wakey, wakey," the stupid old git's voice said.

Ignore him. He's not there. I'm in my bed at home having a nightmare. If I cling on to that belief, in a minute I'll wake up.

A sharp something traced round the outline of her eye. Knowing what it was; the bastards had taken great delight in showing her the instrument, then going into graphic detail about its use, her stomach twisted with fear.

"Open your eyes. We know you're awake and we need to have more discussions." The stupid cow must also have crept into the room.

If I could get my hands round her throat... if I could get my hands round either of their throats, they wouldn't be so bloody cocky.

"I'll count to ten," said Stan.

They'd introduced themselves by their first names when they'd abducted her like long lost relatives. Maria couldn't believe she'd been kidnapped, tied down on a freezing table, straps securing her, and then they'd talked to her as though they were having a normal conversation over a cup of tea. The incongruity of it all was driving her mad.

"Listen to Stan, he means what he says. Open your eyes, answer our questions and things will get a lot better."

"I notice you didn't say I could go home," said Maria, her voice sullen and obstinate, her eyes slowly opening, the hope of her being in her own bed and just having a normal nightmare floated away like bonfire smoke in the wind. She made the most of this pain free time. When they started on her again, all the bravado would zoom from her body like a rocket breaking free from the earth's atmosphere, along with her screams. Not that she could yell, the tape over her mouth when they started 'the treatment' as they called it, muffled most of the sound, but inside her head, throughout her whole body, her nerves, bones and the very core of her being shrieked for the pain to stop.

"You never know," said Muriel. "If we get what we want, and you make a few promises that you won't tell who we are, you could soon be home and comfortable in a very short time."

They're lying. They won't let me go 'cos the moment I was out of here I'd be up the cop shop shouting blue murder and they know it.

"Stan, Muriel, how many times do I have to tell you? I don't know and I don't know anyone who knows. I swear on my mother's grave that if I knew I would tell you. Why should I lie here suffering this agony?"

"Look at poor Nigel and Don, that's just what they said. Now you're a handsome woman, you don't want to end up like them, do you?" said Stan and the wheedling note in his voice grated on Maria's nerves.

Maria fought very hard not to glance at the ghastly heads, now resembling macabre puppets from a horror film, propped on some sort of stainless steel upright support, but she couldn't control her eyes, the horror was like a magnet. The heads had collapsed in on themselves even in the time Maria had first encountered the grisly tableau. The eyeholes were now black and she could see something wriggling around inside them and knew maggots were doing their best to demolish the green and rotting remains. At first the smell had made her vomit but she barely noticed that now. She'd read somewhere that the brain deals with smells very quickly and you soon become immune.

Bloody good use that knowledge is in this sodding predicament.

"Look, Stan," Maria explained for the umpteenth time, "I don't know... " The woman stopped. A brainwave flooded her mind; the threat of more excruciating pain and imminent death had sent a surge of adrenalin through her body, feeding the brain and giving her an idea that might just save her life. "I've just remembered something. Donald and Nigel might not have known but what about the fourth person who got away?" Maria struggled to recall his name, after all, if she was going to make out she knew him that well, she ought to know his name.

Muriel fell for it, and supplied the information from their extensive research. "You mean Joseph Bates."

"Yes, Jo." The shortened form of his name made him sound like a friend. She normally wouldn't know the other cell member's names, but had heard their names during the interview by the police after the cells failed Operation Heigh-ho. "It totally escaped my mind. I'm sure he could help you. I believe he told me himself that he'd been directly involved. I didn't approve of it at all; I told the cops so at the time."

"You told the police." Stan's face came into view as he thrust himself into her face. "They never said anything about it."

"Well, they wouldn't, would they," interrupted Maria. "If you think you really know how the cops work, you're mistaken. If it's too much like hard work, they don't want to know."

"We did keep onto them," said Muriel. She peered at Maria from the other side of the table and her voice was sorrowful. "Said they'd put all resources into it but to no avail. The case isn't closed, will never be closed, but according to them, those resources have to be allocated to more pressing, recent cases."

"The bastards! I told you so." Maria was ecstatic; they were hooked.

"But we can't trace Joseph Bates," said Stan. "We've tried everything and he seems to have disappeared off the face of the earth.

"I'm not sure where he is at the moment," said Maria, her brain cells still working overtime in her survival process, "But I know how we can draw him in."

The two faces leaned over her, only inches away from her face, in their eagerness to hear her words. Maria controlled the panic seeping in now the gush of life-saving chemicals had passed their peak, leaving her momentarily floundering. She'd have to wing it! Having absolutely no idea how to draw him in, in truth she hardly knew him, but necessity proved a hard master. Hard concentration would supply her with a convincing story until she could escape this nightmare.

"Money. He's mad on money. That's how we'll trap him."

The stupid gits nodded enthusiastically, and didn't argue with her phrase 'we'll have to draw him in'. She needed to be part of this 'gang' if she was going to *ever* get free.

Chapter 31

The SOCO team arrived at the same time as Dan and DC Luke Steiner at Sonning Heath Woods. Luke was with the duty officer alerted by a frantic call from a young police officer dispatched from the small, local police station in response to a 999. The young man was obviously more used to drunken youths and minor quarrels, and not prepared for what he saw. Luke was just leaving the police station in answer to the call when Dan arrived for work and so accompanied his DC to what sounded, by the grisly details given by the shocked young officer, a macabre scene.

When they arrived at the site, the young policeman stood with an equally pale faced man holding an impatient dog on a leash, both visibly shaken and distressed.

"Tell me the events, PC..." said Dan to the police officer, taking his arm and drawing him aside from the man.

"PC Sam Austen. I answered the 999.The gentleman with the dog..." He consulted his notebook. "A Mr John Brooker, was taking his dog for a walk. The dog started sniffing around and Mr. Brooker discovered the bodies."

"Bodies? More than one?"

"Two bodies. Lying side by side, holding hands."

"OK. Luke, go and talk to Mr Brooker. See if he noticed anything or anybody around the immediate area."

Dan looked towards the probable crime scene, the SOCO

were already preserving the wider area with the cordon. He could see they were going to be in this 'wider area' and he ordered Luke, Mr Brooker and the PC to walk further away with him, leaving the SOCOs to do their work. He knew the importance of having a broad uncontaminated location.

He continued to question the PC but it was obvious he knew nothing other than he'd answered the emergency call, had met Mr Brooker at the edge of the woods and then shown the site containing the two bodies. After confirming that PC Austen had obtained the relevant details, Dan suggested the two of them remove themselves even farther away. He handed the young police officer a flask of coffee he'd made for the late evening shift due to the temperamental performance of the team's electric kettle, deducing their need was greater than his.

"Go and sit by on that fallen log. The coffee should still be hot. You both look as though you need a drink."

"Don't suppose there's any brandy in it, sir?"

Dan chuckled. "'Fraid not, son. I'd have put a slug in if I'd known it was for medicinal purposes."

Luke, who had been peering impatiently over the cordon off area, wandered over to Dan.

"When we going to be able to get a look, boss?"

"Let's don some scrubs. Long as we don't get in their way, we'll check what's immediately obvious." Pulling on the protective garments was never an easy manoeuvre over top clothes; Dan glanced around and checked with Luke as to whether he had seen the pathologist.

"Not seen him. Left a message for DI Cole telling him as much as I could make out from Austen's phone call. Will he attend?"

"Maybe, maybe not. He's tied up with the Michelle case. We'll see what we have first then I'll phone and update him. Ready?"

The two officers walked to the cordon, showing their identification passes to a young woman as she logged them into the area. She, naturally, was also wearing the protective outfit and despite the hat pulled low over her brow, looked like she was just out of school which made Dan feel decidedly old.

The inner cordon and tent to preserve and shield the bodies weren't yet in place, and the two attending SOCOs agreed to let Dan and Luke view the bodies provided they keep to the dedicated path just laid down. Two bodies were clearly visible, a thin layer of soil not able to conceal the horror.

"Holy shite, boss," muttered Luke, putting his hand over his mouth, vainly hoping it might control the violent shifting of his stomach contents.

"Bloody hell, did an animal get to them?" said Dan, also covering his mouth, as though that would halt the feelings of nausea that sweeping over him. He felt like an inexperienced, new recruit.

"No, the cuts look clean on initial inspection," answered one of the crime scene officers who had assumed Dan was asking him. "They look neatly butchered. On first inspection I'd say there's no indication of an animal chewing them. Looks like an expert has been at work."

"Expert?"

"Cuts as clean as lamb chops on the butcher's slab." Dan glanced at the man, not amused by what he thought was an insensitive remark, but the tone and the part of his face showing above his mask, were serious.

The two police officers leaned down to have a closer look, controlling their initial horror, and forcing themselves to be professional. The bodies, lying side by side, were holding hands. Their faces were a bloody mess and identification would be difficult even from someone who knew them.

"Jesus," winced Luke, shaking his head at the horror before him. "Their noses and ears are missing though you can see, even amongst the carnage; one of them's a black guy." Straightening up, he pointed to the large congealed pools of blood covering both genital areas. "I don't care to think about what happened there."

"Their mouths are half open. If you look... maté, can you focus that torch on their faces?" Dan asked the SOCO standing nearest to him. "Look, if you peer in, I've got a horrible feeling what should be at the top of their legs, hidden by a zip, has been stuffed into their mouths."

"I've seen some ghastly sights, I think this beats all. What sick bastard would do this?" Luke took a deep breath to steady his nerves.

"One positive thing, they've still got their hands, so if we have their prints on file, IDing them'll be easy. Looks like a different MO to the two other sets of body parts we've being investigating. Interesting to know what the pathologist comes up with."

As if on cue, the familiar voice of the pathologist boomed like thunder over the area.

"What have we got here then?" Dan and Luke straightened up from their studies and moved aside to let Dr. MacFarlane, or Dr MacDeath as he was nicknamed by the crime team, gain access to the bodies. The police officers nodded at him; both had worked with him on previous cases and knew he had performed the post mortems on Donald Taylor and Nigel Matthews.

"We're certainly keeping you busy, Doc," said Dan.

"You certainly are, lads," he muttered, hands on his knees, eyes squinting in the poor light."

"Any chance of getting some light over here? Dark as a power cut in hell," his voice bellowed again. The pathologist didn't seem capable of a speaking with a soft voice.

"Just fixing them up now," a voice came out of the gloom. "Ask and it shall be given." Bright lights flared and the grisly details stood out clearly for the on-lookers to see.

No-one spoke as the pathologist trod carefully around the narrow dedicated path, viewing the body from all angles, leaning over so far that Dan thought he may well topple onto the bodies. As he inspected, he was making grunting noises, lots of 'huh huhs', interspaced with a tuneless whistling sound.

"Photographers finished?" he called out to the duty PC.

"Yes, sir, just."

After his initial close inspection, he knelt down and began to gently move their limbs, testing for rigor mortis. When he produced his thermometer, knowing temperatures are gauged by inserting the instrument into the rectum, Dan and Luke decided to quit the area.

Outside the outer cordon, Luke stripped off his protective clothing.

"I thought a temperature couldn't be taken if clothing had to be removed as that risks contamination," said Luke, folding the trousers up and dropping them in the collection bag offered by the young girl.

"I've heard he hates having us breathe down his neck while he works so he always gets that out because he knows most officers don't lust after watching a thermometer being thrust up some poor dead soul's arse."

"What? So we walk away?"

Dan nodded as he got out his mobile.

"I'd better update the Gov now. Christ; he's going to go ballistic. He's going to start quoting statistics."

"What statistics, boss?"

"The ones about the normal number of murders in this town and what's happening at the moment."

"It's a bit like a Lynda Le Plant novel. Mind you, surely this is exceptional. It's not the norm, you know, black on black, kids stabbing each other or a bloke murdering his misses for shagging around. These murders are well outside that norm."

Dan sighed as the ringing continued, "Still makes the stats and our clear up rate look pretty crap. I think our beloved leader's going to have to re-think his budget allocation for overtime."

Cole didn't answer his phone again and the call was redirected to the duty officer who took a message.

"Yeah," said Luke as Dan snapped his mobile shut, "and the bags under our eyes are going to hit suitcase size with the lack of sleep."

"C'este la vie."

"Bugger that, boss, got a fag? It's gonna be a long night."

"Good point, Luke. No fags I'm afraid. Send young Austen off to get that flask topped up. There's a Macdonald's down the road."

"Two cheeseburgers?"

"Four, could be a long night." As Luke hurried over to PC Austen and Mr. Brooker, Dan called after him, revising the food order. "Get those two burgers as well if they fancy a bite. My treat. Tell him to hurry, in case DI Cole gets my message and decides to view the scene. Tell them both to keep away from the cordoned off area. Burger wrappers contaminating the crime scene don't bode well for promotion."

As Luke wandered over to PC Austen to give the food orders, Dan turned and contemplated the crime scene. With instant re-call, he visualised the details of what he had seen when he'd previously examined the area. Mulling over in his mind the things of no importance, he dismissed them for immediate consideration. He then stored away other facts in the filing cabinet at the back of his mind for later retrieval and contemplation.

Carefully considering the circumstances, he analysed what was missing and then what was present and may be pertinent to the investigation.

Digging his hands deep into his overcoat pockets, as his concentration deepened, two furrows appeared between his eyebrows. His colleagues called this contemplation the 'Diamond Brain Coma' but they never interrupted these thoughts!

Dan spotted that two men in white suits were now erecting the inner cordon and a blue tent to shield the bodies. Once again donning scrubs, he walked again to outer barrier, lifted it and bending almost double to gain access to the crime scene, needing to check whether Dr Mac Death had formed any early conclusions. He also wanted to view the site again; he called it his 'one time look'. Although there were photographs to examine later, he always found that the image ironed onto his brain during his first examination was the most revealing. Momentarily he experienced the urge for a cigarette. He shrugged the feeling away, he had to focus and not be distracted!

Chapter 32

1989

"You're not serious, Sharon. What's so important about a few clothes?" said Stuart. He couldn't believe she was determined to go back to her rooms to pick up her meagre belongings. They'd been dossing temporarily with a friend of Sharon's. Dana used to be on the game but after she met her present boyfriend, she'd packed up the drugs and prostitution and settled down with Pete. The couple had given Sharon and Stuart a lift to her old accommodation and parked round the corner in their old van.

"They're all I have and I don't see why that wanker should have them." answered Sharon, referring to Winston, her now ex-pimp. He lived on the ground floor of a Victorian house. Sharon and some of his other girls had various rooms on the floors above. Naturally, being a mean bastard in the girls' opinion, he charged them rent.

"It's eleven o'clock. He'll be out checking on the girls. If we go round the side there's a fire escape that we can use. It goes right past the balcony outside my room."

"Balcony. That's posh."

"Shuddup. You up for this or not?"

"Lead on. I knew you'd be trouble."

179

The two walked quietly along the alleyway by the side of the building. There were no lights in the house except a chink showing through a slit in curtains covering the basement window.

"Who lives down there?" whispered Stuart. Sharon shrugged and shook her head. Beckoning him to follow her, she pointed to a rusty ladder that masqueraded as a fire escape.

"That ol' thing?" Stuart said, shaking his head. "You're joking, it wouldn't support a flea."

"Ssh, speak quietly. The ladder'll be fine. Just jump. Get hold of the bottom rung. It eases down OK. Used it before once when I forgot my door key."

Sharon went first and on reaching her floor level eased her leg over her balcony and beckoned for the rent boy to join her. Trying the door, she swore when she found it locked.

"Don't tell me. You haven't brought the key. Typical unprepared woman."

"Only ever had keys for the front door and my room. This one wasn't locked before."

"Luckily for you, I'm a master of all trades." Drawing something from his pocket, he squatted down and inserted it into the lock. Jiggling it round, Sharon heard a click.

"Voila!! For an ex-rent boy I'm well clever," Stuart said in a terrible French accent, opening the door with a flourish.

"How the hell did you do that?" she asked.

He tapped the side of his nose. "Ask no questions, hear no lies."

"You're a nutter," she whispered as she pushed past him into the room.

"Ungrateful cow," he retorted softly. Sharon giggled.

"Where's the light?"

"Don't put that on. I know where everything is." Going to a wardrobe, she pulled out a scruffy canvas bag and started stuffing clothes into it. A strange wailing noise made them both freeze.

"Christ, what's that? The hairs are sticking up on my neck." said Stuart, eyes as big as saucers. "It's coming from the corner. The place's haunted. "

"It's an old house. Full of creaks and the wind groans in the chimneys. Really eerie sometimes. I've never heard that sound before. God, there it is again." They both held their breath and listened. Sharon whispered, "It's coming from that old fireplace. I think the chimney comes all the way up from the basement."

Walking to the fireplace, she pulled the cover from the opening and bend over concentrating on the noises emanating from the fireplace.

"Sounds like your urban fox. A funny wailing," said Stuart.

"That's not a fox. That's a child crying."

"Some-one got a kid in this place?" The sound whimpered up the chimney again and muffled voices mixed in with it.

"Bloody hell," swore Sharon. "That's Winston. Who's he got down there?"

Stuart shrugged. "Just get those clothes packed and let's skiddaddle."

Sharon straightened up. Memories of her childhood washed in front of her. She'd had no-one there for her; maybe she was here for a reason. "No, this is fate."

"Fuck fate, let's just split."

"No, we go and find out what's going on down there."

"You're totally mad, man. You've been gone for seven days. He'll kill you."

Looking around for a weapon to defend herself, she picked up an old poker and coal shovel lying in the grate.

"I was going to throw these out. Glad I didn't. I'll take the poker. You have the shovel. We'll go armed then."

"Oh, great. What the hell do we do with these? If it's Winston, he'll be fucking carrying. Gun versus shovel, guh, what do I prefer?"

"We'll have to hit him before he shoots us then, won't

we?" The girl hit the poker against her other hand. "This is well solid. It's big enough to knock some-one out." She walked to the bedroom door and opened it carefully, peering along the dark landing. Looking back over her shoulder, she whispered, "You coming or not, you poofter?"

Stuart groaned as she hurried from the room.

"Gott im Himmel, what did I ever do to deserve this mad cow?" Following closely behind her, muttering that his lifestyle had been complicated enough, now he was going to get himself killed. "Shite. It just gets better and better with this total idiot."

Chapter 33

Dan walked into the meeting room with his folder tucked under his armpit after updating DI Cole. He had left his bosses' office with the proverbial flea in his ear because of the lack of progress in solving or connecting the cases with hard evidence.

"We've got more bloody bodies turning up in the last couple of months than in five years." Cole was red in the face with frustration, and as Dan had predicted to Luke at the crime screen of the two bodies, had started quoting statistics. His foxy eyes had flashed and he had smoked three cigarettes in a row. Even Dan didn't have the courage to point out smoking on the premises was illegal, although he noticed despite the cold weather, the office window was wide open. As Cole finished one, he lit a fresh one with the butt. Dan, still struggling to kick the habit, tried to draw the smoke in without seeming too obvious.

Dan understood why he was getting it the neck; Cole's superior were also reprimanding him. The blame cascaded down from the top like custard poured over a pudding, and eventually thumped onto his shoulders. He had learned long ago to keep quiet when the boss went on the rampage. When he had first worked for Cole, he had foolishly tried to justify his position, but now knew he could never match the lash of Cole's tongue. Far better to inwardly wince, keep quiet and take it like a man. When the DI emptied the rage, they would then begin talking future plans.

Looking round the room Dan was relieved to see more staff present than at the last big get-together.

"OK, listen up. If we're all to still have jobs at Christmas, we're going to have to get our brain cells working and see the links to these cases and bloody solve them."

"You're still seeing links then?" asked Tom Carter.

"Yes but the details of those links aren't clear. I have some ideas I want to run pass you. Maybe with some fresh ideas from our colleagues returned from the flu, perhaps we'll start seeing the light. Welcome back, hope you're now germ free?" Dan looked at six officers who had returned recently after the bout of flu decimating the station's staff numbers. The men grinned and nodded and one in particular raised his hand in acknowledgement.

"I'm not assigned to this case, Dan. Just thought I'd sit in while my team is digging up some information on the robbery we're assigned to. Maybe as you said, come up with some fresh ideas, if that's OK with you?" DS Paul Fletcher had gone off sick the morning that Nigel Matthew's body parts were uncovered. Being an older and more experienced officer, normally he would have led the murder case. Due to his illness, the assignment had fallen on Dan's shoulders.

"Thanks, Paul. Yes, heard you're heading up the robbery investigation at the main post office. You're very welcome. Fresh eyes are always good. Any ideas will be great 'cos we're going no-where. Fresh face, fresh ideas. We've got a lot of supposition but sod-all facts or evidence."

Dan turned to the white board now re-arranged to three columns. He pointed to the left column topped with photos of Nigel Matthews and Donald Taylor.

"OK, let's go over this again. Nigel Mathews' body parts found hidden in a small wooded area of Elmpark by a Lucy Hamilton who was out jogging. She took a short cut through the woods and her dog dug up the bones. Two weeks later a joker leaves a bag of similar body parts outside the same Lucy Hamilton's flat. Turns out these two 'bodies' knew each other and were ID'd as two of the four that got away on the entrapment technicality after the failed Operation Rawhide. Body number two belonged to Donald Taylor."

Dan then pointed to two pictures beneath the top ones, and continued, "Maria Grainger and Joseph Bates. The other two released. If the top two murders were payback, then we need to contact Grainger and Bates to warn them they may also be in danger.

"Maria Grainger's neighbours confirm she returned from a holiday in Spain but hasn't been seen since. We're still trying to run Bates to ground. Despite numerous interviews and enquiries to local known nonces, nothing's come up that moves our enquiry forward. OK so far?"

"So apart from the fact the four of them were involved in this operation and they got away on a technicality, there's no other connection, no clear motive?" asked Paul.

"No, but what leads us to believe it *may* be retribution is that although the operation was unsuccessful in terms of arresting anyone except these four, their plans for a mass abduction of kids was terminated."

"Yeah, I remember now," interrupted Paul. "Those four were the only ones captured. The rest slipped the noose and conveniently got alibis by the time they were rounded up."

"That's right. Unfortunately, one child, Jordan Turner, did disappear and his body has never been found."

"You think this pay back, ie the motive, is linked then to the child's disappearance?"

Dan shrugged. "Seems weak on its own, I know. Jordan was from a single parent family and we're trying to locate the mother but she also seems to have disappeared. The neighbours at her address here in Reading say she may have moved up north. Where exactly, they don't know. We can't locate Grainger and Bates. The massive black hole syndrome, sucking everybody in and never re-appearing. If it was revenge, then the only people in the public domain as far as this child's disappearance goes, are these four. So the perpetrator's motive... is payback. "

Moving back to the white board, Dan pointed at Michelle Foster's picture at the top of the centre column.

"Michelle Foster. Abducted on October 12th. No-one saw or knows anything. Despite extensive enquiries the investigation's stalled. Out of the blue, she turns up. We find out she was abducted by two men, Uncle John and Uncle Roger. She's just a child, so her description didn't help us; even showing photos of known nonces got us nowhere."

"Was she harmed in any way?" asked Paul.

"A detailed medical examination confirms she wasn't raped although she was sore in the genital area. The results suggest interference but no actual penile penetration. She told us they gave her a pretty dress, but no pretty knickers, her words, and they took photos. They told her she was going to have a friend join them soon and then the two 'Uncles' said they would have real fun."

Hostile murmuring emanating from the police officers forced Dan to hold up his hand.

"OK, let's focus. Anger doesn't produce results." His eyes swept the room, emphasising his point. "In the meantime we find out a young boy, aged ten, a Genghis Simpson, had been approached by a man in a chat room who wanted to meet him to 'get him into films'. Said the kid could earn a lot of money. Fortunately it was reported to us by his teacher, Lucy Hamilton."

"Another link then," said Paul. "This Lucy Hamilton."

Dan stared at his colleague, raising his eyebrows enquiringly.

"Involved with the two body parts of our Nigel and Don and then turns out she's Genghis's teacher. Genghis, you're kidding me. Anyway, is anyone investigating this Lucy Hamilton?"

"Yes. Meena's done a thorough background check and

she's clean as virgin snow." He didn't add his suspicions about the spotless inspection on her past, he wanted to focus on what he thought at this point was more important.

Paul obviously wasn't going to let this go. "Think about it. This Genghis Khan... "

"Simpson."

"Whatever. Suddenly a kid in her class gets chatted up. How do we know she's not involved? Maybe gave out his name to whoever was chatting to this kid. You say she hasn't any form? Nothing."

"No, not a dicky bird. Meena, who never leaves a stone unturned, checked her out thoroughly. She appears an innocent bystander who's caught up in this. We have done a thorough background check naturally. In fact she's Miss Ultra Clean. Not even so much as a parking ticket. However, naturally we keep an open mind." He turned and let his eyes rove over the room, before he added, "Another kid at the school told Lucy... Miss Hamilton, that Genghis was being chatted up. That's how Miss Hamilton got involved. Can I carry on; we're drifting away from the story line?"

Dan avoided Meena's eyes as he turned back to the white board, but he could feel them piercing his back.

"OK, third column. Two bodies found on Sonning Heath. You can see from the photos at the crime scene they've been badly mutilated. Noses, ears, and genitals removed very neatly. The pathologist's report confirms the MOs are different to Matthew and Taylor's. Inside one of the gentlemen's pockets was note explaining their demise. I'll read the photocopy. I would suspect the author intends to be helpful and hopes we stop chasing our tails in regard to Michelle."

Dan held up the note contained in a plastic bag, flourishing it in a theatrical fashion, he read,

'These men have been disobedient. They knew the rules which they flagrantly broke so they have been punished, paying the ultimate price. Their deaths were painful. We set

the girl free. That's the end of it.'

"No signature naturally. No DNA, clean as a whistle. Produced on a computer, so no handwriting to go on. OK, any thoughts on what this is all about?"

"You talked about revenge, boss. This is revenge. Maybe someone is going around knocking off all the nonces they know about," suggested Meena.

"Got anything from their finger prints? At least with these two, their hands were intact," said Jim Davison, who had walked in a few minutes previously with coffees balanced on a tray.

"Yes, we got a hit with one set of prints. They belonged to a John Thomas, a well-known nonce. Maybe Michelle's 'Uncle John'."

The name produced ripples of laughter through the room and a few comments that Dan was kidding. "Steady up, I'm serious, my fellow officers. A nice, plain Welsh name. Anyway, he had form. One count of suspected child molesting although nothing proved; the family were fed up with the do-gooder judge and the welfare people blocking the case. They moved from the area. He was also caught loitering around a school and got off with a warning." Dan shook his head with frustration. "Let off. Christ, what does it take? We've hoping Michelle will know him from his photo."

"Well, he won't be hanging around any more schools, boss, I'm pleased to say." called out Luke Steiner.

"And the other little chappy he was holding hands so lovingly with, boss, anything there?" said Tom.

"No, nothing on the finger prints data base for him. We're sending off his DNA but if we haven't got prints on file," He shrugged. "I'm not hopeful anything will come of that."

"So whoever killed them, for whatever reason, returned the girl. Maybe it is a retribution thing." said Meena.

"How would anyone know what this John Thomas and his mate were doing unless they were involved? The four released nonces, now their names were in the public domain, but how would anyone know about the latest two killed? The MOs are plainly different and Dr. McDeath categorically rules out the two sets of murders being carried out by the same person or persons," said Dan. He took the last cup of coffee from the tray on the table near the white board and sipped it.

"We know that Lawman, supposedly dead keen to meet Genghis, didn't turn up for the meet. D'you reckon one of them could be him...Lawman?" said Meena, pointing at the photos on the right of the white board? "After all, Michelle alleges that the two 'uncles' told her they were going to get her a play mate. I hate to even think about what that means.

"Is it possible after the date with Genghis was set up, Lawman and his accomplice were topped before the actual meeting in the park took place? That would explain why Lawman never showed. Then the person or persons seeking revenge let Michelle go. What did you say the note stated, 'that's the end of it'?" Meena sat back in her seat and crossed her arms, please with her explanation.

"You might have something there," affirmed Dan, sipping more coffee and looking over the top of the plastic cup. "This is my theory regarding the note. See how this grabs you. I think whoever wrote the note may have made an unintentional mistake. Think about this phrase used in the note, 'They know the rules'."

The room was silent as the officers digested and thought about this.

"I see," said Paul, his forefinger tapping his chin. "Rules for what. Maybe revenge for Michelle, whose abduction was not in their plans. They played outside their laid down rules, whatever they were. "

"Yes." said Dan, his voice laced with excitement. "Maybe they didn't want attention for a reason. As you know, and this doesn't get out of this room on pain of death, the officer investigating a paedophile ring says those he's involved with

189

are totally up their own arses, excuse the pun.

"Full of themselves, all having unique code names, formal meetings and such like. Their activities two years ago, although foiled to a certain extent, we suspect are up and running again. Except for the four arrests, the rest scattered and lay low. Informants now believe this paedophile cell has reformed over the last year, thinking the time is safe for them to have another go."

Dan paced up and down in front of the board, his face and body animated as he explained his deductions. He continued, "Information from other police forces indicate they also have evidence suggesting cells in their areas being monitored are doing the same. If this is the case, then the leaders wouldn't want anyone doing their own thing ie John Thomas and his mate. Hence, 'breaking the rules'. Those rules stipulating everyone keeps a low profile until the times right.

"Whoever wrote that note wrote the truth as it was, revenge for their foolish actions, but in his arrogance didn't realise that the phrase was a giveaway. If they weren't 'abiding by rules'; rules for what? Their rules! If that phrase hadn't put that in the letter, then it might just have looked like a case of vengeance. Think about 'that will be the end of it'."

"That's what they want us to think," said Meena, excitement shining on her face now.

"After the initial furore of Michelle being returned, we all know the huge number of resources focused of finding her will be scaled down and used elsewhere. Michelle's returned and we have the kidnappers. The team will inevitably be scaled down. 'The end of it'," added Tom Carter.

"Yes," said Dan, turning to look at the speaker. "We're not going to stop looking for the murderers, but we all know our resources were mainly concentrated on looking for the child and that, perhaps, is what they're banking on. Eventually, as the story comes off the front pages as it were, other things occur and become front page news. Probably they're hoping it'll be the same for us, other cases come up, resources re-allocated. The task force numbers will drop because Michelle came home."

"So, you believe its revenge for the two acting outside the plan and the note's a cover up, a sort of diversion in a way." said Tom. "I can see your point but just coming to that conclusion on one sentence is a bit thin."

"True, but isn't that how crimes are often solved." Dan shrugged. "Loads of hard work, a bit of intuition, and then the criminal makes one small mistake. The puzzle, totally fragmented, suddenly starts to slot into place. It'll be prudent to give out the idea this task force is running down now that Michelle is back. That way, these people'll believe they're in the clear and no harm has been done, so they carry on with their plans."

"But how does that link to the first two murders, Mathews and Taylor?" said Meena. "I can't see how they're linked."

"I think the connection is that they are nonces, plain and simple. Matthews and Taylor may have been in the original gang and their names were in the public domain. Maybe revenge is the motive; maybe not from the cell. Perhaps someone else had it in for them. That's why I think it imperative we contact Grainger and Bates because they're probably in danger too from the infamous 'Stan and Muriel'. We don't know whether they are connected with this cell in any way. Stan and Muriel were the signatures on notes left with the two body parts, one which Lucy Hamilton found in the wood and the other outside her apartment," he explained to the newly returned officers.

"There's that name again, Lucy Hamilton!" interrupted Paul Fletcher. "Me, I'd be all over her like a rash. *Nobody's that clean!*"

Dan scowled at him for a moment but never replied. Turning to Meena, aware he should be winding up the briefing, asked, "You were looking into tracing the mother of the missing boy. Still nothing?"

Meena shook her head. "Nope. Like you said, it's like a black hole is swallowing up these people. We know her address and I asked the local boys from her origins to get back to me. I'll give them another ring to see if they've come up with anything yet."

"Good." Dan turned back to the team. "So, low profile on this one, giving the impression we've lost our momentum, but understand that is definitely not the case. I don't want to interfere and blow a case out of the water for another enquiry but we still need to crack these murders. Crimes need to be solved, whatever else is going on."

The room was silent as the officers thought about his words. When Dan asked if there were any question or other theories, a few shook their heads but no-one spoke.

"OK, now we're getting more up to strength in terms of staff, I've re-scheduled some jobs." Dan pointed to a stack of papers stack on the desk next to his file. "Actions. I've put finger to PC, ignore the typing mistakes, so you all know what you should be doing and where everyone else is at any time. Grab a copy before you leave. Meena, can I see you before you go."

Dan waited until the others had left the room.

"You say you still have nothing on the missing boy's mother, Jordan Turner?"

"No, boss. As I said earlier, I'll chase it up again."

"Have you considered she might have got married? You say she was a single mum. Maybe we shouldn't be looking for a..."

"Tessa Turner."

"Maybe she's a Tessa Smith, Jones, Blake, whatever. Check with the Public Records."

"Will do, boss. Anything else?"

Dan was silent for a moment. He turned and looked deeply into her eyes.

"I want you and Luke to go and see Lucy Hamilton.

You're right, three things is too much of a coincidence. I want you to dig, and dig, make her think. There's a connection. Family, friends, something in her past."

"You don't want to do this, boss? "

"No, I want fresh eyes on this. There's a link, but I'm damned if I can see it. I need to stand back if I'm to see things clearly. Get back to me if you dig up anything interesting."

He walked from the room. Meena sensed his depression, his broad shoulders were dipped and the usual cheerful demeanour had evaporated. The lack of progress was obviously getting to him, and she didn't doubt the men from above were coming down on him like a collapsing house of bricks in an earthquake, and he was shielding the team from the tremors.

Chapter 34

"Well your ideas don't seem to have worked." Stan was putting a cup of tea down on the coffee table in front of Maria. "All this time and we haven't heard a dickey bird."

"You've got to give it time, Stan." Maria's situation had improved considerably but she knew things could revert back in a short space of time. She was working on building a good relationship with the couple besides feeding them bizarre ideas how to track down Joseph Bates. "OK, we've only tried one thing, putting an advert in local newspapers, hinting it'd be to his benefit to contact the box number you've set up."

"It's been a week and we've made no progress. I think you're clutching at straws," whined Muriel.

You're such a negative old cow. When I get out of here are you going to suffer! I know someone in the cell who'll eat you up for breakfast – literally.

Maria smiled at Muriel, the deception wasn't easy but was necessary if she was to survive.

"Muriel, dear, he could be on holiday, working away, anything. Anyway, I have a few more ideas. I know he didn't come from the Reading area originally. I'm sure though he lived somewhere in Berkshire. If you'd let me make a few phone calls I know someone who'd be able to tell us where exactly he came from, even if they can't give a local address.

Then we check in that area's telephone directory or check the electoral register and we'll soon run him to earth.

"At the same time we can run an advert in that local newspaper and be much more specific about what he can gain. We can say a long forgotten Aunt from Australia has left him a million pound or something"

"I've never heard such a load of bloody rubbish in my life," said Stan. He stood up, shaking his head with exasperation. "I think Muriel's right, you're desperate and coming up with a load of rubbish. Drink your tea before I chop your bloody hand off."

Maria, leaning forward with her free hand trembling at his threat, finished her tea. Her other hand and both feet were handcuffed to the arm and legs of the chair. They had blindfolded her, tied her hands behind her, and taken her from the cold metal bed to the chair. Why they had blindfolded her she had no idea, but supposed it was so she wouldn't know the layout of the house. They'd also tied her ankles with a short amount of rope so she could shuffle but not run away. She felt like a shackled prisoner on death row in a film she'd once seen about an American Deep South Penitentiary. This had been going on for four days whilst Maria frantically dredged up her suggestions.

In truth, Maria hadn't known Joseph Bates that well. Members weren't encouraged to be friendly outside the cell and particularly whilst Operation Hobbledehoy Day was imminent. Brother Samson, the cell leader, had explained it was for security and that familiarity bred mistakes. Personally she'd thought he talked a load of bollocks, but nodded and appeared to agree to ensure her inclusion in the plan for the forthcoming orgy of childish delights.

Consequently, although she could pick Bates out in a crowd quite successfully, despite the stupid masks, except by chance knowing he was a racing fanatic, and that he came from the Didcot area, she didn't know anything else about him. She only knew these things because she'd once overheard him say he travelled from there to Newbury racecourse or to a local greyhound stadium.

She particularly remembered that incident because Brother Samson had walked into the room and Bates had quickly shut up, knowing he shouldn't be socialising. To save her life however, she was making out she knew him intimately and fabricating fictitious facts to convince stupid Stan and Muriel.

"OK, I know what definitely will rope him in. Horseracing. Dog racing. He loves them and reads the Racing Post constantly. We place an advert in there to his advantage etc and he'll race to the starting blocks, believe me."

"Umm, OK, but this is your last chance. If we don't know his location in another couple of days, your time is up," said Stan, thumping the teacup down on the table, slurping some of the contents into the saucer.

"An advertisement. Can't imagine that'll be cheap," said Muriel. "Things like that are well outside our budget."

"It won't be cheap," agreed Maria. "It depends how desperate you are. You tell me you want to find Jo, then it'll cost."

"You reckon you know him so well, think of another way," said Stan.

Maria could see by their faces they weren't enamoured by her suggestion, but she had nothing else up her sleeve. Still winging it, she knew it was only by the slimmest chance she wasn't still on the steel bed suffering agonies. Once again the emergency chemicals rushed round her body, feeding her brain, giving her ideas. She had never counted herself as one of life's creative personalities, but these last few days her imagination had worked overtime.

"I feel so sure this idea will work, I'll pay for the advert." Maria watched their faces and knew she'd scored another point and was back in their good books. She pushed the thought home. "I know you're desperate to find him and I'm certain Jo will be able to help you. I don't care how much the advert costs; I'll pay if it'll help." She sipped her drink and could almost hear their brain cells clicking together, testing the validity of her suggestion. Strike while the iron's hot. "Get me a pen and paper and I'll outline the advert that'll haul him in."

Luckily Maria's dad had liked the horses and most of his life had read a racing paper. He could only afford a small bet once a week and an extra flutter on the Grand National or something special; now Maria thanked her lucky stars that this might be enough knowledge to save her life.

Placing the pen and paper in front of her, Stan stood back, waiting for Maria to write something, unaware that she was straining her brain to remember the sorts of things she recalled being in the journal besides the details of the race meetings.

"Here we go, this'll work." Maria put the end of the pen in her mouth, pretending to be thinking about the words she was going to write whereas in reality, she had no idea where to start. "I tell you what, I'll write down what I think and if you buy the Racing Post tomorrow, we'll check what I've written is acceptable."

"And won't be suspicious to anyone," said Muriel thoughtfully

"Naturally," agreed Maria, smiling kindly, her thoughts in total contrast to her words or expression. She leaned over the paper and started to write. Once she started, the words flowed and when she'd finished, she was proud of her efforts. She read out the result. 'Another winner for... the Joseph Bates Stables... Contact... we'll insert a telephone number here... Prize Money available £1,000,000... UND2KL.'"

"Sounds reasonable. What does that last bit mean?" said Stan.

"It's a code. Jo will understand it." Maria, even though fighting for her life, was reluctant to tell them the meaning. The cell had improvised certain code words to use in emergencies. These messages went to a mobile phone kept at a secret location known only to Brother Samson. He checked this phone frequently in case he needed information regarding potentially dangerous situations. The number was committed to memory. The leader threatened the cell members to tell no-one the codes or their meanings, on pain of death.

Maria realised this situation was threatening her on her pain of death, so sod the instructions from Brother Samson.

"That particular expression means 'urgent you contact that telephone number'. If he sees it, he'll ring and then we can reel him in." She constantly used the royal 'we', subtly brainwashing them to include her in their conspiracy.

"OK, we give it another week. We've waited this long, I suppose another seven days won't matter. Mind you, it's costing us a fortune feeding you," said Muriel, her face screwed up with annoyance.

I've never bloody hated anyone so much in all my life. Jeez, when I get out of this place, I'm going to take great delight in wringing your scrawny neck.

"Muriel, dear, I'm so sorry. I never thought of that. How selfish of me. If I can have my handbag, I'll write you a cheque to cover the costs. Just glad to help." Maria smiled, pleased how her surface showed one set of feelings and completely obscured the rage and dislike that festered like a poisonous wound inside her. *One day soon...*

The beaming face veiled the hate but also the fear of what this murderous couple would do if Bates didn't respond. Maria wished she believed in prayer.

Chapter 35

Lucy closed the door behind the two police officers. She leaned her head against the cool panel of the door, and took a deep breath.

Will this nightmare never end?

Recalling the last hour, she felt sick, and the despair washed over her in a wave of desolation.

DC Mesbah, with a colleague she introduced as DC Luke Steiner, had just left. She had explained on their arrival that they needed to check her statements. The words of the interview, mainly led by DC Steiner, swirled like a whirlwind around in her head.

"To recap," he had begun, "you were out jogging with your dog on Oct 5th when you took a short cut through a wooded area at the side of Elmpark, where you lost sight of your dog. When you eventually found him, he was digging under a hedgerow where he discovered a severed hand, and other body parts. Is that correct?" When she nodded her agreement, Luke continued. "Then on Oct 28th, a pupil of yours at your school, a Genghis Simpson had some concerning news. This was brought to your attention by another of your pupils, Jade Thomson, that Genghis had confided in her he had been approached by a man over the internet calling himself Lawman, and proposing they meet."

Lucy recalled interrupting him, and although anxious,

she could feel her temper rising, annoyance crawling up her backbone like biting red ants.

"Right. You don't have to go on. I presume you are also going to bring up the fact that a second bag of body parts was dumped outside my door. That a note from 'Stan and Muriel', addressed to me was attached to the bag. That a couple watch me but haven't actually done anything other than watch, and therefore we can't assume they're the elusive Stan and Muriel. Now with this latest incident, what I believe you're trying to say is that I'm top of some list making me a suspect or an unfortunate bystander, reluctantly dragged into this nightmare." *And you've no idea how this nightmare could escalate if...*

Luke did not answer her statement. Giving her time to cool down, he attempted a sympathetic half smile, as though understanding her frustration. Looking directly at Lucy, and being a man first and a police officer second, fleetingly decided that she had the sexiest eyes he'd seen in a long time. The long, dark eyelashes surrounding her brunette eyes were nearly on a par with Meena's, the station's sex queen as the male police officers surreptitiously dubbed her, none of them brave enough to say this to her face. Lucy's complexion, pale compared to Meena's, was the only thing that stopped her looking Middle Eastern.

Meena coughed and as Luke glanced at her, she glared, using her 'concentrate and stop ogling' look which many of the male police officers had experienced at times. He was not to know that Lucy, having been stared at by Dan Blake in a similar way and made to feel guilty, now interpreted the look as suggesting he also found her culpable on all counts.

"It's just coincidence, you know. Higgins found the body parts. I don't know this couple, Stan and Muriel. How could I know anything about who Genghis communicates with?"

"Lucy, I understand how you feel but we have a series of murders we believe are connected. In both cases you were involved..."

"But..."

"I didn't say implicated... why we are here today is to get you to think. I want you to go over in your mind where you think you could fit in with all this. Coincidences are for fiction; somehow, somewhere, you have a place in this puzzle. Let's start with the exercise you take. You go running quite regularly and you say that you have noticed a couple watching you. You gave a good description to DS Blake, but told looking isn't a crime."

"It might not be, but if I'm part of this puzzle, then why don't you at least track this couple down, get their names and address and see just how they do fit in. Whether they are the Stan and Muriel or just innocent bystanders like me."

"We may well do that."

The police officers continued to question her for another hour, but despite penetrating questions, they got no additional information and the interview finished with Luke and Meena tired with frustration.

Lucy, glad to close the front door after them, felt depressed and beginning to think she had periods of blackouts she couldn't recall, during which she went round killing people and chopping them up for firewood! She felt tearful, afraid and confused she should be in this situation and badly needed a drink to steady her nerves.

Pouring herself a white wine, rather early in the evening but she needed the succour it might bring, she walked with the glass to the window and absentmindedly looked at the view. She sipped, not seeing the heavy clouds, pregnant with rain but not giving birth at the moment.

Considering her options, her mind whirled with the unpleasant possibilities that some nosy journalist might start digging. If her face got into the news once more, she was sure the coincidences would start to add up to a very exciting story, and if she wasn't co-operative to the press, they would dig and dig until something juicy turned up. She'd been assured she was safe, but... putting down her wine on the telephone table, she dialled his number. Even after all these years, she didn't have to check it. It was ingrained into her very soul.

"Hello." His voice hadn't changed; deep, neutral, in control.

"I think I'm in trouble."

"You're not panicking?"

"No... yes... maybe."

"Meet at the usual place. 1830. Day after tomorrow, Sunday, OK?"

"Yes."

The phone went dead.

Chapter36

"Get anything from the Lucy Hamilton interview?" asked Dan.

"Boss, she's either the best actress in the UK or she's totally innocent, wrong place, wrong time as you said," said Luke, running his fingers through his hair with frustration. "Get some coffee, Meena, be a sweetie."

"Get it yourself," snapped his colleague. "I may be a female, I may be Asian but in this station I'm a police officer. Equal Opps and all that if you recall."

Luke got to his feet, grumbling. "Stroppy women, don't know their place."

"Whoa, you've been watching too many 'Life on Mars' episodes on the tele. Thirty years ago policewomen were the underdog. You might not have noticed, but nowadays things have changed. By the way, I've changed the broken kettle again; we don't have to settle for the crap from the machine."

"I remember when you first joined the force, young lady. Swear words never passed your lovely lips." said Dan, enjoying the banter between Meena and Luke.

"Yes, well, I've caught a lot of bad habits. As Luke's a man and therefore can't do two things at once, boss, shall I update you with the interview?" At Dan's smirk followed by a nod, she continued. "As Luke said, she's either a cool customer, a good liar or both or she really is totally innocent.

We asked all the questions you suggested but she has no idea how she got involved with this. This latest incident makes three connections. The two body parts and the Genghis incident. What the hell is the connection?"

Luke, who had been listening but not commenting as he made the drinks, walked over and placed the two coffees on Dan's desk. He walked back for his cup and as he sat down next to Meena, facing Dan, said,

"Hey, maybe a combination of both. Perhaps she's involved for some reason, say, in the dumping of the body bits, although as yet she doesn't know why. Regarding Genghis and the Lawman contact, she heard about it just because she's his teacher. I know Cole hates those words, fate, chance, coincidence but sometimes twists of fate do happen."

Dan, elbows on his desk and sipping his coffee, looked perplexed.

"Could be. Christ, we've got bodies all over the place, kids being abducted, chatted up and no leads and yet Lucy seems to be the central point."

"We've got the 'Stan and Muriel' lead." said Meena, attempting to be positive. "We've now ID'd the first two bodies. We know Michelle was abducted by 'Uncle John' and 'Uncle Roger' and that one of the second pair of bodies was a John Thomas... "

"True. Just to update, I've received more information on that." interrupted Dan, "Michelle has positively ID'd Uncle John as being John Thomas. She's also confirmed 'Uncle Roger' from a sketch. She even recalled that Uncle Roger had a big nose, whereas the police artist didn't have that detail to work on."

"Any nonces we know called Roger?" said Luke.

"We're running it through the system as we speak." Dan turned back to Luke. "Perhaps you're right, Lucy Hamilton is involved in a part... and the other is... chance." He leaned back in his chair, steepling his fingers and staring into space.

"What we need is the Theory of Everything, then maybe it'd fall into place."

"The Theory of what?" said Luke.

"Everything," said Meena. "Einstein produced the General Theory of Relativity but thought the Theory of Everything was a film."

"Yes, it was but... "

"OK, said Luke impatiently, "what exactly is this General Theory of Relativity?"

Dan grinned. "It's actually the Theory of General Relativity. Einstein realised that massive objects caused a distortion in space-time. So his theory predicted that the space-time around Earth would be warped and twisted by the planets..." Seeing the lost look on Luke's face, he laughed, and continued. "OK that's not relevant to my theory, which..."

"Boss, I think you're getting on your soap box again and it's not relevant here," admonished Meena. She turned to Luke. "The boss studied physics at University. I don't know why he became a copper when he could have been earning a fortune as a scientific bod."

Luke, hooked now, wanted to know more. "So tell me about your theory. You've got a theory that will do what?"

"OK, Einstein's theory explains the connection between space and time. Physical laws are the same everywhere in the universe... well, except in the centre off a black hole where math proves the laws break down , but... " He held up his hands to ward off Meena's frustrated expression. "All I'm postulating with *my* theory, if the police have a Theory of Everything with the final answer equalling so many factors, ie evidence, facts, motives, verification, knowledge, relative variables into those factors, we'll be able to forecast the correct outcome."

"It might mean we don't have a job," Cole's voice suddenly said he tossed a large file onto Dan's desk. "I don't think any scientific theory will make up for good police work, so if you three have finished, why don't you do some."

Luke and Meena jumped to their feet. Dan remained at his desk.

"They were updating me, Guv, with the Lucy Hamilton interview and I was telling them that Michelle had ID'd John Thomas and his mate Roger."

"Hum, you and your bloody particle physics," retorted Cole, not side-lined by Dan's explanation. "Just look at that file and get back to me." DI Cole strode from the room leaving Luke and Meena staring admiringly at Dan.

"You're brave, boss," said Meena. "He scares me to death."

Dan grinned and shrugged. He now knew when Cole was serious or not. "Anything else to report?"

"Yes, boss," said Luke. "I think we need to investigate this couple who are allegedly watching Lucy. They don't appear to have done anything but watch. OK, that's not an offence so difficult to take any action, but if we could get Lucy to identify them and then have an unofficial word. See exactly what they are about. Just seems this couple may also be at the centre of something but we're not investigating that area. I know we're still up to our eyes in this case, but now Michelle's back, perhaps we could spare Mel or Meena to go running with Lucy. Or if not actually go running, be prepared to respond quickly should Lucy see them and then we have an unofficial chat."

"You're right, Luke. I think we do need to check them out. It won't do any harm for us to talk to them. Find out exactly their role is. See if they're linked to the infamous 'Stan and Muriel'. You up for that, Meena? Fancy a spot of running. You seemed to hit it off with Lucy when you both went to Genghis Simpson's house"

"Sounds good. I'll liaise with Lucy. Mel's definitely not into running but she'll be a good back up should I not be available."

"OK, I'll let you sort that out."

As Meena and Luke left, Dan opened the file on his desk but wasn't seeing the words. His mind was working on the Police Theory of Everything, fantasizing that if he discovered this elusive concept, he could well become the Police Commissioner. Then he could work on the Scientific Theory of Everything and win the Nobel Prize. He rubbed his hands together.

Now that'll impress the mysterious Lucy Hamilton. He sat back in his chair, surprised at this thought. *Be careful, Blake, maybe she's not as innocent as she maintains.*

Suddenly he craved a cigarette and a coffee, he hated not being in control. He didn't know that Lucy was suffering from the same problem.

Chapter 37

Lucy drove her car into the car park in Henley-on-Thames, and parked on the fifth floor. Glancing in all directions as she got out of the car, and despite knowing she was being paranoid about being watched, she couldn't control her obsession. She took the lift to the bottom floor and hurried to the mall café in the high street, still unable to stop glancing behind to make sure no-one was following.

Spotting him in the corner as soon as she entered the coffee aromatic café, she sauntered slowly around the tightly packed tables and chairs. He'd been staring at his cup and stirring his coffee as she moved towards him, but Lucy knew he was aware of her presence the moment she'd entered. He never missed anything. Neither greeted the other as she sat down. They just stared at each other.

The past years hadn't been kind to him. His fair ginger hair was now very thin; she could see his pink scalp, and the lines beneath and around his eyes were deeper than ever. He looked an old man, much older than his fifty three years.

He nodded at the waitress for her attention. Lucy ordered her drink before he said, "You haven't changed."

She didn't have the heart to be truthful, and replied, "Neither have you."

He laughed and she remembered the deep throaty sound that had put her at her ease so many times.

"Oh, I think I have." His eyes wandered over her face and hair. "I loved your natural colour. Deep chestnut hair. Dark hair suits you but it's a bit of a contrast compared to your pale skin." He peered in closer. "You're wearing coloured contact lenses as well." She nodded. He leaned back in his chair. "Different hair colour, different colour eyes, and you've lost... what... a few stones in weight?"

She nodded.

"Suits you." He bent and sipped his coffee. "Well, I know you but I'd have been hard pushed to recognise you. Why the panic now, after so long?"

The waitress put her coffee cup on the table, and Lucy took a long, slow sip before she drew a deep breath and told him all that had happened over the last few weeks. She left nothing out. He didn't interrupt her once for clarification, just intermittently sipped his drink, his eyes riveted on her face, occasionally nodding. When she ended her tale, she finished her almost cold coffee in one gulp, and felt as though a huge burden had flown off into interstellar space, leaving her earthbound and relieved.

For the next hour, interspaced with lunch consisting of cheese and pickle sandwiches and another coffee each, he asked her endless penetrating questions. Lucy marvelled at how he always seems to grasp any concept so clearly and was then able to make basic and sensible deductions.

Pushing his plate and cup to the side of the table, he gave her his conclusions.

"I'll ask the right persons some pertinent questions just to be sure. However, from what you have told me, and assuming what you have gone through is not a plot of some sort, and I just can't think it is, it's just bad luck. There are too many variables, I think you should not panic and run.

"That will stir up the proverbial hornet's nest, questions will be asked as to why an innocent person would run. One thing can lead to another." He took her hand, inspected it for a few seconds as he had when she was eleven and they

209

had first met. Looking up, he smiled and said. "Stay with it. You've done really well. It sounds like you have a good job, a good friend in Freddy, Higgins, and an OK life in general. I do agree it sounds weird that the second lot of bones were left outside your apartment. That wasn't coincidence. I can find out what the police's thinking is on that. Must have a quiet word in the right person's ear just to check that. Now, in case there is some weirdo trying to get your attention, as that DS... "

"Blake."

"Yes, as DS Blake advised, be careful and don't put yourself in a position of possible danger. You're sensible enough to know how to behave. You say he's often at the gym, yet you're sure he's not interested in getting fit." He chucked and picking up his cup, he drained the last of his drink. " Maybe he fancies *you,* yet while you're a witness, he's not going to get too involved. " He looked at her keenly, before continuing. "What do I advise? It's simple. Enjoy your life. In the meantime, I'll do some digging. I'll phone you if there's anything to worry about. If you don't hear from me, there's nothing to worry about. Go home, Lucy, enjoy your life."

She stood up and together they left the café. He went to walk away, but hesitated.

"What's wrong?" Her heart plummeted. Some sixth sense warned her of bad news.

"Well... I wouldn't have told you if we hadn't met. As we have, I think it unfair not to mention it. She's up for parole."

Lucy felt the colour empty from her face like sand dropping through an egg timer. She couldn't speak; the horror filled her being, riding through her like a plague of red, spiteful, biting ants plunging along her veins.

He took her arm and drew her to the side of the café window. "Damn, I shouldn't have told you. I can categorically swear to you she will never, ever be released. I only said it because almost certainly the news media will get hold of the story. I was wondering how to warn you. When you phoned... it seemed easier to tell you to your face."

"Why didn't you tell me earlier?"

"I needed to hear your story without that side issue. As I've said, she will remain locked up forever. Just be prepared in case it gets into the papers. Promise me not to worry about it." He stared at her until she promised, albeit with a quavering voice.

He leaned forward and kissed her cheek, the first time he had ever done that. "You've been through worse than this and survived. Remember how the family hounded you through the trial and afterwards until we got you away. You were unbelievably strong for such a young 'un. Even the judge remarked on your steadfastness despite the verbal attacks from the family during the trial. You were strong. Be strong now. This is nothing compared... have faith, you'll get through it." He turned and walked away, not looking back. She knew he had to act like that. He had made her cope with unbelievable events.

I'm not going to let him down. I will hack this.

She wasn't to know how her resolve would be tested by one stupid act.

Chapter 38

"Jo, someone's taking your name in vain."

Joseph Bates stopped licking the end of the pencil he'd been using to ring his choice of the horses running in the two fifteen race at Newton Abbott. There was only National Hunt racing this time of year and although his first love was flat racing, he still studied form and placed bets.

"What?"

"Here in the Racing Post. An advert about the Joseph Bates Stables. Never even 'eard of them, have you?"

Joseph took his elbows off the shelf in the betting shop, closed his paper, walked across the betting shop to Teddy Collins and took the paper from his hands.

"Where?"

"There. Top left." Teddy pointed with a grubby forefinger and Joseph winced at his black rimmed nails. Being very pernickety about his hands and nails which were antiseptically clean, Jo was always aware of others' poor hygiene habits. He shuddered and made a point of moving away from Teddy whose odour suggested his body was no cleaner than his hands.

Joseph washed his hands at least every half an hour, more if he touched anyone and if possible, showered three times a day. His parents told him he had some sort of disorder and was regularly shut in the under stairs cupboard as punishment. After that, his father reckoned he was ripe pickings and took young Joseph to the 'dark room' and then sexually abused him. The dark room's claim to fame was that the curtains were always closed to stop anyone seeing what went on.

This behaviour stopped when Joseph realised he was bigger than his dad. He'd run away at fourteen and lived on the streets for two years. Eventually he caught sight of himself in a shop window, noticing how he'd grown and his shoulders had almost doubled in width despite his poor diet. He went back home, beat up his dad, slapped his mum until she begged for mercy and threatened them both if they reported it he would go to the police with his version of events. He was in no position to take his younger brother Matthew with him for his own safety, but he warned them if Matt so much as stepped one foot in the 'dark room', he'd kill them both.

He phoned home every month to check on Matt's safety until he discovered his brother had died of a heroin overdose on his seventeenth birthday. After that his parent's lives were of no interest to him.

Joseph knew he was cursed. Although he hated his father, he had enough of his genes to like sex with kids himself. At first he sought treatment but the urge grew faster than the cure and he disappeared into the ether, hanging round schools and sometimes exposing himself in parks until he had met Brother and become initiated into the Reading cell and the safe delights it offered.

After the shambles of Operation Heigh-ho, and the lucky escape by a ludicrous old bugger who ruled he'd 'been entrapped' or some such stupid term, Jo disappeared from the Reading area and returned to his roots in Didcot.

Joseph read the advert again. Two interesting points were the million pounds allegedly on offer and the code at the end indicating it was imperative he call a certain known telephone number.

"Coincidence or what, Jo?" the grubby Teddy asked.

"Dunno. Probably. Can I borrow this?" At Teddy's nod, Joseph took the page and returned to his stool by the betting shelf. Analysing the advert and looking for catches, his brow wrinkled as he decided exactly what it really meant and what his options were? He knew the advert aimed specifically at him. Clearly listing his name and the code term he was ninety nine percent sure no other existing Joseph Bates would understand. The fact that the notice was in the racing paper meant someone knew his liking for the horses and betting in general. It must be a member from the Reading cell although he didn't think Brother Sampson was aware of his hobby.

"Probably can't do no 'arm to ring that number," said Teddy, sidling up to his mate, pound notes whirling in front of his eyes. If Jo got rich, he knew he could bum a few quid from him since they'd been mates a long time. The fact they only actually met in the bookies because they were both fanatics conveniently escaped Teddy's thinking.

Joseph appeared to ignore him but Teddy's fawning words were similar to his own thoughts.

It can't do no 'arm, as Ted puts it so poetically. If it's a mistake and there really is a winning stable with my name, I just put down the phone. Don't have to use my mobile. I can ring from a phone box. Might be for some strange reason I can't fathom, I'm about to make a load of dosh.

He hurried from the betting shop, ignoring Teddy's plea to know where he was going. The first phone box he came across was broken, and anyway, a casual glance over his shoulder told him Teddy was following. Quickening his pace and dodging in and out of shops, Joseph eventually shook Teddy off his trail in the large shopping centre just outside the town centre.

There were plenty of phone booths there. His hand trembled as he dialled the number. When a woman's voice answered with just a guarded 'yes', he didn't give his name. He hadn't completely forgotten his training. If it was someone from the cell, they would recognise his reply.

"Answering as requested. Secure or otherwise?"

There was silence for a moment and then a quavery voice said, "Hang on. I think I know who you want."

There was more silence at the end of the phone and he was about to replace the receiver when an excited voice said, "Jo, is that you? Secure is the word."

Still cautious but recalling the voice although not able to put a face to it, he said, "Who's that?"

"Jo, this is your lucky day. It's Maria Grainger." She lowered her voice. "You probably would remember me as Naomi. You're the Scarlet Pimpernel. Only know you're real name because of our unfortunate run-in with the law." Aware that Stan and Muriel's ears were madly flapping, she raised her voice as she continued. " I know where to get hold of more cash available than you ever dreamt about, but I need just a little help. I thought of you and your special skills."

He was still suspicious. *I remember her. Tall, good looking. Too gobby for my liking. Thought she was God's gift. Naomi, that's right...really Maria. Didn't know her that well. Why she think of me? Special skills?*

"What special skills. Why me?"

"I can't explain too well over the phone. You working?" At his 'no', she continued. "Just come to this address. It won't do any harm will it? Just a day out of your life or you'll pass up the opportunity of being a very rich man. No complications. Just a few hours work, no strings attached, and you'll walk away and won't ever have to work again. Believe it or not, it's not even illegal. Don't tell a soul though; people are unbelievably greedy if they thought they might get in on being rich."

"I dunno. Sounds weird to me. Where have I got to come? Just for an hour maybe."

Joseph couldn't see Maria punching the air with her success and Stan and Muriel's excited face. He naturally didn't know he'd sealed his fate.

Chapter 39

Meena, bent over with her hands on her thighs, was panting heavily.

"You OK?" said Lucy, concern painted over her face. Meena couldn't answer, her bright red complexion completely obliterating the normal dark golden colour of her skin. "We'll rest. There's a park bench just over there, let's sit down."

Lucy walked slowly over to the seat whilst Meena straightened up, groaned, and limped after her. She flopped down; leaning backwards and stretching out her limbs in the hope of the cold air circulating would more effectively cool her down. The police woman looked at the sky.

"The drizzle's thankfully stopped, but those clouds look dodgy."

"The forecast is for the rain to move away. If it rains again, I promise you we'll go home."

Sitting down next to her, Lucy admired the outlook. Despite the low slung cumulus clouds heavy with moisture, but jealously hanging on to their burden, the view stretching into the distance, sprinkled with oaks, large shrubs and small groves lining the park boundaries, would provide a scene an artist would yearn to paint.

Knowing they would get cold and stiff if they rested too long in the damp atmosphere, Lucy turned to her companion to check on her recovery.

"Bring any water with you?"

Meena shook her head at the question, still unable to speak although feeling a great deal better. The stitch in her side had gone, and the sensation she would explode like a dying sun had ceased.

Lucy handed her the water bottle she unclipped from her waistband. "Sip it slowly. You must keep your water intake up. I should have reminded you to bring some. We mustn't get too cold."

"I'm not fit," said the police woman, sounding depressed." I thought I was. At Police College I came top of my group in the keep-fit sessions. Too much drinking coffee and sitting at a desk since then. I must make an effort to get to the gym more often. "

"Don't beat yourself up, we've been running round this damn park quite some time. Isn't it typical, they always seem to be walking in the park yet because I want them to be here, they're not, and I haven't seen them in days."

"So, as far as you recall, they were always in the park when you were out jogging?"

"Not always. At least I don't think so. I mean, until I realised they were watching me, I took no notice. They might have been here, but like other people I often see, I took them for granted."

"You said the other people you saw, who do you mean?"

"If you use the same running facility, particularly if you regularly use a local park say, I'd often see the same people. I don't know them; we just nod. There's people walking their dogs, others jogging."

"The weather might well be keeping them in. I can't say I'd enjoy spending my week-ends running in the rain and it being so cold."

"Hardly rain; not even drizzle yet. I've run in worse, but you soon warm up once you get going. Then it's great to go back home for a hot shower."

"Higgins certainly didn't think the weather was good. I liked the way he steadfastly refused to leave his basket and come running."

"He's a fair weather runner. I'm always telling him that."

"Who looks after him while you're at work or doesn't he mind lazing at home all day?"

Lucy laughed. "He'd like to be lazy but I won't allow him to be. We go for a walk before and straight after work. I give up my lunch hour for him unless I'm doing playground duty. It only takes ten minutes to drive home and I take him to the green at the end of the road with my poop bag. If I'm doing playground duty, I pay the daughter of a friend who lives nearby. She loves walking him and its pocket money for her." Lucy laughed and shook her head. "He never goes moody with her, she tells me. Walks without a tantrum."

"Poor Higgins, fit whether he wants to be or not." Meena glanced round. "I'm OK now, what should we do now? If they're not going to show again, I think we ought to stop for the day. I'm due back at the station at two."

When Lucy didn't reply, Meena glanced at her but her attention was elsewhere. Lucy was looking down the path to the left.

"Would you believe it?" Lucy muttered. "Talk of the devil, here they come."

The women drew in breaths of excitement as the elderly couple rounded the corner, their terrier dog pulling the man along by the lead. Meena, without being too obvious, watched the couple as they approached.

They are elderly. About the right age to be Stan and Muriel. Maybe too old to be murderers.

"How are you going to approach this?" whispered Lucy. She was shivering and couldn't decide if it was excitement or fear.

"Leave it to me." Meena stood up, "I'm going to ask them to sit down. I assume they're too elderly to bolt so when they do, just walk a few metres away. Far enough so they can see you clearly, but not too near so they feel intimidated and won't talk."

"OK, although I can't imagine people who chop up bodies would be intimidated by me."

As the couple drew level with them, Lucy walked off and Meena stood up and greeted the couple, remarking on the dank day and wouldn't the sun be a welcome visitor?

"You're right there, young lady," said the man, raising his hat as he talked in an old-fashioned gesture of good manners that Meena found appealing. "Winter's creeping in fast. I noticed Christmas paraphernalia inching into the shops, and it's not even fire work night."

"Have you been jogging?" asked his companion. "Your face certainly has a rosy glow to it."

"Yes, I have. I'm exhausted."

"Good for young people to exercise," he said. "We come here most days. Take young Algie here for a walk. When I retired we decided to get a dog. Makes you go out walking.

"Good idea." Meena fished her warrant card from her track suit trouser pocket and showed it. "I'm DC Meena Mesbah. I wonder if you would be good enough to talk to me on a matter that I'm involved with. Just a few questions that might prove helpful to a police enquiry."

"Police matter," said the woman, eyes lighting up. "How exciting. How can we help?"

"I know it's cold and damp, but would you mind sitting on this bench with me to answer the questions. Hopefully it won't take too long and I don't want you to freeze in the process."

"Don't worry, we're both wrapped up warm," the man said. "Come October, on go the thermals so we're always as warm as toast. Good invention they were. Anyway, enough wittering on, how can we help?"

Feeling rather thrown by their friendly and helpful attitude, Meena didn't know where to begin. There was no evidence to suggest the couple were in any way involved in the murders other than the fact a couple had signed themselves Stan and Muriel on the note to Lucy, and the names themselves suggested they belonged to an elderly couple, but that was a loose connection. The other involvement was that Lucy had noticed the couple were constantly in the park and had been told they were watching her. These facts didn't fill Meena with confidence in an interview situation, albeit it was an informal one which the couple seemed delighted to participate in.

She pushed her misgivings aside, and got out her notebook from the opposite pocket in her tracksuit bottoms.

"I'll start with you, sir, if I may. Can I ask your name?"

"Ron Pierce and this is my lovely wife of fifty three years, Janet. Happily married for all that time although she still nags me about not putting the toilet seat down."

Janet giggled and dug Ron in the ribs, assuming a 'you are a cheeky boy, Ron' face. Their names, assuming the ones supplied were correct, dug a bigger muddy hole for Meena's self-assurance that these were the notorious Stan and Muriel, and her confidence slid surely and unfalteringly into the slippery aperture.

The policewoman swallowed, straightened her back, and doggedly continued.

"Thank you, Mr Pierce. I'm involved in a murder enquiry and I would like to ask you a few questions that might assist? I must tell you that you..."

Before she could explain that this was an informal conversation, the talkative Ron interrupted, "Murder! I can't believe what's going on in this town. Reading used to be a sleepy market town when I was a kid. You could walk down Broad Street with your mates on a Saturday night after a couple of beers, quite safe and sound. Now I wouldn't dare; you'd get your throat slit if you looked at anyone at what they thought was the wrong way. Murder. Crickey, I've read about four murders in as many months. It's frightening, that's what it is. I reckon it's all down to damn drugs."

"Yes, thank you, you may well be right. Save you and Janet getting too cold, I'll just continue with the questions. Can you recall where you were during the day of October 5th and the evening of October 20th?"

The couple glanced at each other, eyes widening, and Meena detected for the first time they looked concerned about this situation. Guilt or surprise, she had no way of knowing.

"What? Those two dates, weeks go," said Janet, her voice wavering." How would we possible know where we were? I've absolutely no idea."

"What's this about? We were trying to be helpful now you're making us feel guilty of something. Unless for some reason you think we were somewhere and might have seen something, is that it?" Ron put his arm protectively round his wife's shoulders.

"Sir, you are not under arrest and are free to leave here at any time. However, it might assist in our enquiries if you would answer my questions. Is there any way that you could find out where you were on those two dates and someone could substantiate them."

"Unless you tell us what this is about we're going home. You're frightening my Janet and this isn't a joke. We're an elderly couple and I don't enjoy being questioned like this by the police as though we're guilty. Tell us what this is about or I'm going home and talking to my MP."

"I'm sorry Mr Pierce. I didn't mean or want to upset you or your wife. As I explained, this is a murder enquiry and we have reason to believe you may be able to help with our enquiries. I'll start from another tack if I may. You see the young lady standing away to the left. Can I ask you if either of you know this person?"

The couple glanced round and looked at Lucy. Ron, still seeming somewhat belligerent by the questioning, snapped,

"Yes, we don't know her exactly, but we often see her in the park."

"Thank you. Can I ask if you know her name?"

At this question, Meena noticed Ron hesitate and glance at Janet. When he answered 'no' she could tell he was lying.

"This young lady is rather concerned that she feels you watch her as she runs. Perhaps you wouldn't mind explaining why you are watching her?"

The couple, now looking very puzzled, glanced at each other again. Janet, now braver, quoted, "Even a cat can look at a king."

"This person is concerned because she has become unfortunately involved in this murder enquiry and we, the police, are following various leads. One of these leads suggests that you may have a motive for watching her and your answer could help us with our enquiries."

"When was watching a crime? Anyway, we weren't watching Lucy, we were watching Pharaoh."

The last word surprised Meena, but she knew she had to continue even though she felt she was skating on the proverbial thin ice.

"I thought you didn't know her name."

Ron, looking sulky and annoyed at being caught out, explained. "Surely it's not a hanging offence. We just snitched a look. It's not the end of the world; we were looking after Pharaoh's interest that's all."

Meena, totally bemused by their answers, sensed she was barking up the wrong tree with the alacrity of a monkey, beckoned over Lucy and after introducing her, said to Ron. "I think we'd better go back to the beginning. If you'd be good enough to explain exactly what was going on... with Pharaoh."

"As I said, we were watching out for Pharaoh. Pharaoh the Third to be exact." He turned to Lucy. "Your dog. When he was running he was a four times champion. Belonged then to my nephew and when his, Pharoah's that is, running days were over, he bloody dumped him, the sod, just like he did to others he'd had. We made him tell us where he'd left him, but before we eventually traced him, the RSPCA had found him and he'd been put into the kennels. You got him a week or so before we arrived. The kennels wouldn't give us your name, but assured us they'd done all the checks to verify you'd be a good owner. Following the guidelines about correct diet and exercise."

"We know you've had an abandoned greyhound before and it had died a year or so before," interrupted Janet, taking over the story. "It was listed in their note book. Well, when the lady went off to check something, we peeked in the notebook and found your name and address. Naughty, I know, but we just had to make sure Pharaoh was really OK. We hoped with your flat being so near the park, you'd take him for walks here. First time we came and looked, there you were, running with him. He looked so happy. So we just bring Algie, that's this little one," Janet rattled their dog's lead who turned and put his head on her lap, "for his walkies, we come and see if Pharaoh's still enjoying himself. I notice he doesn't like the cold and wet any more than he used to."

Lucy, feeling the relief pour from her like rain from a sloping roof, said, "No, you're right there. He refused to come out today because it looked too much like rain. He peers out of the window to the balcony would you believe? I ask you, how does a dog know when rain's due, but he does? He's better than the forecasters on the TV."

"He was always a fair weather dog," said Janet. Lucy nodded and laughed at the expression she'd used so often herself. "Never performed well in the wet but otherwise he could run like the wind. We're just thrilled he's got an owner that obviously loves him and encourages him to do the exercise he's bred for."

Lucy apologised for her mistake and the couple appeared quite mollified. Meena explained that all leads had to be followed up and confirmed, and obviously if their story was verified, then she was also sorry for the error. The couple had no hard feelings and when Lucy invited them round for tea to re-acquaint themselves with the now Higgins, the four parted good friends.

As Meena and Lucy walked back to her flat, Meena having had more than enough running for one day, warned Lucy not to be alone when the couple called on her.

"Surely you don't still suspect them now?"

"No I don't but my experience has taught me that people can swear on their precious child's head they're totally innocent and then been proved guilty as hell."

"DC Mesbah, I do believe this job is turning you into a cynic."

"Miss Lucy Hamilton, you're absolutely right."

The two women laughed aloud, Lucy with relief she wasn't being stalked and Meena because the interview hadn't been a total disaster.

Chapter 40

On joining Dan at the bar, Adam asked, "What's your poison?"

Dan lifted the glass to his lips and finished off the last inch of beer. "My treat. You still drinking Guinness or are the English pubs still pouring them too quickly for the likes of you?"

"You're bloody right. Shove the black nectar into the glass like they're in a race. Hardly got a head on it. Sacrilege. What're you drinking?"

"Local one. It's good."

"Ok, I'll try it. Get me two."

Dan raised his eyebrows quizzically.

"I've got to catch up with you." Adam rubbed his hands together in anticipation.

Dan smiled but didn't comment. His Irish friend's capacity to drink and remain sober was almost legendary at the station. Celebrating victories, many officers had tried either to outdo or keep up with Adam, but none had yet succeeded.

Neither men spoke as they waited for the three pints and two packets of peanuts. The year before they had worked closely together on a case, and from the beginning of their association were at ease in each other's company and felt no need for small talk.

Picking up their drinks and snacks, Dan nodded towards an empty table in the far corner of the room and the two ambled over. They didn't look or act like policemen, as was their intention.

The silence continued until Adam had downed his first pint in one go. Dan leaned back in his chair, arms folded, watching the feat, a tiny grin flickering at the corners of his mouth. As Adam put the empty glass on the table, belched quietly and said,

"Now we're evens."

"Good. Tell me, what's going down?"

Adam, elbows on the table, rubbed his eyes and said,

"Holy Mary, I'm feckin' knackered. Right, what's going down? Well, I'll tell you, I'm in as deep as a turd in a sewer with the bastard." Dan didn't interrupt. He silently agreed his friend did indeed look tired, and appreciated Adam's undercover work was draining. Adam sipped his second pint slowly but didn't continue until half of the pint had slid down his throat. "That's better. Something's happened. I'm not sure what; he won't tell me details. I've been invited to a meeting."

"What sort of meeting?"

"Don't know. Tomas is excited about something. His body language is a giveaway. He's buzzing, feckin' hyped up; keyed up like an electric saw. As I told you before, he thinks I've got form. He obviously fell for the ploy and I reckon he's had it verified, and it checked out OK 'cos we get thicker and friendlier every day."

"Does he still think you're a civil servant?"

"Yes, and I reckon he's confirmed that as well. Still, as it'll appear kosher, he trusts me more and more. Now he thinks he knows my inclinations he's asked me if I'm up for something big? Course I say yes. He grins. Christ, I feckin' hate his grin. I could put me fist into his feckin' teeth. Anyway, I get to thinking, if it's something big and your theory about John Thomas and Uncle Roger is correct, then maybe they're two men short for this operation. Another person would be very useful if numbers were a requisite."

"So whatever it is, you reckon you're going to be clued up at this meeting?"

"Not sure. He used the word initiation."

"Jeez, I don't like the sound of that. Maybe its pull out time. Perhaps when you find out where and when this meeting is, we should go in and pull them in then and there."

"Dan, come off it. We're so close. If we lose our nerve now, all the work from the last few years since the last botched op is for nothing. We've got to keep our nerve."

"You could be in real danger. John Thomas and Roger have proved that. The way they were murdered was horrific. If they find out about you, they won't think twice about killing you."

Adam drained the last of his pint and walked to the bar for two more drinks. Once again the two men slaked their thirst before the conversation continued.

"They won't find out unless you tell them." Adam said, as though the conversation hadn't been interrupted. "We've covered every angle. I've supposedly been banged up for a load of nonce offences and the records are as authentic as it's humanly possible to make them. I'm a civil servant, going to work every day and sitting behind me feckin' desk with a load of chattering women. Believe me, that part's nearly as bad as keeping company with a feckin' nonce. I'm not giving up all those months of me life so you can lose your nerve now."

"I'm not losing my nerve. I'm concerned for you. This isn't just a case of a load of perverts flashing their dicks at kids; it's a serious case and I don't want an officer losing his life. We now know they will stop at nothing."

"Holy Mary, we both know under cover's dangerous. I've been in worse situations. Put a tail on me then if you've the manpower. Their security's as tight as a duck's arse. When I'm called to this meeting, you can bet your life I'm not going to know where or when. I'll be taken there at a moment's notice. If you can spare a tail, then you'll know where I am."

"Don't worry, we'll find the man power. As soon as I leave here, I shall be on to Cole to get it authorised. If he says we haven't got enough people, I'll do it myself."

"Want another?"

"No, three's my limit. We haven't all got hollow Irish legs. Can I get you one?"

"Why not! What about we finish off the evening with a double Jamesons. Come on, we don't get to date very often."

"Fuck you. OK, why not. My shout."

Adam stood up. "No way. Anyone man enough to drink a treble Jameson's, it's my treat."

"You said a double," Dan said to his retreating back.

"Any news on Uncle Roger in the files?" said Adam as he placed the large whiskies on the table.

"We got four hits with a Roger. Two were up north and the third's banged up. That leaves a Roger Caine who would you believe resides in Caversham. He's got form but is not at his listed address; hasn't been seen for a few weeks. His dear old mum, he lived with her, had already reported him missing apparently. When we went round there she thought we had news of his whereabouts."

"Which you had but not quite what she expected."

"Yes, Tom said she was a dear old soul."

"She identify the body?"

"No, a brother did."

"And it's our man?"

"Yes. Uncle Roger is Roger Caine. As I said, you be careful, we don't want you ending up with your nose, ears and bollocks cut off."

"Don't worry, me lad, I have no intentions of that happening."

The treble whiskey gave Dan a false sense of his immortality and he foolishly insisted on two more trebles.

When Adam poured him into his taxi, Dan prayed he wasn't going to honk carrot coloured puke all over the back of the driver.

Chapter 41

Jo Bates hesitated, and then decided he had nothing to lose. Glancing round, he could see no-one around in this 'back-and-beyond-nowhere-hick-place'. The country road was empty and with darkness falling, he felt uneasy despite more re-assurances from Maria when he'd phoned her again this morning for directions to the house. On answering his call, she'd sounded excited, urging him to come late afternoon to meet the backers of this financially rewarding project; once again recommending he tell no-one where he was going and assuring him before nightfall he would be a millionaire.

The dwelling was a typical, beginning of the century small cottage although he did notice there were cellar windows which he thought may not be usual for a property built to house farm labourers. There was a plaster circle with a date over the front door presumably depicting the date the cottages' erection but in the fading light, he couldn't read it. Noticing lights on in the house next door, he felt more secure knowing there were people he could contact quickly should he find himself in some sort of predicament.

He knocked on the door, for some reason expecting a hollow sound to echo through the house as happened in horror movies, but the noise was normal and didn't come across as sinister in the least. After a minute had passed and no-one had answered the firm, constant rapping with his knuckles, he noticed a bell on the door side and rang that, hearing the noise clearly reverberate through the house.

No quick response to that, then no-one's home or they're bloody deaf.

Within seconds a light came on in the hall and he heard footsteps and then a bolt drawn back. For some reason, his heart was beating fast but his jangling nerves settled instantly when an old lady wearing a welcoming smile peered round the door.

"Hello, dear, you must be Jo Bates that Maria is expecting?" At his nod and gruff 'yes', she opened the door fully and welcomed him in. "Come straight through to the dining room, dear. I've just this instant made a pot of tea. It's a bit of a journey here, I know, but you're very welcome and I'm sure you won't regret it. Sit here."

She indicated a seat at a small dining room table that was neatly laid up with a spotless white tablecloth and a tray containing a floral teapot and four matching cups. She poured his tea, indicating the sugar bowl and said she would go and get Maria. He became aware of loud talking from nearby as though someone hard of hearing was listening to the television programme.

Christ, that's all I need. Some old biddy as deaf as a post and gobby Maria. This had better be worth it or someone is going to be very sorry. Bloody train and bus fare cost a tidy sum.

As he sipped his tea he heard someone come into the room. Before he could even turn round a muscled arm was across his chest and something clamped onto his lower face. Being a strong man, he twisted away but the hold tightened and the pad pushed back over his nose. He wriggled like an eel, forcing himself not to breathe the strong smelling fumes but eventually, feeling he was going to burst if he didn't, he took a breath. The room swam and he heard wind whistling in his ears.

"Hello, Jo, time to wake up." He ignored the voice.

Bloody Christine bringing my morning cuppa. Stupid cow, it's still dark. She'll get a thump if she's woken me up that early.

His eyes flashed open. *Christine! I've been divorced for seven years*. It wasn't dark and he definitely wasn't in his bed and Christine hadn't suddenly come back into his life, thank God.

He was in a brightly lit room, and would have peered round checking his situation if he could move his head but something was stopping him. Trying to shift his arms and legs produced the same result. With the small amount of movement available to him, he wriggled his fingers, attempting to feel what he was lying on. It was cold and hard and certainly not as comfortable as his double bed at home with the sprung mattress for extra comfort.

The memory of why he was here washed into his brain, flooding his thoughts with confusion and apprehension.

"Maria," he screamed. "Bloody Maria, where are you? What the fuck's this all about?"

If it was possible to jerk he would have, as the face of the old lady who had previously opened the front door loomed into view and startled him.

"What the hell...?"

"Sorry about the treatment, dear. Hubby and I are a bit old and frail, you know, and unless you were subdued and tied down, we obviously wouldn't get any co-operation."

"What the hell's going on here? Where's that bloody Maria? I never should have trusted that lying cow. Wait until I get my hands on her. Where is she?"

"She's a bit tied up at the moment. Now, I'm Muriel and as soon as he comes in I'll introduce my hubby, Stan."

"Are you going to tell me what's going on? This is kidnapping. Tying me down like this and holding me against my wishes."

"Aah, here comes Stan." The woman pinched her fingers over her nostrils and Joseph realised why as the most evil smell he'd ever experienced attacked his nostrils. There were no words within his vocabulary he could recall to describe it. The nearest he could bring to mind was rancid meat and dog shit mixed together and those were perfume compared to this stench. He gagged.

Muriel face disappeared and Stan's appeared, eyes squinting as he peered at him.

"Good evening, Jo. I believe the trouble and strife has told you my name. Later on you may get to see Maria but at the moment I'd like to introduce two old mates of yours. I use the word 'old' purposely although when you see them you may use other terms. It's just that you need to see them in their present state, because it may very well make your decision a lot easier as to whether to co-operate or not. We've just two questions to ask you. How and if you answer them will depend on whether or not you die, and whether or not you die in an excruciating pain or relatively pain free."

"What the frigging hell are you talking about? Just let me go, I know nothing that warrants this bloody treatment. And what the fuck is that foul smell?"

"Patience, patience."

He couldn't see, but Joseph could hear the old woman's voice.

"OK, here we go. Now things are getting a bit difficult because these two mates of you are fast decaying. I've managed to get hold of these two glass cases, although I noticed Nigel's beginning to leak out of his. Right, here's Nigel."

Joseph didn't want to look, but the glass case, held just six inches from his eyes with the couple standing either side, supporting it. At first he looked away but then guessed he was just putting off the inevitable. What he saw churned up his lunchtime fish and chips in his stomach like a revolving concrete mixer, and lumps rose up into his throat. He mewed like a kitten.

"Damn, even with the decay Nigel's still heavy. Just a

quick look at Don. He seems to have withstood the ravages of the worms rather better." Stan smirked as he spoke. "Wearing quite well is old Don."

"Perhaps he took his vitamins, good boy," the woman cackled.

The second oozing mass in front of his eyes ensured that the half-digested dinner erupted out of his mouth like Vesuvius in full fury, splashing the bottom of the glass container, giving the green rotting skull splashes of carrot colour.

"Right, we won't waste any more time," said Stan, removing the two containers of horrors from sight. "As I said, we have two questions we urgently need to ask. If you give us what we want you may not end up like those two. They wouldn't tell us, so believe me how they suffered would have made the agonies of the tortures inflicted in the middle ages seem like tickling. I used to own and work in an abattoir so I have the experience and tools that can cut through flesh and bone like a knife through butter."

Joseph shook violently and the pain that shot down his left arm and through his chest made him wonder if he were about to have a heart attack, and his intuition told him even that possible excruciating pain may be the lesser of two evils.

Chapter 42

1989

They crept as quietly as possible down the stairs but no matter how lightly they trod, each stair creaked and groaned.

"Sounds like a ghost house from a film. Where's the basement door?" he whispered.

"Never seen one. Maybe inside his flat."

She attempted to open her pimp's apartment door but it held firm. Looking at Stuart, she smiled sweetly and raised her eyebrows. Shaking his head in exasperation, he got out the tool kit again and once more it only took him seconds to open the door. The child's whimpering was clearer now and the muffled voices continued.

"So far so good," Sharon whispered. "They haven't heard us."

Creeping along a passageway smelling of damp and stale tobacco smoke which led into a living room crammed full of tatty furniture, still no door was evident that might lead down to the cellar.

"My Gran had a cupboard in her old cottage that used to house the basement door," Stuart whispered, pointing to a cupboard door in the far corner. "I'll have a gander in there."

On opening the cupboard door, inside there was another

door that was slightly ajar.

"Voila."

"I wish you'd shut up saying that, you're getting on my nerves," giggled Sharon, her grin and voice belaying her words.

"It's just that I'm so impressed with my cleverness," said Stuart, breathing on his nails and rubbing them on his shirt. "Anyway, have you seen enough, can we now clear off?"

"Sod off, we've come this far, I'm going to get to the bottom of this. If they've got a kid, knowing that bastard Winston..." Sharon didn't finish but carefully opened the door and started to ease herself down the stairs

Stuart grimaced as she crept down, expecting the stairs to be as noisy as the previous ones, but luck was on their side, and except one squeak on the third step from the bottom, she made a soundless descent.

He watched as she got onto her knees and peered through the keyhole and groaned when she, without taking her eye away from the hole, frantically beckoned him down.

As he got to the bottom stair, she straightened up, mouthed, "Ready," and he watched in disbelief as she quietly turned the doorknob and as the door creaked opened, charged through the door into a brilliantly lit room, yelling like a banshee.

"Oh fuck," he groaned, "I've got to go in and save the stupid tart. I'm gonna get killed."

He followed her in, deciding if she could yell like an idiot and hope to scare and freeze a thug into docility, he might as well use the same stupid ploy.

The bright lights of the room blinded him momentarily but he recovered quickly and laughed hysterically as he watched the slight young girl bash her poker into Winston's groin and as he went down, a sharp blow to the head then laid him flat on the floor, his arms flailing like a string puppet as he fell. His fall knocked over a camera supported by a tripod that smashed noisily onto the floor, taking a light stand with it.

Frozen with astonishment at the events, a young man not much older than Stuart stared at him and then at the shovel in his hand. Stuart shrugged an apology, raising the weapon to demolish the opposition. He didn't have to strike, however, because the young man snapped into action and jumping over the broken camera, agilely ducked past Stuart and could be heard thundering up the stairs.

"Leave him," yelled Sharon as Stuart turned to give chase. "Get the boy. Let's split pronto." She pointed to a heap of clothing on the floor. "Grab the clothes."

A naked boy sat on a table brightly illuminated by two large lamps focused on him. His eyes, wide and amazed, somehow matched his ginger hair sticking out at all angles, making him look like a young, startled Einstein.

Stuart dragging the boy and with Sharon pushing from behind, the three of them pounded up the stairs

"What the fuck do we do now, you idiot?" he asked as they tumbled through the front door that had presumably left ajar by the fleeing youth. The three belted down the road into the side alley where they'd gone to climb to the flat.

"Take off your leather jacket." Sharon, puffed out from the sprint, wheezed at her companion.

"What?"

"He's freezing. He's naked."

As the girl helped the shivering, traumatised boy into the jacket and his jeans, she looked very pleased with herself.

"I know who he is."

"Who?"

"The kid I read about in the papers what got abducted from Cranwell Park, not ten minutes' drive from here. That's right isn't it," she asked the youngster. "Did those men take you from the park? Take you away from your mummy?"

"No, they took me away from Elsie, Nanny's friend."

"OK, kid, you're going home. Let's high-tail it back to the van."

Chapter 43

Dan felt he'd spent too much time again by the water dispenser. Although all the members in the gym were focusing with their usual intense-verging-on-the-insane concentrations on the torture machines spread around the room, he knew it would be obvious to anyone who should notice that he was skiving, and had no intentions of exercising and becoming fit. If they noticed his obsession with drinking water, they must think him very strange and wasting his joining fee.

He glanced at the clock and was sure it had stopped. It said eight fifteen but when he'd glanced at it what seemed like two hours ago, it had read ten past eight. It seemed the clock in the gym always ran slowly and he decided it's time keeping was out-of-sync with the rest of the world.

Adam had telephoned him earlier saying he'd been contacted by Tomas and told to be outside the gym at seven ready to go to the initiation ceremony. Dan had parked his car at six o' clock in a quiet corner of the gym car park. Luke was with him, eating a bag of chips. Noticing the lack of CCTV cameras, Tomas obviously deemed the pick-up point as safe. Dan intended to follow the vehicle when it came to pick up his colleague but after waiting for over an hour and a half, and neither Adam nor any transport appeared, Dan's frustration had grown to boiling point.

Sending Luke home, as he was due later on duty outside

Adam's house, he had decided to wait in the gym to see if either Adam or Tomas appeared. When neither had, his anxiety then spiralled. He could not contact Adam on his mobile as they'd agreed even a guarded conversation may rouse suspicion if he was with Tomas or any of his compatriots.

Walking back to the changing room, he wandered round the lockers to check no-one was present. He retrieved his mobile from his locker and selected DC Mel Stubbs contact number who was on surveillance duty outside Adam's house. Talking to her previously before his stakeout in the gym car park, she'd confirmed lights were on in the house and she had not seen him leave since he had arrived home from his 'Civil Service job'.

"What's happening your end now?" Dan asked her when she answered.

"Nothing. He's still here, or at least the lights are still on in the house. He's late for his date."

"Yeah, I know. He should've been here by seven. I want you to phone his home number, check his whereabouts. If he answers ask him what's going on? Check whether there's been a change of plan?"

"OK, what if the baby sitter answers?"

"It'll be his mum. She's over fairly permanently from Ireland looking after the twins as you probably know. Say you need to speak to him, the office's computers on the blink or something. Find out where he is? Get back to me as soon as."

"OK, boss."

Dan wandered impatiently round the changing room, then back into the gym to check whether Tomas had arrived at his office or Adam had put in an appearance. Keeping his mobile in his pocket, despite polite notices requesting not to bring mobiles into the workout area. If Mel phoned, he needed to react quickly.

Again he couldn't enthuse about any exercise and

although he was gazing at the frenzied activity of sweaty bodies, his mind was elsewhere. If somehow Adam was taken to the initiation ceremony, he certainly hadn't gone by the front door which in itself was worrying. There would be no way of knowing where he was and although undercover work was dangerous, and the officers involved accepted that as part and parcel of the job, it didn't stop Dan from being concerned.

His mobile buzzed. He walked back along the corridor to the changing room.

"Yes," he snapped.

"I've spoken to his mum, boss," said Mel, the worry in her voice matching Dan's concern. "Apparently he was just getting on his coat about 18.30 when someone knocked on the back door. He answered it, his mum heard a woman's voice but never saw who it was. Adam wanted to say goodbye to her and the kids who were ready for bed. She heard the woman insist he come straightaway, then and there. Apparently Adam looked round quickly and said goodbye as he was yanked out of the door by... I quote... " Mel assumed a Southern Irish accent. "By a very rude woman. Not letting a man say goodbye properly to his family."

Shit. Wonder... Maybe... Dan thoughts were in turmoil.

"Boss, you still there?"

"Yeah, sorry." He pulled himself together, knowing he needed to be clear headed. "OK. He's gone almost two hours. When's Luke's shift start?"

"Ten."

"Update him. He's on his way home now. I want him on duty promptly and inform me immediately Adam returns. Remember the arrangement, he puts milk bottles out should something like this occurs and we didn't clock his return. I'll be here or somewhere local. I want to speak to him as soon as."

"OK, boss."

Dan, thoroughly depressed, wandered back into the gym,

intending to go and join in the watch. *Something's bloody amiss.* As he pulled on his jumper and jeans, he could feel his heart beating like a pneumatic drill.

Chapter 44

Adam walked straight to the kitchen sink, filled his pint glass his mam had washed up and placed upside down previously on the draining board and knocked back the drink in one go. Splashing his face with the cold water until his skin tingled, he felt he had washed away the dirt of the evening.

The sick feeling still plagued his stomach, but he at least felt more refreshed. Retrieving a glass and a bottle of Jameson's whiskey from the sideboard in the dining room, he walked back into the kitchen, poured himself a treble and downed that in one as well.

Right, that's done the feckin' trick.

As the complex flavours of toasted wood, spice and sherry glided down his throat and the gentle heat spread through his chest, he poured himself another slug. Breathing in the heady aroma, he waited for the first drink to complete its task of relaxing him before he brought the second drink to his lips. As the glass touched his mouth, the sharp rapping on the door caused him to jump and some of the precious liquid splashed down his shirt.

Shite, whose that? Not those feckin' nonces again!

Cautiously opening the back door, his relief on seeing Dan was enormous.

"Holy Mary, I nearly had a heart attack." He hissed, aware of his sleeping children and a mother who had a devilish temper if roused from her slumbers.

"Sorry, mate." whispered Dan in return, glad of the warmth of the room as he walked in. "Just arrived home ready to join Luke when he phoned to say he saw you put the milk bottles out. He never clocked you coming in though."

"They dropped me round the corner. There's an hidden alleyway you can use to get to my house. They came for me that way."

"Alleyway! You never bloody mentioned that."

"It's a bit of a meander and over-grown. Hardly ever used. Never thought they'd know it. Must have checked it out previously. They don't miss a thing."

"So the part about them picking you up at the gym was just a blind?" Dan looked closely at Adam who merely shrugged and sipped his drink. "You OK?"

Adam chuckled. "Sure, you eejit, you're such a feckin' nurse-maid."

"It's my job. Tell me, what's so funny?"

Adam walked into the dining room and got another glass which he filled and handed to Dan before he spoke.

"No thanks. I'm driving."

"Drink it. I hate feckin' drinking on my own."

Dan dutifully sipped the drink while Adam told him about the evening.

"They knocked the back door before I could warn Mel. Had me out of here in a second and into their vehicle parked round the corner."

"What type of vehicle?"

"Black Range rover, at least it looked black at night, darkened windows."

"Registration number?"

"T7 GAT. Probably false plates."

"I'll check. Where'd you go? Manage to get the address?"

"I was blindfolded once I was in the car. We drove quite a way. Maybe half an hour although that might have been a blind, if you excuse the pun, to confuse me."

"Yes, you could have driven back to where you started."

"Not quite. We definitely hit a main road. I could hear lorries. Then we turned off left and were on a country road. Quiet, twisty. When we got out I was still blindfolded but I heard an owl and the wind in the trees."

He laughed again, putting his head back as he did and Dan smirked, the merriment becoming infectious, despite the seriousness of the situation.

"Anyway, I've been to a feckin' tea party."

"A what?"

"As soon as we got into the house... "

"Who picked you up, by the way?"

"Two of them. A man and a woman. They kept their heads down but I'd recognise them. My blindfold was changed for a mask when we got there. We're in a huge house. Beautifully furnished. Big hall, polished wooden floor and a Persian carpet that cost more than you earn in a month. I was met by Tomas who's also wearing a mask, stupid prick. As though I wouldn't recognise him. He beckons me into this room. Antique looking chairs covered in expensive looking material. In the middle was a coffee table with this tea set. What do you call that fine stuff, Katherine was always raving about it."

"Bone china."

"Yeah, feckin' bone china tea pot and matching cups. There was some people already there. All wearing stupid masks. There was a young fellow, early twenties, pony tail. Wolfbane they called him. " Adam chortled again."

"Get on with it. It's bloody late."

"Get that drink down your throat, matey. The night's young for fellows like us. Kip on the sofa," said Adam, topping his companion's empty glass up again. Dan could have sworn he hadn't drunk the contents but as there was no-one else in the room, he concluded he had.

"They're so up their own arses. They think they're infallible and that's what'll be their undoing. Bone china tea party! Code names! Masks! Feckin' ponces. The two that picked me up were introduced as Delilah and Excalibur."

Dan, writing the names in a notebook as Adam mentioned them, said, "That's all you did, drink tea."

"Yeah. Tomas introduced me to the others. The woman, Delilah, had long black hair, parted in the middle like the proverbial witch from a kid's fairy tale. Smoked like a chimney and you could see it in her teeth. Gums shrunk back, teeth yellow. Ugly cow."

"She speaks very highly of you."

Adam finished his drink and topped it up before he continued. "Don't look like that. This is medicinal."

"I'm not judging, mate, believe me. Go on."

"We drank the tea as they interrogated me. All of them, quick fire questions, not giving you time to make anything up. They asked all sorts. Where I was born? My form? How long I'd been banged up? Which prison? Who were my cellmates? What was my particular inclination, boys, girls, either, both? Feckin' wankers."

"You reckon you passed?"

"Sure. You made me go over it a thousand times. I'm word perfect."

"Bet you're glad I did. Otherwise you'd be dead meat by now."

"I know."

"Learn anything more about the operation they're planning?"

"No, but I've been invited to a meeting in the next week or so to be, quote, updated."

"When exactly? Same place?"

Adam shrugged. "They wouldn't say. Just said to carry on as normal but be prepared to be picked up at a moment's notice. I tell you, they're not infallible because, like I said, they're so up their own arses, but you have to give them ten out of ten for trying. Their security I mean."

"OK. I'll need you to come in and look through some

photos of nonces. See if you recognise anyone without their pretty masks on. Anything else?"

When the Irishman shook his head, Dan got out his mobile. "I'll tell Luke to go home and the team to stand down till tomorrow. What time you going to work?"

"We do feckin' flexi. Civil Servants have it easy. I get in as late as possible. Say ten o'clock. Anyway, invite Luke in for a drink. He deserves it, sitting out there in the cold."

Luke didn't need any persuasion, although being cautious, he also came in through the back door.

Dan fell onto the sofa at three o'clock, leaving Luke and Adam getting to the bottom of a second bottle of whiskey, and talking absolute slurring drivel.

Chapter 45

Maria was trembling. She could hear the thumping and chopping sounds coming from the cellar which housed the torture table. Hearing the carnage was as bad as actually seeing Jo's body being cut up into 'manageable sizes', using Stan's description.

Stupid sod. Bloody keeling over from a heart attack.

Jo had suffered his first seizure when he first tied down and threatened, but Muriel who apparently used to be a nurse, had tended him through the night, and the next day he'd seemed better.

How the hell I didn't snarl she was no damn Florence Nightingale who should care for people and not bloody torture them. Wicked cow.

However Maria, still hoping that if she worked with and not against them she might earn her freedom, had used her usual ploy and smiled and sympathised. She'd agreed that Jo was just damn awkward when the next day he suffered a massive heart attack and had died in front of Stan's eyes just as he was showing him the circular saw he intended to use if the questions weren't answered.

Stupid buggers. He'd obviously got a dodgy ticker, and the thick sod flashes that hateful instrument at him. If it hadn't put me back into a bloody awful situation, I'd have laughed.

Maria couldn't control the tremors twitching through her body, but was concentrating on how to get back in control of the situation.

Jo Bates was my last hope. Still, they don't know that, so maybe I can draw someone else into the net. Who would know the answers to their questions? I know, but if that doesn't work out, there'll be more torture and I'm a dead 'un for sure.

Maria had to face the truth. All along she was aware who probably could answer the questions Stan and Muriel were asking, but Brother Samson ruled the cell with a rod of iron and if anyone stepped out of line, it was curtains for them. Still, if it was fear of him versus the circular saw and the hook that extracted your eyeballs, there was no contest, and death by Stan was more imminent than Brother's retribution for grassing.

With Jo's demise I've had run out of other ideas so there's no alternative than to draw Brother Samson into the net and let him take his chance against Stan and frigging Muriel.

Maria still found it unbelievable that such a frail old couple could kidnap three well-built younger men, and she herself was no pushover. If they had an accomplice, then she hadn't seen or heard him. Maybe Stan's days as a butcher and Muriel's days as a nurse, humping fat slobs around, had made them unusually fit. She shrugged away the thoughts; if she was to save her skin, she needed to form a plan to entice Brother into a trap.

Delilah! His bloody pet, Delilah! That should entice him if anything can.

No-one in the cell knew for sure, but if they had an opportunity to gossip, most of the cell reckoned Brother was 'giving her one'. Rumour had it they went back years; when the cells were first formed.

The scandalmongers also tittle-tattled that years ago Delilah been involved with two men in the abduction of a young boy which had gone wrong. Two teenagers had somehow rescued the kidnapped boy. The Brotherhood, although in its infancy, still had rigid rules laid down which you ignored at your peril and that meant you didn't decide, on a fanciful whim, to go and abduct a child without their say so. It was too dangerous and foolhardy. The men were nastily murdered after they were imprisoned. The Brotherhood's fingers stretched everywhere, being banged up was no protection for anyone.

Delilah was forgiven because it was rumoured she was led astray by older and more experienced men. She had been Brother's close companion ever since. Allegedly in her youth she'd been a stunner, but Maria couldn't see any of her beauty left now, even with a mask hiding most of her face. Her mouth, normally smeared with a leer, plus her crooked, yellow teeth was bad enough, but her eyes peering through the masks slits emitted evil. Knowing she was far from an angel herself, even Maria sensed the radiating malevolence.

Snapping out of her daydreaming, she smiled as Muriel walked into the room with a tray of coffees which placed on the small table in front of the chair to which she was still firmly tied.

"My goodness, our Stan certainly is making a racket. Good job Alison next door is stone deaf and her Keith is working nights," Muriel said as though just commenting on the weather. "I think they'd be banging on our door otherwise."

"Doesn't seem to wake the baby either," agreed Maria, still desperate to remain in their good books but unable to stop irony colouring her words.

"I know. Such a dear little soul. He must be a good sleeper."

She's so thick, she didn't even notice the sarcasm luckily. Must be more controlled in future.

"I'm so sorry you didn't get your questions answered. I've been sat here wracking my brains, and I've come up with a brainwave."

"I don't know, dear. So far your ideas haven't come to much. I think dear old Stan is going to run out of patience."

"Yes, but if you ever want to accomplish your life's ambition, then you mustn't give in. Delilah!"

"Who?"

"She was rather close to Jo. I could never stand her. A really horrible woman but if anyone knows what you want, it'll be her."

"What's her surname? Will she be in the phone book?"

Maria didn't dare tell Muriel that Delilah was a code name and she didn't know her actual first name let alone her surname. All the desperate prisoner could do was play for time, just extending her life by the hour; she wasn't even playing for days now. She had an awful feeling her end was near, and prayed it would be quick.

"Can't quite recall her surname but if you give me a local book for the Reading area, I'm sure she lived in Tilehurst. I could go through it carefully. I'm sure I'd recognise the name if I saw it."

Muriel sipped her coffee, seeming unmoved by the loud sounds from the cellar, and gazed at Maria over the rim of the cup. She sucked at her coffee and made slurping noises which Maria found disgusting but continued to disguise her feelings with a sympathetic and friendly face. Muriel carefully placed the cup back into the saucer and stood up.

"OK. Last chance. I'll get the phone book. You've got another day to help us. I just think you're making up these names to play for time."

"Thanks, Muriel. I swear on my sister's children's heads, you won't regret this. I may take a little time but Delilah will be the answer to our prayers."

I swear my hate for you will give me strength to break these straps, then I'll put my hands round your skinny neck and squeeze till you're purple, you stupid bat.

As Muriel left the room, Maria called after her, "Thanks for the coffee. It's delicious."

Chapter 46

Seth and Michael Ayre were identical twins and it was obvious. Both had jet-black curly hair worn long onto their shoulders. Their eyes, dark as their hair, held the same twinkle enabling them to melt girls' hearts, and more mature women who should know better.

They didn't know their true father and their mother kept quiet on the subject as she was unsure who had sired them as she had been 'extremely friendly' in her youth. She strongly suspected it was a young Romany who frequented the local pub for a few months and took full advantage of her responsive nature. The gypsies had moved on by the autumn after Daisy had spent a fruitful summer in the hayfield beneath the dark and handsome lover. The resultant children, with their brunette hair and flashing eyes certainly bore a strong resemblance to the wanderer. As they grew older, Daisy became more certain of their father as they both exhibited highly lustful and usually successful leanings towards anything female.

Despite these highly sexual natures, and other characteristics that ensured there were no long lasting emotional ties with any girlfriends, Daisy herself couldn't have had two more devoted supporters.

She had eventually married when the boys were twelve years old, but the man turned out to be a drunk and a bully.

The first time he beat up their mother, and afterwards swore he was sorry and it would never happen again, they all forgave him. On the fifth occasion, even with youth still sitting on their shoulders, the twins knew they could tolerate a happy drunk who fell into bed and snored loudly all night, but a man, who drank, and then beat up his wife, and the kids if they didn't run fast enough, was the proverbial leopard whose spots would remain firmly in place until the next time.

After this last event, the man eventually fell asleep on the sofa after giving Daisy a severe beating. The twins, having locked themselves in the cellar as their mother warned them to do during such occasions, were therefore fit and well and out for revenge.

When 'father' awoke later he was tied, gagged and being dragged out of the house on the twins homemade go-cart. The downpour fortunately tipping out of the sky like giants emptying their rain buckets ensured no witnesses on such a depressing night. Despite his struggles and muted screams under the gag, it didn't prevent his toppling into the local slurry lake that had formed at the bottom of a long abandoned gravel pit.

After five years the council filled the pit and then built a housing estate on the reclaimed site. The twins, after a few months of sweating in case their stepfather's body should be discovered, breathed with relief and thought it hilarious and ironic that the council awarded the family a larger house on this site. The number of children in the family had now expanded to six, all with different fathers, and the previous two-bedroom council house couldn't cope. The twins hoped the new accommodation was directly above the bastard's body.

Daisy never worried, or had any idea about where the 'bullying bugger' was, so she slept very soundly in her innocence, unaware she was probably sixty feet above his body.

The twins, now twenty, and long-term unemployed, still

couldn't keep their trouser zips done up. The local populace deemed them local villains, but not given to violence. They considered themselves more local Robin Hoods to the extent that they left the poor alone but the rich were easy pickings. Their younger siblings adored them and at Christmas, Seth and Michael always miraculously produced the family Yuletide tree about two or three weeks prior to the event, giving the youngsters ample time to decorate it.

Recently the young men had heard on the television news there would be a shortage of Christmas trees this coming season, and decided there would be no disappointed kids in their house, so left instantly to obtain this seasonal adornment before stocks ran out.

A local farmer in the Burghfield area on the outskirts of Reading, in an attempt to boost his meagre income now dairy farming wasn't so profitable, had put aside a proportion of his land to growing various types of pine trees. After fifteen years, by undercutting most of the supermarkets and other local suppliers, had become well known for his reasonable priced trees, and had many repeat customers. Not that the farmer counted his crop, and was unaware that for many years he had been supplying the Ayre family with the lush green pine that stood in the bay window of their house; its luxurious foliage always being the envy of the neighbours.

This year, however, Daisy was becoming 'green' and declared she wanted a tree with roots ensuring she could plant it in the back garden after the festive occasion.

The twins, still the loving offspring who idolised their mum, were willing to obey even this whim without question. The only difficulty their mother's 'green' phase presented was that the tree gathering might take a little longer. Instead of taking a small chopper, and the job taking ten minutes at the most, it meant the two of them taking spades and carefully digging round the roots because mum had specifically declared if roots were broken, the tree would probably die.

So at midnight on a cold and rainy night in November,

in the middle of the farmer's small wood, well away from the road where no passers-by would notice the torchlight, the twins started digging. Seth held the torch whilst Michael dug and then they swopped places after ten minutes. It was Seth's second go and he had bent down to check on what was stopping his spade getting round the edge of the target tree roots.

"It's tarpaulin or something," he explained to his brother who had remarked he wasn't putting his back into the job. "There's a bit of a stink to it as well."

"I can't smell anything. Can't you get the tree out without bothering about that? We'll be here all bloody night."

"Mike, use your eyes. The bloody roots are wrapped round it. Get your arse down here and help me. Did you bring that small fork and trowel thing?"

"Yes. Move over. Let me do it. Christ, if you want a job done, do it your fucking self."

The brothers swopped positions and Seth could hear Michael heaving and panting from the effort. He was dying to say 'I told you so' but decided as this job was taking longer than planned he wouldn't provoke an argument. Another half an hour passed before Seth, who had again replaced his exhausted brother, managed to heave the tarpaulin from the hole. As he did, it unwrapped itself and a small skeleton tumbled onto the ground.

Seth jumped up, crying, "Jesus H, what the fuck?"

Michael shone the beam onto the skull and then slowly brought the beam down the body. Most of the clothing had rotted away and he could see small bones poking through the remains of blue jeans and a plaid shirt

"My God, what are we going to do?"

"We can't report it. The bizzies are going to wonder what the fuck we were doing here at this hour."

"It's bloody obvious, 'ennit. We're nicking Christmas trees."

Seth bent and touched the skull. "Poor little bugger.

Who'd do this? It's small. Just a child."

Michael dashed his hand over his eyes. He didn't want Seth to see his tears.

"He's been lying here all this time. His mum probably not knowing. We can't leave him. How long do you reckon he's been here?"

"No idea but he's not going to be here for much longer. Take off your scarf."

"What?"

"We walk back to the car. The car's out of sight so we bung the tree in the boot. If we tie the scarf to the nearest point at the edge of the wood so they've only got to walk straight to the body, even the thick plods'll find him easy enough. You nicked the scarf today so nobody's going to recognise it as yours."

"What about... what is it, DNA?"

"You've never been nicked, so there'll be nothing on record. Anyway, when we tell the plod it's a kid's body, there'll have a fucking posse out here in five minutes, and we'll be long gone. 'Spec the rain'll wash away any DNA."

"I don't want no animal chewing on him. I know he can't feel it but..."

"Yeah, I know, mate. Poor little sod. Could have been our Jack, heaven forbid."

"Murdering bastard. I hope who ever done it burns forever in hell."

Both men wiped away the tears.

Chapter 47

Lucy was feeling decidedly tipsy. She, Peter and Freddy had been to the pub to celebrate Freddy's thirty-second birthday.

They had decided the celebration would take place in their local pub because it was within staggering distance home. Knowing both the land-lord and the usual customers as it was their customary watering hole, Freddy had hoped he might well get a few 'free birthday treats'. His conclusions had proved correct and as an extra indulgence, the landlord agreed to a 'lock–in' that had lasted until one in the morning. The three of them plus seven other customers had lurched, giggling loudly, into the street.

Freddy invited the seven back to his flat for more drinks, but Lucy was relieved with their refusal, knowing they would surely end up drinking in her flat instead. She already had enough red wine and beer stains on her carpet from Freddy's so-called generous 'mein-host' nature.

Staggering into the lift and shushing the two men to stop laughing so loudly, she quickly hit the 'four' button, Freddy's floor. She was quite prepared to propel the men into their accommodation and walk down the stairs to her flat , knowing full well if Freddy started drinking in her flat, she'd never manage to eject him and as usual he'd collapse on the sofa. Although Peter was a good influence on Freddy, he wasn't a strong enough character to alter Freddy's ingrained bad habits yet. Lucy hoped that would come in time.

When Peter guided the key with an unsteady hand to the keyhole and Freddy realised it was his own flat, he refused to enter, vowing loudly he must escort Lucy home.

"She only lives downstairs, you idiot. Anyway, do what you want," hissed Peter, more sensitive to the neighbour's needs. "I'm going to bed so don't forget your own key. I'm not getting up at bloody dawn to let you in."

"Oh, so touchy, temperamental cow," Freddy said as the door closed in his face.

"Ssh, Freddy. Birthday or not, keep your voice down, people are in bed," Lucy stage whispered, not realising how efficiently noise, even whispered, carries in a nocturnal silence.

An urgent and firm knocking on their wall from Freddy's neighbour, a Mr. and Mrs. Brown not known for their sense of humour, caused more giggling from Freddy. They were not appreciative of Freddy since he had told them he was a 'raving queer' to their constant, nosey enquiries about when he was ever going to settle down and get married? Mrs Brown had drawn herself up like he'd told her he had the plague, muttering about 'living next to perverts' and hadn't spoken directly to him since. They had then taken every opportunity to be indirectly unpleasant, making snide remarks about him if they passed. Unfortunately for them, they couldn't have picked a more worthy opponent. Freddy, albeit possessing an irrepressible sense of humour combined with a heart of gold, to racists and bigots he was a formidable neighbour and foe.

Lucy dragged Freddy away as he blew a raspberry through the Brown's letterbox and they both hurried unsteadily down the stairs to floor three. Lucy gave into the inevitable; Freddy would be kipping on her sofa.

Her arm through Freddy's, she hauled him to her door, determined to hurry him noiselessly and quickly into her flat, lest she fall out with her neighbours too. The black plastic bag outside her door, ominous in its familiarity, sobered them both instantly.

"Fucking hell," Freddy muttered. "That's not my birthday present, I know."

Putting his arm round his friend's shoulders, he pulled her to him, fully expecting to have to take control of the situation if she became frightened and hysterical. He was therefore amazed at her reaction.

She pulled away from him, put her hands on her hips, stamped her foot, and with consideration for the neighbour's feelings gone in an instant, said loudly "I'm bloody fed up with this."

Freddy eyes opened like blackcurrant gob-stoppers, no words issuing from his open but silent mouth. He watched in amazement as she hunted through her shoulder-bag for the front door key, muttering, "Right, enough's enough. Whoever the tosser is that keeps leaving these sodding body parts at my front door, can take a running jump. I'm pissed off to ten."

As she walked through the front door, she turned back to Freddy who was attempting to lift the bag, and snapped.

"Don't touch that and don't bring it in here. I'm phoning the police straight away so don't even read the note."

Freddy glanced at an envelope stapled to the top of the bag. He wouldn't have dared even touch it; he'd never seen his friend so angry.

It didn't help when at that moment Higgins, who had been sound asleep in his basket in the kitchen, awoken by his mistress's voice sounding the same as when he'd nicked and eaten a whole packet of digestive biscuits from the breakfast bar, bounded out to meet them, hoping his enthusiasm would put her in a better frame of mind. The smell of fresh bones for breakfast put him in a good mood and he woofed his approval as he leapt onto the plastic container.

Freddy left Lucy to contain her pet as he dialled 999.

"Life is full of fucking bones at the moment, and my

mates really pissed off with it," was his unhelpful explanation to the young policewoman who was on night duty. She wasn't amused at what she thought was an idiot , and if not a professional woman, might well have put down the phone.

Lucy, after pushing Higgins into the kitchen and closing the door, snatched the phone from Freddy and gave a more lucid explanation.

WPC Trinder who had only been in the job four weeks since she had left police college, silently deciding the world was a terrible place, assured Lucy of a speedy police presence.

Chapter 48

Meena pushed through the foliage at the edge of the wood and stood back as the photographer recorded the scarf tied to a tree. She then eased her way through to the edge of the yellow ribbon depicting the crime scene area. The tent protecting the body remains was being erected.

Spotting Dan talking to a woman wearing a long bright red plastic mac', sensible attire in the lashing rain, Meena stood behind him and waited until the conversation finished. As the woman walked away she recognised her as the assistant pathologist to Dr McDeath.

"She finished already?" Meena asked Dan as he turned round.

"No, she's getting her scrubs on in the back of her van as it's so wet." He pulled up his collar, tucking his head into his raincoat, hoping that might stop the rain from trickling down his neck. "God, this is a bad enough job without it pissing with rain." He peered at her. "Anyway, what are you doing here? Thought you were on a week's leave?"

"No, just a couple of days off. My cousin got married."

"Is she as lovely as you, DC Mesbah. Thought you'd have been snapped up by now."

"Don't you start! It's bad enough hearing it endlessly from my mum without you..."

"Oh, touchy."

Meena ignored the banter and asked if they had anything to ID the body?

"Not that I'm aware of. SOCOs are still doing their work. I've briefly spoken to one of them. At first glance, looks like the remains of a child between five and ten. Until the pathologist does her bit, I think with the time that's probably passed since the poor little soul's been here, nothing's obvious at the moment."

"What's happened to Dr. McDeath."

"He's got the 'flu bug now. Thought it had finished its rounds but clearly not. Tom's gone off sick too."

"Yes, I heard. There are no instances of missing local children in recent years that haven't been found that I can recall." She paused. "You say the body's been here some time. Jordan... umm... Turner, his name came up recently funnily enough. You reckon it could be him?"

Dan shrugged. "Could be. Who knows?" Looking towards the now erected crime scene tent, he turned back Meena. "Reminds me, d'you ever discover what happened to his mother?"

"I put a note on your desk before I left. Your idea about the Records Office was a good one. She didn't get married though. She died."

Dan's eyebrows rose in surprise. "She was young. What, late twenties?"

"Committed suicide eighteen months ago. Just over six months after Jordan went missing."

"Pour soul. Still, if this little 'un is Jordan, without her DNA we might have a job ID-ing him. I recall you saying she was a single parent so chances are we won't know who the father is."

"Even if it was publicised that we need him to come forward, he might not have known she was pregnant."

"If he's married now, he's not going to admit he's the father." Dan turned back to watching the activities inside the cordon. Meena knew he would be straining at the leash to get inside and inspect the scene and was surprised he hadn't already done so.

"I'm surprised you're still here?"

"Here?" He looked at her questioningly.

"Outside the cordon. Normally..."

"I've already seen the body. I've been here for hours. Just removed the scrubs before you got here." He paused and Meena didn't interrupt. She knew when the boss was in deep thinking mode. He turned and gave her one of his eye piercing looks that made her weak at the knees. "She got any parents?"

"Who?"

"Jordan's mum. If they're still round, or maybe brothers or sisters, that might help with the DNA. Probably a near enough match to confirm he's a family member."

"I'll retrieve the file again and check. I found out she came from Bucklebury, a little village, in Berkshire. I'd contacted the local police for help. I can speak to them again and see if any of her family still live in the locality. I'll retrieve her medical records a well."

"Good."

"Boss, you said you've been here hours. Anyone else here?"

"DC Steiner. I sent him back to update the guv. There's nothing more he could do here for the moment. I wanted him to get an ID on the scarf, any DNA, although I don't think it'd have been left it if there was a chance of that. Plus the rain would have not upped our chances there. I told him to listen again to the telephone call reporting finding the body. Fat chance we'll ID the voice."

"We might if we put it out on the air."

"Yes, we can try that but if he, the voice on the phone, just found the body, there's probably not much more he'll know."

"What was he doing here?"

"Nicking a tree for Christmas from the hole left in the

ground. Anyway, why did you ask how long I'd been here?"

"If you've been here for hours, I suspect you could use a hot drink. Stashed in my car at this moment is a thermos full of hot coffee. How does that sound?"

"DC Mesbah you will make someone a wonderful wife. Why don't you fetch it before I freeze to death?"

As she walked to her car, he called after her, "Are you rich?"

She looked back, puzzled. "No, why?"

"Shame. Rich and very thoughtful and kind, I'd have married you myself but a poor DS like myself will need a rich wife."

She smiled at his banter, but quickly turned away so he wouldn't see the hurt on her face.

CHAPTER 49

Lucy was limping through the park with Higgins having turned her ankle the previous evening. Life felt such a bummer. Even the sun fighting and gradually winning the battle to pierce supposed unconquerable clouds didn't lift her spirits.

The bag of body parts left on her doorstep had been the final straw. The previous encounters had shocked and alarmed her, but this last unpleasant event put her in a changed frame of mind. From this point there was no going back. Whoever was inflicting this on her had forced her to a point of no return. Anger marched through her veins like an army of determined red ants, hell bent on destruction. If she ever discovered the perpetrator of these annoying, malicious acts, payback time wouldn't be pleasant! Also there was the worry that this would focus the police's attention on her even more. Despite his re-assuring words... .*Stop it, act like the innocent party you are!*

Her mind returned to last night. The details in the note she'd refused to let Freddy read had been similar to the one left with the second bag of body parts, give or take the odd word, so didn't throw any more clues as to who were the unseen Stan and Muriel.

She hobbled to a seat and watched as Higgins ran round the delights of the park, sniffing at bushes, tree roots and bench supports or the other places where his kind had left their calling marks. Lifting her ankle she slowly rotated it. Somehow during the previous evening's celebrations she'd twisted it but she couldn't recall where or when. She'd only become conscious of the pain when her foot had taken her weight as she alighted from bed this morning. Her anger the previous night at the bag left outside her door had also ensured a sore ankle had not caught her attention.

It was after three a.m. when she had eventually climbed into bed. Seven hours later when Higgins was licking her face informing her he was hungry, she felt as though she had just dozed off. Despite the heavy head, she knew Higgins had his lavatorial needs, and hoped at the same time the fresh air would clear her head. Freddy, as usual, was gone although she did notice a cup of tea, long since cold, on her bedside table and guessed he had left it there.

Her thumping headache, in terms of intensity, matched the pain in her foot so she felt life was treating her none too well at the moment. Knowing she deserved the hangover, but in truth, most of the pain was probably due to the police inquisition rather than the drinking.

Interviewed by two officers she had not met before, Lucy decided their 'equivalent police bedside manner' was on a par with the first officer, DI Cole, whom she had first met when Higgins had dug up the bones in the park grove. DCs Mel Stubbs and Jim Davison, as they had introduced themselves, had certainly made her feel she personally had chopped up the latest body.

Freddy bore no resemblance to the normal staunch defending champion he had been when Dan had interviewed her. Before the police officers and their crime scene entourage had even arrived, Freddy had fallen into a deep drunken stupor on her sofa and even the insistent finger poking and grating voice of DC Stubbs failed to raise him.

Lucy pulled her coat tightly around her, failing to keep out the mean wind that blew through the park, and mulled over the frustration she'd felt during the police interrogation.

I agreed with their insinuations, that I was somehow bloody implicated in this charade, didn't I? How many sodding times did I have to tell them I had no idea of what my involvement was? I must have told them fifty times that I had already gone over and over it with their colleagues, Meena and Luke something or other. As for wanting me to come down to the station, I bloody was not having that if they weren't going to arrest me. I told them, interview me all night here but no way I'm going to the police station. Still, they seem to calm down once I'd made them a few coffees.

Lucy glanced up and down the pathway that ran through the middle of the park but couldn't see Higgins. Shivering, she drew up the collar of her long woollen coat which didn't get many outings, because mostly she ran in her tracksuit or used a short bomber jacket in her car. Thankful she was wearing the warm garment, because despite the sun's gamely efforts, the thick wool was allowing the spiteful cold and dampness to penetrate her bones. Deciding she'd had enough fresh air, and a cup of tea would improve her disposition, she stood up to limp home to her warm flat.

"Higgins," she called, glancing around her for the inquisitive dog. "Come on. Home time, it's freezing."

Normally the fair weather dog would have bounded back to her immediately, tongue hanging out and with a look of relief on his face that a doggy biscuit might be on the horizon. Lucy was instantly uneasy; memories of the last time she lost sight of him for a time filled her mind.

Don't panic. It's just coincidence. He's around somewhere.

She slowly turned through three hundred and sixty degrees, scanning each sector for her pet, but with no success. As each forty five degree zone produced no sign of the dog, the panic began to rise, filling her chest with painful lumps of concrete. Attempting to reassure herself that flukes of fate like this could not possibly occur twice to the same person, Lucy soon felt these hopeful efforts fade away into insubstantial granules of sand. The chest concrete turned to tempered steel, and panic took over.

"Higgins, where are you? Come here!" This time she shrieked and a woman who had just jogged past her, stopped and called back enquiring if she was alright?

"Thanks. Oh God, my dog's gone missing. This happened before and..."

The woman, dressed unsuitably in shorts and running top but displaying a warm glowing skin, walked back to Lucy. Panting heavily from her exertions, hands on her hips, she asked Lucy what sort of dog she had?

"A brown greyhound. Fully grown."

"Mm, didn't think anything of it at the time, just thought the dog was being awkward."

"What do you mean?"

The woman, who introduced herself as Caroline, pointed back to where she had just run. "Back there, near the north park entrance. I saw a man pulling a very reluctant dog out of the park. A greyhound."

Lucy felt the colour and heat drain out of her body. Her legs trembled, collapsed under her and she dropped back to the seat.

"Can you describe the man?" she asked, her voice unsteady with dread.

"Mm, not really."

"Was he wearing running clothes, ordinary day clothes?"

"Let me think. Dark brown hair, medium height. About as tall as you, maybe a little taller. Late twenties, early thirties maybe. Oh, yes, he was wearing running gear, red top and shorts. That's why I noticed him. I've seen him running around before I think. Don't know him though."

Lucy stood up and winced as the pain from her ankle shot through her leg.

"Can I do anything? Maybe run back and see if I can spot them again?"

Lucy stared at her. "No thanks. You've been very helpful. I'll sort it out."

"Are you sure? It's no trouble."

"No, I'm sure. Thanks. I can manage."

Lucy limped away as the woman reluctantly turned and continued her run. Now Lucy knew why all this 'body parts' was happening to her.

Someone wants my attention. Well, now he's bloody got it. This is war! No-one takes my dog without a fight!

Part 3
After shocks

Chapter 50

Brother Samson walked into the room and took his place at the head of the table. Smoothing his hair that he grew long at the side and then combed over his balding head, he lifted up his head, attempting to look important, in charge, and a person whose decisions were never challenged. Placing his files on the table before him, he slowly looked round at the masked members of his cell sitting before him. It was etiquette at such a meeting to display respect; no word said before he had spoken. Even before he joined them, the members weren't to address each other. If anyone thought this unnecessary, no-one dared voice an opinion.

All cell members were aware that anyone who broke rules, ranging from mere bad manners at a meeting to breaking the strict guidelines on conduct outside the meetings, retribution was swift and final. The brainwashing was carried out for a purpose; no-one dared step out of line to endanger the success of Operation Hobbledehoy.

"We are reduced to five in this team. However, five reliable members of the Brotherhood. As you all know, we're six members short." Someone gasped and Brother's head shot round to the source of the sound but the perpetrator lowered his head and didn't speak. "With Operation Hobbledehoy so near, we obviously cannot make up that number easily and therefore our operations on that day would have been reduced. However, I have made alternative plans and we will use the locations considered to be the best places for a successful operation. Also, I've been busy and my hard work has been fruitful. Two more initiates will be joining us."

"Now! When we're so near the final day?" a voice dared to speak, continuing, "Our planning did not include 'novices.'" He spoke in an educated manner, his demeanour and way of dressing supporting that he came from upper class stock.

"Hawk. You grow braver every day. Once you would not have challenged my words."

"Brother, I do so for the good of the Brotherhood, not to usurp you or our plans. Are these 'initiates' prepared, trained and sufficiently aware of the dangers to be trusted at such short notice? You warned us so often about foolish actions, loose words, ill-prepared thoughts. Our training, like an army squad, has taken months. Now you talk of novices."

Brother stared hard at Hawk. Hawk's words, although dissenting, showed clear thinking.

I do believe he's ready to be the Brother of another group. After Hobbledehoy is completed, I'll speak to the Elders about the matter.

"Thank you for voicing your concern, Hawk. Have no fear. The two newcomers have been coached by the best, as you were. They lack some of your experience, I grant you. They will have lesser tasks. Delilah, you will be promoted to carry out Lawman's task." The woman merely nodded. In the team she was the only one who showed no fear in his presence but even she was careful about her behaviour. Brother turned and dramatically flourished his hand towards the door. "Now would you like to meet your new Brother and Sister?"

"They're here? Already!" said Delilah.

"Naturally. Time is short. We must make the final preparations; they need to be included." With that, Brother walked to the door and ushered in the newcomers. They were also wearing masks. It didn't hide the fact that the female particularly was very young.

"A teenager," gasped Wolfbane, his astonishment making him brave.

"Our new sister is twenty one. Age is not important. It's dedication that matters." The leader turned to the man who stood next to her. He was tall, dark haired man whose unusually pale blue eyes were obvious even through the eyeholes of his mask. "Our new brother here is not much older than you were when you were recruited, Wolfbane. You were eager and able enough. These are your new companions, Dione and Viking. Now greet each other."

Despite their reluctance, the five members of the brotherhood embraced the newcomers with formal handshakes as though they were new members of a business circle. Brother invited them to join the group, introducing the others by their code names.

"Dione, Viking, you know we use code names and masks for security reasons. We are successful because of those precautions. If anyone should be apprehended, then he or she cannot supply information they do not have. When the important day arrives, I will supply the senior members of each team with essential information and they will contact their team members and then, and only then, will everyone be aware of the other member's identity.

"The final details will be given out at a secure place. You will be told of the others in your team, your destination, and your prey targets. Photographs will be available, also clear details of the strategy to ensure our success. You will then know the full plans and our meeting place after the operation where we will reap the benefits of our months of planning and waiting."

Viking, the new recruit, looked round to see if anyone was going to ask a question. He controlled himself not to laugh at the silliness of masks and code names, and forced himself to focus. The leader had not invited questions, and their fear and uneasy respect for him was almost tangible as it hung in the air like invisible bubbles of trepidation.

Viking was braver than these stupid 'eejits'. "You say we will be given this knowledge the day before the great day?" he asked, the soft musical lilt of his Irish accent somehow at odds with the occasion. "I'm new, so I apologise if you think I'm impertinent and my question out of order. I've waited a long time and am eager to get started but I don't want to let you down. Will Dione, who's as much a novice as I am... will we be given any more training?"

"I understand your eagerness," said Brother," but you must learn that impatience breeds danger. Don't worry, the plans are well laid, and everything will be made clear. I and others have vetted both you and Dione and found you suitable for the task. You won't need more training. The leaders of the groups are very experienced and the target areas have been well researched as have the Prey themselves.

"This is not just a local operation as you know. This is nationwide and everything is in place. Watertight plans. We need the authorities caught unaware, without suspects and totally disorganised by the sheer scale of the operation. This will be achieved if the plans are followed without question."

Brother Samson turned away, and continued,

"Excalibur, hand out the Agenda for today's meeting. Viking, Dione, remember even these brief notes never leave this room. Once the meeting is finished, we burn them, not even shred them. Even that can mean danger. Shredding can be sifted and reconfigured. Burning is the only way that ensures total safety."

"With these security safeguards we ensure we don't get caught," said Delilah. "No loose tongues. We talk to no-one, kapish?" She stared at the newcomers, her aggressive glare making it obvious she didn't appreciate their presence.

"Relax, Delilah, our new friends have been thoroughly schooled. They understand the rules and they have been told the outcome of breaking them." He turned back to Dione and Viking. "We keep nothing in writing. We do not phone each other on our normal phones. Always our messages are in pre-arranged but constantly changing codes. At the end of this meeting, you will both be given these codes to learn by heart. As I said, nothing in writing. Now, we need to move on. Excalibur, the agenda!"

The agendas were distributed and the meeting began. It lasted an hour, coffee and biscuits being brought in by a young girl later who had not attended the meeting. Although masked, the disguise didn't hide her youth. Viking found it difficult not to stare. Her mousey fair hair was caught up in a ponytail and was dressed in jeans and casual top. Adam estimated she was no more than fourteen or fifteen.

He was caught between choking with disgust on his coffee or laughing hysterically at the stupidity of it all. *Agendas! Coffee! Stupid wankers!* If their ideas were not so horrifying he'd have given in to his instincts to stand up, tell them they were a load of arrogant, evil tossers who deserved to be hung very slowly by their necks until well and truly dead.

As a police officer doing his duty, although at the moment hating every second of it, he finished his coffee and prayed his face was not a mirror for his true thoughts.

Chapter 51

Lucy limped to one of the park gate where Caroline had reported she'd last seen Higgins, but neither he nor his abductor was in sight. Walking through the gates she inspected the road beyond but except for a half-empty corporation bus swishing past and wetting her feet, she saw nothing.

Gritting her teeth against the discomfort of her ankle, she hurried to the next entrance; on the way scrutinising the road beyond through various breaks in the decrepit boundary fencing. There was no sign of him or the person who had enticed him into the car. The park had three or four other entrances; Lucy silently cursed that in her panic she had not asked for more specific details from Caroline who had pointed generally to the north where two openings were near each other. Higgins could easily have been dragged through anyone of these or the breaks in the perimeter.

Checking her watch, panic racked her body when she realised at least twenty minutes had passed since his disappearance.

Walking through the second north gate, she glanced up and down the road again, tears of desperation oozing from her eyes and down her cheeks. Dashing them away hastily, knowing self-pity wasn't going to help.

Two cars approached and she peered into them as they

passed, but only contained two couples and their children, none of whom even glanced in her direction. The cold plus the icy drizzle now falling, the failed sun sulking and now snuggled up in bed beneath its grey duvet, all contributed towards the total ruin of Lucy's day. Unusual for a Sunday morning, even the regular joggers were absent, but as the drizzle became more vicious and grew sharper nails which scratched her face, Lucy was sympathetic with their decisions to stay home. The weather was as foul as her mood, and her search progress nil.

Taking out her mobile she phoned Freddy. She didn't know what she expected him to do but even talking to someone would help. In her heart she was sure her friend, despite his hangover, would come and help her search or at the least come up with a good idea. His mobile continued to ring but even his answering service didn't activate to receive a message. To complete the bad day, an unsympathetic message interrupted her call informing her that her credit was running low and her phoned went dead.

Hell and damnation. What have I done to deserve this? I'm kind to old ladies. Always put a quid in charity boxes. Someone up there doesn't like me or Hig.

The panic returned again. With dropping shoulders and more tears trickling from her eyes, she felt very alone. She wondered whether Higgins was frightened and the trickle threatened to become an avalanche. Breathing deeply, she straightened up her shoulders, realising that being a total wuss was not going to save her dog. She forced herself to concentrate on positive thoughts. Her actions worked; within a minute a bolt of adrenalin coursed into her brain and her thoughts sharpened.

Red top and shorts. Caroline said he wore red. Where've I seen that?

Lucy, frowning deeply, focused her mind on the people she most frequently saw when she ran. No-one just wore red but at the same time something annoyingly relevant but elusive hid round a corner in her brain, but just would not peek out and let her recall the fact.

Still deliberating, she ignored the old and scratched Fiesta driving along the road in her direction. Pulling up beside her, when some-one rolled down the window, and a pleasant voice asked, "Looking for your dog?", she snapped back to the present.

At his words, anxiety clenched its hands round Lucy's heart, and a feeling this wasn't good yet not knowing why. Recognising his face as a fellow jogger, she recalled the conversation in the dark park when this same young man had told her he'd noticed a couple watching her.

He smiled. "It's Jake. Remember me. We pass and wave and we talked in the park one night. You were out running with your grumpy friend and Higgins."

Relief swept over Lucy. "Yes, Jake, of course."

"You OK? You look worried."

"Yes, I'm actually distraught. I've lost Higgins. Someone's taken him."

"Aah, I thought so. When was that? About half an hour ago?"

Lucy leant down by the car; the falling moisture had been determined to find the narrow gap between her coat and neck and was now coldly licking her back. Her hair, which she hadn't bothered to tie into the normal ponytail, was wet and hanging round her face. Unconsciously wiping the water from her eyes, not caring now about the weather, how cold she felt, or her appearance; news about Higgins, good or bad, was paramount.

"Yes, maybe twenty minutes or so. Have you seen anything?"

"For goodness sake, get out of the rain. You're soaking. Anyway, I think I've seen something. Maybe I can help."

Lucy got into the car, glad of the warmth issuing from the still running engine. As soon as she closed the door, the heat from her breath steamed up the car windows.

"What did you see?" she asked eagerly.

"I was running back to my car after jogging. Saw someone dragging a dog into his car. Thought it was funny; the dog looked just like yours. He'd driven away before I could say anything. I know where the bloke lives. We'll go straight there."

As he spoke, Jake put the car into gear and sped away. Lucy blinked and shook herself. A niggle wriggled like a worm at the back of her mind, then slithered snakelike towards her rational thinking area, forcing logic to take over. A forgotten monochromic scene lodged before her eyes. Her thoughts jumbled and tumbled into an abyss of apprehension for her stupidity.

Colours aren't easily discernible in the dark! That night, the moon had peered round the cloud... I... unconsciously... noted his unusual ensemble. Oh, dear, this is stupid. I'm so stupid. Caroline said the guy was dressed in red today. Jake was in red that night, you silly cow!

Glancing cautiously across to Jake, dread terrorising her pounding heart, she saw his black tracksuit. The jacket was half-undone, her eyes trailed up the path of the zip, and a red running top clearly showed.

Her heartbeats went into over-drive. She considered jumping from the car but if, for whatever reason Jake had taken Higgins, not staying might mean she'd never see her pet again.

"They weren't watching me at all, were they?" she said, her voice steady but in complete contrast to her shaking body and desperate reasoning.

"Who?"

"The couple in the park."

"Oh, they were."

"Yes, but they weren't watching me."

"Not you exactly, they were watching... Higgins. I asked them."

"So who was watching me?"

"Ah, well, that was me," he admitted

Jake turned to look at her, a chilling smile hovering round his mouth. Lucy stared into his eyes, her imagination zoomed into overload. *Oh my God, I'm sitting next to a serial killer... or maybe... even worse... he's my family. Either way... this is really bad.*

Chapter 52

Within fifteen minutes, Jake and Lucy arrived at their destination. She'd often driven past the end of the road on her way to school. He drove the car onto a parking space next to an old-fashioned cottage. Above the front door doorway there was a circular brick plaque with the date of 1900 engraved in the centre. Both this cottages and the one next door look solidly built with decorative brickwork suggesting it came from an era when builders took a pride in their work even if only erecting lowly homes.

This far into the country Lucy assumed they were tied cottages built for farm labourers as they had passed a farm on the drive to the house. Looking up and down the country lane, she noticed on either side of the dwellings there were signs that at one time there had been more houses, although now there were just footings where they had once stood.

"Home, sweet home," Jake joked. "Come on inside and meet the family."

Getting out of the car, he hurried round to open the door for Lucy. Saying nothing although her mind was racing with uncertainty, she thought his humour weird and out of place under the circumstances. Even though he hadn't strictly abducted her, he'd given her no choice if she wanted to safely retrieve Higgins.

About to ask who lived here, she didn't have to put

her question into words because the front door opened and a woman wearing a welcoming smile beckoned them in. Lucy estimated she was into her late sixties and didn't seem flummoxed that she was wearing a fluffy pink dressing gown and matching slippers which were strange for almost the middle of the day. The rain had stopped but the dark grumpy skies gave the impression a cantankerous afternoon was fast approaching.

Maybe she's getting ready for bed. Lucy felt a hysterical giggle gurgle in her throat.

"Hello, so pleased to meet you," the woman greeted, pumping Lucy's hand as she spoke, offering no explanation of her unusual dress at this time of the day. "You must be the famous Lucy we've heard so much about. I'm Muriel Turner."

Before Lucy could query her own fame or whether this person was the 'Muriel of the body-parts note', the woman invited her into a side room. She was amazed to see a woman tied with leather straps to an armchair, yet again Muriel seemed unfazed by this unusual situation and offered no explanation. Convinced she'd entered the crazy world of Alice in Wonderland where everything was not all that it seemed, Lucy felt hysteria bubble up again. She wasn't sure if she would laugh or cry when it popped to the surface.

"Let me introduce everyone." Muriel indicated a man drinking from a cup and sitting on an armchair opposite the restrained woman. "This is Stan, my hubby, Jakey's uncle and I'm his aunt." Stan put down his cup, stood up and shook Lucy's hand with a firm grip that supposedly indicated a reliable character, but Lucy thought this assumption wasn't valid considering the circumstances.

"Nice to meet you after all this time. Both Muriel and I are delighted you've made our Jake such a happy man." He winked conspiratorially at Lucy. "Nothing like a bit of romance to put a smile on someone's face."

"And our Jake has been walking round like the proverbial

cat with two tails and six extra helpings of Whiskas," added Muriel.

Lucy felt her head spin with confusion but decided if she was to find out exactly what this crazy situation was all about, initially silence was her best ally. She smiled politely and said she was pleased to meet them both, praying her face and voice provided a sincerity not present within the tiniest cell of her body.

"Now meet Maria, who has been helping us with our enquiries as Jake will have explained to you." Maria wriggled the fingers of her left hand to greet Lucy, her face stretched into a smile that expressed the same artificiality as Lucy's own countenance.

"Hi, Lucy, nice to meet you."

No-one offered to explain why Maria was so tethered, and Jake certainly hadn't mentioned it. Lucy decided that either during romantic moments with Jake of which she had no recall, he would have explained the circumstances, or she was currently suffering from a very bad nervous breakdown and this whole episode was a psychotic illusion of her unbalanced mind. When she felt an urge to giggle again about the absurdity of the situation, she settled on the latter option; she was definitely unbalanced.

"I'll get you a coffee, sweetheart," Jake said, disappearing into the kitchen. The affectionate label, despite her vow of 'let's be cool and see what happens', caught Lucy by surprise, and her eyebrows disobeyed her intentions and shot up into her hair line.

Higgins' bark filled the air and Lucy's head turned towards the source of the noise.

"Higgins, where is he? Is he OK, you haven't hurt him have you?"

This time it was both Muriel and Stan's turn for raised eyebrows. "What made you say that, dear?" said Muriel. "Why should we hurt him when you asked us, well Jake, to look after him? He and Judy, our dog, hit it off straight away.

They're friend already."

"What? I... " Again, despite the craziness of the situation, the necessary lifesaving chemicals required for Mach 3 speed survival thinking flooded Lucy's brains. *Whatever's going on with this looney family, I have to play along.*

"Sorry, what made me say that? His bark made me jump. I don't know what I was thinking."

The explanation, including the tone, wasn't convincing, but fortunately neither Muriel nor Stan questioned it. Lucy furtively glanced at Maria who wasn't adding to the conversation, but her large frightened eyes and the merest nod of approval indicted to Lucy her playing along was the right avenue to take. Maria's eyes then flitted to the table and Lucy's followed the direction. Besides two empty coffee cups there was a tea plate covered in cake crumbs and lying diagonally across it, a knife. It was a small kitchen knife with a wooden handle and a sharp looking blade.

"You're taking time with Lucy's coffee, Jake." Muriel stood up. "He's useless in the kitchen, you know. I'd better go and do it. It'll be undrinkable otherwise." As the woman walked towards the kitchen she called back to Stan. "Bring the cups, lovey, I'll wash them up."

As Stan rose to his feet, Maria suddenly spoke. "Oh, Stan, take a look at this wrist again. I think it's either coming loose or something. It's rubbing my wrist, it feels slack."

Stan walked round and bent over Maria's wrist. As he did, the woman glared over his back at Lucy, nodding towards the knife on the coffee table. Lucy didn't need a second flash of eyes, deciphering the implication, the knife was off the table and slipped into the inside of her sock in an instant.

"Looks OK to me," said Stan.

"OK, maybe you're right. Just felt loose that's all," Maria said.

Stan picked up the two cups and the plate and both women drew in breaths in case he should notice the missing knife, but he stacked the crockery and headed into the kitchen. Before Lucy could ask Maria what was going on, Jake walked in with her coffee and placed it on the table.

"There you are, darling."

"Jake." Lucy's hissed. "What's going on? Where's Higgins and why do Stan and Muriel think we're... "

"Engaged. I told them the news, I hope you don't mind."

"Engaged. Bloody engaged. What the hell are you talking about?"

Jake's eyes opened wide, the shock causing his mouth to fall open. "Lucy, language! You don't normally swear. What has come over you?"

"Don't swear!" Lucy felt all the oaths she had ever used bubbling up to her throat, hovering impatiently, ready to be shot into the air like arrows from a bow. "You don't know anything about me, let along whether I swear or not and if I bloody want to... "

"Lucy," Maria urged. "Look at me." Lucy's head swung round, her eyes lashing like whips, ready to flay the woman's face. "Steady. Just think." Her words were firm, their eyes locked. She transferred her meaning in the glance as clearly as if relaying the message in legible photons along a light wave.

In an instant, Maria's unspoken advice cooled her temper. Turning back to Jake, she swallowed, beamed her brightest and with what she hoped was her most winning smile, said sweetly, "Sorry, Jake, love. I don't know what came over me." She leaned over and took his hand. "Honestly, darling, I'm so sorry. It's just Higgins. I heard his bark and it sounded so pathetic. You know what I'm like when I'm not with him. We miss each other so much, just like you and me. Please can I see him now? Pretty please."

Jake gazed at her, all his love and obsession spilling over into a stupid grin that Lucy wanted so much to wipe off his face. However, needs must. She just repeated her 'pretty please' to see him.

"I'll get him," he said and walked out of the room, the gooey smile plastered all over his face.

"Christ, you're not really engaged to that looney?" hissed Maria.

"You're joking. I've only met him once before today. Does he live with Uncle Stan and Auntie Muriel?"

Maria shrugged her shoulders," Don't know, never seen him before today." She looked round as she heard footsteps in the hall. "Atta girl for the acting then, he's fooled and they all think he's your boyfriend." was all Maria had time to mutter before Stan walked back into the room. Now there were two women acting for a Brit Award in order to save their lives.

Chapter 53

Lucy, although not tied up like Maria, still felt like a prisoner, even if neither Jake nor the elderly couple treated her like one. She did notice, however, that whenever left on her own with Maria, Jake took Higgins out of the room. Despite his confusion over their supposed relationship, he was sensible enough to know she would not leave without her dog.

Conversation with Maria was also difficult, but occasionally the two of them were alone and had the opportunity to talk. Their first dialogue left Lucy gobsmacked and very concerned.

"What are you here for?" hissed Lucy. "Tied up like that. This is the craziest situation I've ever been in."

"They're total loonies," Maria whispered back. "They abducted me, using some kind of anaesthetic, and I ended up here. I wondered how two old cronies managed it but now I've met their mate I realise he was probably involved."

"But why?"

"They think I was involved with the disappearance of their grandson, Jordan. I wasn't but they didn't believe me. Before me they kidnapped two men. Christ, you've never seen anything like it. They've kept their heads, all mouldy and green and the maggots are beginning to munch away. The crazies make out they're talking, like hand puppets. Frigging total wierdos. The heads got so squelchy they told me they had to put them in the freezer. They must chop up the bodies. I heard them chopping up Jo. God knows what they do with the bits."

Lucy felt sick. She knew very well what they did with the body parts but before she could say anything, Jake walked back into the room. Acting like the attentive fiancée he now imagined he was, Lucy realised she also had to go along with the farce. Jake had explained earlier his aunt and uncle and had raised him after his mother had passed away, so Lucy deduced that he'd inherited the 'mad gene' and was as dotty as they obviously were. If Maria's words were true, then he could turn on a sixpence, and the 'lover' become a 'murderer'.

She'd only ever had the one conversation with Jake the night she and Freddy had jogged in the park, although she had seen him and waved often enough. In some crazy way he imagined that meant a serious romance. Lucy had read about people with obsessions, that, if thwarted in their delusions, could become dangerous. For the sake of acting for a few hours, and hoping that escape was only that length of time away, then she'd act the sweetheart. It might make her furious deep down to perform this way, but she had Higgins to consider as well.

When left alone again, Lucy restarted their conversation.

"Why did they kill the men?"

Maria lifted her shoulders in a gesture of 'ask-me-another'. "They were convinced they knew where their grandson was, or at the least, where his body was, but I don't think they did because presumably if they had known, they'd have told them rather than be tortured and killed. Four of us; them two, me and another person I'll tell you about, were taken to court on a trumped up charge. We were innocent and we all got off.

"These crazies decided that British justice was left very much wanting and the bizzies hadn't made any effort to locate their grandson. Then Jordan's mum committed suicide, they say from grief, but if she was as mad as them, who knows? They were broken hearted. First the lad and then their daughter. I can understand that, but it doesn't give them the right to murder the way they did. So they kidnap this Nigel and Donald but they couldn't tell them anything. So chop chop, the end of them."

"But you're still here."

"Yes, well I decided to help out. Joseph Bates, the fourth person arrested and then released, was proving difficult to find. I stopped them making mincemeat of me by convincing them I could trace him. Unfortunately for him, I succeeded. Really I was just playing for time. Hoping somebody would rescue me. Anyway, he came here, and... umm... well, he died of fright I'm afraid,"

"Maria... " Lucy was about to say that her actions had virtually signed his death warrant but knew instantly she was being judgemental. If threatened in a similar manner as Maria, who could say for sure she wouldn't have acted the same way. She hoped not, but until it happens, who could tell.

Sensing Lucy's disapproval, Maria attempted to justify her position. "To be honest, from things I'd overheard him say," she lied, "I think he was involved with Jordan's disappearance. I didn't want to get him killed, I just hoped he'd find a way to help me and we'd escape together."

"What happened then? They chopped him up anyway."

"I know. I heard, it was awful."

"Oh my God, he was alive when..."

"No, he keeled over with a heart attack. I didn't know he had a dodgy ticker or I never would have helped them trace him."

"So neither of us is safe because although I'm playing the fiancée at the moment, I'm also just playing for time. The moment he realises I'm not serious, things could change. "

"Yeah, I know. When they're not around, if you could cut my straps, maybe we could leg it together."

Again, the discussion was interrupted and the women had to be patient.

Stan and Muriel popped in and out of the room quite frequently, on one of these occasions Muriel told Lucy her room was ready if she wanted to freshen up at any time. Jake had brought 'her case' containing her pyjamas, toothbrush and clean clothes. By this time, Lucy, realising her impression of being watched when out jogging in the park was in fact, correct, didn't doubt the clothes he provided would be a good fit.

Insisting Higgins have his late night constitutional to do his business, she took him into the back garden accompanied by Jake who blithely talked of their marriage plans. Lucy felt it all so surreal. Like an actor in a badly written farce, she played her part and acted out her role with an adoring smile on her face.

If she hoped they would escape from the garden, she was wrong. Although the area was large as old country gardens often are, it was securely fenced. There were dark fields at the back and she guessed they all knew the area better than she. Lights peeped through the neighbours closed curtains but if all this kidnapping and chopping had gone on, the neighbours were either deaf, as mad as her captors or in league with them. Either way, Lucy decided she couldn't look to them for help, she was going to have to get herself out of this mess!

Chapter 54

The expression on Dan's face was one of extreme bafflement.

Luke placed a cup of coffee on his bosses desk. "Boss, you look as though some one's asked you a million dollar prize question and you can't answer it," He and Meena then pulled up chairs at his desk for a discussion.

"You're right. Well, not so much a question, as a conversation" He leaned back in his chair, tapping his teeth with a pencil. Taking a deep breath, he leaned forward and said quietly, "OK, for your ears only, and it doesn't get out of this room. I've just had the weirdest conversation with our esteemed leader.

"I'd finished updating him and was collecting my files ready to leave, when he said, Lucy Hamilton, where is she in terms of your suspect list? I told him, certainly not at the top, but all these things that keep happening to her, she certainly hasn't dropped off the list. Also that Meen'd done a check on her and it was almost suspicious that she was so clean." He sipped his coffee, the lines denoting puzzlement still deep and making a V shape between his eyebrows. "Then he says, all casual like, 'Drop her off your suspect list. Unless some indisputable evidence arises regarding her guilt, drop her from your list.'"

Meena leaned forward, her posture and bewildered face identical to Dan's. "What?" She turned to Luke, her eyes large and questioning.

"I know, " said Dan. "I tried to question him, but he just cut me short with that steely voice that sounds like it's been tempered in the fires of hell. 'No questions. I don't know anything myself. I can only tell you that from on high, and I mean just beneath God, the word is we drop any investigation on her, and inform your detectives on the case.'" He looked at their expressions. He sipped his coffee before he continued, "So, I can't help you further. I believe Cole when he says he doesn't know. Oh, that's right, as I left, he added, 'Might be an idea to keep an eye on her. Somebody's obviously got it in for her.' Then he just looked down as though to say, no more questions!"

"Do'you think... "

"I don't think anything, Luke. It's puzzling but we're not going to ever find out, unless she knows and tells us, which I doubt. So, we stop wasting time on her, and move on."

The silence in the room was almost palpable. The three police officers stared at each other, each with their own confused thoughts until Dan said,

"Ok, let's move on. Let's hear what you've got to report before I update you."

After Luke and Meena had left, Dan walked to the window of his office. Peering at the clouds scudding across the late autumn sky and intermittently covering the stars, a sudden urge for a cigarette swept over him. He hadn't thought about a cigarette in a few weeks now, and the desire surprised him. Deciding he'd better get a sweet coffee before he weakened, he hurried to the machine which dispensed drinks the taste of which bore no resemblance to the label, but it was better than nothing.

He winced as he sipped the brew, and his conversation with Cole crossed his mind. There could be many reasons why he had been told to not further investigate and consider Lucy Hamilton, and he didn't intend to waste time worrying about it, but he didn't like mysteries.

Shrugging the problem away as he returned to his office, he realised some good may come from it. At last, admitting to himself that despite her strange keep fit obsession, he did find her attractive. As a suspect, if he were to behave professionally, he would have to have stayed away from her.

Mm, now maybe a date, whenever I have a spare two minutes, won't be out of the question.

Chapter 55

It wasn't until mid-morning on the next day that Maria and Lucy managed to continue their conversation.

"If you can cut my straps with that knife, we can leg it fast," murmured Maria, aware of the need to speak quietly. "You've still got it with you I suppose. It wasn't missed?"

"No, still got it. Stan and Muriel have no reason to think I'm going to bolt. They believe Jake's bullshit that I'm the delightful fiancée. Jake seems to trust his illusion too. " She heard a noise and stopped in case some-one was coming into the room but no-one entered She continued, "Two things. Firstly, I'm not going anywhere without Higgins. Jake doesn't leave him here with me unless he's here too, so obviously I'm not totally trusted. Secondly, although the knife looks sharp, it'll take ages to cut through those straps. They look like thick leather. Things like that'll probably blunt the knife quickly."

"What'll we do then? I'm desperate. At the moment, you're safe but that won't last forever."

"I know. What about I sneak into your bedroom during the night. Which is your room?"

"Next to yours, I think. Left of the bathroom. What's the betting your door will be locked?"

"True. I should have tested it last night. I thought I wouldn't sleep but I went out like a light."

"Did you actually drink the Horlicks?"

"Yes, was it...?"

"I think so. I don't drink it anymore. I'm sure they slip in a Mickey Finn or whatever it's called."

"OK, if they're sensible the bedroom door will be locked. When we go to bed, could you cause a diversion and maybe they'll forget to lock my door. Do they tie you to your bed?"

"Yes I'm securely strapped. I'll could try a diversion but I can't see they would forget to lock the door."

"Mmm, maybe what I'll have to do is just escape on my own, it's the only option. Maybe without Higgins in case he starts to bark. I don't want to leave him but perhaps that's the way I'll save him. " Lucy saw the look of terror on Maria's face. "Both of you, save both of you I mean. I swear on all that's holy and on Higgin's head, I'll have the police back here in less than an hour."

"Swear!"

"Swear, promise and give you my solemn oath."

Maria grinned. "Fucking guides honour."

"Definitely and f-ing scouts honour too."

That evening Lucy did not drink the Horlicks, tipping it into a pot plant holder when an opportunity arose. Slipping out of bed when the house became quiet and everyone obviously in bed, she discovered Maria was right, the door and window were securely locked.

Chapter 56

Dan, chewing his lip, and then running his fingers through his hair making the spikes more severe and upright than normal, was bursting with frustration and doubt. Adam had been gone all the previous evening. It was now ten in the morning and despite the surveillance outside his house, he had not appeared.

His mother, when questioned, said that she'd gone to bed at ten thirty. Adam had told her he was going to watch a football match he'd recorded from the television before he retired for the night. She had heard nothing during the night but when he didn't appear for his breakfast by eight o' clock, she checked his room, but he wasn't there and his bed looked unused. There was no note and normally if he had left unexpectedly, he wrote an explanation updating her on his situation. Although Adam had warned Dan he might leave quickly, it still didn't explain how he had slipped the surveillance and it didn't ease Dan's concern.

His mobile rang and he pounced on it, praying it was Adam with good news. "Blake." The anxiety made his voice sharp as he answered.

"Dan, its Fred."

Taken by surprise, Dan couldn't think who the hell 'Fred' was. "Who?"

"Freddy Heath. Lucy's friend."

"Oh, how can I help?"

"It's Luce. She's missing."

"What do you mean? You had a row or something?"

"No, at my birthday bash, Saturday night, we got smashed. Then, surprise fucking surprise, we have another sackful of body parts left at her front door, as you probably know by now. 'Fraid I'd passed out on her sofa by the time your lot arrived to question us and examine the area. They were going to take over the whole of her flat as a crime scene area but I think your boss, Cole is it, said there was no need. Seems by morning, except a taped off area outside her flat and a Plod keeping tabs, things were back to normal."

"When did she go missing then?"

"I kipped on her sofa. Took her a cup of tea in about eight, she was still asleep, and I buggered off to my flat and slept for the rest of the morning. When I went down late afternoon to check, your Mr Plod said she'd gone out with the dog about half past ten."

"She was going running?"

"Apparently not. She was limping and told your uniformed mate she'd twisted her ankle but had to take Higgins for his morning constitutional. She hobbled off with Hig and a poop bag or whatever it's called."

"And this was when, yesterday?"

"No, day before yesterday. I reported her missing when she didn't return by Sunday night. I spoke to a policewoman who took all the details. I'm going to see her tomorrow with a list I've compiled of where she could be or anyone who might know. The policewoman was helpful and suggested I ought to consider that as an adult, Lucy has the right to go off somewhere. Asked me again if she had anyone she was likely to visit?"

"And has she?"

"Not that I know of. She doesn't answer her mobile. She hasn't been to work. I phoned the school and they hadn't heard from her. She never misses school, ever. I've a key to her place so this morning Pete and I looked for her private phone book. She scribbles friends' numbers in there, although most of her numbers are probably on her mobile. She's told me she hasn't any family. Clearly doesn't want to talk about it so I don't push. Anyway, she just wouldn't go off without telling me."

"It does seem strange... " Dan recalled his conversation with her when she said she felt she was being watched when out jogging. He'd dismissed it from his mind with all that had been happening. A feeling of guilt stalked round and then bit into his innards.

Cole's words that she was almost certainly not a suspect, and in fact, to keep an eye on her if possible. *What the fuck does this mean?* At that moment the phone on Dan's desk went and he pointed at it, indicating to Meena to answer it. "Look, give it till tonight. I'll talk to you then. When're you home?"

"I'm working mornings and evenings. I'm usually home about two thirty, then I work seven till nine. I just thought as you know her, maybe you could push it along a bit."

"I'll chase it up but I'm sure everything's being done that should be. The matter of missing people is taking seriously. When you finish work, give me a call." Out of the corner of his eye he could see Meena pointing to the phone and mouthing that it was important. "Just before you go, has Lucy got the telephone number of the people who were supposed to be watching her and turns out they weren't."

"I suppose so. She's talked to them I know, and they came round last week for a meal. DC Meena Mesbah checked their alibis for the dates of the body parts being put outside Lucy's door and apparently they were ballroom dancing. It's their hobby. "

"OK, but still, look in the phone book and contact them if their number's listed. Seems they're in the park with their dog a great deal, so they might have seen something. It's worth a try."

"Do you think... ?

"I don't know. It's another angle to check. I've got to go. Call me later. If she's not back by then, we'll make it really official."

Dan closed his mobile and forcing himself to focus on his present situation. It now seemed two people he cared about were missing. He was surprised by that thought. Trying to push Lucy Hamilton to the back of his mind, but he knew he was obviously failing.

Taking the phone from Meena, he raised his eyebrows in a 'who is it' look, she mouthed, "Mel, on surveillance."

"Mel, what's happening?"

"Boss, he's just been dropped off at the end of the road. Just gone in the house. I didn't get the registration number of the vehicle, too far away. It was a black Range Rover with blacked out windows, I saw that much. You said not to try and contact him."

"That's right. Sit tight. He'll probably go to his job soon. I'll phone him, but I don't want you to lose sight of him. You been there all night?"

"No, came on at six."

"OK, keep me updated if anything changes."

"Right, boss."

Dan sat back in his chair, relieved at least one of the missing was accounted for. He had no idea what had happened to Lucy, but with all that had been going on in her life, he had a bad feeling about it. Feeling guilty again that he'd never given her concern another thought, he knew for the moment he must concentrate on the present enquiry, and once again pushed her from his mind.

He dialled a phone kept at Adam's home used exclusively for updating the undercover operation.

"Yes?" were the only words spoken.

"It's Dan. Safe to talk?"

"Not really. Other ears. I'm OK. See you at my desk, so

to speak."

"How long?"

"Give me an hour."

Meena placed a coffee on his desk. "Everything OK?"

"He's back. I'm going to see him at his so-called job in an hour. Any news yet on the third lot of body parts, the ones left at Lucy Hamilton's flat?"

"No. No ID yet. No head or hands again so we'll have to wait for DNA results. Probably won't be quick unless you can contact your mate again. Dr. McDeath's back, still sneezing dramatically all over the place apparently."

"Why the hell do these things turn up on Lucy's doorstep?" Dan mused softly. He looked up at Meena. "What is going on? Freddy Heath's reported her missing?"

"What! Since when?"

"Day before yesterday. She took her dog for a walk and hasn't been seen since."

"With all that's happened, that's dodgy. Has he officially reported it?"

"Yes but was told not to panic. Going through the official channels apparently. It'll be taken seriously. She could have just decided to split for a time."

"True. Happens all the time. Two hundred thousand people a year go missing without explanation."

"I know and you know that, but Heath's convinced there's no way she'd act in that way. Never went to school which is very worrying in itself."

"What can we do?"

"I've asked Heath to contact the couple who we suspected were watching her... um."

"Ron and Janet Pierce. But why?"

"I don't know. It's somewhere to start. I know they appear to be innocent bystanders but we have to begin somewhere."

"Do you want me to search her apartment?"

"Maybe you could find out whose dealing with it and check how far the investigation's progressed." Dan leaned back in his chair, frowning and tapping his teeth with a pencil. Glancing back to Meena, he muttered, "Freddy's adamant she wouldn't just go missing and I think he's right. With what we now know, Cole's mysterious statement, I get the feeling she's not happy with all this attention she's getting with all these body parts being dumped. I don't know why she's concerned about the attention, but... " Dan looked out of the window at the grey sky, still annoyed that he was so bothered about her, and that his feelings had nothing to do with Cole's warning.

"Boss, I can see you're worried. I'm off in an hour; can I get into her apartment? Maybe give it the once over, just to see if there's anything that might give us a clue."

"Check with the official channels first. I don't suppose they'll mind some support but we don't want to tread on their toes. If they OK it, Freddy Heath has a key. I'll give you his mobile number, arrange to meet him. You happy doing this in your own time?"

"Why not? Lucy and I got on really well. She deserves a bit of extra."

"You're a good mate to me, Meena."

Meena turned away. She didn't want to her boss to see the effect the 'mate' expression had.

"Drink your coffee, boss. Don't let it get cold." Her heart was heavy and so was Dan's, for different reasons.

Chapter 57

Meena impatiently looked at her watch as though it would somehow make Freddy Heath appear. When she had phoned him at work and explained Dan had talked to her about Lucy's disappearance, she felt it prudent to move on this as quickly as possible. The policewoman dealing with the case had been quite happy for Meena to help in whatever way she could so long as Meena updated her regarding any progress.

Meena wanted to examine Lucy's flat in case there was some clue as to where she had gone, and Freddy had promised he would join her outside the flat at just after three, and it was now almost half past. Standing on the landing outside the flat, the crime scene tape and police officer now gone, she tapped her foot impatiently.

Come on, come on. I've got things to do.

As though on cue, she heard the lift as it hummed its way up. Freddy, looking harassed, emerged through the lift doors.

"Sorry, there's an accident on the road near the gym, the traffic's piling back for bloody miles." He dropped his leather holdall on the floor and searched his pockets. "Not there, bugger. Aah, I know. The brain's better than the memory." With that, he felt inside his jacket for his wallet and produced the key from a zipped pocket. "Ah ha! Voila as ze Frenchies say."

Despite her impatience, Meena smiled at his expression and understood why Lucy was so fond of him. A natural comic and his turn of phrases obviously made him good company and, the police officer had to agree with Lucy's words when previously talking about him, irresistible.

The flat had a chill to it when they entered. In her job, Meena had previously entered people's homes when they were reported missing, and invariably noticed that a property didn't have to be empty for long before the presence of the owner evaporated like mist as the sun appears, and the place became a cold, unfriendly dwelling.

"No Higgins," Meena noticed.

"No, I'd checked he wasn't here and starving. Almost certainly he's with her. See, here's her shoulder bag," said Freddy. "She doesn't usually take it running, so I'm not surprised it's still here. I looked in it when I started to get worried when she didn't return and went through looking to see if she kept her diary in it."

"You know she kept one then?"

"Yes, but I've only seen her put telephone numbers or addresses in it. I think she only uses it for appointments. It was tucked in the back pocket but there was nothing listed for last Sunday."

"Did she take her mobile with her?"

"Yes, but I can't get any reply. She must be in trouble. I know her. There's no way she'd go missing like this."

"Has she family that she could've visited or maybe had to visit; family illness or something."

"She never talks about them except to say she has no-one. They're all dead. She obviously doesn't want to talk so I don't push."

"OK, I'll have a look through her flat but if she went missing, not of her own volition, might be nothing that'll help."

"I've had a quick look; didn't like to go through her drawers or anything, seemed not nice. It was tidy as usual."

Freddy's face was unusually serious and his disquiet spread to Meena. "Fancy a coffee? I've just bought some fresh milk."

At Meena's nod, he disappeared into the kitchen. As the policewoman walked into Lucy's bedroom and spotted an open bureau which might prove interesting, her mobile rang.

"Meena Mesbah, by all that's holy," a familiar Northern Irish voice replied to her name. "How the devil are you? Patrick Collins, your favourite fan from Police College."

"Hello, Patrick, I keep hearing about your successes. You OK?"

"Sure. I've just come on duty and read the note left about your enquiry on the Jordan Turner family."

"You working at Newbury then?"

"Yes, been here about four months. I know we've been a bit tardy getting back to you with previous enquiries, but half the staff have been off with the flu thing and we've had two big robberies. Up to our eyes I'm afraid."

"I understand, but I could do with finding out about the Turner family. His mum committed suicide and the body of a male child has been discovered. We're trying to track down who he is. If we can get DNA from a close family member, maybe we can rule him out or confirm its Jordan."

"OK, seeing your name, and hoping this will stand me in your good books, I've done a quick bit of asking around. One of our lads hails from the Bucklebury area, and knew the family. Must be your lucky day, your favourite classmate finding out this info. It'll cost you."

"Haven't changed, Patrick. Chasing everything in a skirt. Come on, give me the details."

"OK, I've scanned and emailed copies of the files to you, and hopefully they'll prove useful. Apparently the Jordan family were a weird lot. Jordan's mum, Shenda Turner was unmarried, and a real nut case. Into drugs, seems her parents tended to care for the kid most of the time. When his mother was around, which wasn't often, she'd take him back. She lived in a council flat near her parents. The kid wasn't happy and he ran away a couple of times."

"But he was only seven, wasn't he?"

"Yes, I think that's what the file said. Anyway, he disappeared again about the time the nonces' operation was broken up, not all that successful for us in terms of arrests as I understand. So it was assumed, rightly or wrongly, the bastards had got him but nothing's been proved."

"Thanks for that. Any details on the grandparents?"

"Yep, let me read it. They were a Stan and Muriel Turner." At those word, something wintry cold and menacing crept up Meena's back. "Anyway, Meena, I hope that helps."

"That's great. Thanks a million."

"Like I said, it'll cost. How about that date you never would agree to when we were at college?"

"Patrick, if this info is as helpful as I think, I may well agree. You've emailed me with the details. Anything else while we're talking?"

"Let me look." Meena could hear Patrick breathing as he scanned the information. "Oh, yes. Might not be relevant. A cousin of the mother's lived at the grandparents address and also used to look after the kid. Jake Carter. Anyway, the whole family moved to your area; we don't have a current address."

"Jake Carter. Ok, haven't heard that one. I'm really grateful for you getting back to me so quickly, Patrick. We'll talk."

Meena hurriedly finished the conversation, because as grateful as she as with Patrick's prompt reply, she didn't want once again to be in a situation of continually fighting off his attentions as she had when they had attended police college.

"Who d'you say? That name. Jake Carter," said Freddy. Meena looked up, aware he was standing with the coffee cup in his hand.

"Yes, why, do you know him?"

"No, but..." Freddy frowned, lines appearing between his eyebrows. He muttered the name again, desperately trying to recall the qualm that hid itself away. The niggle, like a flasher, suddenly leapt out and revealed itself. "Christ, I know. He's a jogger. We met him in the park. He's the one told Luce she was being watched."

"But she wasn't. Well, not with sinister motive."

"No, you're right." Freddy stared at Meena, his mind whirling with possibilities. "Maybe if he was watching them watching her, he wouldn't necessarily know they were checking on Higgins and not Lucy."

Meena didn't reply. She stared back at Freddy. Her large eyes drilled into his. Sensing she was deliberating and not really looking at him he didn't feel discomforted. He didn't interrupt, allowing her mind to fit the puzzle together.

"So," she finally said. "We have Stan and Muriel Turner, the missing lad's grandparents...and with same names on the notes to Lucy. We have Jake who tells Lucy she's being watched. A person with the same name is the cousin of the mother of the missing Jordon. Three lots of body parts and a missing woman, Maria Grainger. Three plus one is four and those are the four arrested during the police operation when Jordan went missing. Dan could be right, retribution. But how did Lucy get into this situation?"

"Think about this," contributed Freddy. "How would he, Jake, know the couple were supposedly watching Lucy unless... maybe he was watching her and then spotted them doing the same? Now, supposedly he had his reasons, but unless he knows them, the watching couple I mean, and my experience with Luce is that joggers don't have time for seeing what others are about, they're too busy madly exercising, then..."

Meena came out of her contemplations. She looked at Freddy and muttered. "Because he was the one watching her! But why would he tell Lucy about Janet and Ron?"

Freddy shrugged. "Maybe to divert attention from what

was really going on? Lucy told me even after she found out about Janet and Ron, she still felt as though she was being watched." Freddy walked round the bedroom, his face a picture of misery. "I told her she was being paranoid, a daft bitch. Christ, it was a joke, but I could bite my stupid tongue out."

"Don't beat yourself up Freddy. From what I've seen, she considers you as her main protector in this world. If she went out with Higgins last Sunday, then she'll have taken him to the park. Someone must have seen something. If we can get a local paper, local TV station, to advertise the fact she's disappeared, someone will come out of the woodwork and have seen something. I'll see if we can get it authorised." She paused, recalling the strange conversation between DI Cole and Dan about Lucy being dropped from the suspect list. Knowing this was not public knowledge, she continued, "There may even be CCTV in the area. We'll check that too."

Freddy looked at her, all his normal confidence missing, his face almost childlike in its misery. "Really? You think that'll help?"

"Come on, we'll quickly recce the flat in case there's something that will help and give us a clue. Finding Mr Jake Carter will help for sure and that'll probably lead us to the infamous Stan and Muriel."

"And Lucy."

"Definitely Lucy... and Higgins."

Chapter 58

Adam was playing golf with his dad who kept hitting his ball into sand bunkers and despite wild swings, just couldn't get it out. They were both laughing; it was only a social game and the resultant score wouldn't matter. Suddenly his dad's watch started ringing, deafeningly loud and persistent. The noise went on and wouldn't stop.

Adam jerked awake, realising he had been dreaming. It was still dark. He struggled through heavy lids, still puffy with sleep, to see the electronic numbers on his clock. They read 01:30.

"Feck, who the hell's ringing my doorbell at this time?"

The meaning of his words hit home, and he jumped out of bed. Pulling on discarded pants and jeans dropped on the floor as he'd climbed into bed, he hurried downstairs. This early, he prayed the surveillance team were watchful. Carefully opening the front door and peering round he saw nobody. The ringing sounded again and he realised the noise was coming from the back door bell.

Trying to shake the sleepy feeling away; his silly mistake making him realise he wasn't truly awake and alert, and he needed to be. This time he begged God to be very, very kind and make the team very, very observant. Opening the door to a tall man Adam recognised him even though he'd never seen him before without his mask.

"You've got five minutes," said Hawk, pushing past Adam into the kitchen. "Anyone here besides you?"

"I told Tomas... I mean Brother Samson, I live with my mother."

Hawk leaned on the back door, arms crossed with an arrogant look on his face that Adam would like very much to slap off.

"Will she wake?" Adam shook his head to the question. "Five minutes, that's all."

Adam hurried up the stairs. He wasn't worried about the twins waking. He envied them their lack of anxiety about life and as long as they were in bed with their favourite toys, they were usually sound asleep within five minutes and a bomb blast couldn't rouse them. They had forgotten about their mother already, although mechanically quoting 'Mummy' if asked who the lady was smiling broadly in the photo that stood on the sideboard. Adam felt it was sad in one way, but also glad because their short memories protected them from the long term hurt of losing their mum at such a young age.

Putting on the trainers designed with a tracking device in the heel should the surveillance team lose him, he grabbed his leather bomber jacket and picked up the back pack of essentials he'd been warned to prepare for a speedy departure. From his top drawer he took a prepared note telling his mother not to worry, he'd only be gone two or three days, and only in what she felt was a dire emergency, phone the listed number. It was Dan Blake's mobile phone. He'd forgotten to leave the note when he'd gone missing before, and had been nagged something chronic on his return.

When selected for the undercover assignment, it was decided he didn't need to move house, as he might not manage to insinuate his way into the cell and it would have then been unnecessary upheaval for the children. His mother, a widow with no other family responsibilities back in the old country, had moved in with him just after Kathryn had died to care for the twins. The four of them had only recently moved into the house and consequently the neighbours didn't know he was a police officer. As the assignment was just underway, he had warned his mother to tell anyone who asked that he was a Civil Servant working locally at the Government Statistical Office.

He'd expected her to question his request, but perhaps because her husband had been in the Guardai in Ireland during the troubles, knowing the detriment of a loose tongue, she merely shrugged and murmured, "Men, more nuisance than they're worth', and had carried on stacking the 'devilish modern fangled dishwasher'. He noticed she never asked further questions and the dishwasher was in constant use.

As Adam tiptoed past the twin's bedroom he threw them a kiss, silently praying it wouldn't be too long before he saw them again. Hurrying into the kitchen, he didn't want Hawk poking his nose in any of the rooms; he was relieved to see him still leaning on the back door.

Without another word spoken, the men exited together by the back door, which Adam locked, slipping the key back through the cat flap, a relic from the previous owner. He expected them to take the back alley as they had previously but instead he followed Hawk round the side of his semi-detached house to the front. They turned to the left and walked into the corner shop car park where the same type of vehicle waited that had picked him up before. Adam noticed the registration plate was different now. He wondered if they had two similar cars or the plate changed purposely.

Delilah, also not masked, was the driver and when the men entered the car, she merely nodded at Hawk and ignored Adam. He knew she didn't like him and as a 'novice' he shouldn't be involved in their operation. The dislike was mutual, and Adam relished the moment when he could look into her eyes as he interviewed her after her arrest, and she would know the truth. When hate emitted like radioactive waves from her as she vainly tried to poison his person, he would smirk with glee into her face. Never before had Adam experienced such revulsion for another living soul. If evil was personified, it was her, every cell of her body radiated malevolence.

On the previous journey to his 'tea-party' Adam had been blindfolded, but he still knew they were travelling along a different route this time. They left the Caversham area, then travelling along the Oxford Road to Tilehurst. He was surprised when they drove into an area known for its large houses with well-kept gardens that the poorer folk from the council estate a mere mile away, referred to as the 'posh area'.

The Range Rover turned into a long drive lined both sides with trees, looking by their diminutive size as though recently planted. Driving towards, and then around the side of a large unlit house, they parked at the rear. On leaving the car, Adam attempted to check whether the houses were occupied on either side, but despite the time of year, dense garden foliage hid the view. A door opened, but no cone of light spilled out to light the path. Hawk pushed Adam through the door which was then bolted.

Someone switched on the lights, and the room was flooded with brightness causing all the newcomers to blink and frown before their sight adjusted. Adam, expression enigmatic, saw through a fuggy atmosphere seven people sitting round a well-scrubbed wooden table drinking coffee, and three were smoking. No-one was wearing a mask.

His eyes swept around the room, noting that three windows were covered with thick blinds. Someone ordered him to sit in the empty chair to the left of Excalibur. He nodded at Brother Samson and Dione who were the only ones to welcome him with a smile. The young girl, whose tender age had disquieted him at the previous meeting, walked over and placed a cup of coffee before him. Without her mask she looked even more like a schoolgirl.

The rich and dark aroma cleared his head and he was pleasantly surprised to see that it was as he preferred, black, strong. On tasting it, she had even added the requisite amount of sugar. He turned to thank her, but she was already leaving the room. Tomas, but now using his official cell title of Brother Samson, introduced some of the people sitting around the table to Adam as though he had never met them.

Stupid prick, does he really think the masks they wore previously hide who they were?

He smiled politely, again praying that his facial expression was at odds with his thoughts, and nodded politely at Dione, Excalibur, Wolfbane and Delilah. They nodded back except Delilah who continued to ignore him.

"We now welcome three newcomers to the group," said Brother. "Their area has been compromised so they now join our group."

Adam wanted to ask about the jeopardy but thought he'd better hold his tongue. No-one else asked the question so as the newcomer, he appreciated he'd have to be silent and listen. Having successfully penetrated this far into the cell, due mainly to the good luck of members being murdered, he didn't want now to arouse suspicion and undermine his position.

As though reading his thoughts, Tomas explained. "We have strong suspicions that Arthur James School are aware of our scrutiny." Adam's ears picked up. *That's the school that the infamous Genghis attended?* "So I now introduce our Brothers and Sister who were selected to target quarries from there. Garth, Argonaut and Mother Teresa."

After the introductions, Adam felt a hysterical urge to laugh at the stupidity of the situation.

If it wasn't so feckin' serious, I'd piss myself laughing. Talk about inappropriate names. These eejits are such pathetic tossers.

Adam studied the three in turn. Garth was a weedy looking man whose hairstyle doubled with Tomas's. They were both balding but chose to grown their hair from the side of their heads and sweep it over to cover their shining domes. *Do the wankers think we don't know they're bloody bald?* The only difference was, Tomas's hair was dark brown with a sprinkling of grey, and Garth's a light ginger.

Argonaut also bore no resemblance to the suggestion of his name. He was tall, anorexically thin with narrow round shoulders that gave the suggestion his body was going to collapse in on itself. His mottled skin was covered in craggy scars implying acne from an early age and supported Adam's silent deductions that he had an eating disorder. He hadn't even drunk his coffee.

Mother Teresa, however, was the one that tickled the crazy sense of humour for which Adam knew he was famous by his police colleagues. She was on the end of the spectrum when it came to brassy blondes. Her hair sported the much-backcombed look so popular in an earlier era. Its drooping spikes, lacquered into high and knotted fountains, were white blond with splitting ends and attached to blatant black roots. Her lipstick was crimson red and trickled into the sagging lines cornering her mouth. The eyes, heavily lidded and not expertly made up, were daubed with bright blue eye shadow, surrounded by lines that multiplied tenfold when she grimaced a smile.

Holy Mary, forgive me but they don't go overboard on attractive women. Delilah must be knocking forty and ugly as feckin' sin and Blondie's seventy if she's a day and even uglier.

Adam was on the verge of believing he was suffering from a total mental breakdown and forced into an institution, not for the insane, who couldn't help their illnesses, but with a load of crazies who should know better, when Brother Samson called the meeting to order and informed them of their teams.

Forcing himself to concentrate, the police officer focused on the task, needing to remember all the details of who was in which squad. He was not happy to hear he was with Hawk and Delilah. Excalibur was leading the group with Garth and

Mother Teresa whilst Wolfbane's team consisted of Argonaut and Dione.

The first two groups' positions were outside previously scrutinised schools at closing time as the pupils' day finished. The last group's location was in a park where a large tractor shed partially obscured the swings and roundabouts position and made it difficult to check on your child if you were less than vigilant. The mums used to congregate and chat on seats not well placed for supervision. The position was excellent for a fast get away into side streets that the team leader knew intimately.

Brother stood up, and in a pretentious voice that once again gave Adam the urge to smirk about the stupid pomp of the occasion, ordered them to retire to bed even for the short hours left of the night. Only the leaders knew the specific situations of the two schools, the park and final meeting venue once they had secured their prey.

The only privacy allowed was the bathroom so Adam took the opportunity to scribble the names of those in each team and their designated abduction sites in a minute notebook secreted away in a pocket within a pocket in his jacket.

He was rooming with Hawk and Garth. Obviously not troubled with conscience, their heavy breathing indicted they were soon asleep. Adam stayed wide wake for what seemed hours. He prayed, most unusually as he had lost his faith, for his children and his mam's health and safety, for Kathryn's soul and that the surveillance team were doing their jobs conscientiously and with great skill.

The team's been building towards this moment for many months, so my last prayer to anyone who'll listen is for the success of this operation. Should I survive, then the bastards get apprehended, and not one child's life is lost. Amen.

Chapter 59

A piercing scream stabbed through the air like a knife, the echo filling the house with a juddering discord.

"Frigging hell, what's going on now?" said Maria, a cup of tea half way to her mouth.

"Sounds like someone has really hurt themselves," said Lucy. For a change, Higgins was in the room with her and the noise caused him to push even closer to his mistress, whine and put his head on her lap for a comforting stroke.

The three of them had returned from the small dining room where everyone had eaten breakfast. When Lucy had first sat down at the table she thought she wasn't hungry, but she had quickly downed the poached eggs on toast and thoroughly enjoyed it. Even Higgins who Lucy had heard whining from the kitchen during the night, wolfed down his dog biscuits.

Maria, as usual, had her hands strapped down to the armchair sides but they both noticed her ankles hadn't been secured. They had just whispered this may be a good sign when the screech had startled them.

"Well, if they have, that's a bloody good job then." Maria sneered as she spoke. "All the evil things they've done, I hope Stan's chopped off Muriel's head, Jake's dick, for your sake, and then his own hands."

The words were injected with venom but Lucy couldn't

help chortling. From the details Maria had given her when they had the opportunity to talk, though she hadn't suffered quite the physical torture of the other victims, the mental agony inflicted must have been dreadful. Before she could comment further, loud words, hysterical crying and shrieking emanated from the kitchen. Both women strained their ears to hear exactly what had occurred. Although the sound had enough decibels to clearly enter the room, the screaming interruptions of the hysterical conversations produced a disharmony that was undecipherable.

"I do believe Jake's eaten Stan's sweets and fucked his aunt. Things are not happy, I'm glad to say."

Again Maria's sarcasm, against Lucy's better wishes and the situation, caused her to grin.

"Like some higher deity producing a rewarding pay-back, is it?" said Lucy.

"You bet. Still, while they're playing happy families... not," Maria added, "You might as well start cutting the straps. This may well be our best chance and should we get lucky and finish the job, Higgins is with us. We can piss off before they stop their bloody wailing."

"Good thinking." Lucy retrieved the knife from her sock and got to cutting the leather but only a few minutes into the job, it became obvious that the knife was quickly becoming blunt and was no match for the task.

"Shit," was Maria's comment. She couldn't see any real progress despite Lucy's efforts.

"If only I had a knife sharpener I could keep honing it." She carried on using the knife, but the cutting had just become rubbing and her hands ached with the effort. "No good. Hey, they're going upstairs aren't they?"

The women listened as they heard the sound of footsteps on the stairs.

"I'll wait a minute and slip into the kitchen and root around in the dresser drawers. I bet there's a sharpener in there."

She listened at the door and when silence had settled through the house for a few minutes she slipped out of the room. Within minutes she was back in the room.

"Got it?" said Maria needlessly as Lucy showed her the required object and a spoon. "They all upstairs then?"

Lucy set about sharpening the knife before speaking.

"Actually no. Jake's in the kitchen, eyes very red and swollen. Whatever's happened is big time. I just sweetly asked him if he was OK. He just nodded. So I said I'd come for a teaspoon. He even pointed to the drawer. In the front section was the sharpener, so I took that and the spoon which I showed him as I walked past, head down as though I was being sensitive to his feelings and could see he wanted to be alone."

"Good girl. If I get free I'm going to strangle that Muriel."

"Maria, if I get you free, we're running for our lives, final."

"Yeah, well, maybe."

An hour passed but no-one came into the room. By this time, Lucy had managed to almost cut through one of the straps and with a last tug when she slipped her hand underneath, it broke.

Hearing more footsteps going upstairs, they presumed it was Jake. Mumbled conversation filtered from the bedrooms, although the hysteria seemed to have gone. The women were still on their own, so Lucy, although now having to hone the knife more and more frequently, proceeded with cutting the second strap. Her hand was sore with the effort and she was experiencing painful cramps, but knew if they were to escape, it was now or never.

"Oh, thank God for that," said Maria, rubbing the circulation back into her wrists as Lucy finally cut through the last piece of resisting leather.

"Blast, someone's coming," whispered Lucy as heavy footsteps could be heard coming down the stairs. Maria stood up but Lucy pushed her down, hissing. "Stay down.

The straps might not be noticed. Put your arms back where they were."

Just as Maria thumped back down on the chair and re-positioned her arms, Jake, eyes still red and face puffy with crying, came into the room. Carrying a newspaper, he walked to a chair and sat down.

"I should explain. You've obviously heard the... noise."

"Yes," said Lucy, glaring at Maria not to draw attention to herself with sarcastic remarks. Lacing her voice with sympathy, Lucy continued. "I hope no-one hurt themselves too badly or anything?"

Jake just shook his head and held up the paper.

"No doubt Maria has explained why she was kidnapped. My cousin's son disappeared some years ago. Four people, including Maria were arrested, suspected of being involved in a paedophile ring."

"It was all lies," Maria protested.

Jake continued as though she hadn't spoken. "They were let off on a technicality. It broke our hearts. Jordan gone, abducted or murdered, and they get away with it. His body has never been found, and eventually his mum decides she can't take the anguish anymore and commits suicide. Again, the family suffering was terrible. So we decided to dish out our own justice and at the same time perhaps locate where Jordan, or if we faced reality, where his body was.

"The first two people we captured swore they didn't know, but we knew they did so they paid the price. Despite extensive searching, we couldn't locate the fourth person. When we got Maria she confirmed Bates probably would know the answers we needed, and helped us to find him. Unfortunately he died so our progress came to a halt."

Lucy felt an urge to say although she could pity them for their suffering and grief it did not give them the right to torture and kill anyone. However, knowing she wasn't dealing with rational people, forced herself to continue with sympathetic nodding and not speak. Jake held up the paper and turned it so the front page faced them. There was a photograph of a young boy with large headlines that proclaimed. 'Jordan's body found.'

Jake wiped his eyes as tears spilled from them and continued to explain. "The paper has published a report from the police. After examining the area where his body was found, the pathologist's report strongly points to the fact Jordan wasn't abducted. He ran away. A small case containing his clothes was found near the body and inside a note he'd written to his mum but never posted."

"And you bloody murdered three people for nothing, you bastards," hissed Maria.

Lucy put a restraining hand on her arm. "Poor child. Do they know what he did die from?"

"Hypothermia, probably an asthma attack as well. He'd wrapped himself in some tarpaulin, maybe dumped by someone in the woods. It wasn't enough to keep out the cold. He had terrible asthma. The day he went missing the temperature plummeted. Maybe he got lost, laid down to sleep and..." Jake bowed his head. "Unfortunately, they think where he'd laid down was over some sort of old pit and then tumbled in. Whether he was already dead or whether he couldn't get out isn't clear although there were no sign he'd attempted to scramble out."

Maria stood up and although Jake looked up at her, seemed unaware that she was now free from her bonds,

"Well, I'm going. You and sodding Stan and Muriel should be ashamed of yourselves. Murdering three people. Come on, Lucy, let's split."

The last sentence seemed to shake Jake out of his gloom. He looked at Lucy.

"No, darling, you can't leave. Not now, I need you even more now. We made a suicide pact, my aunt, uncle and me. We'd decided when we eventually found Jordan's body and he was properly buried, we'd all go together. Stan and Muriel have gone upstairs but I can't do that now. They want me to claim Jordon's body and bury him properly. Now I've got you so I don't want to die." Standing up, he walked to Lucy and pulled her to him.

"You fucking idiot, she doesn't love you," Maria shouted with frustration. "Don't you understand, it's all in your mind? She doesn't even know you, you stupid obsessed tosser."

With that, Maria marched to the door, flung it open and left. Lucy struggled to free herself but Jake's obsession made him strong. Higgins whined, realising his mistress was distressed, but it wasn't in his nature to attack. Lucy, now desperate and seeing freedom slip through her fingers, wriggled but couldn't free herself and her companion Maria, her last hope, was gone.

Still wrestling to free herself from Jake's embrace, she jumped when she heard a frustrated yell.

"Jake, you stupid shit," Maria screamed from the doorway, "for fuck's sake wake up. She doesn't bloody want you." She strode into the room, pulled Jake's head back by his hair and punched him straight on the nose.

As he fell back onto the sofa holding a nose streaming with blood, Maria grabbed Lucy's hand, yelling, "Now, come on, for God's sake. Higgins, you bloody come too."

As the three of them tumbled through the front door, Lucy, still hobbling slightly from her twisted ankle, shook her hand free from Maria's, whispering, "I can't go. I can't leave them."

Maria turned round, hands on hips. "You stupid cow, why the fuck not?"

"Jake said they went upstairs, maybe to commit suicide? If they've taken tablets, and we get them to the hospital on time, we can save them."

"Good. I hope they die and go to hell. You do the Saint Lucy bit. I'm going home, packing and going to get the first plane to my sister in Spain. I knew I shouldn't have come back." With that, she turned on her heels and hurried along the garden path.

"Maria, my mobile's dead. Phone for an ambulance and the police as soon as you can, please."

Maria turned and looked over her shoulder, shaking her head.

"Stubborn bitch. Phone 999. Jesus H Christ, I must be going soft in my old age."

"Thanks, mate. Look at the road sign for the name of the road." Lucy called out, turning to go back into the house.

Chapter 60

Hawk passed two photos to Adam. One was of a boy about six or seven. His fair hair was cut badly and the police officer suspected his mum had chopped at it. The boy's grin was plastered across his little face and showed a gap where one of his front baby teeth had fallen out. He was looking over his shoulder at something.

"Who took this?" he asked Hawk.

"Me. Couple of weeks ago. Why?"

He studied the top photo before he spoke. "No reason. Just wondered how recent it was." Bringing the bottom photo to the top, his stomach turned when he saw it was a girl, a similar age to the boy. Having twin girls made him super sensitive to the more vulnerable sex although sense dictated at this tender age, boys were at equal risk from predators such as the bastard he sat next to.

He forced his hands not to tremble from anguish and anger as he scrutinised the image. The child was skipping. The rope was over her head and her feet suspended in mid-air. Her blue and white checked school dress was short and the legs beneath looked painfully thin. She was laughing and it appeared as though she was posing because she was looking straight at the camera. Adam's heart hurt as he thought about how she might suffer if he wasn't here now. Hopefully his presence would prevent anything happening to her.

It made all his efforts of creeping round the disgusting Tomas, and the hours he had been forced to act as though he were as vile and base as the cell members, all worthwhile. Revenge was going to be very sweet, he could almost taste it. It was like sugar from a doughnut pasting his lips, making it impossible not to lick them. Hawk, closely watching his scrutinising, misunderstood his action.

"Oh, getting eager are we. Won't be long now," he said to Adam.

"Why these two?" he asked Hawk, eager to take the beast's attention away from his face in case he was unable to control his disgust, and it slipped unbidden onto his face.

"Why not? Why are you here if you don't like it?"

Adam shrugged, sensing Hawk's animosity. Both he and Delilah were as unpredictable and volatile as each other. Maybe the prospects of this operation, besides being thrilling, was also making them nervous. Delilah was sitting in the driving seat and ignoring the two men behind her.

"I never said I didn't like it. How am I to learn if I don't understand the thinking and planning as to why certain schools and kids've been selected."

"We select schools because everyone is so concerned with keeping kids safe, they think this is the last place we'd be. Right under their bloody noses. We've been vetting various schools for some time. Some are better than others."

"Better? In what way?"

"Position mainly. This one for instance doesn't have any surveillance cameras in this street. Some schools allow a good view. For instance, the private school in Caversham was useless. The kids came out the back of the school so we never had a good view. The mums always pick them up in cars. This one's the best for this area. Good views. We can observe them without being seen. Also it's in a poor area. The mums probably work because there's always a few that are late. Then you find some teachers are more vigilant than others."

"Right. And these two then? Mums usually late and teachers not so vigilant?"

"Yep. The boy's teacher's a dodo. The kid's mother's always late. He goes and plays in the bicycle shed or round the side of the school where he can't be seen."

"And the girl?

"Sometimes her mother doesn't turn up at all. She comes out of the class and points as though her mum's just coming through the gates. The teacher lets her go. She wanders home on her own mostly."

"So how do we do this? Do the kids know you?"

"Yes, I've spoken to both of them. Made out I was a replacement teacher. Kids at that age never argue with adults. The boy'll be no problem. I've a toy car he wants. When we get him to the car, looking at the toy just held out of reach so he reaches in, we heave him in, put the pad over his face and he's out for the count and no trouble. Then we follow the girl. Her mother never meets her on Mondays, ever. We wait until she turns into South Street. I'll have her in the car before she knows what's hit her."

The school bell announcing the end of the day rang out. Adam looked in the side mirror. He could see nothing to indicate that the surveillance team were in position. That meant either they were doing an excellent job and were invisible or they had lost him. Although he had the tracking device in his trainers and it was a supposedly state of the art design, Adam didn't have great faith in electronics. He preferred good old-fashioned police work. He felt on his own, whatever happened would be just down to his efforts. He wasn't afraid; he couldn't wait for the action. His repugnance of these people would make him strong.

Adam glanced sideways at Hawk. He was no more than sixty and looked fit and wiry as though he worked out. Adam marveled how he had disguised himself. No-one would recognize him as the smart ex-MP in his usual business suit. His hair had been dyed black and he wore thick rimmed glasses.

Probably has cut rate fees at Tomas's gym although I've never eyeballed him. Well spoken, obviously educated. What the feck does he want with kids? If I passed him on the street, I wouldn't give him a second glance.

Looking away from him in case his loathing for this man and all he represented showed, Adam knew when the time came; his feelings would make him powerful. He visualised putting his hands round the bastard's throat, slowly squeezing the evil life from him. He could visualise those eyes bulging and fearful.

Maybe I'm the wrong man for this job. I'm getting personal, too involved in the wrong way. Too late now, stick with it. Keep detached, keep focused.

Hawk interrupted his thoughts.

"There he is. See him? He's talking to two little boys with blazers on. On the right side of the playground. They're just leaving with their mums. See where I mean?"

"Yeah. He's just gone over to the bike shed, like you said."

"Ok. Stay here. I'll go for him."

Hawk left the car and walked casually over the road and through the school gate. He carried a brief case and a book tucked under his arm. Stopping and looking in one of the books as though, to a casual observer as if was checking some detail, but Adam knew he was actually surveying the area. In a perverse way he admired his acting. The man was totally in character and the police officer realised to the milling parents he was 'invisible' and they weren't giving him a second glance.

Amongst the confusion of parents, he nonchalantly wandered to the child who was crouching down as though looking at something on the bike shed floor. As Hawk arrived by his side, the boy glanced up and then pointed at something. The man bent down next to the boy and scrutinised it too, behaving like an interested teacher or parent.

After a few moments of scrutiny, they both stood up, and Adam could see them laughing together. Hawk then opened the book and showed the boy something. He gazed with great interest and then clapped his hands and grinned, and Adam could feel the hurt coiling like a snake round his heart and once again thanked God he was present.

The pair started to walk together towards the car. Hawk held out his hand and the innocent took it. He was looking up, gazing adoringly at the man who was smiling back. Chatting to the child as though he was his child whom he had met him from school, the pair walked unhurriedly to the car.

For a second Adam felt relief as he thought he glimpsed a woman resembling Meena but a swirl of parents blocked his view. Then Hawk and his prey reached the vehicle, forcing Adam to focus on them.

Delilah, silent through the whole of this episode, started the engine as Hawk opened the door and pointed to the red toy car lying enticingly on the back seat.

"There it is. Just waiting for you. It's my son's but he's outgrown it and he doesn't want it any more. He said you could have it. Can you reach it?"

The boy reached in and before he could utter a sound was deftly lifted from behind and sprawled onto the seat. Hawk pushed in beside him and the pad was over the child's face as soon as the door closed. The windows were dark. It happened so quickly, no-one noticed anything was amiss.

Delilah put the automatic into drive and the car glided away. Just a man picking up his son from school. She didn't rush, everything was in order, and the plan was falling into place.

Adam looked at the boy beside him, his stomach churning as though full of bubbling lava. The boy's struggles were already waning and as he drifted into unconsciousness. Adam took a deep breath to control the volcanic eruption and casually glanced behind him.

"What's wrong? What are you looking at?" Delilah

snapped. She had seen his action in the rear view mirror.

"Nothing. Just checking," he said. *Shit, where are they?* He heard a thump as Hawk pushed the boy's limp body onto the floor and hurt and fury, in equal amounts, raced around Adam's body.

Chapter 61

Freddy was with a client when he heard his mobile ring from inside his jacket pocket hanging on a clothes peg situated just outside the treatment room. He ignored it, the man was lying on his back, and Freddy had straightened and pulled his leg, trying to ease the pain in the man's back. Asking the man to turn over, he began to massage his lower back when the phone rang again.

Ignoring it once more, but now feeling slightly uneasy about its persistence, he still didn't answer it. Having finished the massage and then applied the electrodes from the deep massage tens machine to the customer's lower spine before adjusting the controls, he couldn't resist collecting the mobile when it rang a third time.

"Comfortable with that strength?" he verified to his client. Without waiting for the man's confirmation, Freddy answered the machine.

He almost dropped the phone in amazement when Lucy said, "Hi, Hon, it's me."

"What do you mean, Hi, Hon, it's me. You've been missing four days, now you phone me like you've been on bloody holiday."

"Hmm, you're obviously pleased to hear from me then. Didn't miss me a bit by the sound of it."

"I've been going out of my mind worrying about you.

What the hell happened? Where are you? I can't believe... "

"Listen, take it easy, that's what I'm phoning about. Do you think you can come and pick me up?"

"Bloody sodding hell! Take it easy she says. I've been going out of my mind. Pick you up, course I can, where in God's name are you?"

"Oh, that's a point, I don't know the actual address. Hang on, there's a letter on the telephone table, let me go and look." Freddy heard footsteps as Lucy walked away. "OK, got it. It's 'The Farm Cottage', 2 Orchard Farm Road, Pangbourne, RG... can't read the postcode. It's literally five, ten minutes away, turning of the main road to school. Anyway, there are only two cottages in the whole road."

"Never mind, I'll find it. You OK? I've been going bloody loco."

"I'm fine, sort of. I'll tell you everything when... oh, got to go, the ambulance has just arrived. Oh, and the law. Good old Marie, she must have phoned and told them. See you soon."

With that, Lucy put the phone down and Freddy's emotions turned from relief to annoyance, similar to a parent's reaction when a missing child suddenly appears, sucking a lolly and completely unaware of their frantic feelings.

Freddy walked back into the treatment room and pulled on his tracksuit.

"These pulses are a bit strong," bleated his client.

"Turn the fucking machine down then," he said as he strode from the room.

It took Freddy twenty minutes to arrive at the country road and he couldn't believe Lucy had been so near when during his sleepless nights his imagination had convinced him she'd been abducted by Eastern Block pimps, and was ensconced in a brothel in Tajikistan or somewhere equally remote.

In his haste, as he skidded on two wheels into the country

road he almost hit a policeman who was setting down traffic cones across the road.

"Sorry, sir," said the young policeman wearing a helmet that looked two sizes too big and in Freddy's estimate looking about fourteen years old. "There has been an incident. I'm placing diversion sign at the end of the road. Where do you want to get to?"

"I'm heading for one of those cottages. Looks as though most of your cavalry have beaten me to it."

"Do you live there, sir?" The man was taking a notebook and a radio from his top uniform pocket.

"No, a girl friend of mine whose been missing for four days, has just phoned and asked me to come get her."

"Can I ask your name, sir?"

"Freddy Heath."

"And your address?"

"Oh for God's sake, I only want to pick Lucy up. I've already reported her missing to your lot and they've done sod all about it as far as I can tell . Phone someone important and check. DS Dan Blake. He knows Lucy's and me."

"I will, sir but I'd still be grateful for your address."

Freddy told him through grated teeth, fuming whilst the police-child checked on his radio. After three minutes, Freddy had timed him in seconds on his wristwatch, the officer lifted enough cones for Freddy to ease through, telling him to draw up behind the first police car on the left of the road and wait in his car.

Eventually, another policeman, this one looking no older than nineteen, strolled over from his position by the garden gate and asked Freddy to wait for a few more minutes.

Again Freddy fumed as the few minutes turned to thirty and still no Lucy appeared. Eventually, his patience now worn to a frazzle, he jumped from the car ready to do battle, when two ambulance men carrying a stretcher appeared from the house and placed it into one of the two ambulances directly outside the house between the three police cars.

Freddy couldn't glimpse who was on the stretcher. His stress caused his imagination to leap into overdrive and as the ambulance zoomed off, siren wailing, all Freddy's hopes dissolved that he'd been in time to save Lucy from an attack by predators, and the jolt in his heart was painful.

He was so involved in his hurt and grief, the arms slipping round his waist and the kiss on the cheek took him totally by surprise.

"Thanks for coming, Fred." Lucy tucked her head into his chest. "That was Stan they've just taken away. He's still unconscious but still breathing. I was too late to save Muriel, she's just died."

With that, Lucy broke down and sobbed uncontrollably, the tears and strain from the last four days breaking forth like a broken dam. Higgins, leaning against Lucy, whined and pawed her, trying to comfort his mistress.

Chapter 62

Dan sat with Meena in the front of a navy blue Honda Civic, training his binoculars on the activity of the Range Rover they were trailing. The vehicle had now stopped just passed the school gates in the parents' parking zone. The windows were dark so the passengers couldn't be counted although the tracking sensor confirmed Adam was in the car.

"See anything, Boss?" Meena asked needlessly for the third time.

"No. Can't you see anything from where you're sitting?"

"Yes but... oh, someone's left the car."

"Tall guy, dressed in brown, heading into the school like he owns the place. Hell, he's got some cheek. Check with the others whether they eyeball him."

Dan watched as the tall man casually made his way into the school. He wore brown cords and a smart darker brown leather bomber jacket carrying a brief case with a book tucked under his arm.

"You getting him?" Dan asked the police photographer who sat behind him.

The photographer shuffled over the other side of the car to get a clearer view.

Yep." Mike Barron tended to speak in monosyllables so Dan didn't question him further. The shots he obtained would be top class.

"Shall I take a stroll into the playground yet, boss?" said Meena, getting out of the car when Dan nodded. He watched as she strolled towards the playground, knowing she would blend in perfectly as a parent. Wearing blue jeans, a short navy blue coat and heavy soled boots, no-one would suspect she was a police officer. Normally she tied her hair back in a severe bun but now it was hanging loose, reaching almost to her waist, and as she walked it swayed like a meandering river of gleaming black oil. As she disappeared into the school playground, Dan, via his walkie-talkie, spoke to Luke positioned outside the classrooms as though he was a father waiting for his child.

"See anything Luke? Suspect just left his car and should be in the playground now. Tall, dark hair, dressed in brown, brief case..."

"Got him. He's walking over to the bike shed and I think I see his prey now. Little kid bending down and looking at something. Mike, he getting clear shots?"

"Yes. Got a good view. Meena's in the playground now."

The surveillance team watched as the predator talked to the child and then walked with him towards the Range Rover. Despite their capabilities of being able to easily communicate with each other, all the police officers involved in the operation were speechless with the ease with which the child was lured into the vehicle.

"OK, pick them up," Dan shouted to two other police vehicles sited at either end of the school road. The original plan had been to follow the vehicle back to its base but with a boy on board, despite Adam's presence, the child's safety was in jeopardy and his well-bring was paramount. Meena was still on the other side of the playground and too far away to apprehend the suspect.

As Dan pulled away, a parent who had parked in the area reserved for the teaching staff, decided at that moment to pull out of the school in front of him and then stall her car. Traffic was flowing in the other direction and Dan fumed as he watched the Range Rover pull away and disappear round a corner.

Frantically contacting other police cars, he felt relieved when they both reported they had the vehicle in sight. Frustration then erupted from both drivers when they hit red traffic lights despite coming from different directions and the heavy traffic completely blocking the road and halting all progress. The Range Rover had slipped through the green lights in time and had disappeared.

"OK, don't use sirens," Dan barked. "That'll warn them. Back to the original plan, we pick them up via the tracking device and follow. I don't want to get into a race with the child in their vehicle. Nothing can happen whilst they're moving and an undercover office is present."

Dan listened into his earpiece as the car's direction was relayed to him and the other drivers from the tracking centre.

"OK, got the direction. They've halted on South Street, north of the school but they're moving again now. They've turned east along Caversham Road towards the ring road. Follow at a distance. I'll wait for my two officers from the school," whom he could see hurrying towards the car.

"Take off as soon as you can. We'll be right behind you."

Chapter 63

Freddy made Lucy her second cup of tea since arriving back at her flat. Having been questioned for two hours at the house in Pangbourne, she then agreed to go to the police station for further questioning. It was now six o' clock in the evening and Lucy was exhausted. He had insisted she sit on her sofa and let him wait on her.

"Did you worry about me?" she asked, relieved to be safely home and grateful for her friend's unusual behaviour. Normally Lucy handed out the tea and sympathy. Although she knew Freddy loved her as a sister, he still hid his true feelings with his sardonic wit that sashayed into a sense of humour some might consider acerbic unless you knew him well.

"Not a bit, I'm dead broke and thought if you'd gone for good, who the hell would help me out with the mortgage?" he said, putting the tea cup into her hand and placing a plate with a large slice of lardy cake on the coffee table within easy reach.

"What about Peter? Wouldn't he have helped you out," replied Lucy, glad to play the game and take her mind off the last four days.

"No, he's worse off than me. Tell me what happened then, after he picked you up in the park."

She explained at length all that had happened, finishing

with Maria leaving and explaining she felt unable to flee in case Stan and Muriel had decided to end it all. If she stayed perhaps she could stop or save them if they'd started to put their suicide plan into action.

"You are decidedly mad. Why the hell didn't you leave with this Maria person and call the ambulance once you were safe and clear of the house?"

"It might have been too late then. As it was, it was too late for Muriel."

"Yes, but after all they'd done to you. Left those body parts, nearly scaring you to death. Then taking you captive. They deserve all they got in my opinion."

"You can't blame them. Firstly they have been going out of their mind following their grandson's disappearance and then their daughter's suicide. They were desperate to find either Jordon or at least his body. All three had made a suicide pact some time ago. Then I think it changed when, for whatever reason, Jake got obsessed with me."

"I notice the sod never topped himself. Now he's skipped it, leaving his aunt and uncle to take the punishment if they'd been rescued in time. Great nephew he turned into."

"Stan and Muriel were fine with me. I wasn't threatened by them at all. They really did believe that I was involved with Jake. I wasn't tied down like Maria, but just to make sure I didn't leave, Jake never left Higgins alone with me until that last time. He knew I wouldn't leave without my dog."

"It still was a crap thing to do, leave the body parts outside your door and sign their names."

"I don't think they did that. Right from the beginning I think it was Jake. I reckon he'd dumped the first lot of body parts in the wood, and when I found them, he saw me and decided in his twisted way that it was fate... and the other stuff, more body parts, that was a way of getting my attention."

"Creepy weirdo. How did he come to that conclusion?"

"You're trying to rationalise somebody's actions who's obviously not rational. The whole family are obviously totally barmy. After all, revenge or not, no-one in their right mind would torture people and then chop up the bodies. Maria said they were as nutty as the proverbial fruit cake. They kept the heads of two of the men, then used them... like two gory hand puppets, according to Maria."

Lucy tucked the legs under her on the sofa, and pulled a cushion to her chest. Shaking her head, she continued,

"Still, we shouldn't judge. They were heartbroken and grief-stricken with losing Jordon. Unfortunately for the two men, their photographs appeared in the news just as the lad went missing with the news media vocally drawing their own conclusions that the men were involved, but with no proof, the police forced to release them. That made them guilty in Stan and Muriel's eyes, so they decided to track them down, determined they should tell them where the lad's body was."

"You're too bloody forgiving. They still signed those notes and put the fear of God into you."

"The more I think of it, the more I think they didn't do that either. I reckon Jake wrote those notes. Again, in his own crazy way he was getting my attention."

"Not very nice of him, adding their names. I notice he didn't draw attention to himself. He might be barmy but he's not daft. Still I guess he didn't want to spoil his marriage plans."

"Oh, don't say that." Lucy shivered. "I wonder what happened to Maria? She kept her word and did phone for an ambulance."

"I wouldn't have thought she'd have phoned the police."

"Maybe they automatically come too if there's a potential suicide. She said she was going to catch the earliest plane possible; go and live in Spain with her sister."

"I don't suppose it'll take the police long to track her down. She'll need to be questioned. Still, it's not her that worries me."

336

"What do you mean?"

"It's that loony Jake who's legged it. That's dodgy. I dread to think of what might have happened to you in the park that night I wasn't there."

"Makes me wonder why he pointed out Janet and Ron. He noticed them watching me, but I wonder why he told me?"

"Now you're trying to rationalise. He'd probably noticed them watching you, and that gave him an excuse to talk to you. Probably once you had that conversation, in his quirky brain, he thought you fancied him and got to thinking you were a couple."

"Don't keep talking like that, it gives me the collywobbles. He told me he got into conversation with them, and they told him what they were actually doing. He just lied to me."

"Crazy loon. Don't worry, till he's caught, I'm not letting you out of my sight."

"Dear Freddy, you do love me."

"Listen, I'm protecting my benefactor. Anyway, you're not going back to school till you're over this. It's almost the weekend, what would you like to do?"

"I can't run yet. The ankle's still twingy. I'd love to go the gym for an hour or so tomorrow. It seems months since I've worked out."

"Shit, I thought you were going to say we'd sit in and chill out."

"Lazy! Still, if you're going to keep an eye on me, you'll have to come too. I think even in the few days since I've not been here to keep an eye on you, the waist looks as though it's thickening up again."

"Aah, it's Pete's cooking! That reminds me, there'll be a homemade chicken pie in my flat. He promised he'd cook it for me before he went to work. Fancy some?"

"You bet." She stroked Higgin's soft velvety head lying across her lap. He hadn't left her side since they'd got home. Bending down and kissing him, she said, "And if you're a good boy, you can have some too."

"Not any of mine he can't," said Freddy, back to his normal self. He heard Lucy giggled at his remark and inwardly he smiled contently, thrilled his best friend was safe at home.

Chapter 64

"Not so fast. Turn right here. Pull into that space where the green car's pulling out. That's Brother Samson. He's saving our space. He'll wait further on down the road till he sees we've got the girl and nothing's gone wrong," said Hawk.

Delilah pulled into the space. Adam couldn't believe they weren't fleeing as fast as possible. They were taking a huge chance snatching one child and now after another! He decided the research they'd done before hand plus their meticulous plans lulled them into believing they were well prepared experts.

Still can't get over how feckin' full of themselves they are. Their stupid code names, drinking tea from bloody china cups. Holy Mary, they think they're invincible. Can't wait to see their faces when they're questioned. It'll be the best day of my life.

"She's coming." At Hawk's words, Adam looked over his shoulder. The second victim was skipping down the road. "Damn, she's with someone. Drive away."

As Delilah drove away Adam knew there was a God up there after all.

The woman slowed and took the next left into a side street. "OK, I get out here. You," she snapped at Adam, "come and take over the driving."

Adam watched as she ran along the road, got into the

green car which sped away.

"Which way," he asked Hawk. "Do I follow them?"

"No, straight ahead to the roundabout, straight over and then follow the A4 out of town. Don't speed. We don't want the law stopping us."

As ordered, Adam drove along the Bath Road heading towards Newbury. Eventually he was directed left into the Aldermaston turn-off and then to follow the winding country road for a couple of miles.

Checking constantly in his rear view mirror, he couldn't spot any vehicle belonging to the surveillance team. He'd noticed a Honda following for some time but he couldn't see it now. Spotting a motorbike his hopes rose that they were being followed, but as Hawk ordered him to turn right into a narrow lane, the bike shot past.

Driving on for half a mile, the lane petered out and became a muddy drive leading to an isolated house. It was old, covered in ivy, and the badly chipped bricks suggested it had had seen better days. Wolfbane's was climbing from another car as though he had just arrived. Argonaut was lifting another child's drooping body from the back seat.

"Stop here," Hawk ordered.

Adam wanted to snap back that there wasn't any further they could go but knew he must be patient. The moment the car had halted, Hawk clambered out and lifted the lad carefully out. His limp body hung like a broken scarecrow over his arms.

"Mustn't damage the goods," he said, smiling for the first time.

The happy look was wiped from his face as three cars and two motorbikes swung into view and surrounded the tableau of the four men and the unconscious children.

Chapter 65

When Sharon recalled that day, she realised fate had taken a monstrous hand in her life. Never previously given destiny a second thought, by the end of that special day, she knew for certain that providence shaped your choices and your life.

She and Stuart had made the decision to quit their present life for good. As she had predicted, her girl friend who had retired from the game after meeting her present boyfriend, had kindly accommodated them up in her small flat for the past week, until events had quietened down. During this time they decided to peruse a map of England, decide on a place-name that took their fancy, catch a train and just go!

They both now felt very positive about life in general and their future. Having rescued the young boy and then read in the paper the 'rescuers' were classed as 'shy heroes' by the young boy's guardians, they felt ready to tackle a new life.

Hearing on the television news that the priest, Father Quigley, had been discovered, taken to a local hospital and although badly beaten, was making good progress had relieved Stuart's conscience. The newspapers had a field day speculating about why a 'holy man' was in an area well known to be the meeting places for picking up rent boys.

Sharon had phoned the police with an anonymous tip giving her late address where the young boy had been held captive. She knew the lad wouldn't be able to lead the police to Winston's address and didn't want the bastards to escape. In her opinion, being a pimp was in a whole different league to abducting kids, and she wanted the sod to pay for his deed.

Lounging about in a local supermarket that sold cheap books as well as food, they were in no hurry. They'd scraped enough money together to buy some basic clothes as Sharon's clothes, in their hurry to run, had been left at her flat, and with the police swarming all over the place, there they would have to stay. She was glad that there was nothing in the flat to identify her.

Enjoying the luxury of just wandering around, idly looking at paperbacks to read on the journey, Sharon felt as though a huge weight had gone from her shoulders despite the fact they had virtually no money. Having discovered they were both avid readers, they decided, despite the dwindling supply of cash, to treat themselves to two cheap paperbacks for the train journey to their new future. Trying to decide which type to select, so they could swap books and still enjoy the other story, was proving difficult. Their tastes were different. Stuart liked science fiction and fantasy whilst Sharon preferred romance and historical novels.

Sharon, mind totally focused on reading the front cover of a Cecelia Ahern novel and trying to assess whether Stuart would enjoy her favourite author, froze in her tracks by a familiar child's voice.

"Hello, Mrs Lady,"

"Holy shite," she muttered and ramming her face into the book, started to back away.

The 'voice' followed and pulled at her jumper. "Hello, lady," it insisted.

"Go away," she hissed. The owner of the voice tapped her in the stomach. Peering over the top of the book, her heart pounding, she prayed for a humungous miracle but it appeared her prayers weren't being listened to. The child, more insistent and now poking her very firmly, carried on talking.

"Who're you talking to, darling? I told you not to leave my side," a cross woman's voice said.

I think I'm going to faint, Sharon thought.

Stuart, totally unaware of her predicament, wandered back along the aisle to show her his preference in reading, and speaking in a loud enough voice that Sharon just knew was going to draw even more attention from the persistent kid.

"This is good. You'll like this one."

She knew he then noticed the child because she clearly heard, even from her position of face firmly pressed against the first chapter, a strangled, "Oh, friggin' hell."

From this limited view beneath the book, Sharon peered down and saw a woman's hand reach out and take the child's hand. "Come on, darling, we've got to go home."

"That's them, Nanny."

"What?" The woman's words, sounding as though they were coated with the hardest steel, tempered in the fires of hell, snapped, "What did you say, who's... them?"

Sharon, who couldn't see, and had absolutely no intentions of looking, knew that the woman was peering with great suspicion at a strange girl suffocating under a book and obviously about to do a runner.

"The lady what saved me. And him. He zonked the man that took off my clothes." The boy pointed to the couple. Sharon lowered the book. Stuart's mouth hung open. The three adults were stunned and speechless. Sharon groaned and wondered when this all forgiving loving God, whom

she should have definitely prayed to more often, was going to miraculously sweep her and Stuart away from this nightmare.

The four stood and stared at each other for what seemed like an eternity. Sharon was the first to find her voice. "We never kidnapped him, honest. We found him in a house where I used to live. I'd gone back to fetch some clothes because we're thinking of... Jeez, I'm gabbling. Please believe me; we rescued him, that's all."

Six seconds rolled into six years. Eventually 'Nanny' found her voice.

"That's all? Why didn't you bring him home? All the way home. Why did you send him down the road on his own?"

"We watched him all the way to his house. He was quite safe. Watched him until he got to the door. There was a police car outside." She looked in desperation at Stuart who was looking like a totally useless gimp. " Look, we're... I'm... we were..." she mouthed the word prostitutes. "Do you think the police would've believed we weren't implicated? Course they wouldn't. We'd have been behind bars before you could blink. Honest, lady, we saw what was happening, we whizzed in, zonked 'em on the head as your kid said, and snatched him away. He told us where he lived and we brought him home. That's it."

The woman, looking as though she was listening to a raging maniac, was speechless. The four continued to stare at each other for another eternity, although the boy soon lost interest and opened his comic.

Pulling herself together, the woman said, "OK, if you're really who you say you are, and not implicated in the... " She stage whispered the word 'abduction', "then help us. The two men in custody are denying everything. The police say they need you, if your phone call saying you were there is to be believed, to corroborate my Grandchild's story. "

"They're guilty," whispered Stuart, curving his hand over the side of his mouth to protect the boy's sensitivity.

"We saw everything. Your lad with no clothes on, cameras, bright lights, the lot."

"But we have to get away." Sharon said. She looked at Stuart and they started to back away. "I'm sorry. We could write a statement. Yes, that's what we'll do; we'll explain it all in writing and send it to you."

She grabbed Stuart's hand. "Remember what we said, don't look back." She pulled him but he didn't move.

"What are we running for?" he said, pulling his hand away.

"Because Winston will kill me. Because of the priest. GBH and all that shit, remember?"

Stuart shook his head. "Winston's should be banged up and our evidence could keep it that way. I wasn't worried about GBH, only murder and that didn't happen. There's no connection to me. We gotta stay."

"What about our plans? Our new life."

"That can... will still happen... another day. If we go now, we'll always be looking back, and we'll always be running."

"Why will we?"

"Our guilt. First time in our lives, well my life and I guess in yours, we've got the chance of doing something good. I don't think we should pass it up."

"Shite, never thought I'd listen to a rent boy... I knew you'd be trouble. OK then, but..." The girl grinned as she looked at him. "When we do eventually go, I choose both books."

"Smart arse. It's a deal."

"We'll do it." She turned, grinning with the thought of doing a good deed and feeling positive about the prospect. "What do we have to do?"

"Follow me," The woman said. As the four of them walked out of the supermarket, Sharon noticed the woman look them up and down and was aware of their shabby appearance. She was about to explain why they looked as they did, but decided against it. *Appearances shouldn't count.*

Anyway, her self-consciousness evaporated instantly as the woman continued. "I guess the reward for finding the lad will come in handy."

Chapter 66

DI Roy Cole was waiting for Adam as he emerged from one of the Interview Rooms to ask about progress.

"He's not saying a word so far," explained Adam. "He's known as Hawk. I told you they had stupid names. He wasn't one of the nonce's I ID'd in the mug shots and he won't tell us his real name, but of course, we all know his very well-known face. I didn't recognise him with that stupid mask on, but I do now." He turned and grinned at his boss before continuing. " I thanked the Holy Mother I've been given the opportunity to see the look of horror and bloody disbelief when you caught him, and then I turned up to interview him. Wait till the newspapers get hold of this! It made all the time I spent creeping round that bastard Tomas, and being in this lot's company all worthwhile."

"Think he'll crack?"

"Can't tell. He's pretty full of himself and a hard bastard, despite his public image of being a caring MP always doing charity work, especially kiddy type charity work. Naturally he wouldn't say a word till we got him his lawyer."

"How are the others doing?"

"Not sure. I came out to give him time to talk to his lawyer. DC Steiner's in Interview Room 2. I was going to check his progress."

Adam and Roy Cole walked along the corridor and

stood by Meena who was watching through the one way glass.

Luke and DC Mel Stubbs sat opposite a muscular good-looking young man who grinned nervously, and in doing so showed long, yellow teeth that would have looked good on a tiger.

"His code name's Wolfbane. He's one of the nonces I picked out from the mug shots." Adam whispered to his boss although his soft voice was unnecessary as the door into the room was thick and he wouldn't have been overheard.

"I remember him, Roger Stock. Football coach. Someone reported him but nothing was ever proved. " said Meena.

Both men smiled, remembering Meena's capacity for names and details.

"On the operation he was teamed up with the new recruit Dione who joined the cell at the same time as me. She'll crack, I'm sure. The drawback is that she probably won't know much as she's new." The three of them were then silent as they listened to Luke's questions.

Meena turned to Adam. "Boss, how're we doing over the counties? How many children are still missing?"

"Two in total as far as we know," said DI Cole answering for him.

"Two's bad enough." Adam chewed his finger and had to fight the hate he felt for these perverts and the frustration that this many children had been taken despite the extensive, country wide undercover operation of which he'd been part.

Cole, not normally having a police officer's equivalent of a doctor's bedside manner, sensing his officer's dark mood said softly, "Adam, remember, due to yours and other dedicated undercover officer's work, so far we've stopped nineteen children from being taken and probably eventually murdered after they'd served their purpose. That reminds me, why did you seem to slow down in South Street and then speed away? I read it on Blake's initial report. "

"Hawk was meant to lure a young girl into the car. They'd noted her mother is often late picking her up. The child's wily, makes out to her teacher that she spots her mum as she comes out of school and the teacher lets her go unescorted."

"Stupid arse."

"Yes, but the majority of teachers are very vigilant and often have loads of kids to deal with. Anyway, this particular mum apparently never picks her up on certain days. Again, they'd spotted that. God only knows how they get this information. They must be constantly monitoring, yet nobody's picked it up or reported it. He had a toy car in our vehicle for the boy and sweets and a doll for the girl. Hawk, who'd spoken to her before, made out he was a teacher, was meant to get out and entice her in the car. Just as we pulled up, they spotted the girl talking to someone and they didn't want to take a chance. We have one kid already, the sod sniggered. Feckin' nonces, the lot of them. "

Adam glowered at the man inside the interview room, wanting to rush into the room and pull his tonsils up into his mouth to force him speak. A young police officer walked along the corridor with a tray of drinks and offered them to the three detectives. After thanking him, Adam turned back to Cole. "Any sign of Tomas and the lovely Delilah?"

"No. You state in your initial report that Delilah left the car just after the failed attempt to pick up the girl. Then she switched to Tomas's car."

"I reckon the two of them had a fail-safe plan. Should anything go wrong they'd still escape. If everything went according to plan, they'd have turned up at the rendezvous."

"But should things go tits-up, they could make their getaway leaving the others to take the can."

"Makes you wonder how they knew things had failed. They must have a mole somewhere in a useful position, or some-one watching us that we don't know about." Adam rubbed his eyes. He felt tired but although he'd had a long day, and knew the interviewing would stretch well into the night, the success was giving him a buzz. He asked, "How are the other teams doing? Any details coming in yet?"

"So far, the operations in Hampshire, Dorset and London have been very successful. They've got twelve people in custody. In South London there are the two kids missing I mentioned. We haven't heard from some of the counties but those with undercover officers in place have all reported successful operations."

"Can you imagine if all these children had gone missing at once," Meena murmured. She turned her big eyes to Adam. "It doesn't bear thinking about. I think the Government would have sent in the troops."

"Yeah. Great lot of help that would've been. Right, I've got to get back. Keep me updated," said Cole, giving Adam a 'well done' pat on the back.

"How's Dan getting on?" asked Adam and he and Meena walked along to the third interview room where Dan was questioning Excalibur.

Turning the corner, they met Dan leaving the room, a huge grin plastered over his face. Adam glanced in through the one way glass to check his interviewee.

"Aah, nibbling Excalibur. Always chewing his horrible little nails," said Adam. "I take it he's talking by the grin all over your feckin' chops."

"Can you arrange some tea, mate?" he asked Adam. "He's not singing like the proverbial bird yet, but he will. The lies are coming out, but once he's been tripped up a couple of times, he'll give us all we want. I've interviewed enough people to know he'll squawk soon. He's no intention of going down, so he thinks. He's saying he's an innocent party caught up in something he didn't realise was happening."

"Like hell he didn't. He was caught red-handed."

"You know that, I know that, but my face is full of sympathy for the innocent sod. He thinks I'm his best mate. Get some tea and listen to his singing. It's so sweet and tuneful. We'll soon get enough to bang these buggers up for good, excuse the pun."

After the tea arrived, Meena and Adam listened to Dan continuing with the interview. Excalibur's real name was Roland Causer. He admitted to having form, explaining for the past three years his record had been exemplary, and he still regularly visited his doctor and his Social Worker.

Protesting that he was only accompanying Mother Teresa to visit an old friend, then dragged into this by mistake. On the way to the friends, Teresa had stopped outside a school, explaining she was picking up her niece. His eyes opened hysterically and the nail nibbling reaching frenzy status. The girl voluntarily got into the car, desperation lacing his voice as he continued that they'd then driven to what he thought was the kid's house. They'd had to carry her indoors because she'd had a funny turn. The next thing he knew the police had arrived, and he and his companion arrested. He had no idea what all the fuss was about."

"If you're not part of this cell, why do you call yourself Excalibur?"

There was silence for a minute and the man quietly conferred with his lawyer.

"It's just a nickname. My mates call me that. Just a joke really."

"That's interesting. You say you were just visiting an old friend with another old friend called... " Dan stopped and consulted his notes. "Called... Mother Teresa. Funny, I thought Mother Teresa was a nun, a Saint by all accounts. Died a few a years ago. Your companion looks pretty much alive to me?"

The silence was almost palpable. Excalibur nibbled his nails again, looked at the table whilst considering his position. His ratty little eyes looking shiftily round the room, as though seeking some sort of invisible saviour to redeem him.

"Well?" persisted Dan.

"Yes."

"Yes what? Is that her real name or her... code name?"

Again the man looked uncomfortable and whispered again to his lawyer.

"I just call her that. I'm not sure of her real name."

"Roland, you don't mind me calling you that? If Teresa's an old friend, surely you'd know her real name?"

"I don't know what you mean. I've always called her that."

"Well, she can't be that much of a friend. I mean; I know all my friends names."

"I've always known her as that."

The questioning continued. Roland eventually, despite advice from his lawyer, tripped himself up time and time again with Dan's expert questioning technique.

"OK, Roland. Let me put this to you. We're going nowhere fast. Why don't you make it easy on yourself? Your so-called mates are telling us everything. They have no intention of going down. They're blaming you. Saying you organised this operation. Now are you going to take the fall for your so-called mates or are you going to make things a lot easier for yourself by helping me?"

Adam and Meena, still avidly watching through the window, saw his face change. Roland went silent for a minute, the nibbling of the nails intensified whilst he considered his dark future and then the beans spilled out faster than an upturned tin of Heinz. His lawyer kept putting a warning hand on his clients arm, but he shook it off.

An unexpected bonus for the police was that he told them the names of the people responsible for murdering Lawman and French Larry. His mouth was now well in motion and Meena noticed Dan's eyes were wide open with amazement and pleasure. He'd been working hard to extract a confession, but was surprised how easily the details gushed from Excalibur's mouth.

Adam rubbed his hands together. "Gotcha," he said. "Better get back to Hawk. Can't wait to see his expression this time. Murder and abduction. Holy Mother, thank you.

He still won't be so easy but I've got plenty of time! All the time in the world to make the bastard crack."

Part 4
After math

Chapter 67

Lucy had slept soundly. She remembered crawling into bed, her mind whirling, convinced she'd lie awake all night. Huddling down into the warmth, grateful that she was home and safe, she forced herself to relax. Briefly thinking about Muriel, she firmly pushed those worries from her mind, promising herself that she'd analyse the last four days tomorrow, when refreshed. She heard the rain softly pattering on her windows and felt cosy and secure.

"Lucy, a cup of tea." Sitting up quickly, her heart beating with fear, Lucy gasped with relief when she realised she was in her own room.

"You OK, hon? Look, tea on the bedside table. It's ten o' clock. Not that it matters, stay in bed all day if you want. Poor over-worked Fred'll wait on you as usual."

Lucy flopped back down onto the bed, laughing with joy, and said, "Oh my God, I've just dreamt I was back in that house, Jake had taken Hig for a walk and wouldn't let me go with them."

"Talk of the devil."

Lucy sat up again as she heard the dog pad into the bedroom.

"No," they both echoed as he bent his back legs ready to spring onto the bed. He stopped, turned through one hundred and eighty degrees, flopped onto the carpet, back firmly

356

planted towards his mistress demonstrating his displeasure about her behaviour after all he'd been through!

"I can't see your face, Higs." Lucy paused and sipped her tea. "But I know you're wearing your 'I'm going to sulk at her cruelty for at least half the day' face."

"Fancy breakfast?" asked Freddy.

"Hmm, I can smell something delicious. It can't be you actually cooking, surely?"

Freddy snapped his fingers and on cue Peter walked in with a tray of breakfast and laid it on her lap. The smell of bacon, eggs, fried tomatoes and mushrooms wafted into her nostrils.

"Oh, Peter, you angel. How wonderful, I haven't had a cooked breakfast in bed for years."

Peter bent and kissed her cheek. Whispering in her ear, he told her he was so pleased she was back because he missed her and was worried to death, plus Freddy had been an absolute pain in the arse since she'd gone.

As the men left the room, Freddy told her to kip for the rest of the morning.

"I need more tea to wash down the breakfast," she shouted after their backs.

She ignored Freddy's 'bloody cheeky mare' and attacked her breakfast with relish.

Finishing the second cup of tea, Lucy lay back for five minutes to digest the food, closing her eyes for a moment. When she looked at the clock after what she thought was a doze, she was amazed to see it was almost two o' clock. Leaping out of bed, she pulled back the curtain, and despite the leaden grey sky and pelting rain, her heart soared and she felt like a million dollars.

Peering into the living room on the way to the bathroom, she wasn't surprised to see a football match on the television. Both men were sitting either end of the sofa, elbows on the arms, heads supported on their hands, fast asleep.

"Sunday afternoon as usual," murmured Lucy.

Having showered and changed into her track suit, Lucy felt ready to take on the world. Her ankle felt a lot better although it wasn't ready to take the strain of running, and peering out of the window again and seeing the rain reaching Niagara velocity, she didn't fancy getting wet.

Walking into the living room with a tray containing three mugs of tea, she shouted to the two men, "Wakey, wakey, tea's up and the gym's waiting to be visited'.

"Sod off," mumbled Fred with his usual good grace and turned over.

"Thanks, ducky," said a sleepy Peter, taking the tea mug.

"In an hour, I'm going to the gym," she informed the still sleeping Freddy. "Hurry up, drink your tea. We're going together. You promised."

It took two hours to get Freddy moving but eventually they drove into the gym car park, after dropping Peter off at the hotel where he was working his shift.

"The place seems closed," said Lucy, looking at the windows seemingly staring at them with dark and sombre eyes.

"Good, let's go home," said Freddy, switching the engine back on.

"Hang on, the side door's open. I'll go and check. Maybe they've just had a power failure. That happened a couple of weeks ago when I was here."

A car drew up behind them.

"Someone else has turned up," said Lucy, still looking at the building. "He's obviously expecting it to be open."

"There's only one other car parked so there's not many takers today. I'm not surprised; they're probably watching Man U play Liverpool, which is where I should be."

"Don't fib and stop whinging."

Alighting from the car, Lucy walked towards the side door. The car park was situated behind the main entrance of the gym and the open side door would allow her to slip in and check the situation.

"Right my darling, you're coming with me"

Lucy froze as she heard the words and felt someone grab her arm. Turning, she felt a painful jolt in her chest as she looked into Jake's eyes. Attempting to wrestle and pull her arm away, his firm grip made her efforts futile.

"I've been looking all over for you," he continued. "I was coming to your flat but I saw you drive away just as I got there."

"Jake, I'm not coming with you. Your aunt has died and Stan's in the hospital. They wouldn't tell me how he was as I'm not a relative when I phoned earlier, but that's a bad sign in itself. Don't you care about them? Why worry about me and what I'm doing?"

"Course I care about them, but I also care about you and I know you care about me."

"No she bloody doesn't," said Freddy, firmly removing Jake's grip from Lucy's arm. "When are you going to get it into your thick head that this entire romance thing is just your imagination? Now clear off and leave her alone before I punch your lights out."

Freddy towered at least six inches above Jake, but he stood well back when Jake produced a large chopping instrument which Lucy presumed had previously belonged to Stan.

"Now, Lucy, darling, if you don't want your friend to have a chopper slice open his head, come with me."

Lucy went to move towards Jake, not wanting her friend to be killed, having no doubts that Jake meant what he said.

Freddy held her back. "You're not going anywhere," he said. "Right mate, where do you want it, in the bollocks or on the knee?"

Jake look confused. "What?"

"My foot, you turd," said Freddy as he kicked Jake in the groin. Jake collapsed onto his knees, groaning and holding himself with his left hand, Freddy whipped the chopper out of his right hand. "Right, now you can hold your bollocks with both hands."

At that moment a car drove at top speed into the car park and out got Dan Blake and the dark haired, handsome Irish man whom Lucy had lusted after in the gym.

"Jesus H," spluttered Freddy, shaking his head in bewilderment at the afternoon's activities, "the cavalry's arrived in time for a change."

Chapter 68

The two predators spotted their prey again. So in tune, they had instantaneously chosen the same child during previous forays into the paradise of the park full of children. Everything contributed towards him being the potential quarry. Most Saturdays mornings around ten o'clock an elderly women left him for at least an hour. Her friend with whom she arrived always sat near-by on a park bench but inevitably she either dozed off or had her nose ensconced in a newspaper.

So for an hour the boy was free to run about and play. Today he'd brought a kite with him. That was a bonus and their ticket to an easy snatch. They watched as he kissed and then waved goodbye to the person, who by her age was presumably his grandma, and the friend settled herself on the bench.

Within ten minutes she had dozed off. The watching couple smiled at each other.

The young man and woman sat on the park bench, relaxed and enjoying the frail October warmth left in the sun. To the passers-by, just an ordinary couple having lunch and feeding the opportunistic ducks that waddled over from the pond when they spotted likely punters.

The Hunters, as they liked to call themselves, had no intentions of being caught. They needed to be 'invisible', part of the background. That way, when questions were asked, only the astute recalled them, but not in detail.

Very different to his usual dark business suit, the young man dressed casually for the occasion. A plain brown jacket and tan trousers were his camouflage. His skin smelt of Imperial Leather soap and the faint smell of shampoo from his hair was pleasant to his companion, a young woman with long black hair that gleamed in the sunshine. As she relished her lunchtime sandwich, she threw the crusts to the persistent ducks, but her eyes never left the boy. Her cream blouse and tailored grey trousers suggested a person who, even on a weekend, was neat and smart. Her make-up was subtle and the perfume she wore was a delicate combination of vanilla and cinnamon.

Despite the target prey being ready for plucking, their experience made them cautious. Their arrogance, however, allowed them the time to enjoy the extra visual delights of the other children playing in the park. They gave their potential victims names. That made it personal and more fun.

Today's victim was 'Keith'. The wind was perfect for kite flying but the child had trouble getting it into the air. The girl strolled, seemingly by chance, towards 'Keith' as he struggled with his problem. The man watched as she bewitched the child with her innocent beauty, endearing giggles and offers of help. The bait was irresistible and the child was snared. He was about to know hell at the tender age of eight.

By teatime that day, word had spread and Camberwell was teetering between being in uproar and a daze.

'Keith' was the third child to disappear from the London area in three months. This disappearance was the final straw. The public demanded more action from the police, whilst the newspaper editors rubbed their hands in glee thinking about escalating sales. Heated debates about 'bloody pervert paedophiles' raced up and down the urban streets; worried mothers not allowing their youngsters out of sight.

A minority maintained the unnatural longings of such people were a sickness whilst the vocal majority shouted them down. 'Damn them to hell!'

The emotional demanded the death penalty be reinstated. The more objective argued such punishment was too good for the likes of them; it was finished too quickly. Why shouldn't they suffer like the little children and their families? Stay in solitary confinement forever. Every day, wonder if the warders would turn a blind eye and let one of the other inmates with their quirky code of honour, slip through the protection to catch them unaware in the showers. Then they would know what it was like to suffer.

The perpetrators didn't care about the discussions, the uproar or the daze. They couldn't wait for nightfall and fantasized about the enjoyment to come. By teatime, they were going about the business of being ordinary citizens and shook their heads in unison with their neighbours, despairing at the way the country seemed to be going.

"You OK, mate, you're miles away?" Adam's words filtered into Dan's consciousness.

Dan shook himself, attempting to bring his mind back to the present and focus on the job in hand.

"Sure," he replied quietly. "I'm fine." He turned his head again and gazed back at the passing houses as they drove towards the gym on this wet and windy Sunday afternoon.

Why do I imagine in such detail what those abductors did? How would I know their thoughts, their intentions? All I was thinking about was getting my kite into the air.

The counsellor had said Dan ought to write about his thoughts, his feelings, the nightmares he consequently suffered. He'd explained it was his imagination and his subconscious working overtime to allow him to deal with the horror of what had happened. This type of therapy forced the shock out into the open, to the front of his mind so he wouldn't destructively brood about it, and he would learn to cope with his fears.

Dan believed he hadn't dwelt on it in any way. Just occasionally it went through his mind, thinking about the incident through the eyes of the kidnappers that day. It would slip in when he wasn't expecting it, when he was often thinking about something quite different.

Just as often he thought about his mum lying dead on the beach in Cornwall; awful as that had been at the time, yet now he knew the abduction experience was what had shaped the path of his life. Not long after he was freed he'd made up his mind he was going to join the police force and hunt down fuckers like the two men and the woman. He hadn't thought of them using that descriptive word at the time, he hadn't known such words at such an innocent age, but it hadn't just been a boy's childish fancy because he had never changed his mind. Even after gaining a first in physics at University and being offered a well paid job at Aldermaston, he had stuck to his dream and joined the force. Today he knew he'd made the right choice.

"I just can't believe we got everybody except those two bastards," said Adam, interrupting his day dream. "I told Cole I thought maybe Tomas and the ugly bitch had a fail-safe plan should things go wrong. They'd leave everyone to take the can and hike it away."

His words finally brought Dan's attention fully back to the present. "How would they know anything had gone wrong if they'd scarpered?"

Adam shrugged. "A deep mole or someone monitoring all their activities and reporting back. They always seem a step ahead of us."

"How were they communicating during the operation?"

"Mobiles, but could only use them in emergencies. I don't think anyone had time to use them before we rounded them up."

"Those already in the cottage near Aldermaston might

364

have had time to phone and warn them."

"We checked. There were only two mobiles and neither had been used."

"What made you think they might be at the gym?"

"I don't know for sure. That's why I suggested just you and I go for a drive, just maybe we'll get lucky. We all have to get lucky sometime. After all, as far as I know, Tomas doesn't know about me not being genuine. We know his address and his house is under surveillance, and he hasn't returned there."

"Yes, but we don't know where this Delilah lives, and we don't know any of their bolt holes, so they could have gone anywhere."

Adam tapped the side of his nose. "But Tomas doesn't realise that I was being very vigilant. I noticed he had a locked metal cupboard. Even when we were best of buddies, he was careful not to let me see what was in there. What I'm telling you next is between you and me, matey. The night before they picked me up for their operation, 'fraid me and Luke did a bit of house-breaking. Only it was more in the line of gym-breaking. Now if we're in time, I think maybe we'll get lucky and see if the happy pair has returned to get what's so valuable he keeps it locked away. I think they'll be desperate to retrieve whatever it is that's so important."

"They'll have got it and scarpered by now."

"Maybe but maybe not... especially if they can't get into the cupboard."

"Don't tell me, you nicked his key."

"He such a feckin' idiot. He keeps something important locked away in a metal cupboard but puts the key in the drawer. Admittedly not easy to find unless..."

"You were watching and you do some unlawful house... gym-breaking. Christ, I hope Cole never finds out about your little escapade."

Dan sat up straight in his seat, back in the present and ready for action. He could feel the need for action spiralling through his body like a virulent virus. His head spun with the adrenalin rush. "I thought you said everyone within the cell was warned not to keep anything in writing. What was in the cupboard?"

"Didn't find out. We found the key and then scarpered. Wouldn't bode well for two police officers to be done for breaking and entering. But without the key, Tomas can't get in the cupboard. It's real solid. I know the cell members were told not to keep hard copies but think about it logically. If you've got a big organisation like there's, then there's no way you'll remember everything. In this day and age anything kept on a computer can be retrieved, despite endless passwords and fail safes. No, he thought he was so secure. So, he kept hard-copy files I bet, and just living the ordinary life of a Gym Manager." Adam leaned back in his seat.

Dan was mesmerised by his confidence, unable to take his eyes away from his friend's strange pale eyes, flashing with self-belief. The feeling was contagious, and he grinned in anticipation of their success as Adam continued. "The gym takings are kept in a safe in a corner of his office that's obvious to all and sundry. He wouldn't want that broken into, but he'd rather that happen than his dirty little secrets that live in his cupboard being exposed."

"I've warned Luke and Meena should we need back up pretty quickly."

"Good," murmured Adam excitedly. As they stopped at traffic lights, Adam's fingers were tapping the steering wheel as the energy coursing through him sought for an outlet. "By the way, Luke tells me this morning that the missing woman Lucy Hamilton's turned up. What happened?"

"Yes, Luke updated me too." The car swerved too quickly into the car park and Dan had to catch the top safety handle. "Whoa, watch it, mate. Don't know the details yet but he said Lucy was fine. Jesus... what the hell's going on."

The scene being re-enacted in the car park amazed both of the police officers.

"Lucy and Freddy... what?" Dan looked in amazement at Freddy who was getting the better of a man who dropped to the floor as Freddy's foot connected with him.

"Holy Mary, a punch up." Adam pulled up near the action, switching off his engine. "This is turning into a right craic. Who's the other felluh? Christ, I don't believe it. The tall fellah kicked the other chaps in the balls."

Dan leapt from the car. "Lucy Hamilton what are you doing here? What the hell's going on?"

She swung round and looked round at him at him in amazement, and then relief.

"DS Blake, thank Heaven you're here." She pointed to the figure that doubled up in agony on the ground. "He's Jake. He's the one that took me, kept me locked up. He was going to attack Freddy with that chopper if I didn't go with him again."

"They're inside. That's their car," said Adam, tugging Dan's sleeve having spotted Tomas's car. "We got to get in there."

"Hey, what's more important than this potential murderer," said Freddy, amazed that the officers weren't more impressed with the incident before them.

"OK," said Dan, weighing up the most effective action for keeping the potential attacker restrained and the need to check on the whereabouts of the two paedophiles. "Give me a hand, Adam. Handcuff him to the steering wheel."

Lucy and Freddy watched in amazement as the two officers hoisted the groaning Jake to his feet, sat him in the driver's seat, feet hanging outside the car and firmly cuffed him to the wheel."

"Don't go anywhere. Don't touch anything, especially that," warned Dan, pointing to the chopper. "We've got to go inside the gym. Don't come in at any cost. Phone the station and talk to either DC Luke Steiner or Meena. Report what's happened. Tell them need back up immediately. Tell them the people we want are in the gym. Emphasise... no sirens."

"Oh bugger off then," said Freddy called to the police officers' backs as they walked towards the side entrance. "What wrong, you afraid you'll miss your turn on the rowing machine?"

Chapter 69

I'm desperate for the loo," said Lucy. The rain had stopped but the cold air was definitely getting to her kidneys.

"No way. You heard what Supercop said, we're to wait here until the rest of the Cavalry arrive." said Freddy. He got a chocolate bar out of his pocket and bit into it after offering half to Lucy who shook her head.

"Please let me go," whined Jake. "I promise on my honour I won't ever approach you again, Lucy."

"No," the pair said in unison.

"Please, I'll pay you."

"How much?" said Freddy, popping the last of the chocolate in his mouth.

"Fred!"

"Hold on, ducky. This could be very lucrative."

"Five hundred pounds."

Freddy put out his hand, palm upwards, and raised it a couple of times.

"OK, a thousand, two hundred. That's all I have. That's my total savings."

"Well, tough shit then, matey. I may have been tempted by twenty thousand, but for that paltry amount you can stink in jail for twenty years."

"I'll sell the house. It's mine anyway. Stan and Muriel moved in with me when they moved from Bucklebury."

"How much is it worth?"

"Fred, you can't be serious."

After the incorrigible Fred had winked at his friend, she relaxed and let him play his game. Two minutes later, the bartering still going on, she said,

"I don't care what you say, I'm now desperate for the loo."

"Go in the bushes over there," said Freddy pointing to the perimeter bushes round the car park.

"No way. I promise I'll go straight to the ladies and come straight out again. It's only just down the corridor."

"Straight in. Pee. Straight out."

"Yes, sir," said Lucy, scampering to the side door.

Peering down the dark corridor she listened for voices or some noise that would indicate the policemen's whereabouts, but could hear nothing. Emerging from the ladies toilet she jumped nervously as she collided with a man.

"Lucy, what're you doing here? I thought you'd gone missing. We've been worried sick. Does Freddy know you're here?" At Lucy assurance that all was fine and Freddy was waiting for her outside, Alex said, "Glad you're back and OK." He then grabbed her to him to give her his usual bear hug.

"Anyway, what are you doing here?"

"Hoping to join on that new deal being offered. Fred's nagged me enough to get fit, so here I am. Bloody hypocrite, he hates exercising. The only thing is, despite the advert saying today was the last day for joining for two free months, no-one's here. The front door's locked. No lights on. I walked round the back and noticed the back door open so I slipped in and been having a nose round. I've been walking round for half an hour, looking at all the gizmos. Some of them look like torture machines."

"You didn't see your police mate, DS Blake and a dark haired fellow come in?"

"No. Just looked round the gym though; that looks great.

Then I nosed around the men's changing rooms. Being a carpenter, I got interested in the wooden lockers. Really good job someone made of those." He frowned. "Anyway, Dan's here you say. He's getting keen on this keep fit lark."

Lucy shrugged. "Not sure what's going on.. He ordered me not to come in, said we had to phone his colleagues. We've had a real incident out back. Tell you about it in a minute but I think we ought to scarper. He told us not to come into the gym but I was desperate for the loo. Still, as they're not around, if you slip up to the office, the application forms are in a filing tray on Mr Tomas's desk. Go and get one and we'll quickly leave. No harm done. Then when we're outside you'll never believe what you'll see."

"Sounds interesting. OK, where's the office?"

"I'll show you. It's only through the gym and up some stairs. Come on, but be quick. Dan sounded like he meant no-one was to come in."

"You women never do what you're told."

Dan and Adam entered the gym as quietly as possible.

"If they're in the office, we need to surprise them," murmured Adam.

"But you have to get to it through the gym. Is there another way up?" Dan whispered.

"Not sure. Hopefully they'll be intent on what they are doing." Adam slipped through the swing door which he held it open and eased closed after Dan walked through. He'd noticed previously when he was doing his unauthorised 'gym-breaking' with Luke that the noise echoed up and down the corridor if allowed to swing closed on its own.

Creeping up the stairs they could hear murmuring voices. Adam turned to Dan, signalling a thumbs-up sign. Walking into the room, he leaned on the wall just inside the room whilst Dan leaned on the door frame, arms crossed and relishing in what he was seeing, a frantic search.

Delilah was searching in a desk drawer while Tomas was on his hands and knees searching in the bottom drawer of a filing cabinet.

"Hello, maties, is this what you're looking for?" said Adam, swinging the key to and fro with his outstretched hand.

"Viking, what are you doing here?" Tomas stood up and looked relieved. "You escaped as well?"

"Sure, it was easy. Nothing to it."

The key was still swinging enticingly. Tomas looked puzzled, obviously wondering how Adam came to have it.

Delilah screwed up her eyes and stared at Dan. "Who's he?"

"You know, Delilah. That sounded just like a snarl. Still, come to think of it, I've only ever heard you speak in that manner. What makes you such a bad tempered, evil cow?" Adam grinned, savouring the moment.

"Viking, what's going on? Look, we need the key. There's stuff in here we need. Then we get out of here as soon as we can." Tomas said, sweeping the long hair that he grew sideways to cover his baldness back over his head.

"You fool," hissed Delilah. "Don't you understand, he's not one of us." She glared at Dan. "He's one of those. The bloody law."

Tomas looked confused. His eyes flicked from Delilah to Adam, and then back to Dan.

"The law. I don't understand."

"The bizzies, you idiot. I can smell them a mile away. Criminals call them the filth. Frigging accurate description."

"Criminals! Ha, Delilah, such a hypocrite," smirked Adam. "You don't consider what you attempted to do yesterday somewhat criminal? Holy Mary, you're feckin' amazing."

"I don't care what you think, you Irish bastard." Withdrawing a long knife from her pocket, she waved it menacingly before her, but then gaped in amazement as a tall, thin man with spiky hair sauntered into the room.

Alex, not expecting the current situation, didn't notice the knife and was too busy grinning and looking at Dan.

"Watcha, matey. Come for the application form you promised to pick up for me and as usual never got round to it." When no-one spoke he looked round the room, the threatening knife causing his eyes to open wide with shock. Hurriedly stepping back and standing next to Dan, he asked, "What the fuck's going on here?"

"Shut up," ordered Delilah. "Brother Samson, we go."

As if they had practiced it, Tomas moved to her side, now also wielding a knife and the two moved in unison towards the door.

"Move!" the woman ordered Adam, but when he didn't move, she sidled towards Dan. "If you don't, the red head gets it."

Adam slid along the wall away from her. "Move Dan. We get them later."

"No," said Dan. "Put down your knives. You're going nowhere. We've reinforcements outside. You won't get out of this place."

With that Delilah raised her knife and sprang.

Dan watched as the knife slashed towards him. Slow motion took over. As the knife hacked down, Alex jumped in front of him, and the knife disappeared from Dan's view.

All eyes were on Alex as he sank to his knees.

Someone had pushed Dan aside but he felt nothing. All feeling had gone from his body and a sound of rushing wind filled his ears. As his long-time friend toppled to the floor he twisted gracefully round, slowly falling onto his back.

Alex smiled at Dan, a trickle of blood issuing from the corner of his mouth. The sight shook him into action. Falling to his knees beside him, moaning in disbelief, Dan pushed his hand on the gaping wound in his chest.

"Second time I've saved you," whispered Alex, bubbles of blood issuing from his mouth distorting the words. "You fucking owe me."

"No, no." Dan moaned softly. "Stu', stay with me. Come on, look at me. Stay with me, fight. Fight! Stuart! Stuart!" His words became a scream." No. no, please, look at me. Don't leave me."

In another dimension, in another time, in another world because he didn't want to be in this one, Dan could hear Adam's frantic words as he radioed for an emergency ambulance. He saw the expression go from Stuart's eyes and he knew they saw nothing. He recalled another pair of eyes, blank and empty. His mother lying on the beach, no soul, no life behind her beautiful green eyes. The ambulance would be too late for his friend as well.

He put back his head, full of anguish, and howled like a wolf.

Chapter 70

Lucy sobbed into Freddy's chest. She had not stopped crying since they had eventually arrived home from the awful events in the gym the previous afternoon. Freddy understood the crying was a release and a healing mechanism. After all that had happened to Lucy over the last three months, he suspected she had taken as much as she could, and a lot of tears needed to fall. As he stroked her hair, he silently decided to persuade her to see her doctor for tranquilizers. Knowing there would be a battle royal, Lucy never went to the doctors and abhorred taking tablets, he was determined this time he was going to win.

Sensing she probably needed to talk about the incident to clear it from her mind; he asked her again exactly what had happened when she left him to go into the gym. Every time she'd previously started to explain, the tears would roll down her cheeks and she couldn't finish.

"If you don't want to talk about it, don't worry. I'll tell you what I saw. I waited outside for you when you went to the toilet. After a few minutes I started to worry, you were taking so bloody long. Then Jake, the stupid wanker, started shouting out and making a fuss. By the time I'd convinced him to shut up or he'd get a smack in the chops, I knew you were gone too long, something was wrong. I hurried to the side door when Tomas and an ugly cow of a woman dashed out, nearly knocking me over. They got in his car and were gone in a second. That's when I rushed in and found you lying at the bottom of the stairs."

Lucy sat upright and accepted the proffered tissue from Freddy. Wiping her eyes, she then picked up the teacup from the coffee table and sipped the tea before she continued.

"They knocked me over too. When I came out of the loo I bumped into Sara's Alex. He was wandering around looking a bit lost. He'd turned up to join the gym on the promotional package they'd offered and was confused because he knew it was the last day to sign up but the gym appeared closed. Anyway, no-one appeared to be about but he found a door open, so he wandered in to have a nose round.

"I told him the application forms were probably kept in the manager's office. I showed him where the stairs to his office were and he went up to get one. I heard talking and then suddenly I heard the most dreadful... well, sort of howl. It froze my blood. Like someone was in terrible pain. Then two people came rushing down the stairs and knocked me over."

She paused. Freddy put his hand over hers and felt her trembling. "Don't go on if it's too painful."

"No, I need to say it. Like you, I don't really know what exactly happened. Just after that you rushed in and picked me up. Then the police and the emergency ambulance arrived. You know what happened then, the police pushed us out and we sat in the car for what seemed like forever."

"Yes, I know. Thank God by then one of the officers had whipped Jake away for questioning and we didn't have to listen to him bleating on. Then all those people arrived, what are they called, SOCOs or something."

"It was so awful waiting there and not really knowing what had happened. Thank goodness you were there. I just couldn't talk then. It was a nightmare. When they eventually brought out the stretcher with a body on it I felt sick."

Freddy once again put his arm round Lucy. "I know. Not

knowing who was beneath that sheet."

"Then when I saw Dan Blake come out with his arm all bandaged up and the dark haired man, I knew who..."

Lucy couldn't continue and she fell forward onto her hands and sobbed again. Freddy rubbed her back. He didn't say don't cry. It irritated him when people said that. If you're crying, all the tears need to fall before the healing process begins.

When the sobbing gradually subsided, Freddy continued.

"Apparently Dan didn't even realise he'd been stabbed in the arm."

Lucy once again wiped her eyes. "Who told you that?"

Freddy shrugged. "One of the young police officers putting up the crime-scene tape. When I asked him if Dan Blake was OK, he'd just gone off in the ambulance; the lawman said yes, he thought so. It was a bad gash down his arm but the ambulance man had stemmed the bleeding, temporarily patched him up. He was in such shock with Alex... with what had happened, Dan didn't know he was bleeding all over the place."

"Tomorrow I'll go and see Sara. God, she must be feeling... well, I can't even imagine what she's feeling. I wonder if anyone's with her. I wouldn't care to think she's on her own."

"I'm sure Alex told me neither were in touch with their families. Christ, it's awful. Alex dead, I can't believe it. Maybe I'll phone Sara and go round today. You're not up to it so I'll go on my own. You come tomorrow if you feel up to it."

Lucy smiled at her friend. Once again beneath the tiger's skin, the nestling soft hearted kitten peeked out. "No, we'll both go if she needs us. My tears are nothing compared to what she's going through."

Chapter 71

"I'll be home about five," Lucy called to Sara who had gone upstairs to shower. When she heard Sara's 'OK, see you then', she pulled the door closed and hurried to her car parked in the lay-by round the corner.

Three weeks had passed since Alex had been killed, and Lucy had stayed with Sara ever since she and Freddy had gone to check on her. Freddy had been right, Sara appeared to have no family. She had briefly described her early life. How she had run away from a terrible home life when she was fourteen and had never returned. Lucy silently sympathised, understanding how devastating being on your own without support could feel.

"I eventually met Stuart. He'd left his home in similar circumstances and we've been... were together ever since. We changed our names from Sharon and Stuart because we wanted to start a new life, a complete change. We met Dan when he was eight, and been in contact off and on ever since. Obviously his busy job meant of late we didn't see each other as often as we'd have liked."

There were no more details, and Lucy sensed it wasn't sensitive to enquire for more at this time.

Hurrying to her car, aware the traffic was always heavy in the mornings, she was anxious to get to work on time. Her class were practising for the Christmas pantomime and the fact that Genghis had been selected to play Joseph, and Jade was the Virgin Mary meant humungous amounts of rehearsals were needed.

When Joseph had asked his wife what name they were going to call their son, Jade's version of 'Jesus Christ' had sounded more like an expletive than a mother's fond words, Lucy knew it wasn't going to be easy.

Inserting the key into the car door, grinning inwardly as she thought about how unintentionally funny kids could be, she became aware of someone leaning against a garden wall, and sensed he was watching her. Despite the tranquilisers, she was still jumpy, and opened the door quickly to get into the car.

"Lucy."

Turning, her stomach lurched when someone unexpectedly said her name and she hadn't recognised the voice. She was still suffering from nerves; she looked cautiously towards the direction of the voice.

She relaxed when he realised who it was. Dan Blake looked quite different. His red-gold hair was now close cropped. The absence of the cool spiky look somehow adding to his look of dejection, especially as his grin which had started to work its way into her affection, was missing.

Not really sure what to say to his obvious gloominess, she just asked, "How's the arm?" she said, noticing the sling he was still wearing.

"Fine."

"I checked how you were. Luke told me you were being de-briefed and wouldn't be around for a time."

"Yes, that's right."

The silence between them lengthened. Lucy sensed he was totally miserable but still didn't know what to say, how to comfort him. Putting the key back into the car door lock, she said, "I'm on my way to work."

"Yes, I've seen you park here a couple of times."

Surprised, she turned back to him. "Why didn't you

speak?" He shrugged and looked at the ground, drawing his eyebrows together in a confused frown. She continued, her voice gentle, " "Why haven't you been to see Sara? She's hurt you haven't, you know. Understand you're really good friends. Go back a long way."

Lucy's stomach jolted when she saw his eyes start to glisten.

"I can't. I should have been killed, not Stu... Alex. I know Sara loves me but how can she forgive me for that? Her husband dies instead of me. He saved me, he's saved me twice. She'll never forgive me." His voice was low, loaded with misery and grief.

"No, you're wrong. Think this through," Lucy said quietly. "She knows it wasn't your fault. She's proud of what he did. Said to me it was fate; she really believes that. They were always meant to save you. I don't know the details of the story behind that statement, but don't take that thought away from her. You're right, she loves you. Go and see her. She needs you now."

Dan wiped his eyes with his free hand. "You're not just saying that. She doesn't hate me?"

"No. Go see her now. And remember, it was me who told Alex where the office was, so if anyone is to blame, it was me."

"No, it was never your fault."

"Sense dictates it was nobody's fault. Just terrible hard luck. Now promise me you'll go and see Sara. She needs you." Formally she had always felt he was in control, suddenly the opposite was true, and she was managing the situation..

He nodded and a few seconds passed before the ghost of a smile won its hard fought battle and eased onto his lips.

"OK. I will." He watched while she got into the car and wound down the window.

"The funeral's next week," she said as she did up her seat belt.

"I know. I'll be there." He put his hand on the top of the open car window.

Lucy started the engine. Looking again at him, she said, "I'm stopping with her till then... so, may see you soon."

"I hope to tell you one day how grateful I am you're staying with her. She hasn't any other family."

"I know. It's not a hardship. We get on really well." Glancing up at him, she said. "Umm, been meaning to ask you! The tattoo on your arm, the Chinese writing. What does it stand for?"

His eyes narrowed for a second, and then he blinked the expression away. "Vengeance," he said quietly. "Long story. Alex paid for it for my sixteenth birthday." He gave her one of his penetrating stares but Lucy detected a softening in the gaze, no suspicion just... what? "So I won't forget."

Lucy just nodded. She suddenly knew that one day she would know, but not now, not now.

As she drove away the image of his enigmatic green eyes boring into hers stayed with her all the way to school.

Chapter 72

Lucy stuffed more underwear and clean clothes into the holdall. She was hurrying because she had told Sara it wouldn't take long to go home and pick up clean clothes, and she didn't want to leave her too long on her own.

Hurrying to the sink, she rinsed out Higgins' food bowl that had been soaking in water since she had hurried to Sara's side. She still felt so sad both for poor Alex's death and Sara's heartache, but knew her company was helping her friend through the ordeal. Plus the fact, Higgins was staying too, and his company seemed really good for Sara. She'd even taken him for a short walk during the past two days which was obviously therapeutic. When she returned she had some colour once again in her cheeks.

Freddy and Peter also popped in whenever they could, and Lucy's could tell that Freddy's often sick but always hilarious sense of humour was aiding her.

The ring on the door bell started her. Assuming it was Freddy, although surprised because he had told her he was working until seven in the evening. The gym was under new management, and the new manager, a Miss Byron whom Freddy had previously informed Lucy with a big smirk over his face, that she was obviously as 'bent' as him, but with diagonally opposite inclinations.

Lucy peered through her peep-hole and was surprised to

see the face of a young man whom she didn't recognise and had not seen as a resident of the apartment block. Attaching the safety/security chain, she cautiously opened the door a little and peered round.

"Hi, Miss Hamilton," he asked, holding up a press card. "My name's Sam Peterson, and I work for the local news. I know the nationals have been talking to you about your various ordeals, and you have explained that you didn't want to do a story for them, but... "

"No, I'm sorry but I'm afraid I have to say the same to you."

Attempting to close the door, his foot that had unobtrusively slid forward, preventing her from doing so.

"Miss Hamilton, Lucy. Look, we're just a local rag, rather struggling in this day and age of austerity. Now we can't offer you big bucks like I'm sure the nationals offered, but how about we just do a short story, and pay you a reasonable fee that you can even give to a charity of your choice if you would prefer."

She felt trapped, as she knew he would anticipate how she would feel with such an offer on the table. Besides which, she knew that anyone with no secrets to hide would probably be happy to take up the offer. If she accepted, that would mean unnecessary publicity, and if she refused, it would appear petty and if the paper felt so inclined, they could make a story from her meanness, especially with the charity offer on the table.

Her mind whirled, the adrenalin pumped and a solution which could satisfy both parties popped into her mind. She opened the door a little more.

"Ok, we make a deal. I'm a private person and would hate to be in the public's eye. I'll write a shortish version of what happened which I'll email to you when the police enquiry has finished. If you give me your word you won't distort my words, and I want that in writing, then you can have the exclusive story. No argument or discussion and the money goes to the local dog pound. That must be done discreetly as well."

The reporter's face was an open book. She could practically see the offer being processed through his mind, weighing up whether he could get something more if he persisted. Sense prevailed and he agreed. Before he could ask to come in, which Lucy guessed would be his next ploy; she stuck out her hand for his business card after confirming his email address was on it. Once she had the card, she just said the story would be with him as soon as possible as long as *he didn't hassle her.* She closed the door before he could argue. Annoyed to think that he could get through the security lock that needed a four digit code, she remembered that Jake had managed whilst delivering his nasty gifts, so obviously entry was easy if you were determined.

Leaning back against the door, her heart beating so fast it felt as though it would do an 'Alien' and burst through her chest. Checking her watch, aware that she should be getting back to Sara, she decided one quick phone call may well relieve her anxiety.

As usual he answered quickly, and without any formal preamble. Lucy told him what had just occurred. When she eventually drew breath, he calmly answered that she had made a sensible decision and it seemed the reporter seemed content and hopefully once he had the story she would soon be forgotten in the world where a new story inevitably arose.

"There's nothing as boring as old news. Again, I say, don't panic, there's no reason to."

"Yes, I suppose you're right, but I can't seem to shake it off. The other night I couldn't sleep thinking about the technology of face recognition and if my face got in the newspapers, someone somewhere would apply this know-how to age my face, and despite the changes, I'd be recognised."

Again he re-assured her she was letting her imagination run away and that she should calm down. "What's happened about the cop you said seemed unduly suspicious of you."

"It's weird. He seems to have backed off."

"Good. I made some phone calls. Maybe things cascaded down."

"God, he doesn't know..."

"No, nothing. He may well just have been told you are almost certainly not a suspect and to leave it at that."

"OK." Lucy drew in a big breath with relief. "He's actually... how can I say? Oh, I might as well be truthful. He's... quite attractive. I'd see him at the gym quite often. I thought maybe he was checking up on me, that he was suspicious of... well, I suppose my past. Probably just being irrational."

"Yes, you are. I'll tell you again, you're so deep you could even emigrate safely. I have checked with those that know and you are totally safe. All you have to consider is whether this came to, say, a romantic situation, with him or someone else, can you live the lie. You've done it for all these years, but now you're, shall we say, marriageable age, it's something you need to think about."

"I couldn't deal with the worry of a serious relationship at the moment. It just with all that's happened recently, it makes me realise how vulnerable I am. Anyway, you're right; I have to pull myself together." She paused but he never said anything. "Thanks for listening, re-assuring me. Hopefully I won't have to bother you again."

"You're never a bother. You've coped really well. I hope not to hear from you again, but for all the right reasons."

They said goodbye. Lucy was aware she now must return to Sara's as soon as possible and grabbing her holdall and the car keys, she hurried to the car.

As she drove, his words about living a lie revolved around in her brain like an endless carousel. If she and Dan, or anybody else for that matter, got together, the inevitable questions about family would emerge. Previous boyfriends' enquiries had been easy to ward off, mainly because they were more interested in themselves. She knew that someone like Dan Blake, a policeman, was probably the worst sort of person she could end up with. Suspicious, forever curious, just a part of his job and probably his nature. *Oh well, why worry. It's not like romance was in the air, even if I do quite like him.*

Maybe emigrating's the answer. Freddy, Pete and me, we could have a good life in New Zealand. I'll mention it to them, see what they say.

As she turned into Sara's road, despite her brave thoughts, but her heart felt heavy and a tear trickled down her cheek. *No romance for me once again.*

Chapter 73

Tomas was smoking a cigar and watching the news. As Yvette Van Looy, known as Delilah during the cell meetings, walked into the room, he turned and said, "Hope you didn't open my Rioja. I was saving that for a special occasion."

Pouring a good measure of wine into a cut glass wine glass and placing it on the side table beside him, she said, "If escaping from the bizzies isn't time for celebration, I don't know what is."

Leaning back and taking another draw of his cigar, he said, "Mm, suppose you're right. However, I've some Gran Reserva Fausino I in the cellar. I don't want that to be used, not yet."

"You've got to drink it some time. You're a long time dead." Yvette glanced at the television. "Why're you watching the news again? Surely you've heard it all."

"Extra bits and pieces keep popping up. The whole cell seem to have been arrested." He shrugged as though the matter was unimportant.

"Except us," the woman sniggered. She sipped her wine, washed it round her mouth, savouring the deep red taste of the fruity grape. "Oh, now that's what I call a nice wine. They got everyone you say."

"Yep. Except us," he repeated.

"Mmm." Delilah stood next to the leader of the cell,

absent-mindedly looking at the news, not really hearing what was said. She'd heard it time and time again over the last weeks and was bored with it. She and Tomas had managed to escape, that was the main thing. The news had been full of all the arrests up and down the country. Forty-four of their people had been arrested, and the police had rescued all of the kids

Tomas had told her he'd already heard from six other leaders who had escaped capture. All those leaders, having arranged the fine details of Operation Hobbledehoy, had doubly ensured they would not be in precarious positions should the operation fail as it had previously. Their safety precautions had worked out well. Four other cell leaders had been apprehended and presumably that was because they had not kept themselves as distanced from the actions as was recommended.

Delilah paused, glass midway to her mouth, couldn't resist saying, "We weren't the only ones that 'got away'."

Tomas, drawing deeply on his cigar, his voice painted with irritation, snapped back. "Yes, Miss Perfect, don't rub it in. I'm aware to what you're referring."

Noticing the look on her companion's face, Delilah didn't finish but knew she had made her point.

Tomas said nothing for a few minutes, slowly sipping his drink and gently exhaling the cigar smoke. Delilah couldn't fathom whether he was ignoring her or contemplating her words. When he spoke, his words laced with hate, the women felt shivers of fear run up and down her spine.

"Viking. Now what shall we do about him?"

Yvette sat down beside him on the sofa. She felt braver now and couldn't resist a further dig.

"You let his good looks transfix you from the start. You couldn't resist those weird pale blue eyes. I warned you though, no initiates. "

"Beautiful Viking." Tomas sighed. "We checked him out. He'd done time. Everything."

"If he was an undercover cop, the law can fix your life! I saw by the way you looked at him you wanted him. Christ, he was thirty if he was a day. Twenty bloody years older than your usual taste."

Tomas leaned his head back. "Still, those lovely Scandinavian eyes." He sighed again and then sniggered. "I couldn't be impervious to their beauty. Swedish sapphires straight from heaven."

"Well look where it's got us."

"You don't know anything for sure." He stood up, stubbed out his cigar in an ashtray and then drank the rest of his wine. "This is what we do. We lie low here. No-one but us knows about this place. The only link was my mobile and I've ditched that. As for Viking, beautiful blue eyes or not, we make him and his mate Blake pay."

The woman shook her head with frustration. "Exactly how do we do pay them back when every member of the filth in the whole bloody country is looking for us?"

"Delilah, have faith. We're safe here. We make it seem as though we've gone abroad. We wait, maybe a year. Then we lure them, Viking first, into our trap. And you, Delilah can have the pleasure of cutting off his locks. Delilah cutting of my namesake's locks, rendering him weak and helpless like the Samson of the Old Testament. And I'll have the pleasure of making him suffer the pain of ten hells. Then later we get Blake."

He stretched his arms above his head up and then turned and walked away. Stopping, he half turned and looked over his shoulder, his black eyes glittered evilly as he whispered.

"And when we've got him, then we open the Faustino I, I promise."

As he left the room, Delilah poured herself more wine and turned over the television to watch Crime Watch. *That's always good for a laugh. Stupid cops.*

◆

The Sequel

Opals in the Sky

Due out 2018.

Gerry Tomas and his sidekick Yvette Van Looy have escaped and are out for retribution against the two cops that thwarted their operation to abduct multiple children. They lay low for a year; then kidnap three children as bate to lure the cops into their grasp for their deserved punishment.

What they don't count on is that their third victim, although seemingly uneducated, is a brilliant street-wise kid who doesn't intend to be brought down and intimidated so easily... he has his 'pals', 'Strike and Killer'...

47758277R00237

Printed in Poland
by Amazon Fulfillment
Poland Sp. z o.o., Wrocław